LOST AND FOUND

A HEART OF THE CITY COLLECTION

BY STEENZ

Andrews McMeel
PUBLISHING®

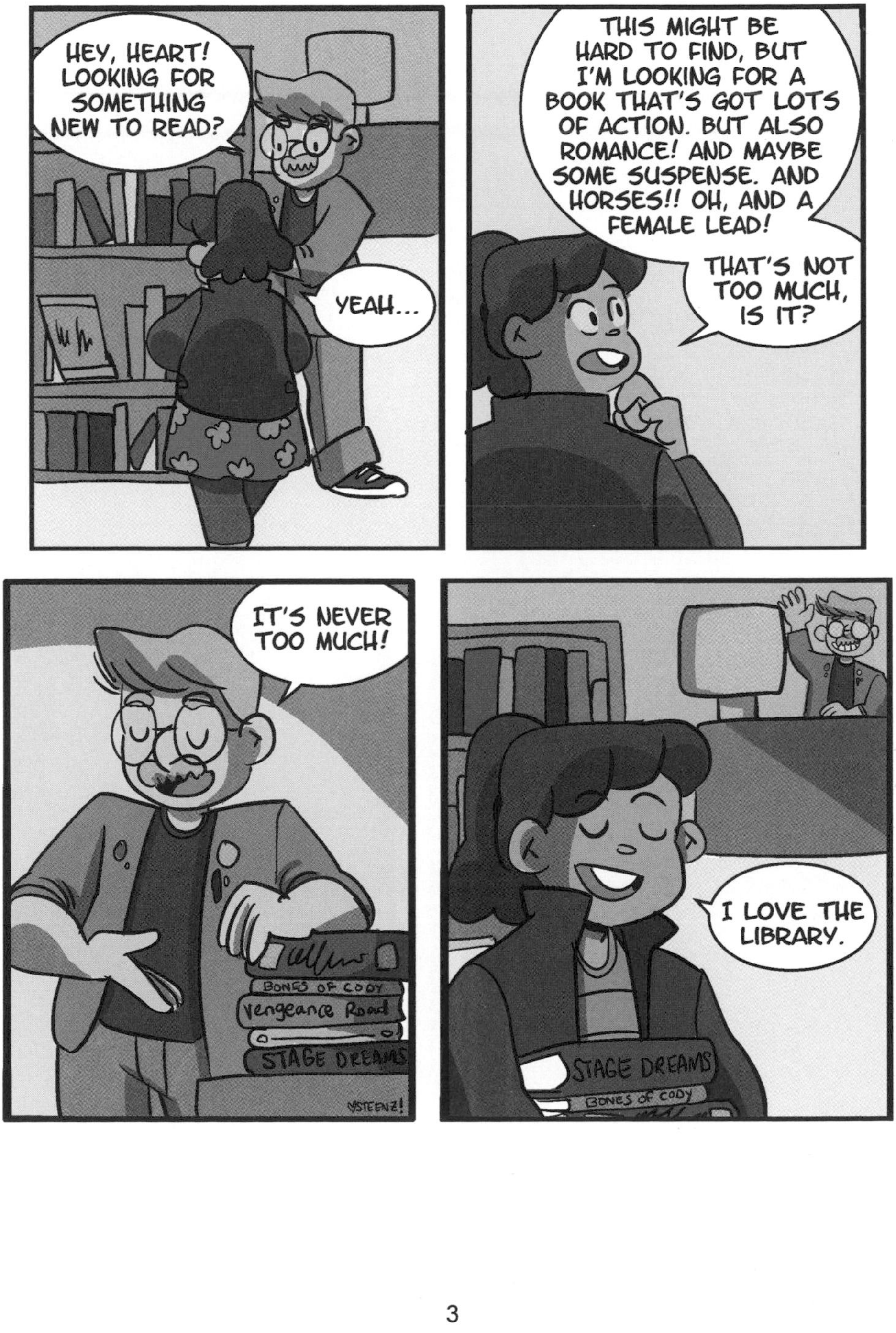
HEY, HEART! LOOKING FOR SOMETHING NEW TO READ?
YEAH...
THIS MIGHT BE HARD TO FIND, BUT I'M LOOKING FOR A BOOK THAT'S GOT LOTS OF ACTION. BUT ALSO ROMANCE! AND MAYBE SOME SUSPENSE. AND HORSES!! OH, AND A FEMALE LEAD!
THAT'S NOT TOO MUCH, IS IT?
IT'S NEVER TOO MUCH!
BONES OF CODY
Vengeance Road
STAGE DREAMS
♡STEENZ!
I LOVE THE LIBRARY.
STAGE DREAMS
BONES OF CODY

GOSH, I'M SO BUSY THIS WEEK.
HEY, AT LEAST YOU HAVE THE WEEKEND TO LOOK FOWARD TO! NO CLASS WORK!
YOU'D THINK THAT, BUT I HAVE FIVE DAYS OF TV TO CATCH UP ON!
♡STEENZ!
SIGH... I'M GONNA HAVE TO GET UP EARLY.

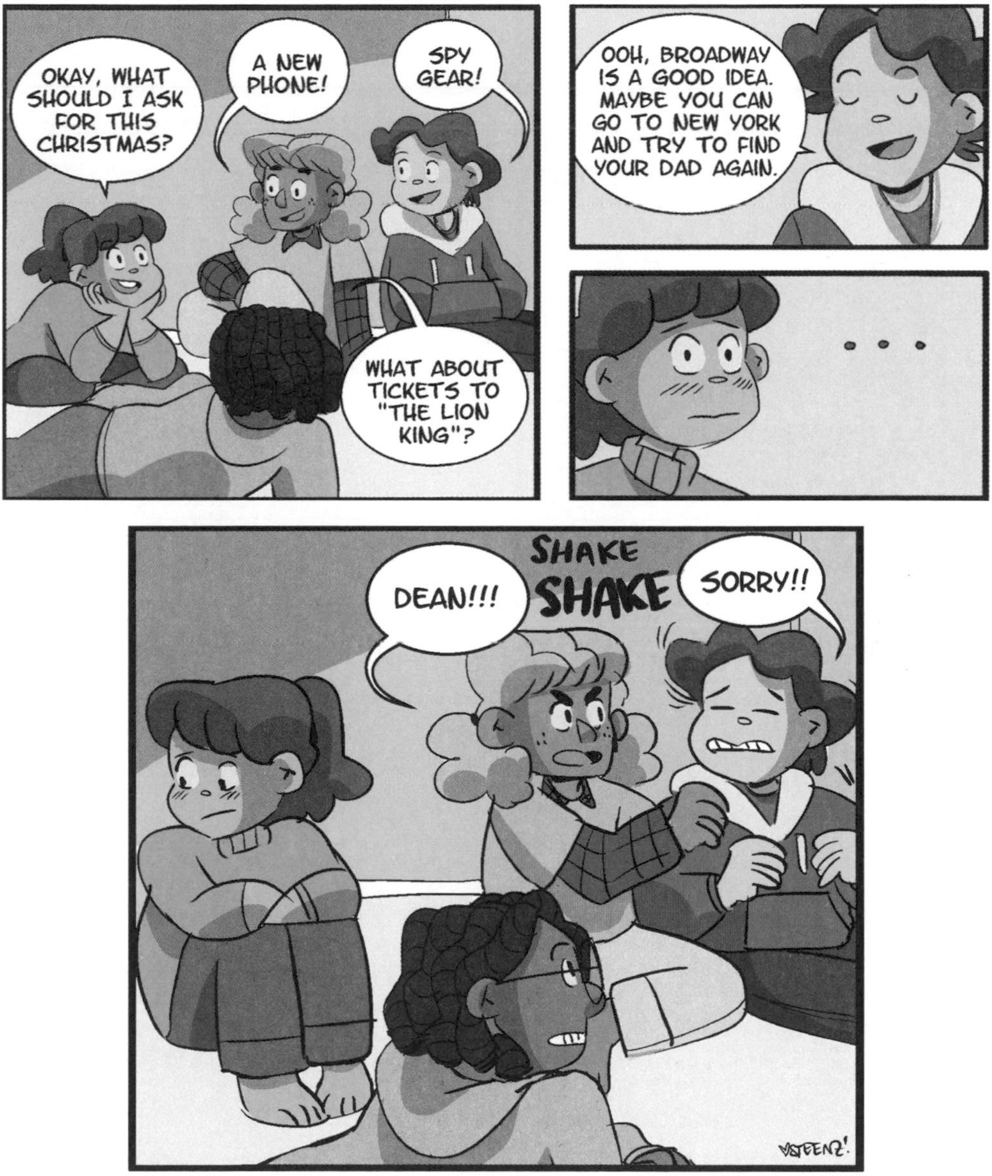
OKAY, WHAT SHOULD I ASK FOR THIS CHRISTMAS?
A NEW PHONE!
SPY GEAR!
WHAT ABOUT TICKETS TO "THE LION KING"?
OOH, BROADWAY IS A GOOD IDEA. MAYBE YOU CAN GO TO NEW YORK AND TRY TO FIND YOUR DAD AGAIN.
. . .
SHAKE
SHAKE
DEAN!!!
SORRY!!

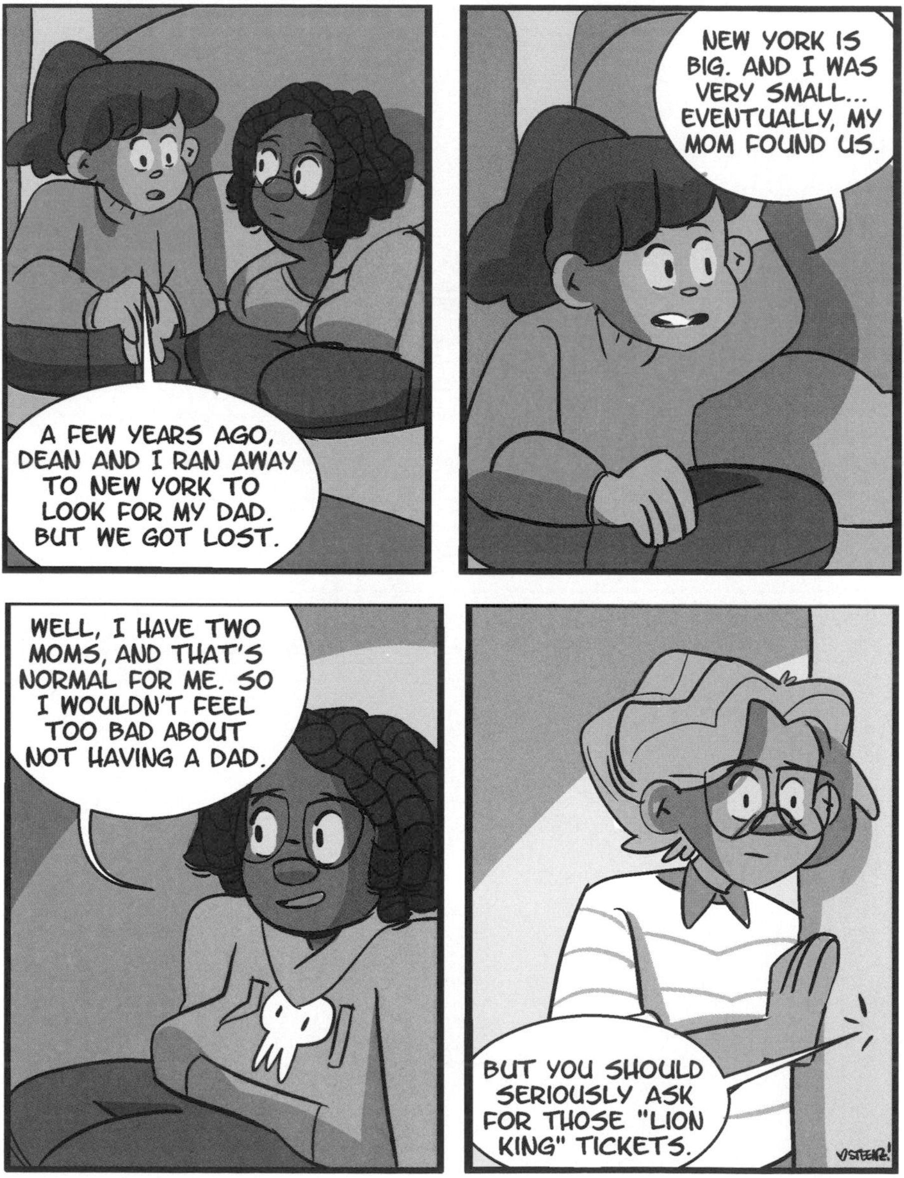
A FEW YEARS AGO, DEAN AND I RAN AWAY TO NEW YORK TO LOOK FOR MY DAD. BUT WE GOT LOST.
NEW YORK IS BIG. AND I WAS VERY SMALL... EVENTUALLY, MY MOM FOUND US.
WELL, I HAVE TWO MOMS, AND THAT'S NORMAL FOR ME. SO I WOULDN'T FEEL TOO BAD ABOUT NOT HAVING A DAD.
BUT YOU SHOULD SERIOUSLY ASK FOR THOSE "LION KING" TICKETS.

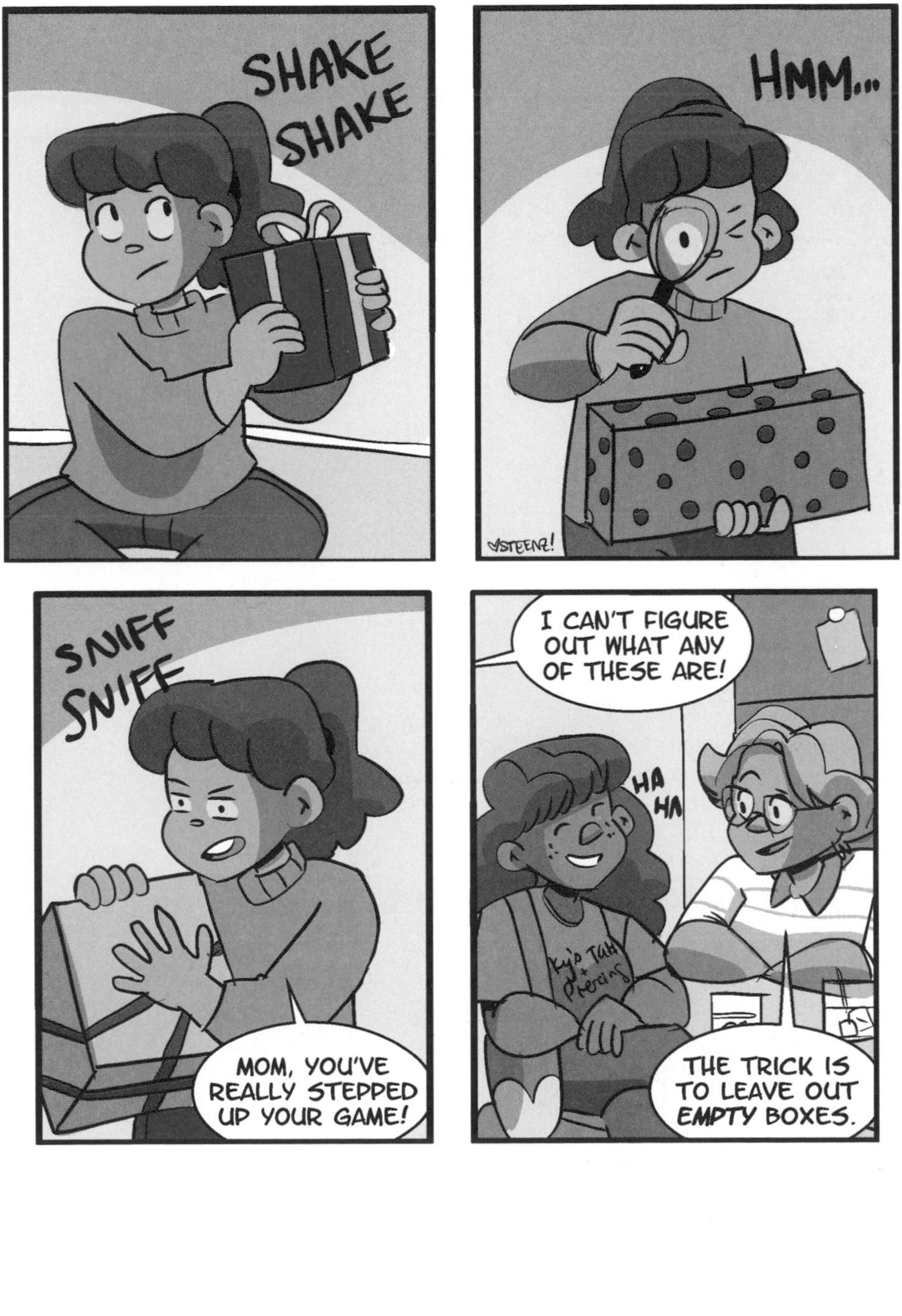
SHAKE
SHAKE
HMM...
STEENZ!
SNIFF
SNIFF
MOM, YOU'VE REALLY STEPPED UP YOUR GAME!
I CAN'T FIGURE OUT WHAT ANY OF THESE ARE!
HA
HA
THE TRICK IS TO LEAVE OUT *EMPTY* BOXES.

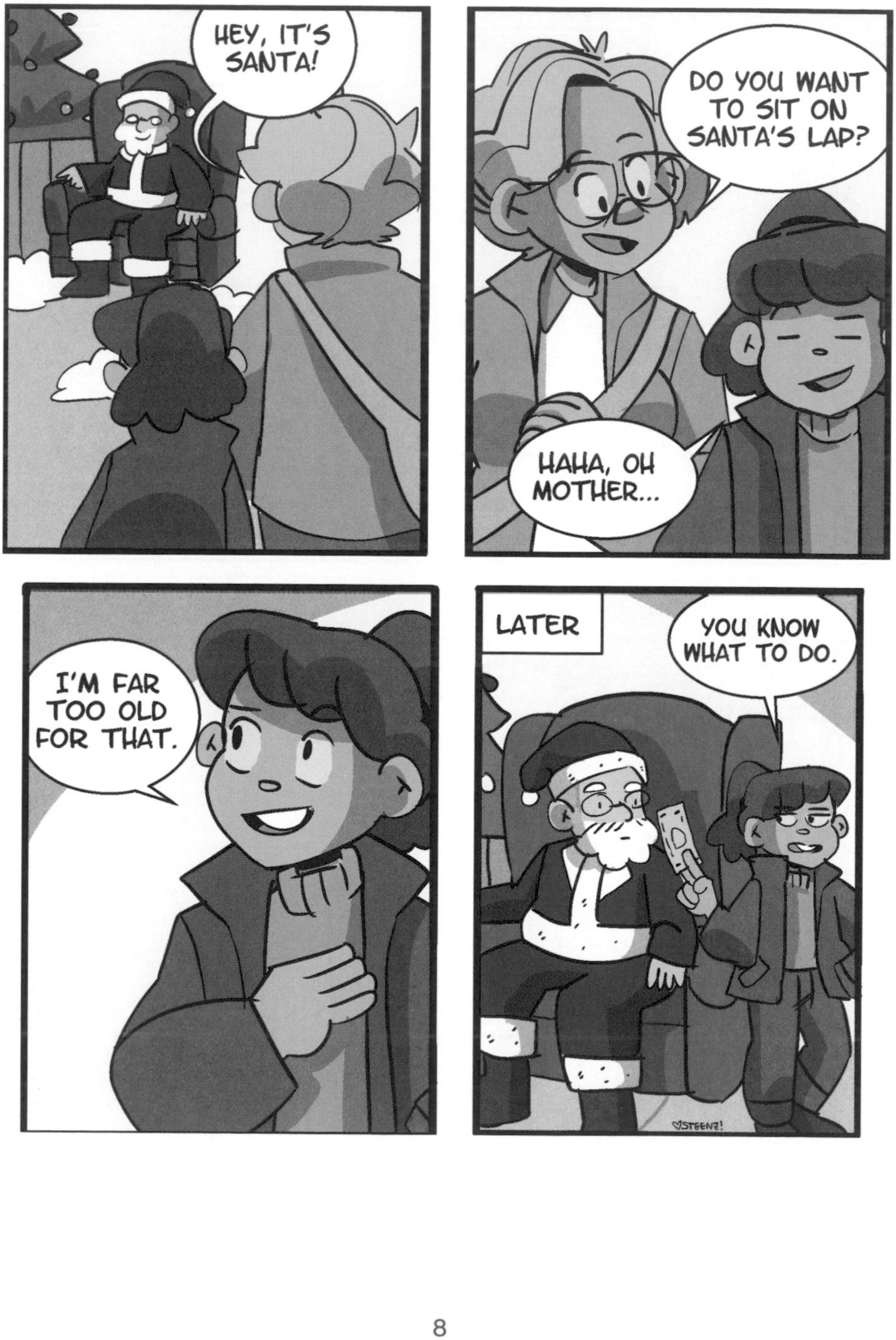
HEY, IT'S SANTA!
DO YOU WANT TO SIT ON SANTA'S LAP?
HAHA, OH MOTHER...
I'M FAR TOO OLD FOR THAT.
LATER
YOU KNOW WHAT TO DO.
STEENZ!

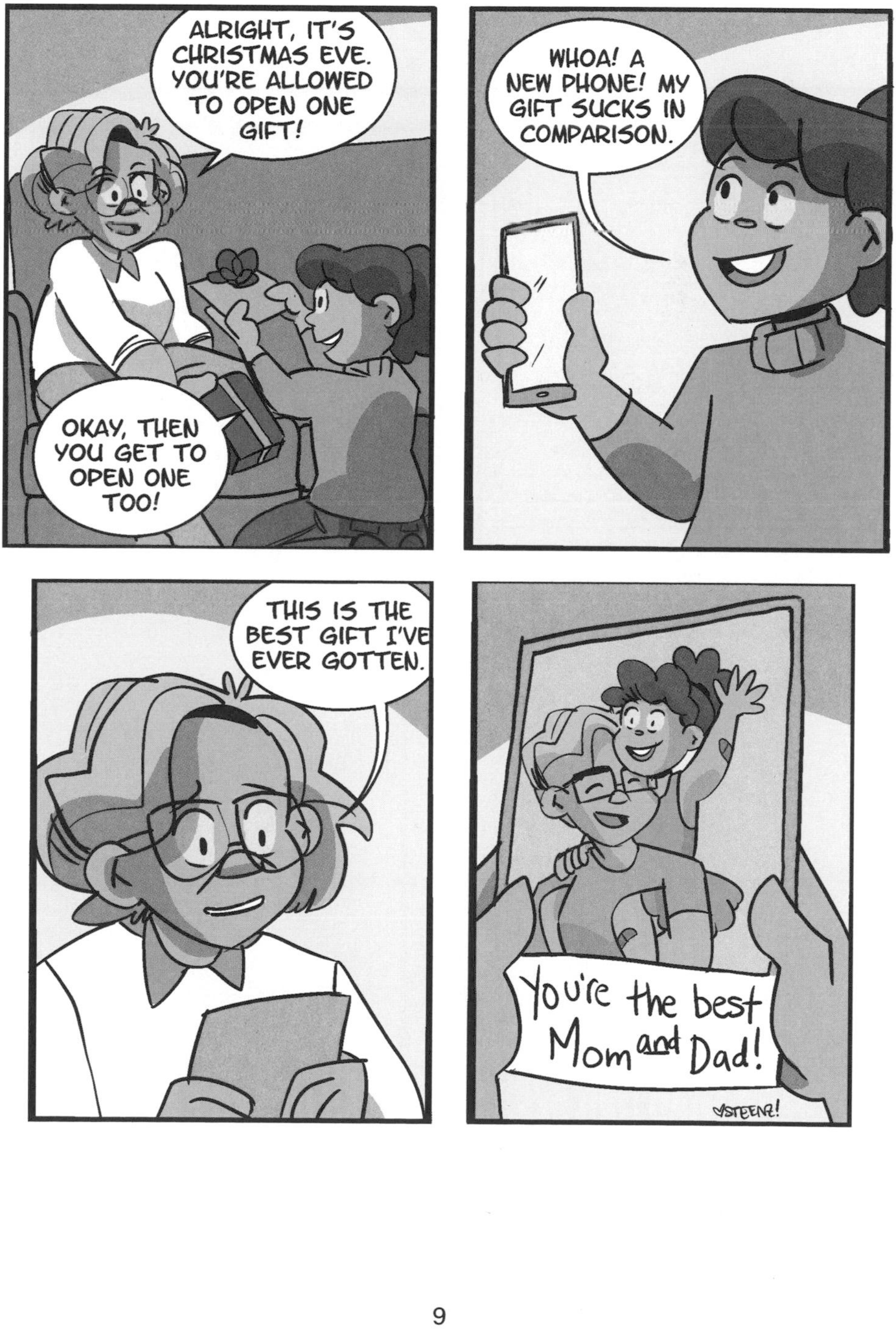
ALRIGHT, IT'S CHRISTMAS EVE. YOU'RE ALLOWED TO OPEN ONE GIFT!
OKAY, THEN YOU GET TO OPEN ONE TOO!
WHOA! A NEW PHONE! MY GIFT SUCKS IN COMPARISON.
THIS IS THE BEST GIFT I'VE EVER GOTTEN.
You're the best Mom and Dad!
STEENZ!

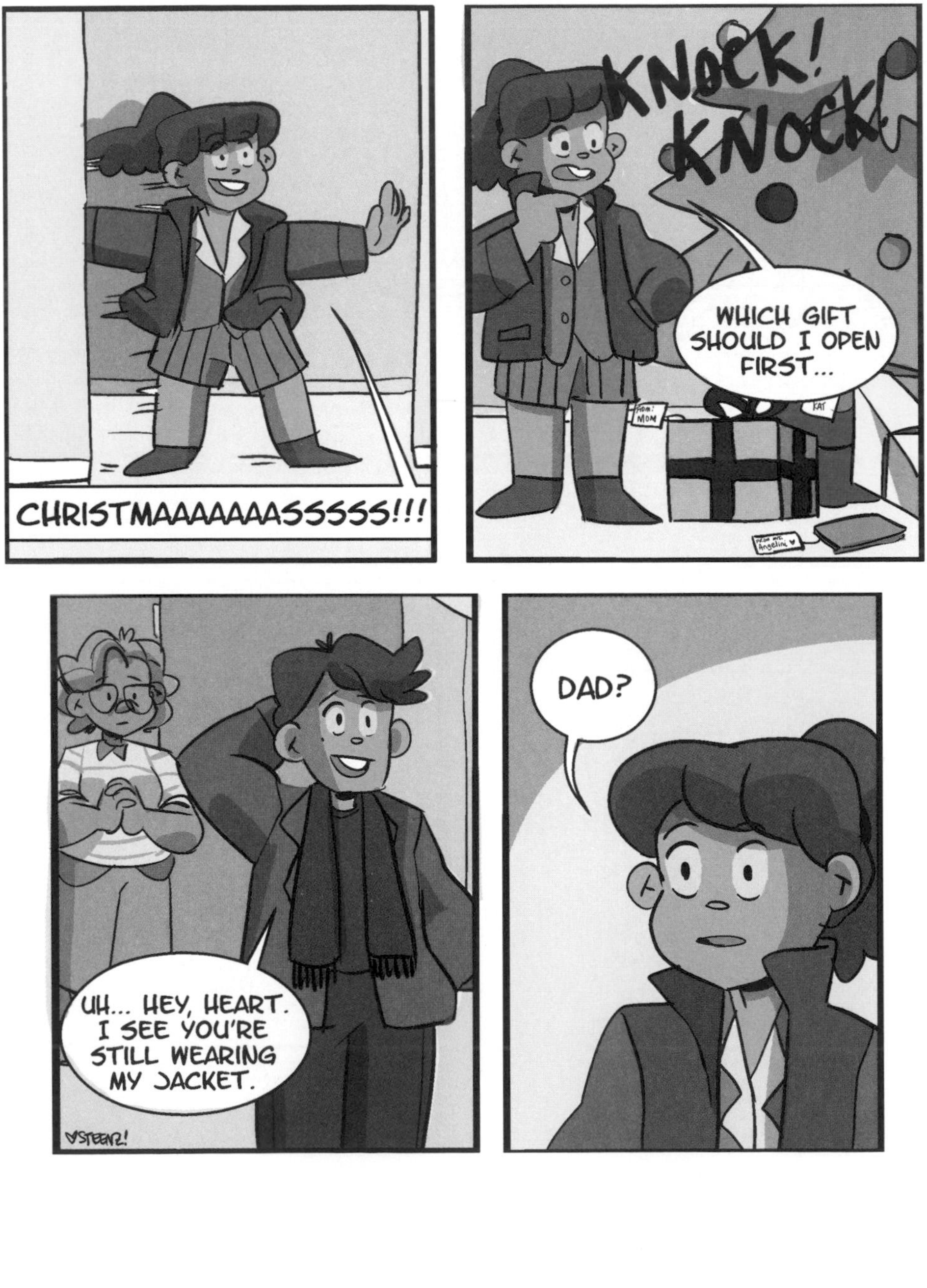
CHRISTMAAAAAAASSSSS!!!
KNOCK! KNOCK!
WHICH GIFT SHOULD I OPEN FIRST...
From: MOM
KAT
UH... HEY, HEART. I SEE YOU'RE STILL WEARING MY JACKET.
DAD?

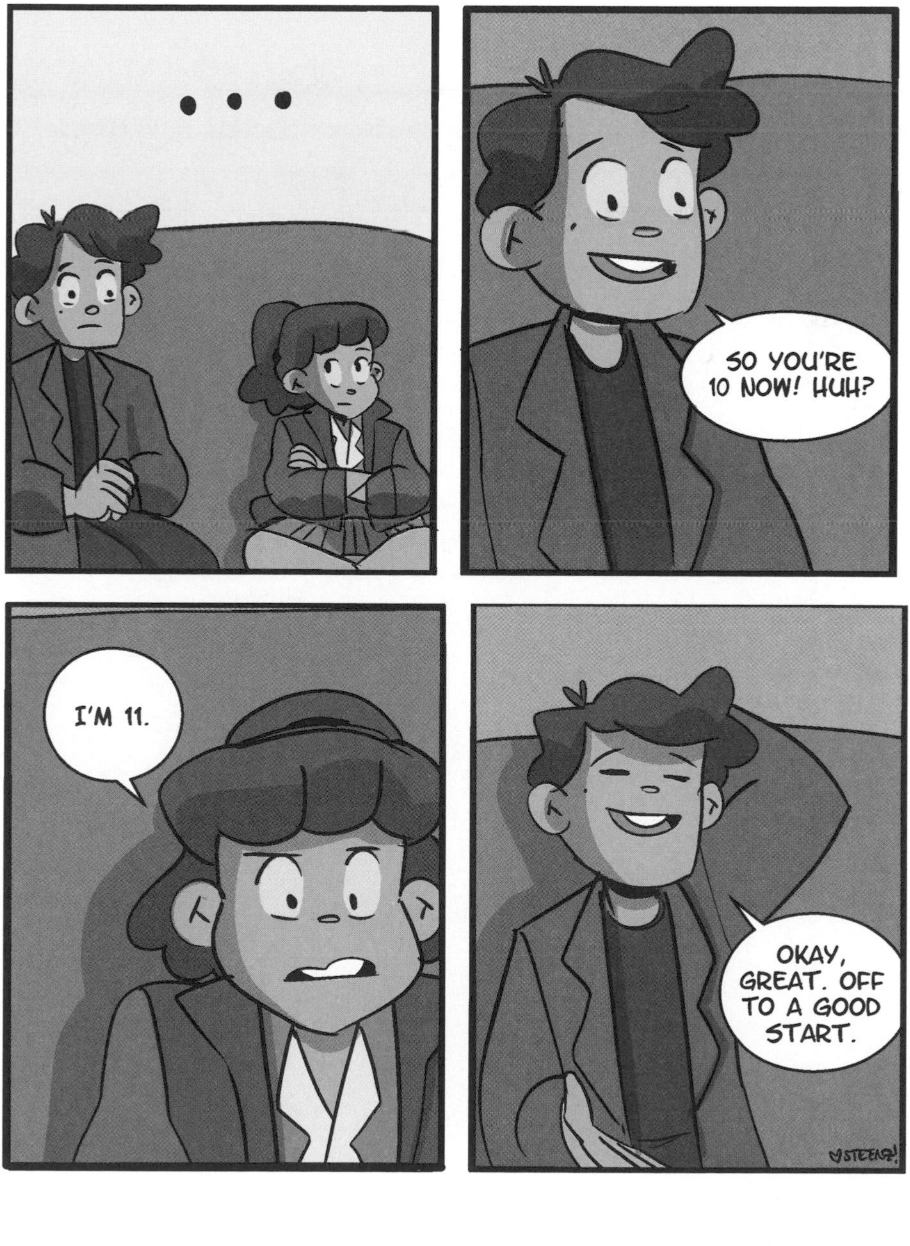
...
SO YOU'RE 10 NOW! HUH?
I'M 11.
OKAY, GREAT. OFF TO A GOOD START.

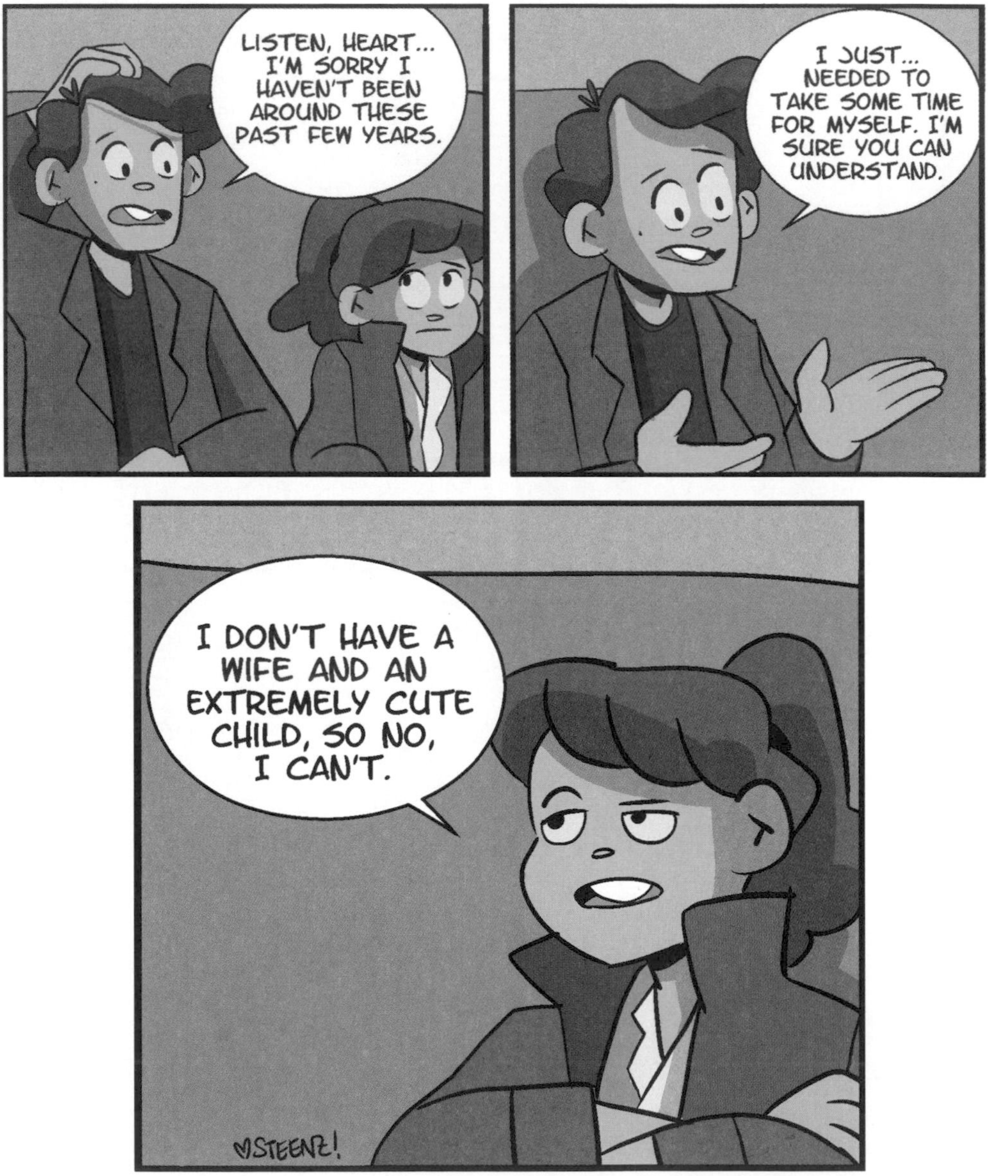
LISTEN, HEART... I'M SORRY I HAVEN'T BEEN AROUND THESE PAST FEW YEARS.
I JUST... NEEDED TO TAKE SOME TIME FOR MYSELF. I'M SURE YOU CAN UNDERSTAND.
I DON'T HAVE A WIFE AND AN EXTREMELY CUTE CHILD, SO NO, I CAN'T.
♡STEENZ!

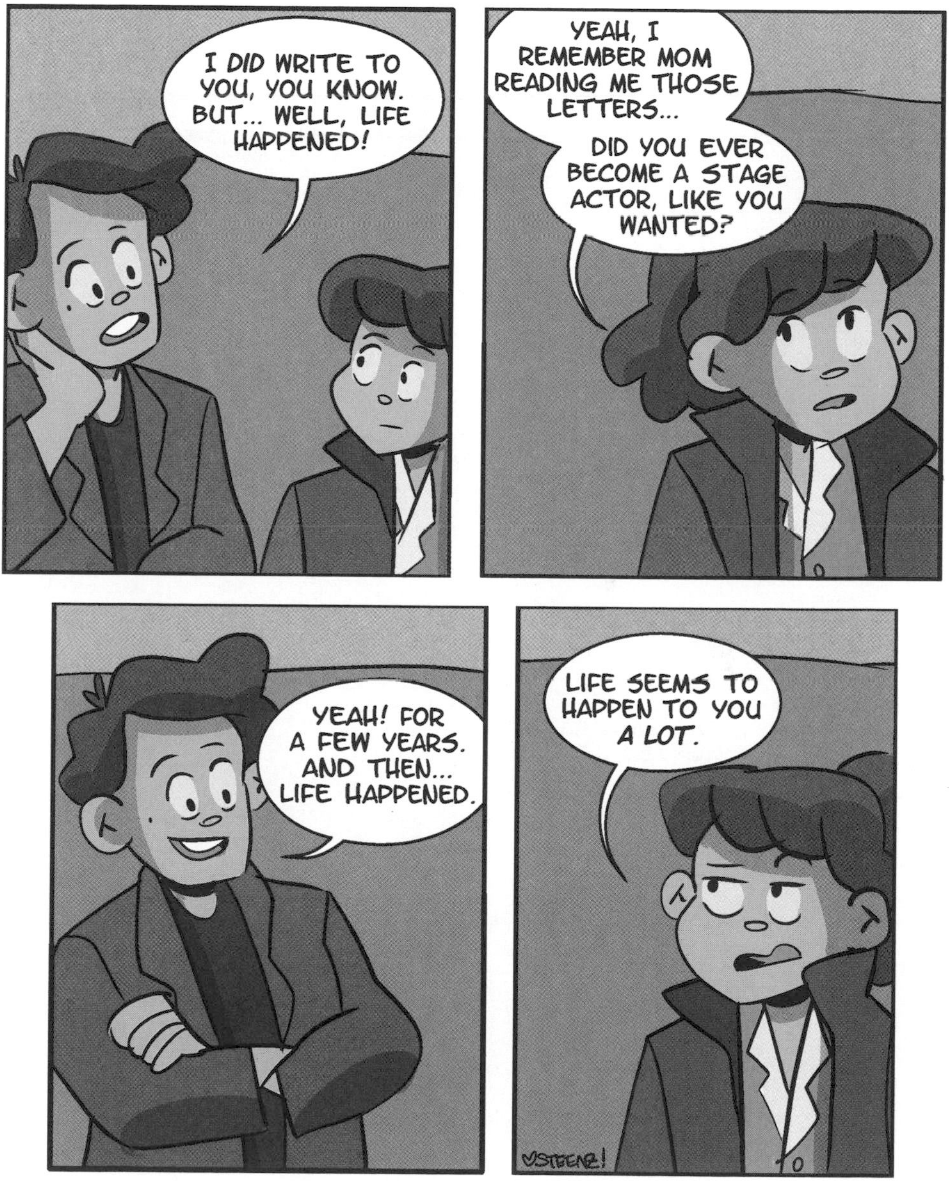
I DID WRITE TO YOU, YOU KNOW. BUT... WELL, LIFE HAPPENED!
YEAH, I REMEMBER MOM READING ME THOSE LETTERS...
DID YOU EVER BECOME A STAGE ACTOR, LIKE YOU WANTED?
YEAH! FOR A FEW YEARS. AND THEN... LIFE HAPPENED.
LIFE SEEMS TO HAPPEN TO YOU A LOT.
STEENZ!

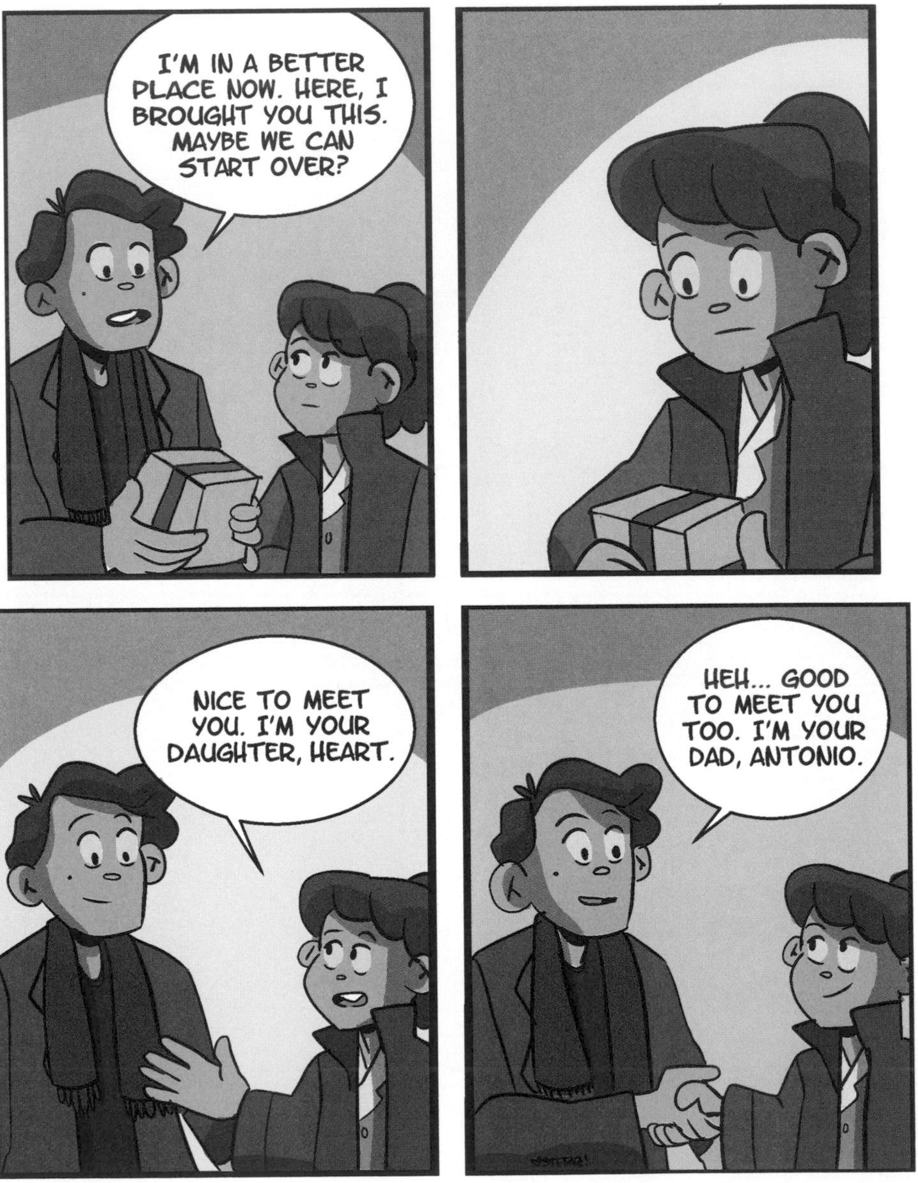
I'M IN A BETTER PLACE NOW. HERE, I BROUGHT YOU THIS. MAYBE WE CAN START OVER?
NICE TO MEET YOU. I'M YOUR DAUGHTER, HEART.
HEH... GOOD TO MEET YOU TOO. I'M YOUR DAD, ANTONIO.

NOW THAT YOU'VE HAD A COUPLE OF DAYS TO THINK ABOUT YOUR DAD, DID YOU WANT TO OPEN THE GIFT HE GOT YOU? START THE YEAR OFF RIGHT?
YEAH, WHY NOT?
HEY!! TICKETS TO "THE LION KING"! HOW DID HE KNOW?
TICKETMOSTER
TICKETMOSTER
LION KING
LION KING
CHIPPY CHIPMINI
I'm sorry for not being around. Merry Christmas
MAYBE HE HAD SPARE TICKETS. OR MAYBE SOMEONE TEXTED HIM AND SAID TO STOP AVOIDING HIS DAUGHTER AND DO THE RIGHT THING. WHO CAN SAY?
♡STEENZ!

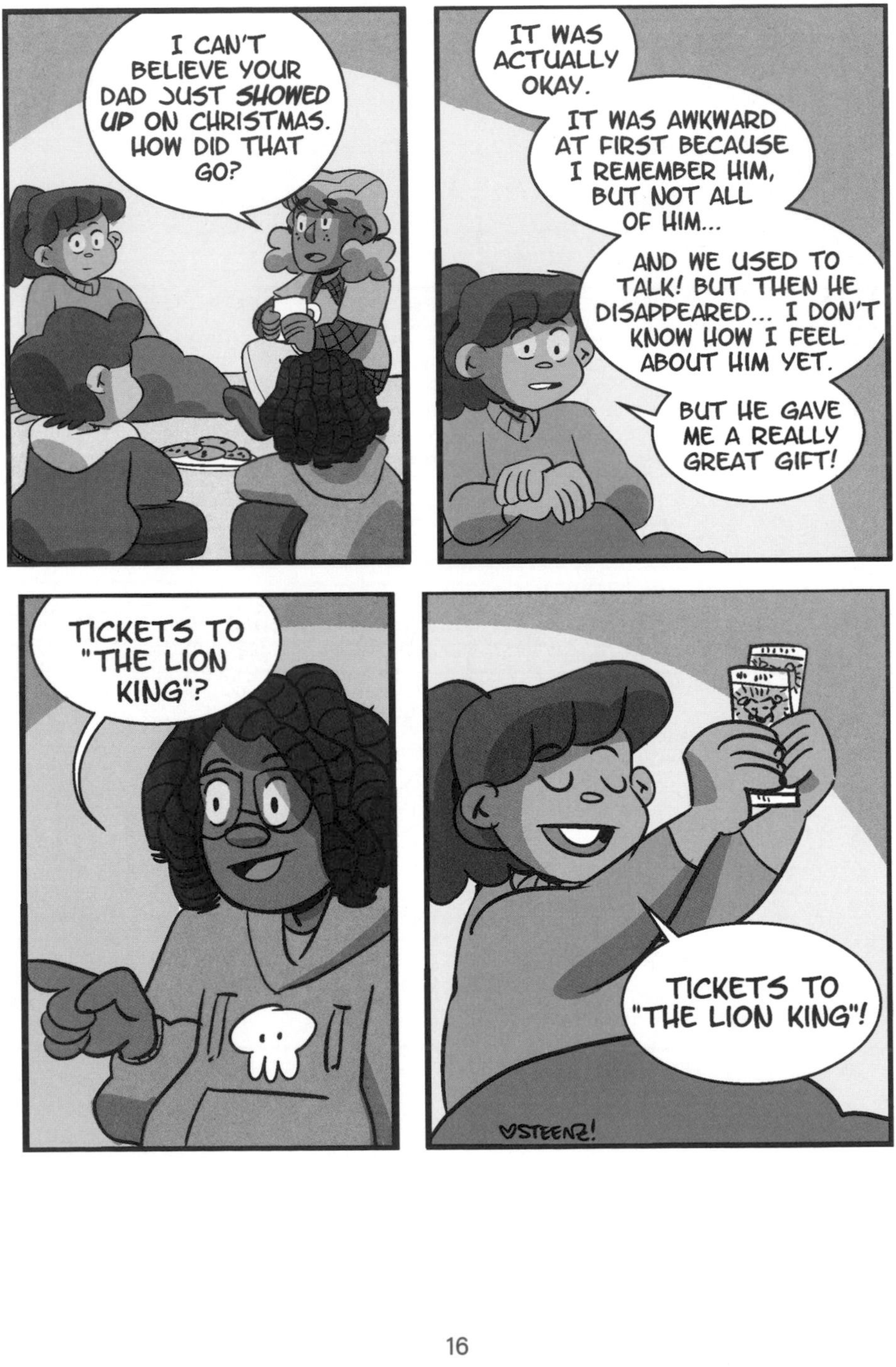
I CAN'T BELIEVE YOUR DAD JUST SHOWED UP ON CHRISTMAS. HOW DID THAT GO?
IT WAS ACTUALLY OKAY.
IT WAS AWKWARD AT FIRST BECAUSE I REMEMBER HIM, BUT NOT ALL OF HIM...
AND WE USED TO TALK! BUT THEN HE DISAPPEARED... I DON'T KNOW HOW I FEEL ABOUT HIM YET.
BUT HE GAVE ME A REALLY GREAT GIFT!
TICKETS TO "THE LION KING"?
TICKETS TO "THE LION KING"!
♡STEENZ!

KAT, YOU'VE GOT TO CLEAN YOUR ROOM. AT LEAST BEFORE CHRISTMAS.
THAT'S NOT FAIR! ALYSSA AND SHARI DON'T HAVE TO CLEAN THEIR ROOMS!
I THINK IT'S DISCRIMINATION AGAINST MIDDLE CHILDREN.
THEIR ROOMS ARE CLEAN!
HOW DO YOU KNOW? YOU'RE IN MY ROOM RIGHT NOW!
CLEAN YOUR ROOM, KAT.
AAAAAUUUUUUUGGGGGHHHHH

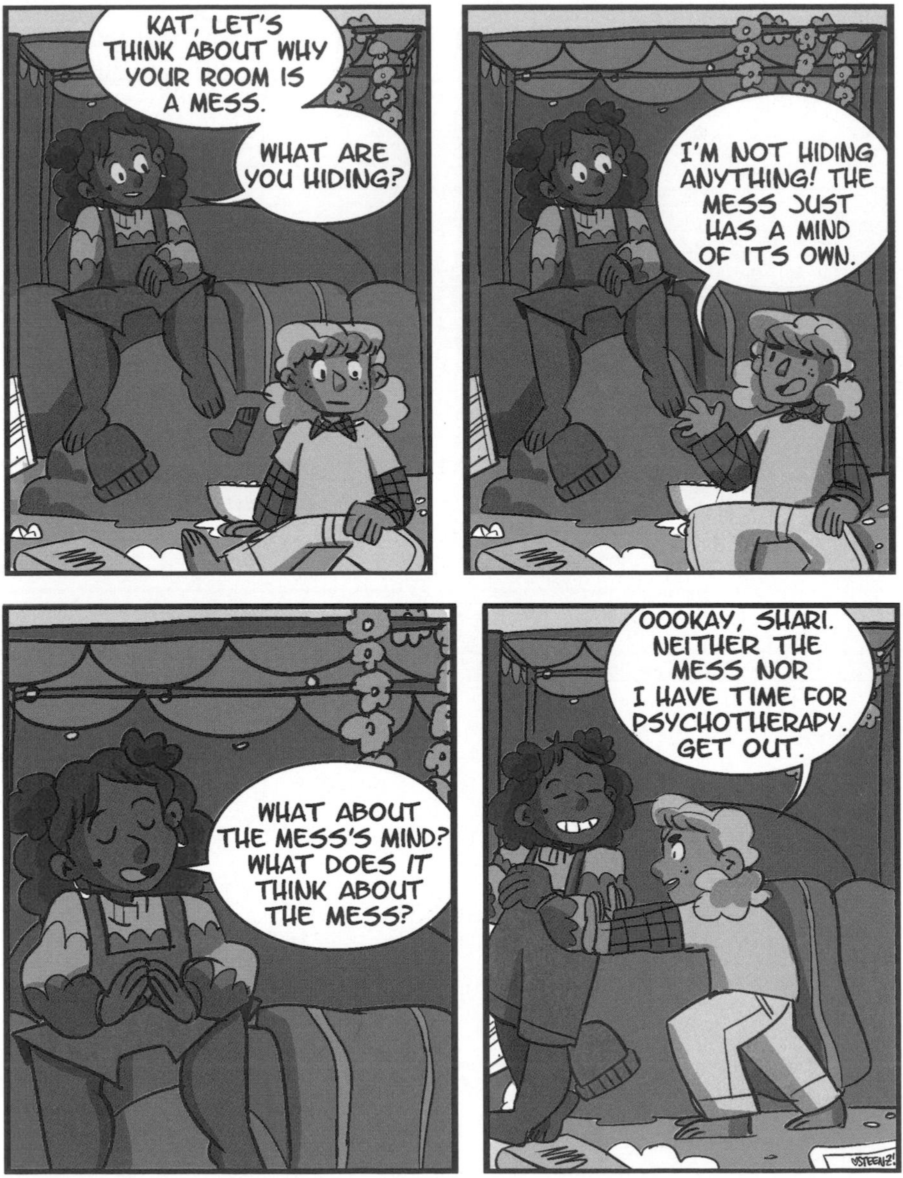
KAT, LET'S THINK ABOUT WHY YOUR ROOM IS A MESS.
WHAT ARE YOU HIDING?
I'M NOT HIDING ANYTHING! THE MESS JUST HAS A MIND OF ITS OWN.
WHAT ABOUT THE MESS'S MIND? WHAT DOES IT THINK ABOUT THE MESS?
OOOKAY, SHARI. NEITHER THE MESS NOR I HAVE TIME FOR PSYCHOTHERAPY. GET OUT.
©STEENZ!

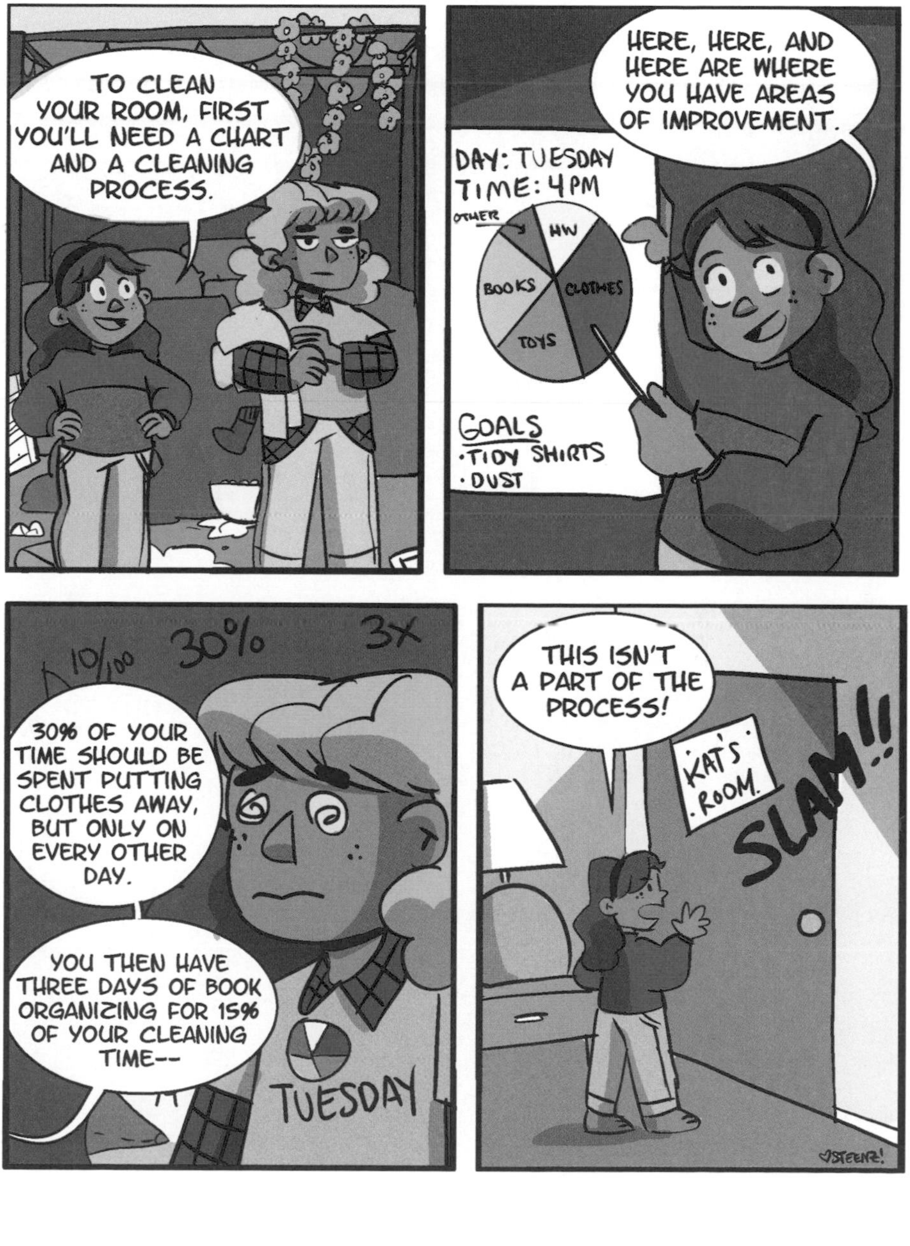
TO CLEAN YOUR ROOM, FIRST YOU'LL NEED A CHART AND A CLEANING PROCESS.
HERE, HERE, AND HERE ARE WHERE YOU HAVE AREAS OF IMPROVEMENT.
DAY: TUESDAY
TIME: 4PM
OTHER
HW
BOOKS
CLOTHES
TOYS
GOALS
·TIDY SHIRTS
·DUST
10/100
30%
3X
30% OF YOUR TIME SHOULD BE SPENT PUTTING CLOTHES AWAY, BUT ONLY ON EVERY OTHER DAY.
YOU THEN HAVE THREE DAYS OF BOOK ORGANIZING FOR 15% OF YOUR CLEANING TIME--
TUESDAY
THIS ISN'T A PART OF THE PROCESS!
KAT'S ROOM.
SLAM!!
♡STEENZ!

UUUGHHH
IT MIGHT BE EASIER TO CLEAN YOUR ROOM IF YOU TAKE IT ONE STEP AT A TIME.
♡STEENZ!
BUT THE *WHOLE ROOM* NEEDS TO BE CLEANED!
THAT'S TRUE. BUT JUST START WITH YOUR BED. CLEAN ONE SECTION A DAY UNTIL IT'S ALL DONE!
THAT SEEMS TOO EASY NOT TO. WHAT'S THE CATCH?
THE CATCH IS THAT YOU'RE CLEANING YOUR ROOM. HAHA.

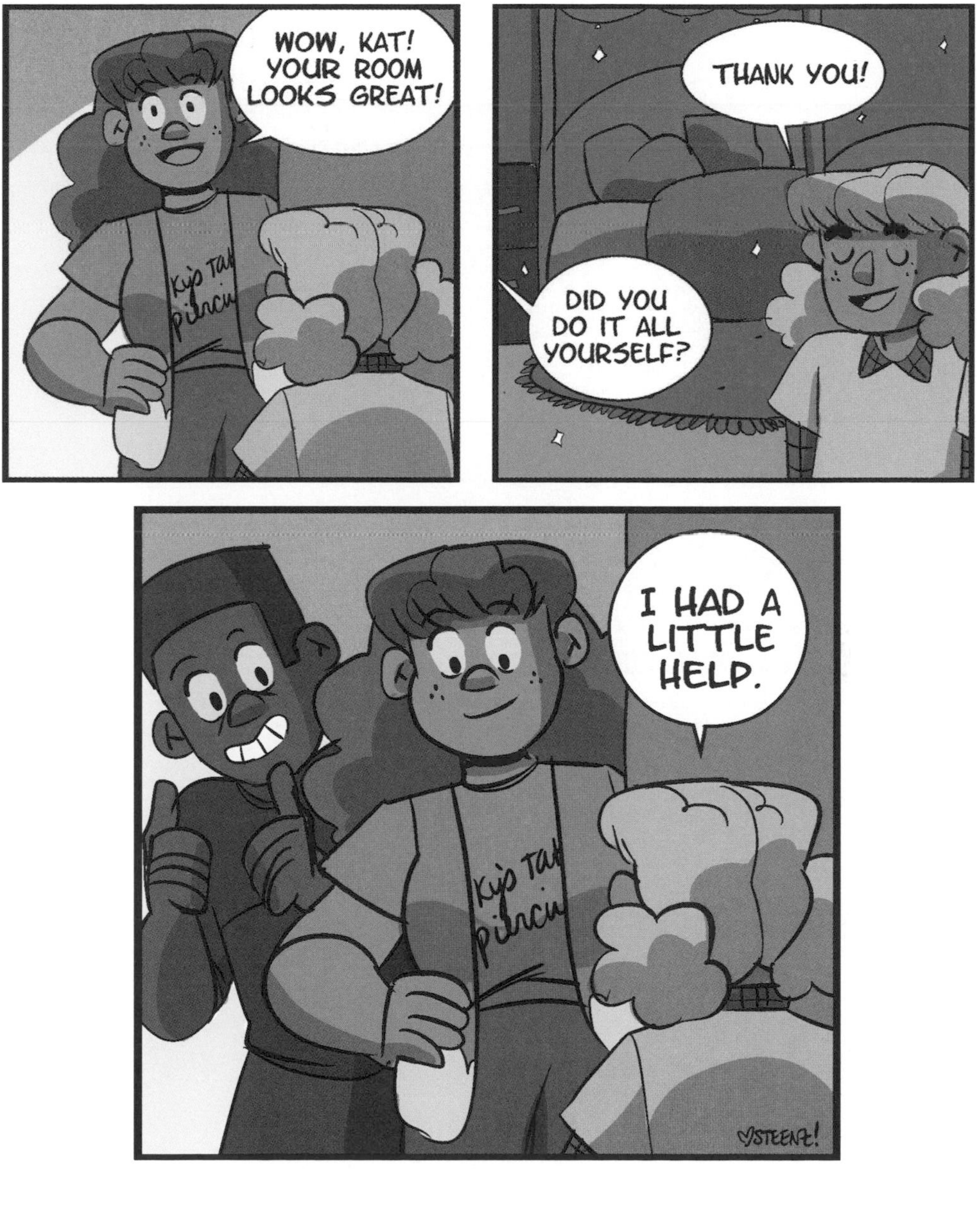
WOW, KAT! YOUR ROOM LOOKS GREAT!
THANK YOU!
DID YOU DO IT ALL YOURSELF?
I HAD A LITTLE HELP.
STEENZ!

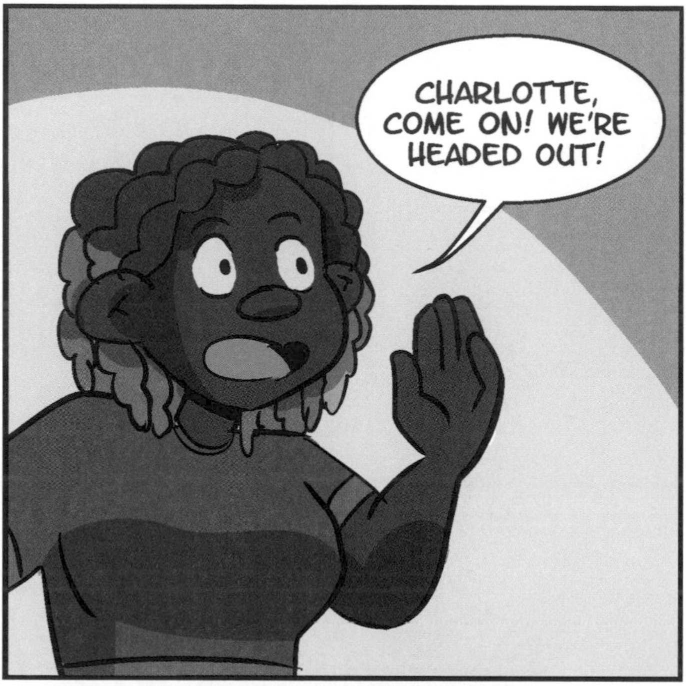
CHARLOTTE, COME ON! WE'RE HEADED OUT!

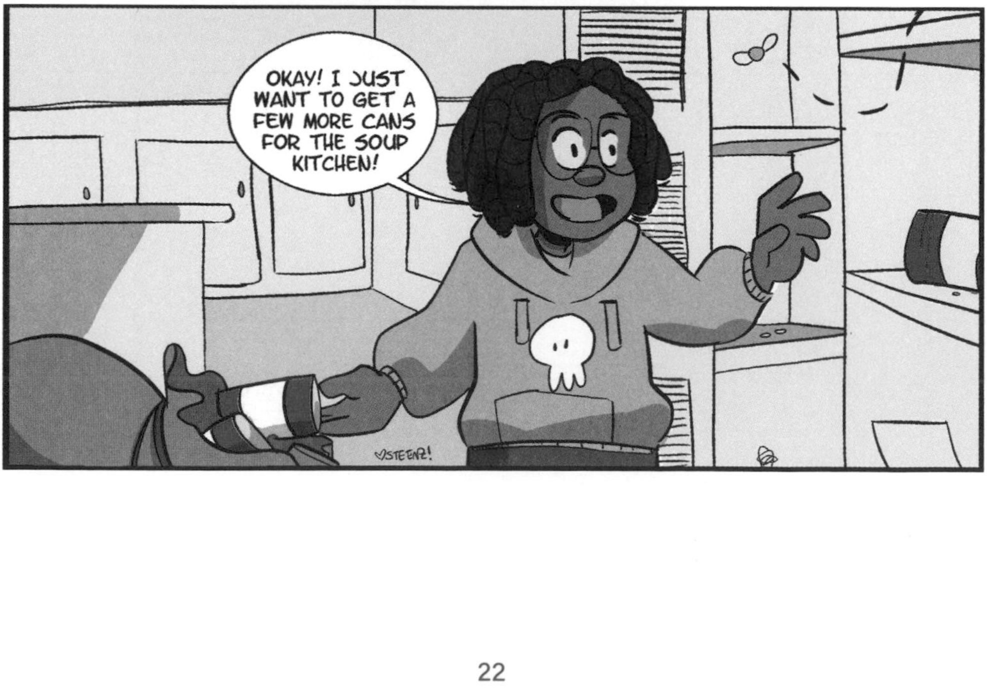
OKAY! I JUST WANT TO GET A FEW MORE CANS FOR THE SOUP KITCHEN!
♡STEENZ!

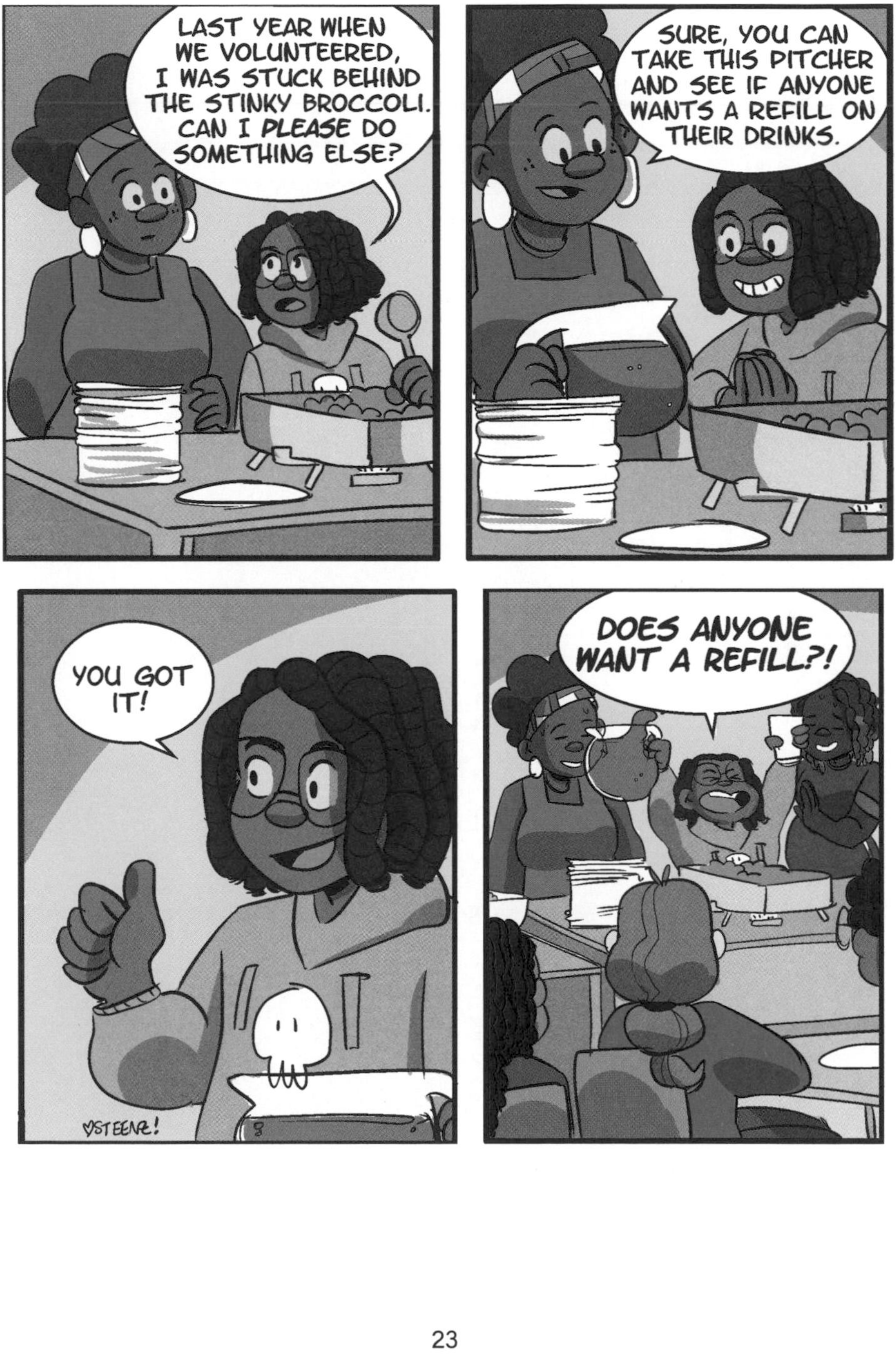
LAST YEAR WHEN WE VOLUNTEERED, I WAS STUCK BEHIND THE STINKY BROCCOLI. CAN I *PLEASE* DO SOMETHING ELSE?
SURE, YOU CAN TAKE THIS PITCHER AND SEE IF ANYONE WANTS A REFILL ON THEIR DRINKS.
YOU GOT IT!
♡STEENZ!
DOES ANYONE WANT A REFILL?!

FOOD BAR THIS WAY!
HEY!!
DON'T I KNOW YOU?!
UH!! NO??
I REALLY GOTTA WORK ON MY VOLUME.

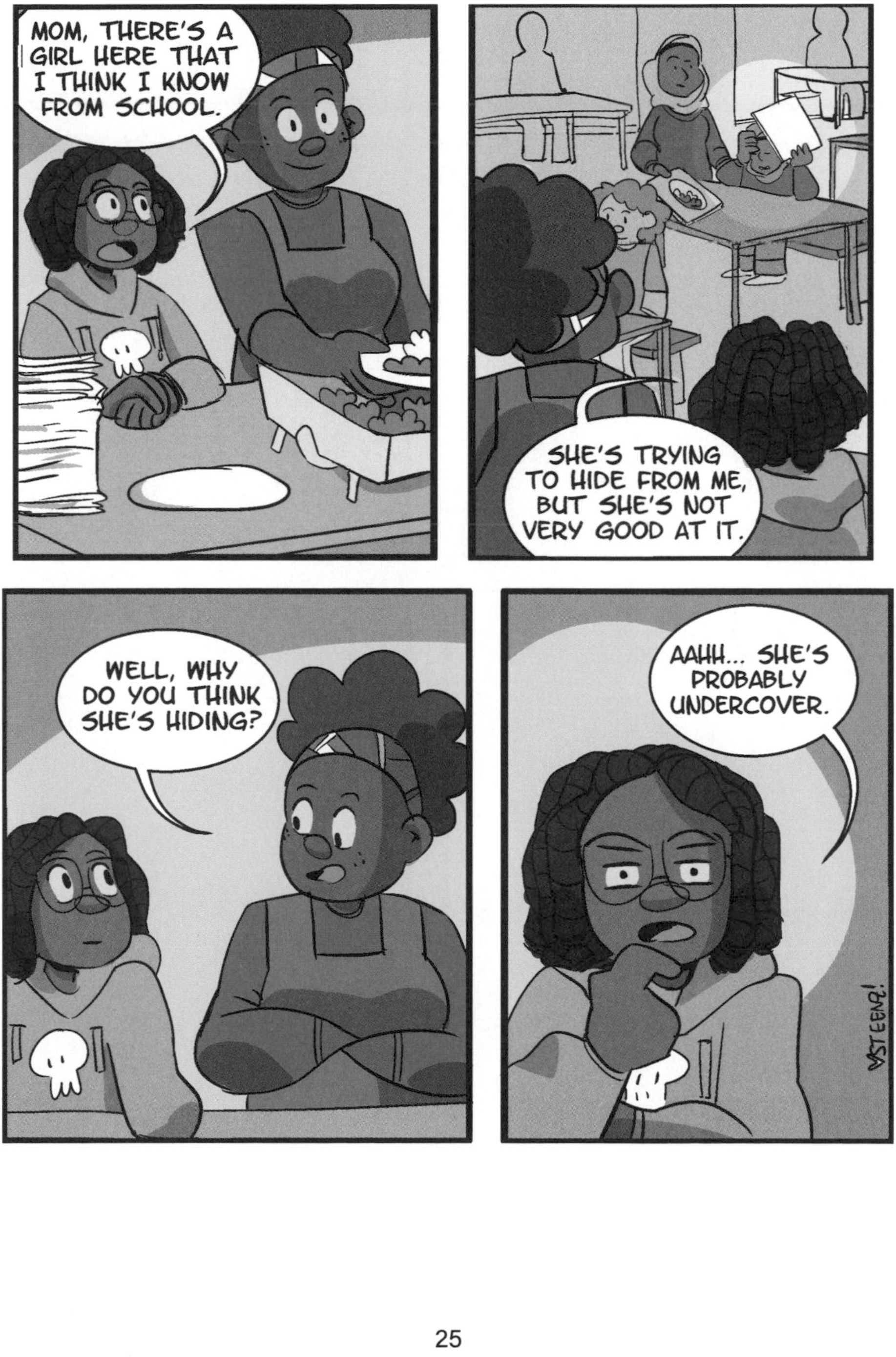
MOM, THERE'S A GIRL HERE THAT I THINK I KNOW FROM SCHOOL.
SHE'S TRYING TO HIDE FROM ME, BUT SHE'S NOT VERY GOOD AT IT.
WELL, WHY DO YOU THINK SHE'S HIDING?
AAHH... SHE'S PROBABLY UNDERCOVER.

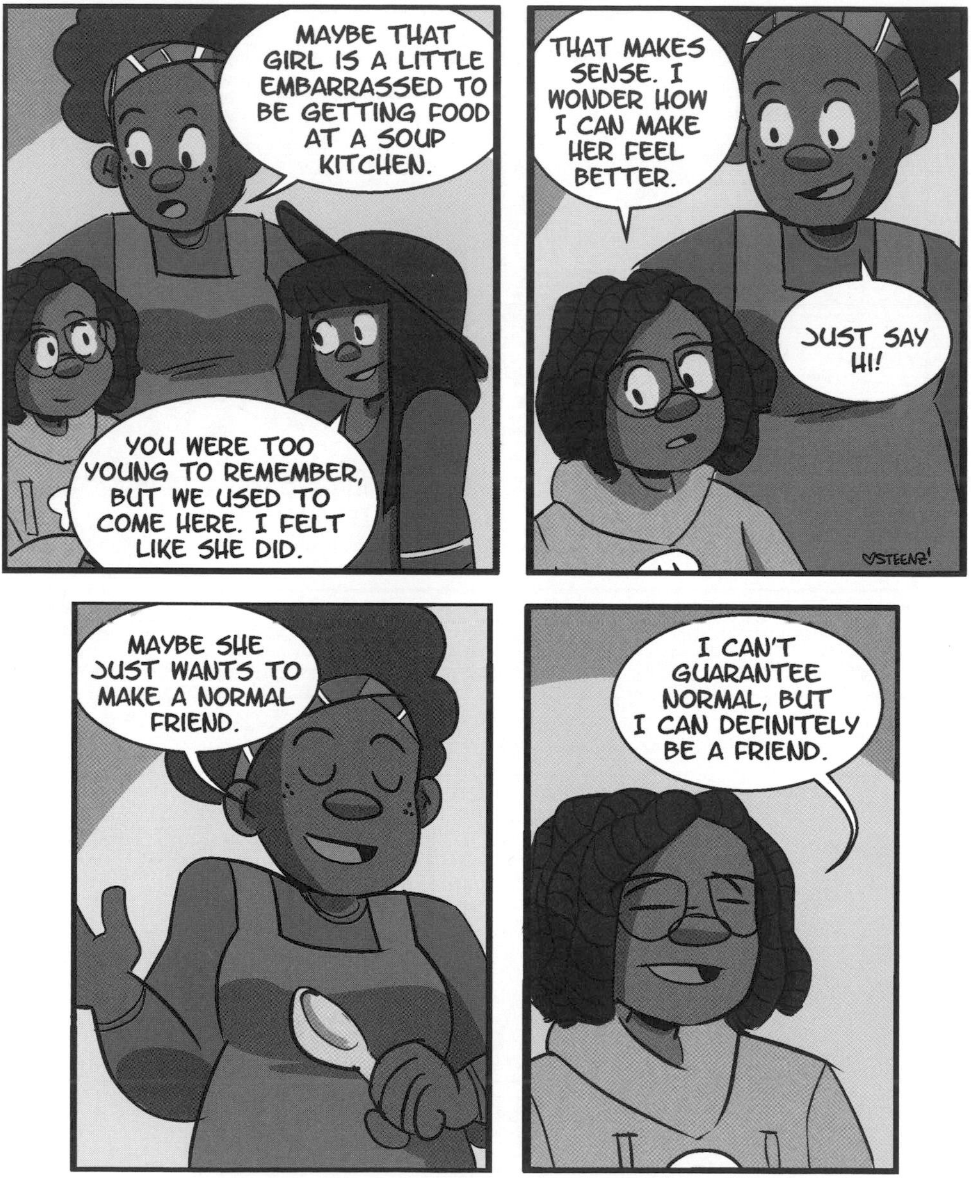
MAYBE THAT GIRL IS A LITTLE EMBARRASSED TO BE GETTING FOOD AT A SOUP KITCHEN.
YOU WERE TOO YOUNG TO REMEMBER, BUT WE USED TO COME HERE. I FELT LIKE SHE DID.
THAT MAKES SENSE. I WONDER HOW I CAN MAKE HER FEEL BETTER.
JUST SAY HI!
♡STEENZ!
MAYBE SHE JUST WANTS TO MAKE A NORMAL FRIEND.
I CAN'T GUARANTEE NORMAL, BUT I CAN DEFINITELY BE A FRIEND.

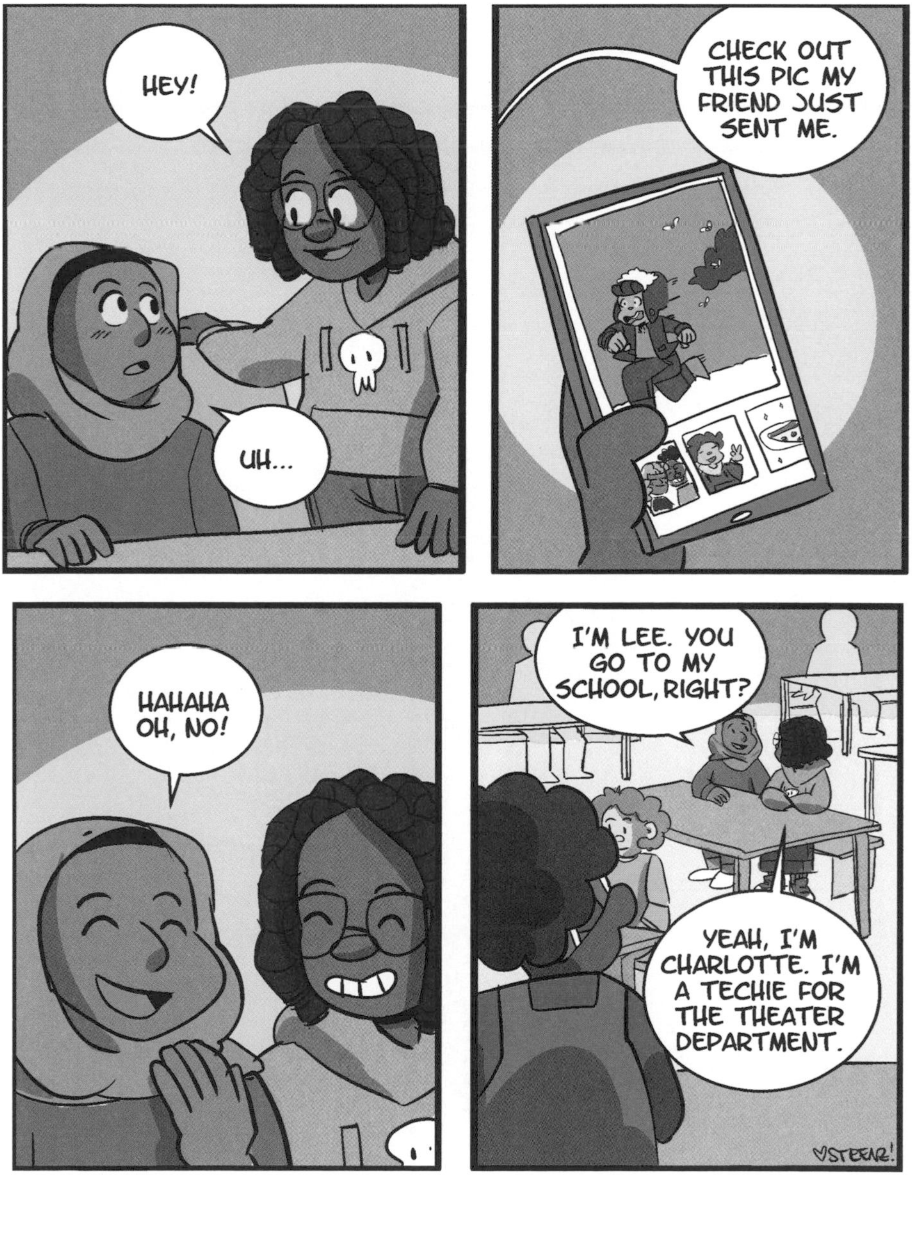
HEY!
UH...
CHECK OUT THIS PIC MY FRIEND JUST SENT ME.
HAHAHA OH, NO!
I'M LEE. YOU GO TO MY SCHOOL, RIGHT?
YEAH, I'M CHARLOTTE. I'M A TECHIE FOR THE THEATER DEPARTMENT.

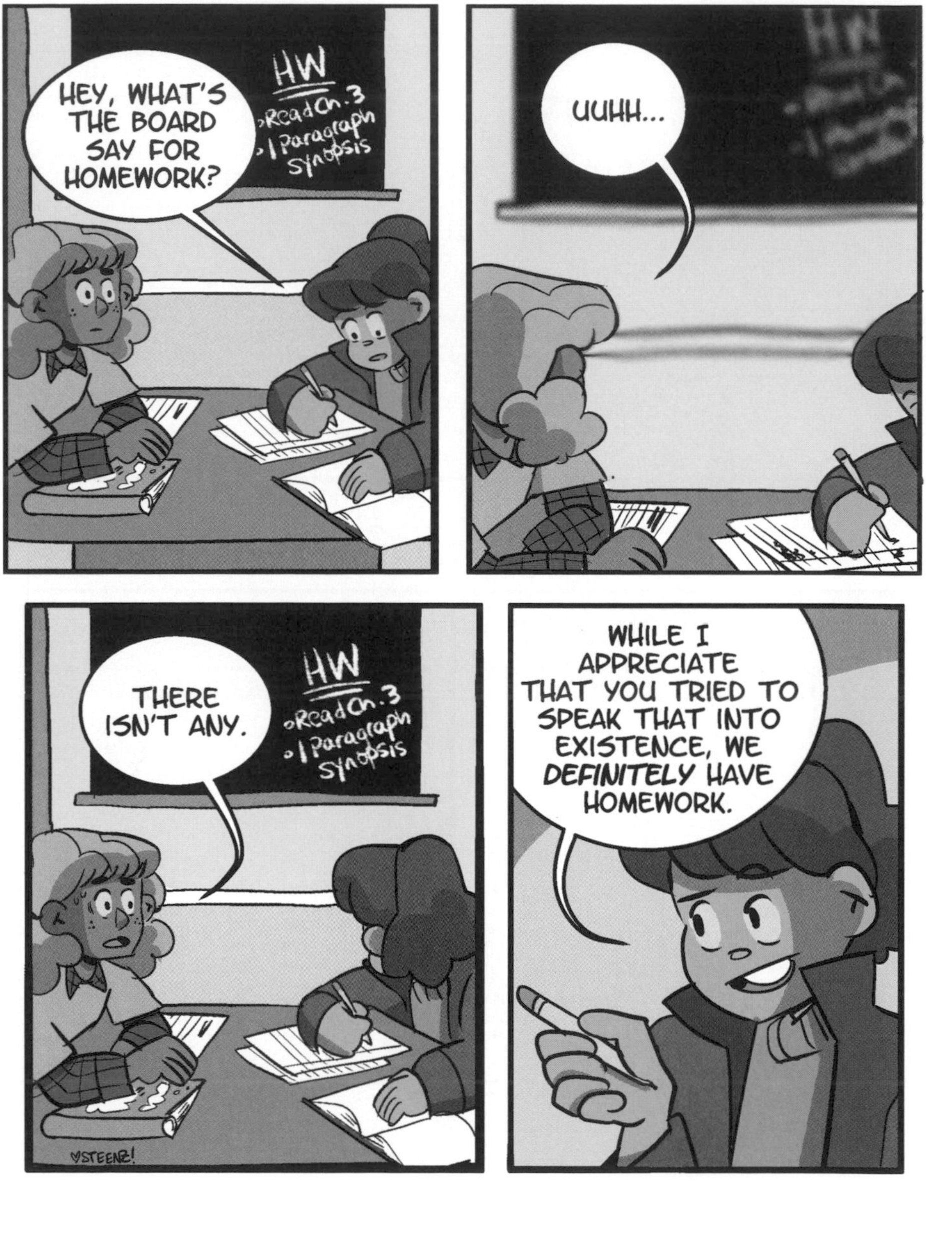
HEY, WHAT'S THE BOARD SAY FOR HOMEWORK?
HW
Read Ch. 3
1 Paragraph Synopsis
UUHH...
THERE ISN'T ANY.
HW
Read Ch. 3
1 Paragraph Synopsis
♡STEENZ!
WHILE I APPRECIATE THAT YOU TRIED TO SPEAK THAT INTO EXISTENCE, WE *DEFINITELY* HAVE HOMEWORK.

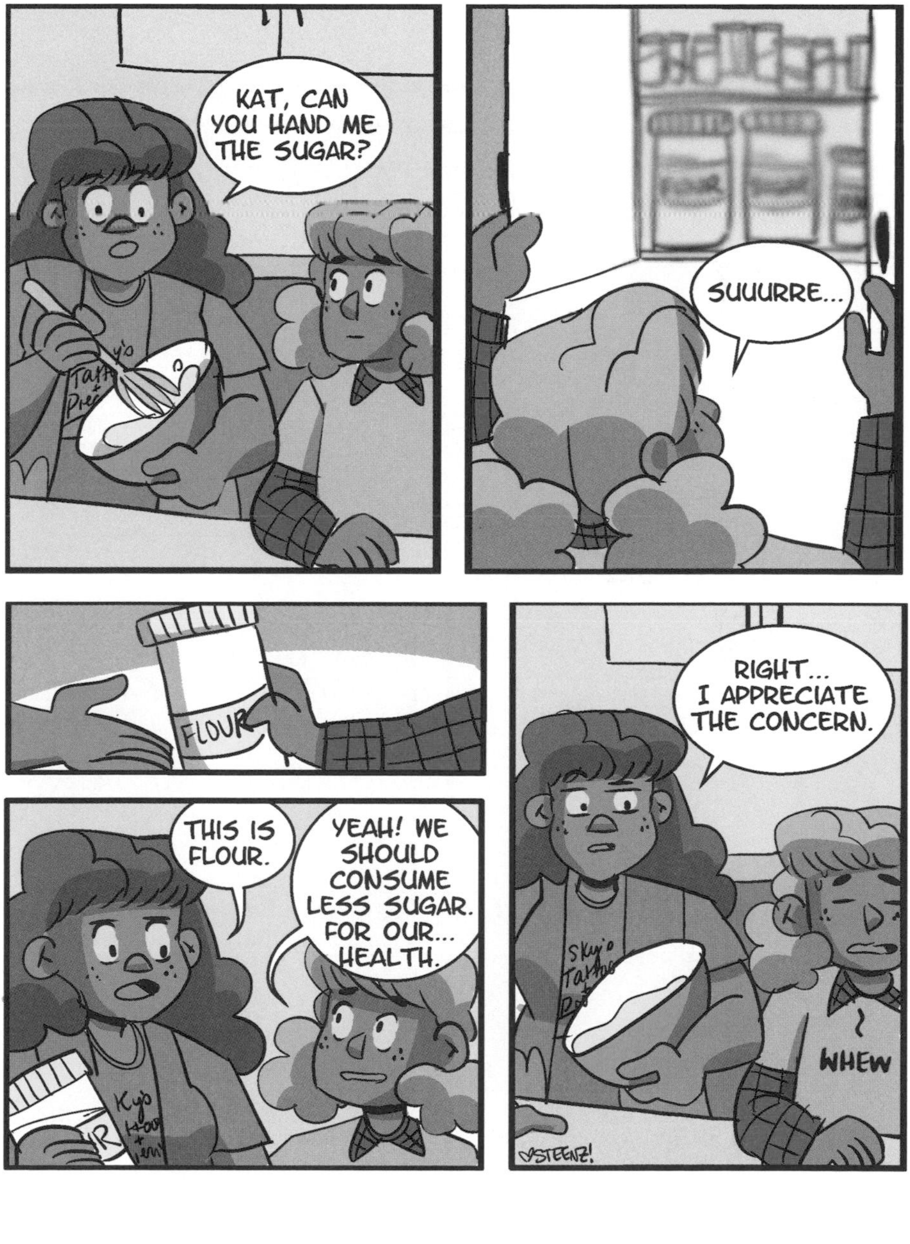
KAT, CAN YOU HAND ME THE SUGAR?
SUUURRE...
FLOUR
THIS IS FLOUR.
YEAH! WE SHOULD CONSUME LESS SUGAR. FOR OUR... HEALTH.
RIGHT... I APPRECIATE THE CONCERN.
WHEW
♡STEENZ!

HHMM...
LET ME DO IT.
PERHAPS MY INTELLECT HAS FINALLY SURPASSED YOURS, KAT.
STEENZ!
OR MAYBE SHE NEEDS GLASSES.
WHY NOT BOTH?

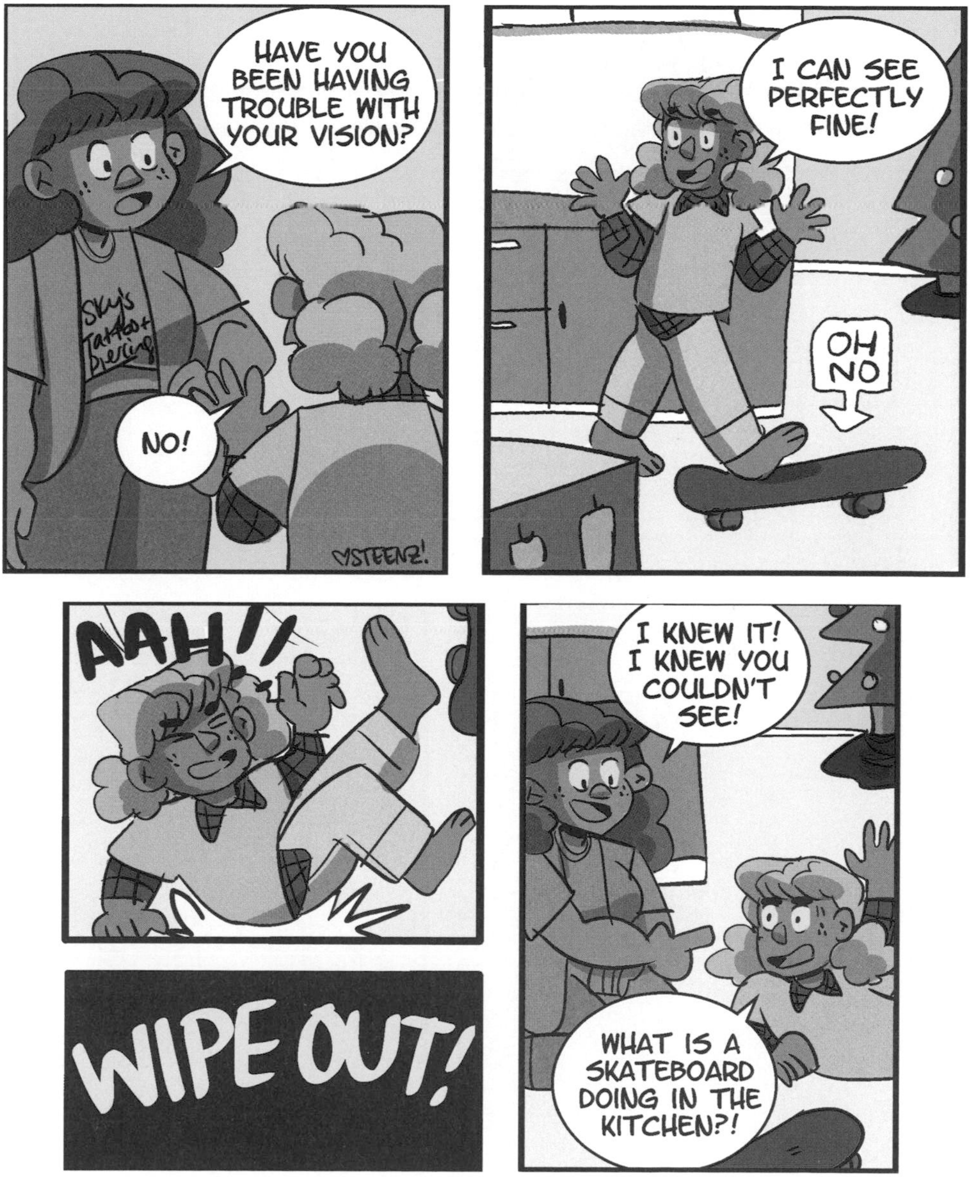
HAVE YOU BEEN HAVING TROUBLE WITH YOUR VISION?
Sky's Tattoo+ Piercing
NO!
STEENZ!
I CAN SEE PERFECTLY FINE!
OH NO
AAH!!
WIPE OUT!
I KNEW IT! I KNEW YOU COULDN'T SEE!
WHAT IS A SKATEBOARD DOING IN THE KITCHEN?!

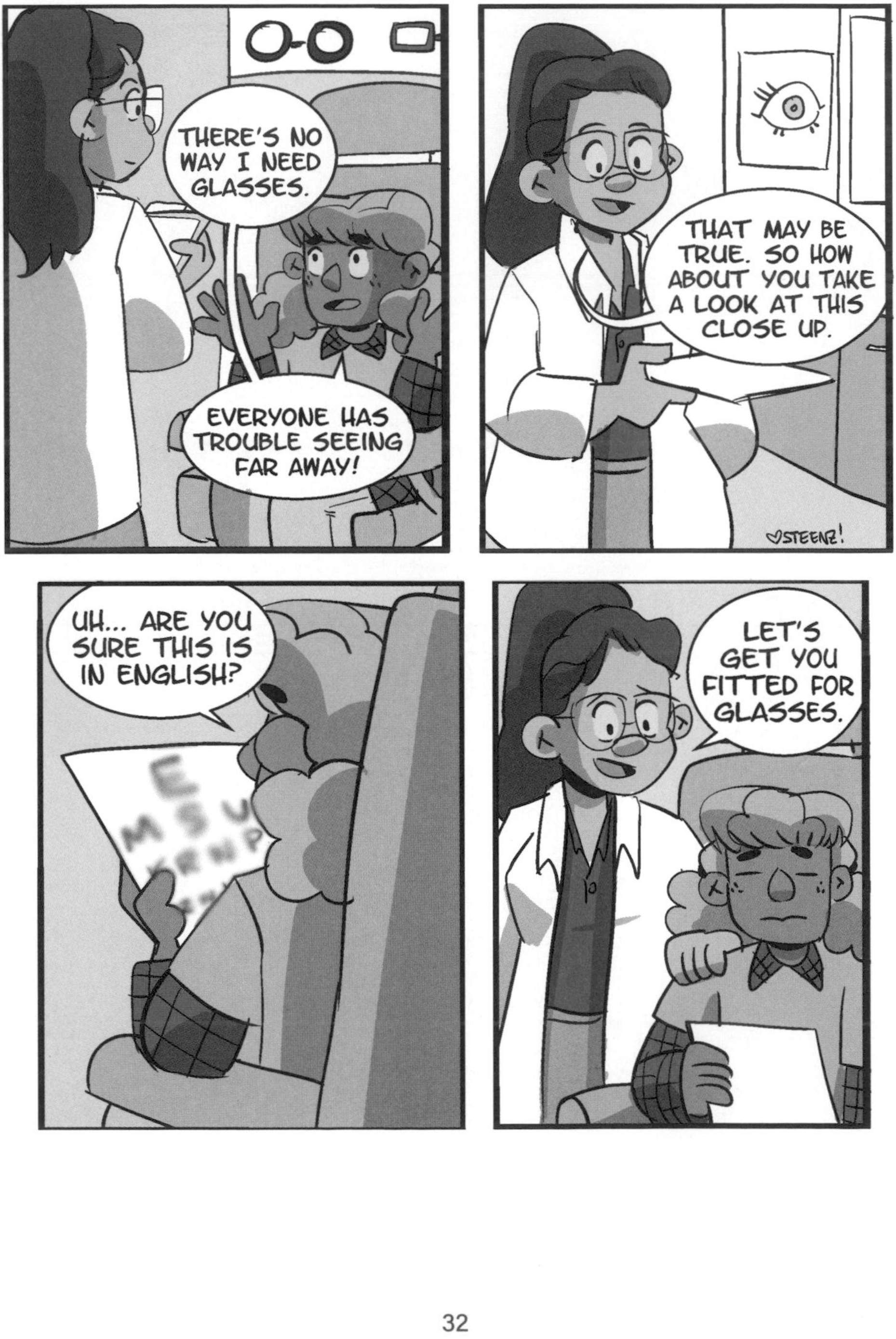
THERE'S NO WAY I NEED GLASSES.
EVERYONE HAS TROUBLE SEEING FAR AWAY!
THAT MAY BE TRUE. SO HOW ABOUT YOU TAKE A LOOK AT THIS CLOSE UP.
♡STEENZ!
UH... ARE YOU SURE THIS IS IN ENGLISH?
LET'S GET YOU FITTED FOR GLASSES.

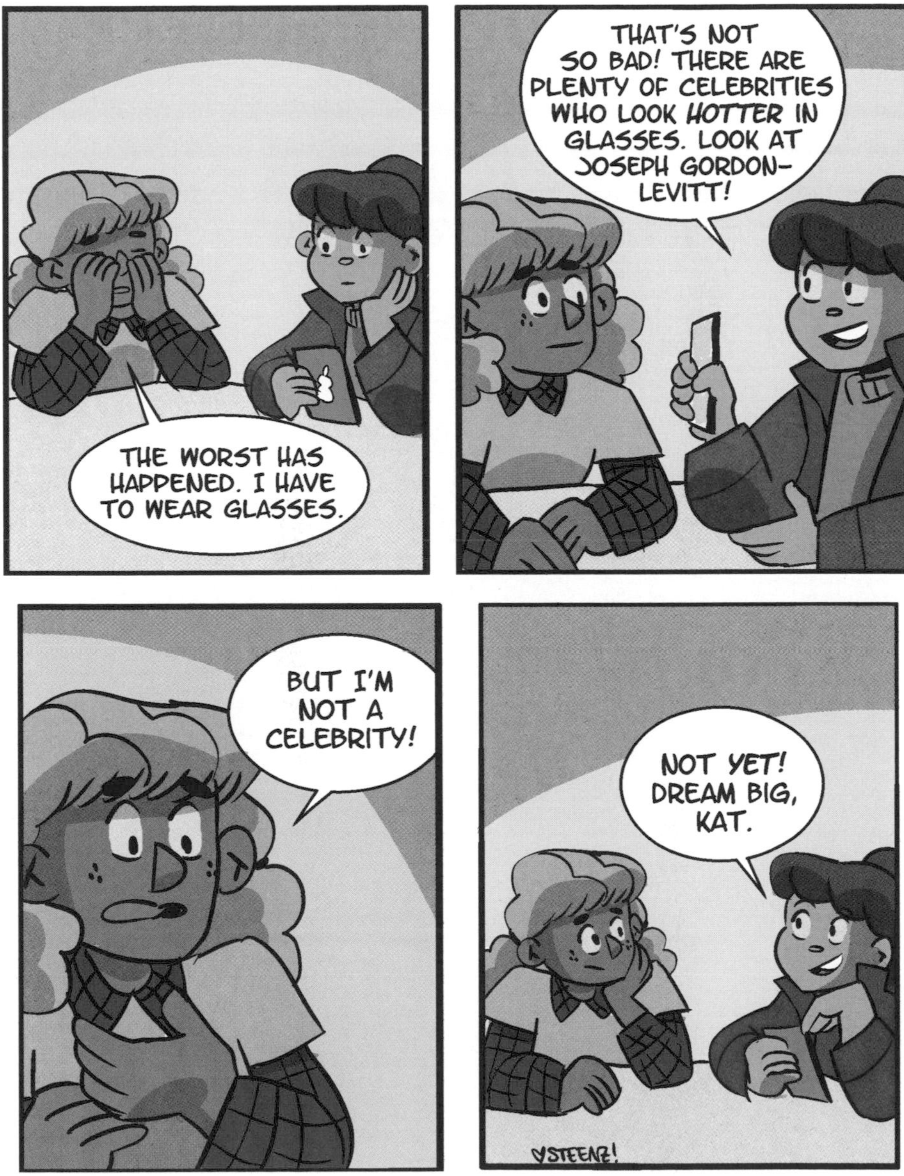
THE WORST HAS HAPPENED. I HAVE TO WEAR GLASSES.
THAT'S NOT SO BAD! THERE ARE PLENTY OF CELEBRITIES WHO LOOK HOTTER IN GLASSES. LOOK AT JOSEPH GORDON-LEVITT!
BUT I'M NOT A CELEBRITY!
NOT YET! DREAM BIG, KAT.
STEENZ!

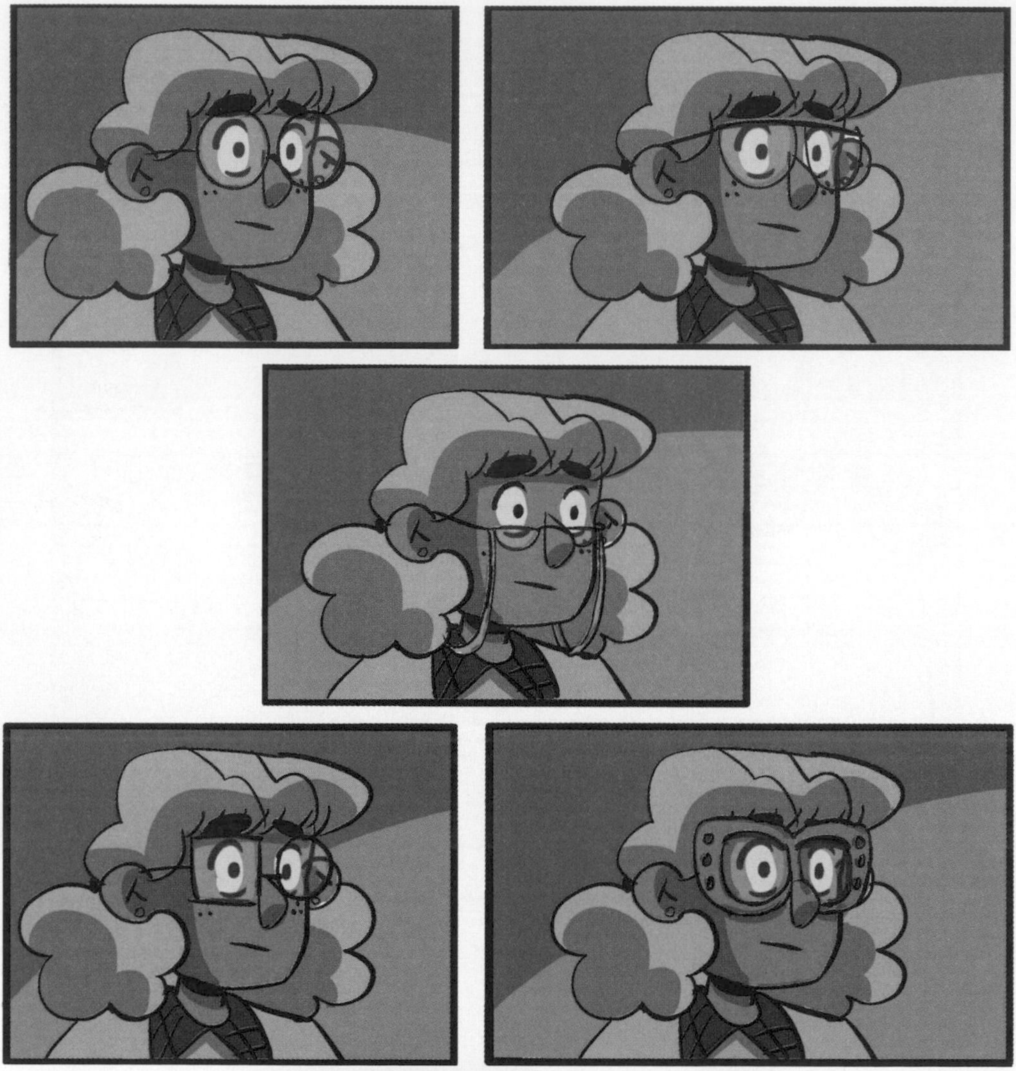
OKAY, I THINK WE'RE GOING IN THE WRONG DIRECTION WITH THESE.
♡STEENZ!

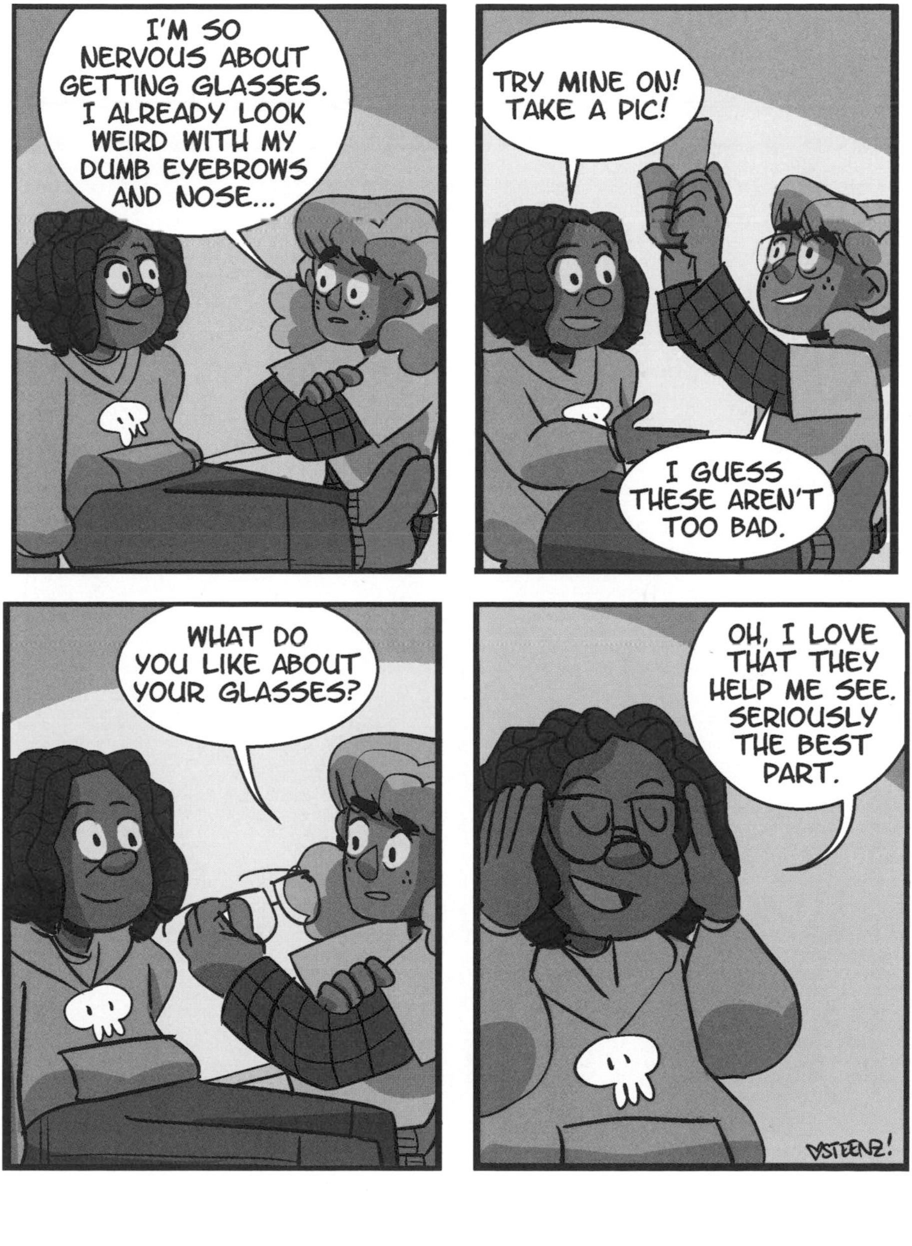
I'M SO NERVOUS ABOUT GETTING GLASSES. I ALREADY LOOK WEIRD WITH MY DUMB EYEBROWS AND NOSE...
TRY MINE ON! TAKE A PIC!
I GUESS THESE AREN'T TOO BAD.
WHAT DO YOU LIKE ABOUT YOUR GLASSES?
OH, I LOVE THAT THEY HELP ME SEE. SERIOUSLY THE BEST PART.
DYSTEENZ!

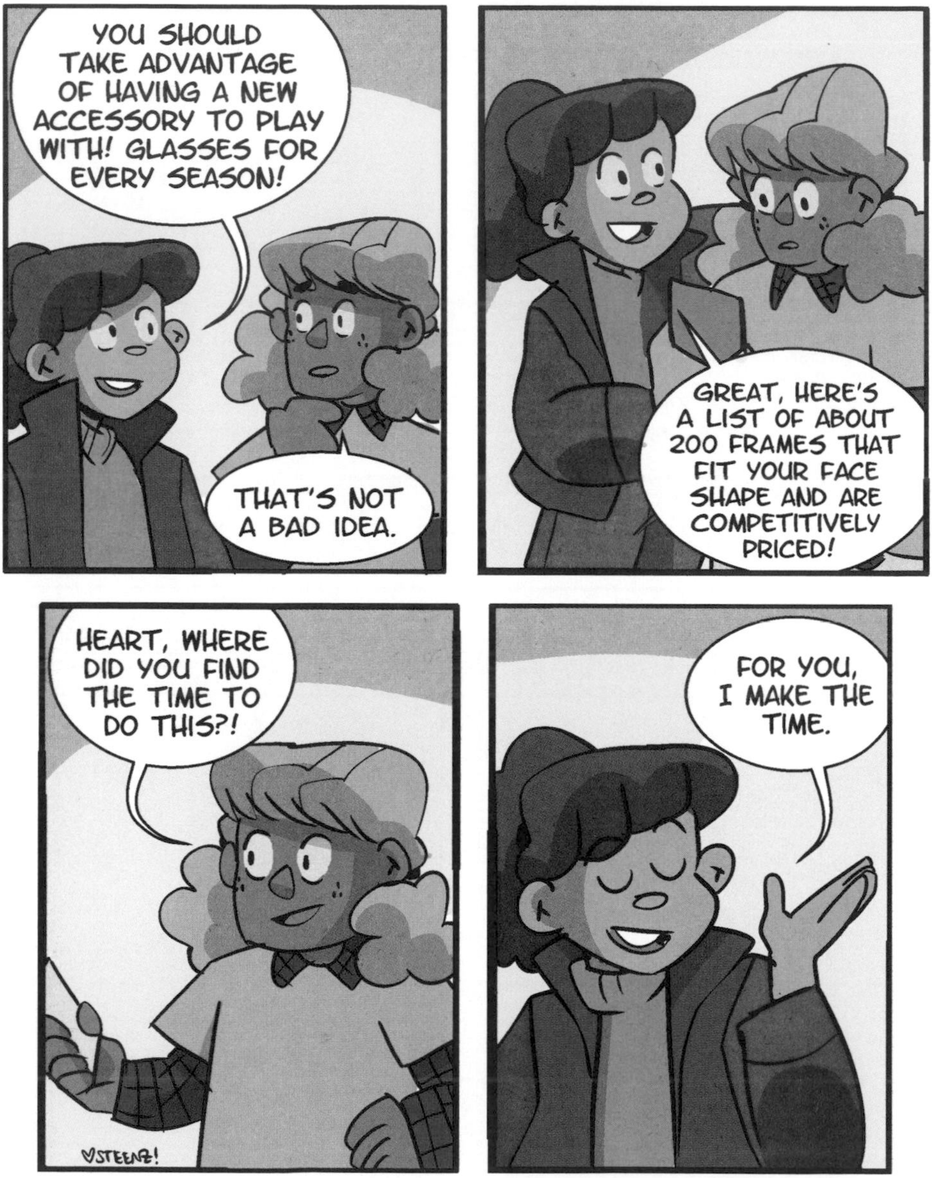
YOU SHOULD TAKE ADVANTAGE OF HAVING A NEW ACCESSORY TO PLAY WITH! GLASSES FOR EVERY SEASON!
THAT'S NOT A BAD IDEA.
GREAT, HERE'S A LIST OF ABOUT 200 FRAMES THAT FIT YOUR FACE SHAPE AND ARE COMPETITIVELY PRICED!
HEART, WHERE DID YOU FIND THE TIME TO DO THIS?!
♡STEENZ!
FOR YOU, I MAKE THE TIME.

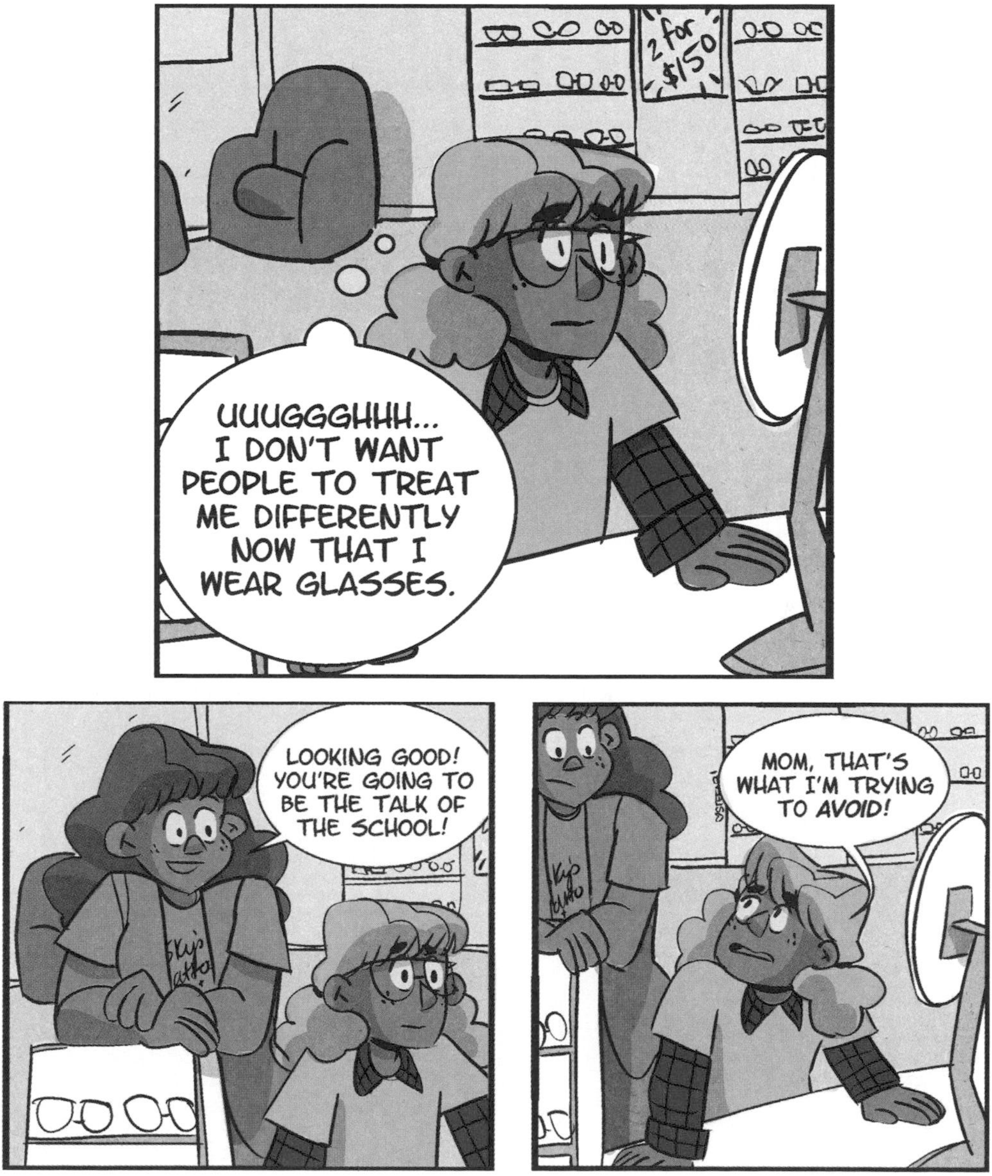
2 for $150
UUUGGGHHH... I DON'T WANT PEOPLE TO TREAT ME DIFFERENTLY NOW THAT I WEAR GLASSES.
LOOKING GOOD! YOU'RE GOING TO BE THE TALK OF THE SCHOOL!
MOM, THAT'S WHAT I'M TRYING TO *AVOID!*

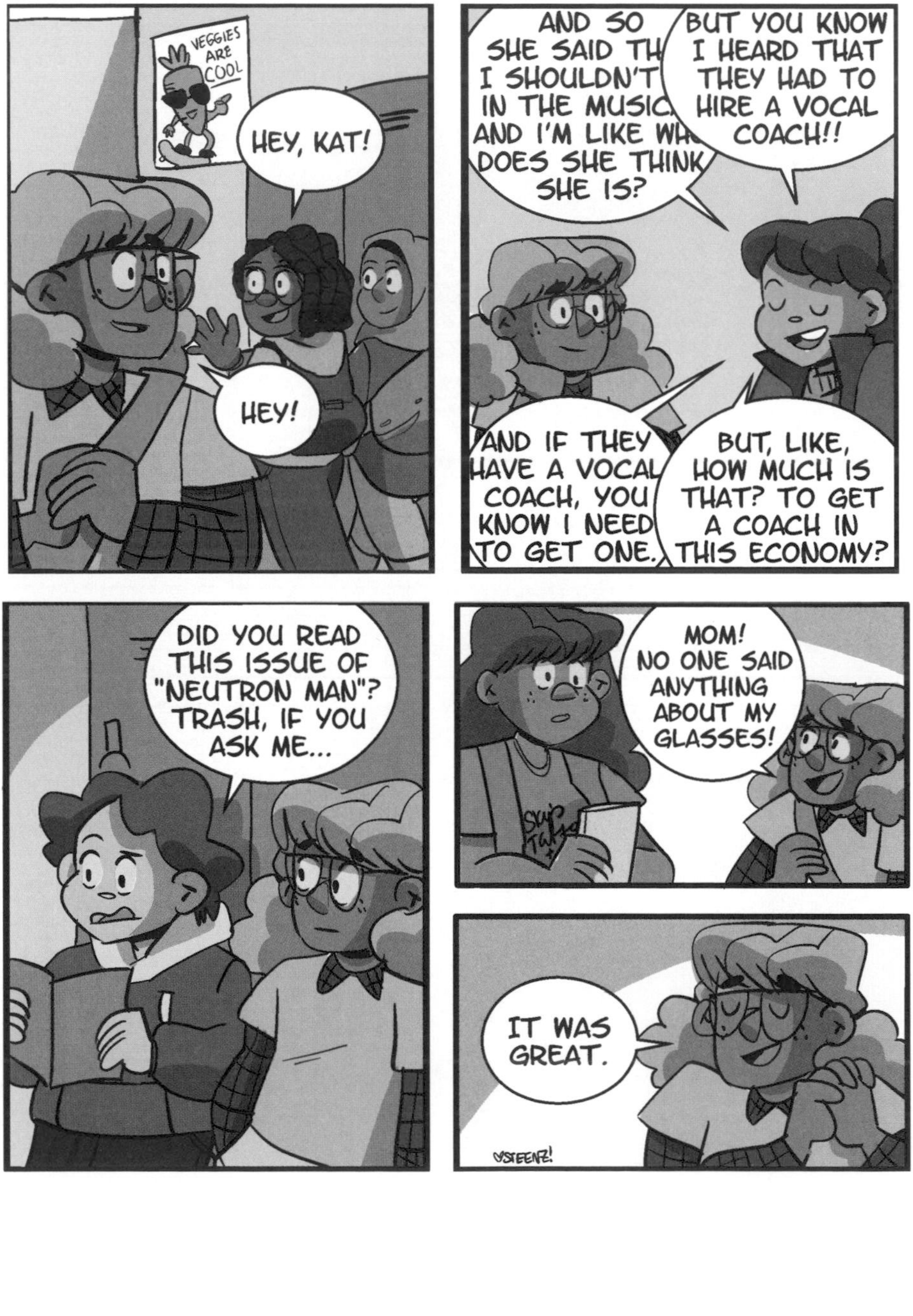
VEGGIES ARE COOL
HEY, KAT!
HEY!
AND SO SHE SAID TH I SHOULDN'T IN THE MUSIC AND I'M LIKE WH DOES SHE THINK SHE IS?
BUT YOU KNOW I HEARD THAT THEY HAD TO HIRE A VOCAL COACH!!
AND IF THEY HAVE A VOCAL COACH, YOU KNOW I NEED TO GET ONE.
BUT, LIKE, HOW MUCH IS THAT? TO GET A COACH IN THIS ECONOMY?
DID YOU READ THIS ISSUE OF "NEUTRON MAN"? TRASH, IF YOU ASK ME...
MOM! NO ONE SAID ANYTHING ABOUT MY GLASSES!
IT WAS GREAT.

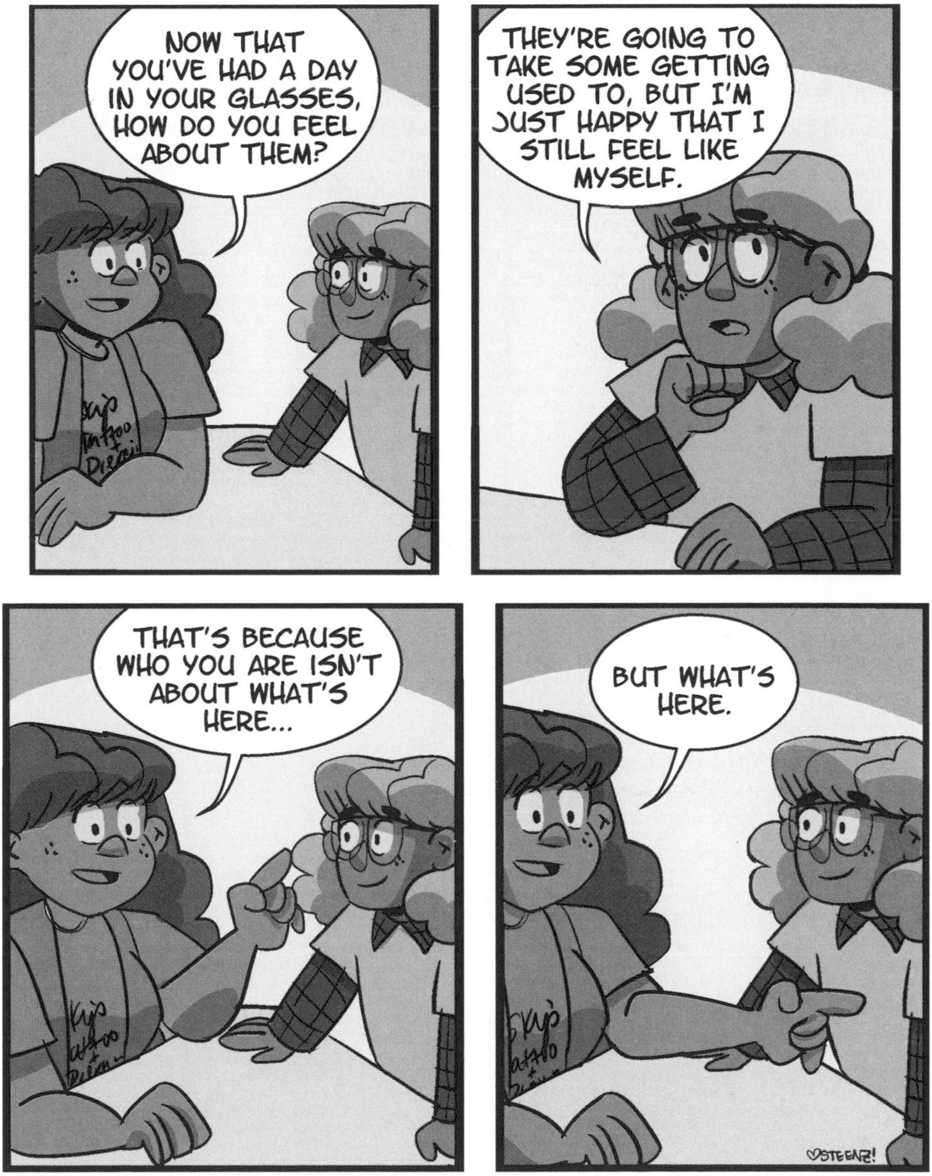
NOW THAT YOU'VE HAD A DAY IN YOUR GLASSES, HOW DO YOU FEEL ABOUT THEM?
THEY'RE GOING TO TAKE SOME GETTING USED TO, BUT I'M JUST HAPPY THAT I STILL FEEL LIKE MYSELF.
THAT'S BECAUSE WHO YOU ARE ISN'T ABOUT WHAT'S HERE...
BUT WHAT'S HERE.
STEENZ!

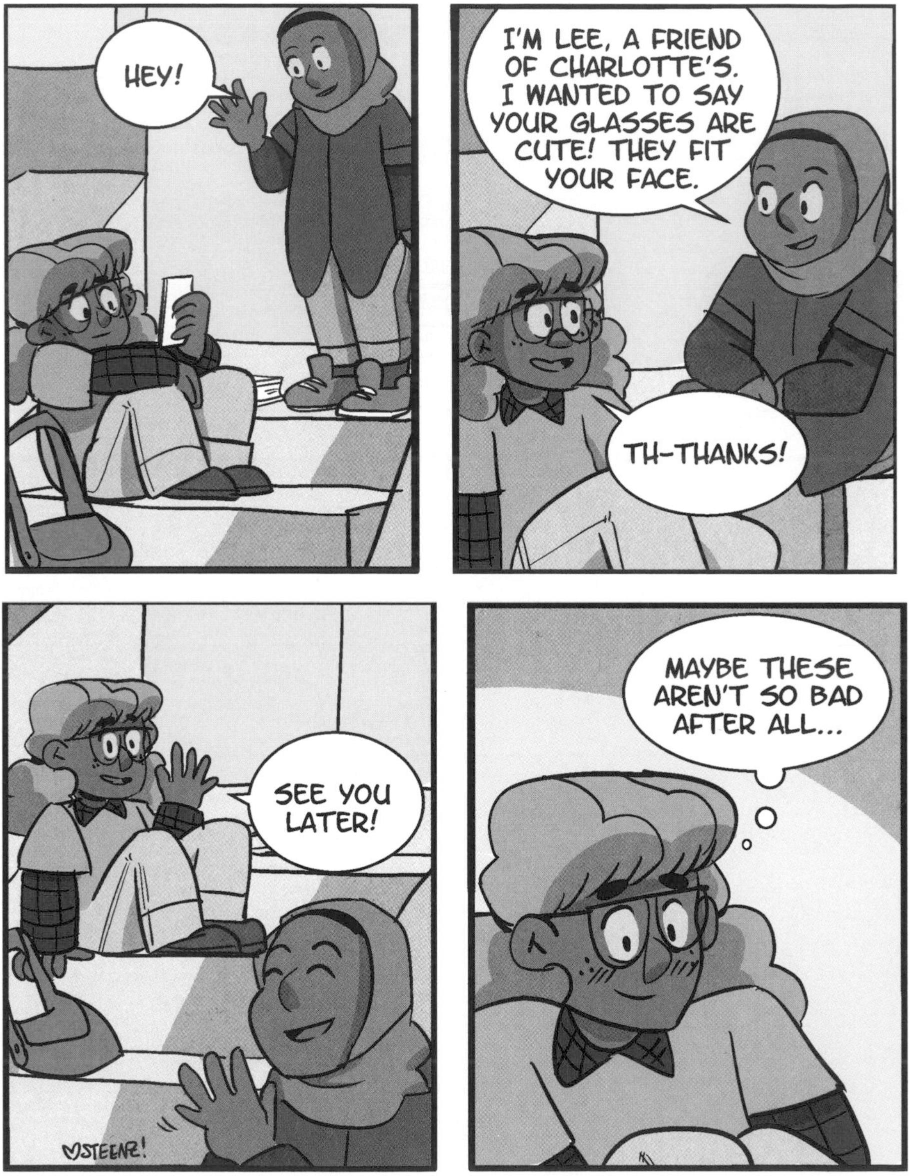
HEY!
I'M LEE, A FRIEND OF CHARLOTTE'S. I WANTED TO SAY YOUR GLASSES ARE CUTE! THEY FIT YOUR FACE.
TH-THANKS!
SEE YOU LATER!
STEENZ!
MAYBE THESE AREN'T SO BAD AFTER ALL...

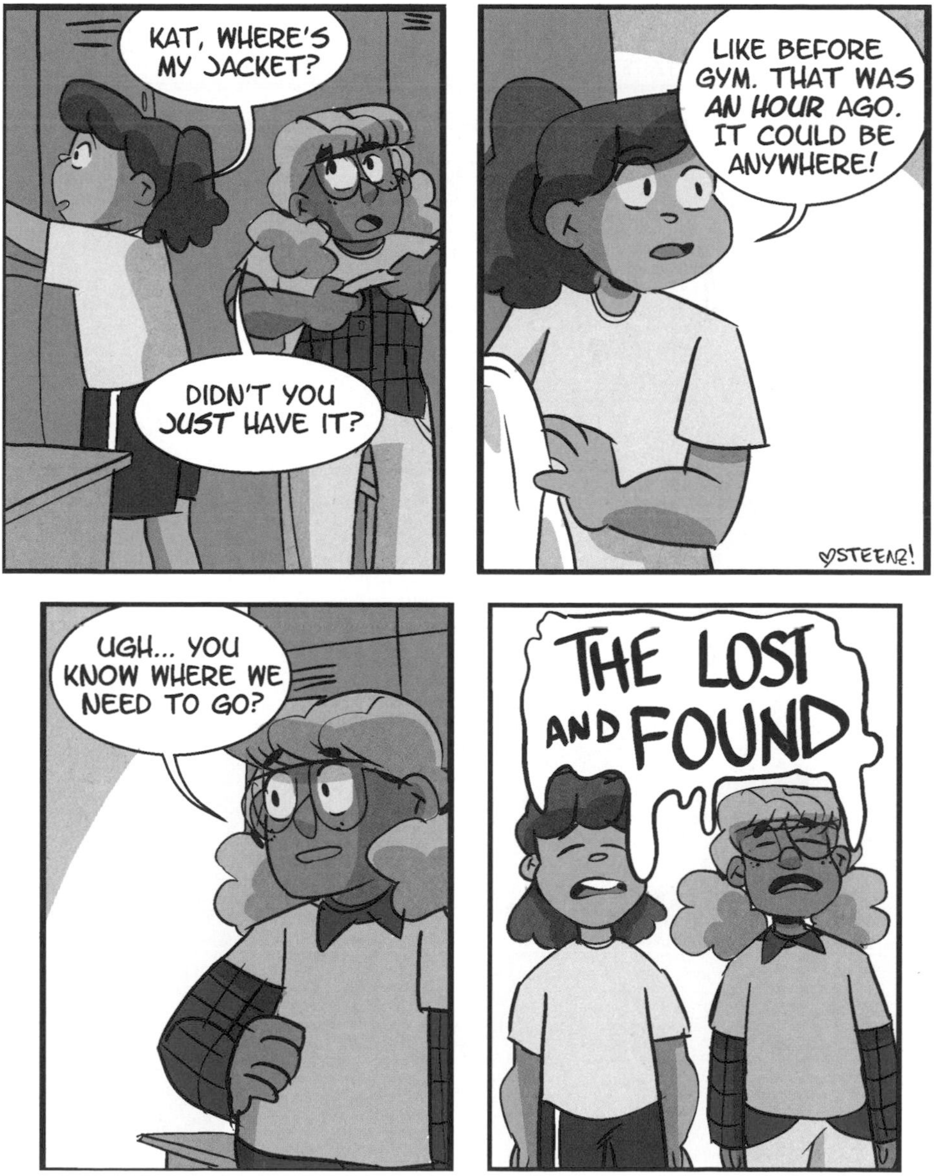
KAT, WHERE'S MY JACKET?
DIDN'T YOU JUST HAVE IT?
LIKE BEFORE GYM. THAT WAS AN HOUR AGO. IT COULD BE ANYWHERE!
♡STEENZ!
UGH... YOU KNOW WHERE WE NEED TO GO?
THE LOST AND FOUND

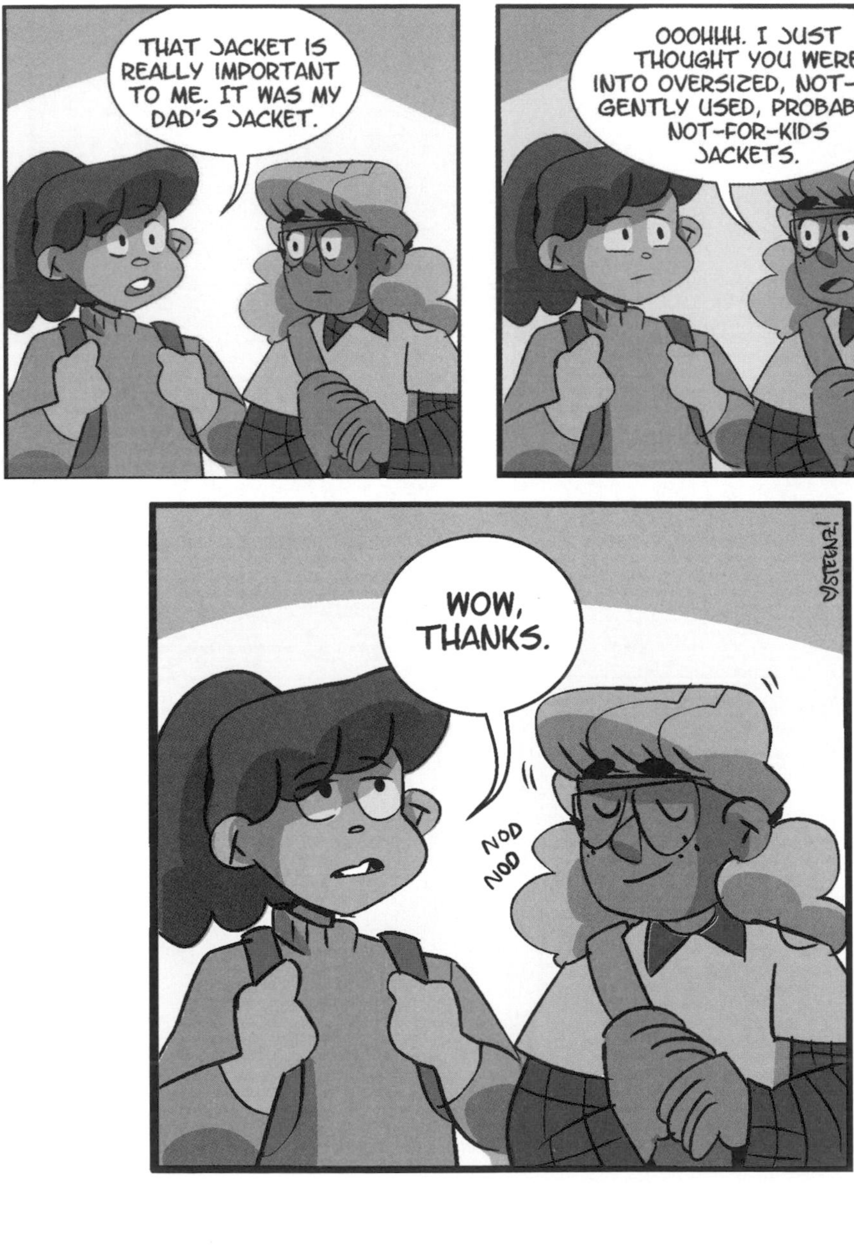
THAT JACKET IS REALLY IMPORTANT TO ME. IT WAS MY DAD'S JACKET.
OOOHHH. I JUST THOUGHT YOU WERE INTO OVERSIZED, NOT-SO-GENTLY USED, PROBABLY-NOT-FOR-KIDS JACKETS.
WOW, THANKS.
NOD NOD

HEY! CAN WE SEE THE LOST AND FOUND?

SURE, ONE SECOND!

WHEN DID YOUR DAD GIVE YOU THAT JACKET?

HHMMM... I THINK I WAS REALLY SMALL. LIKE 4 OR 5 YEARS OLD.

♡STEENZ!

HEART - 4 OR 5 YEARS OLD

MUNCH! CRUNCH!

WELL, WHAT'S MORE IMPORTANT, ANTONIO? US OR YOUR "CAREER"?
STEENZ!
EXCUSE ME!!
I AM TRYING TO GET MY BEAUTY SLEEP.
YOU SEE WHAT YOU'RE DOING? SHE'S TRYING TO GET HER BEAUTY SLEEP!

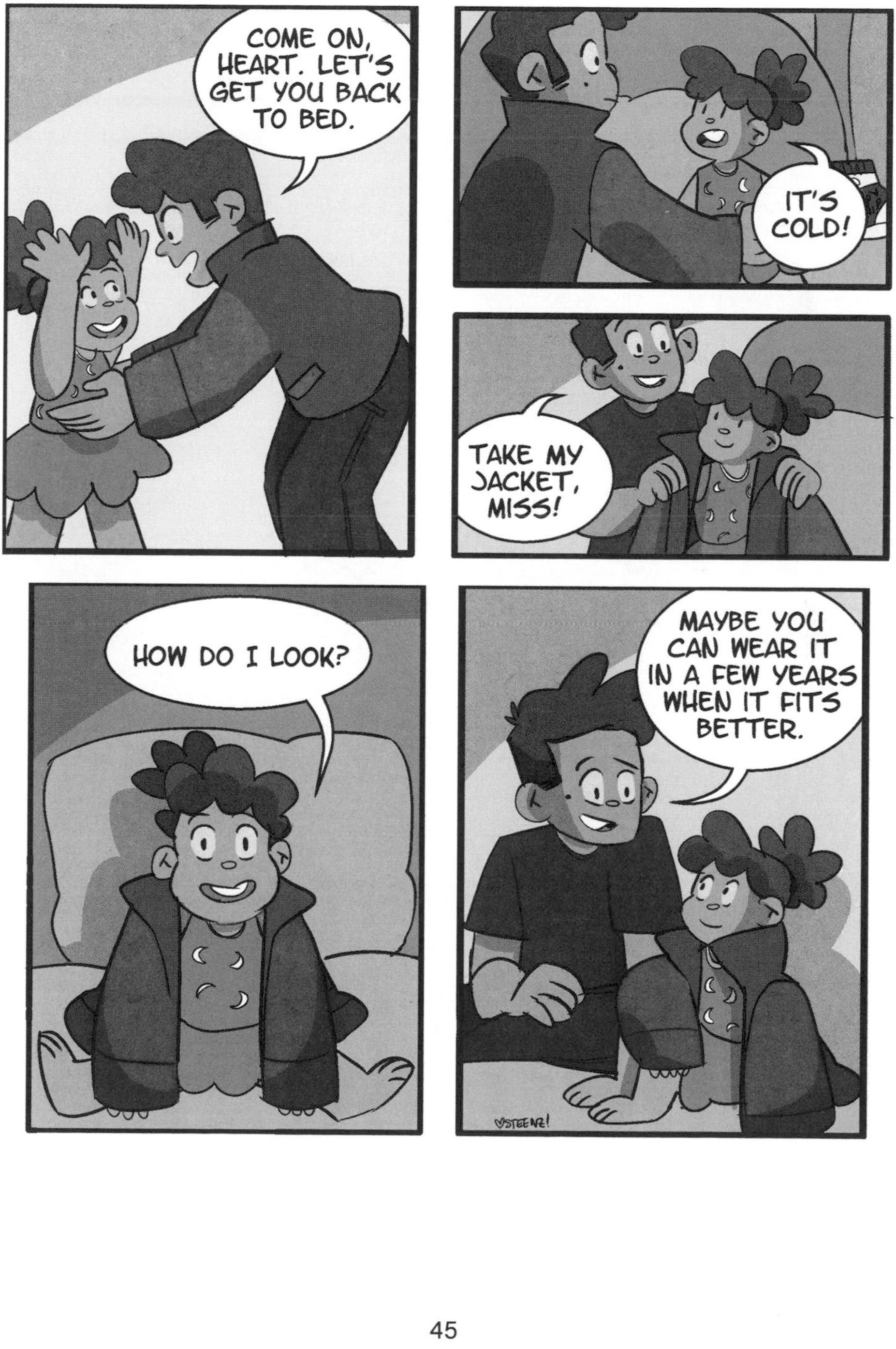
COME ON, HEART. LET'S GET YOU BACK TO BED.
IT'S COLD!
TAKE MY JACKET, MISS!
HOW DO I LOOK?
MAYBE YOU CAN WEAR IT IN A FEW YEARS WHEN IT FITS BETTER.

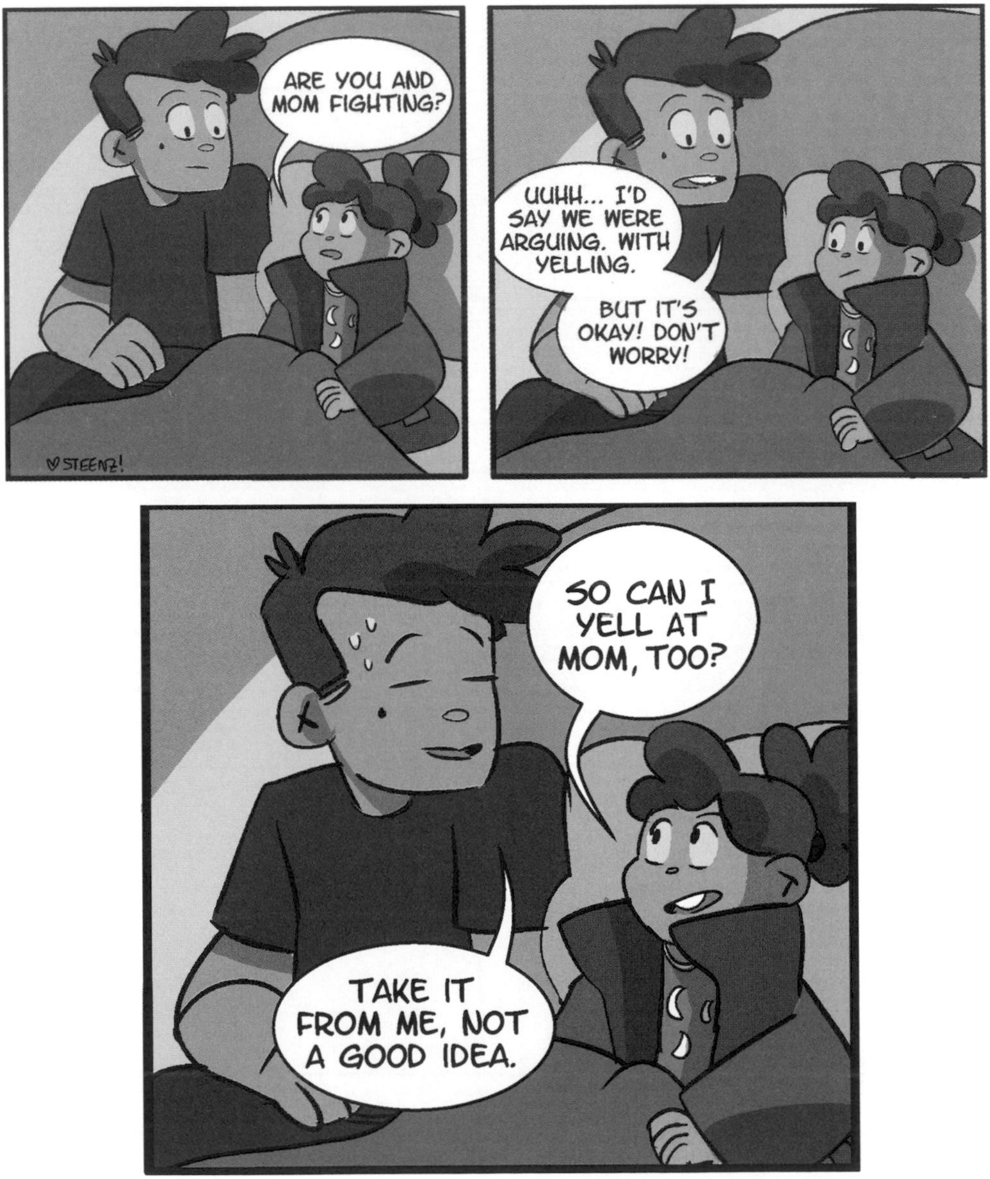
ARE YOU AND MOM FIGHTING?
♡STEENZ!
UUHH... I'D SAY WE WERE ARGUING. WITH YELLING.
BUT IT'S OKAY! DON'T WORRY!
SO CAN I YELL AT MOM, TOO?
TAKE IT FROM ME, NOT A GOOD IDEA.

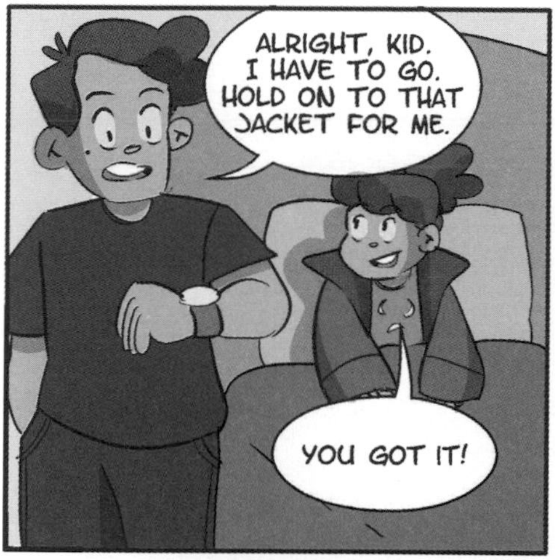
ALRIGHT, KID. I HAVE TO GO. HOLD ON TO THAT JACKET FOR ME.
YOU GOT IT!

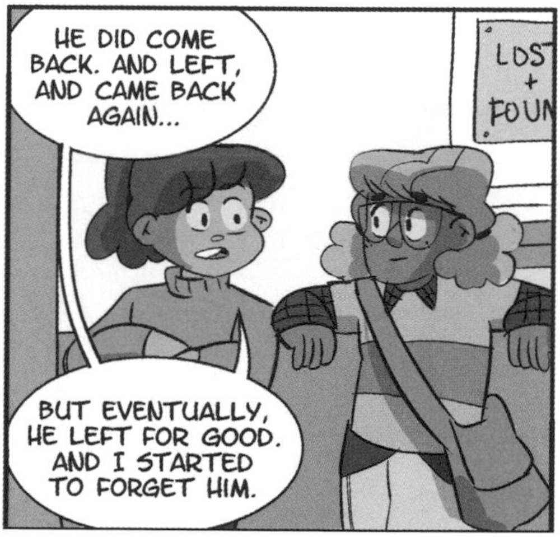
HE DID COME BACK. AND LEFT, AND CAME BACK AGAIN...
LOST + FOUN
BUT EVENTUALLY, HE LEFT FOR GOOD. AND I STARTED TO FORGET HIM.

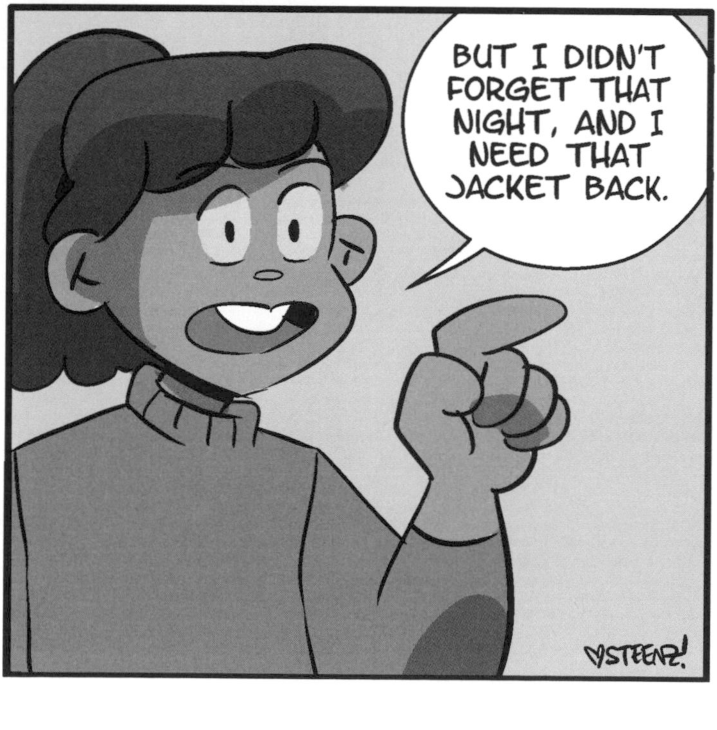
BUT I DIDN'T FORGET THAT NIGHT, AND I NEED THAT JACKET BACK.
STEENZ!

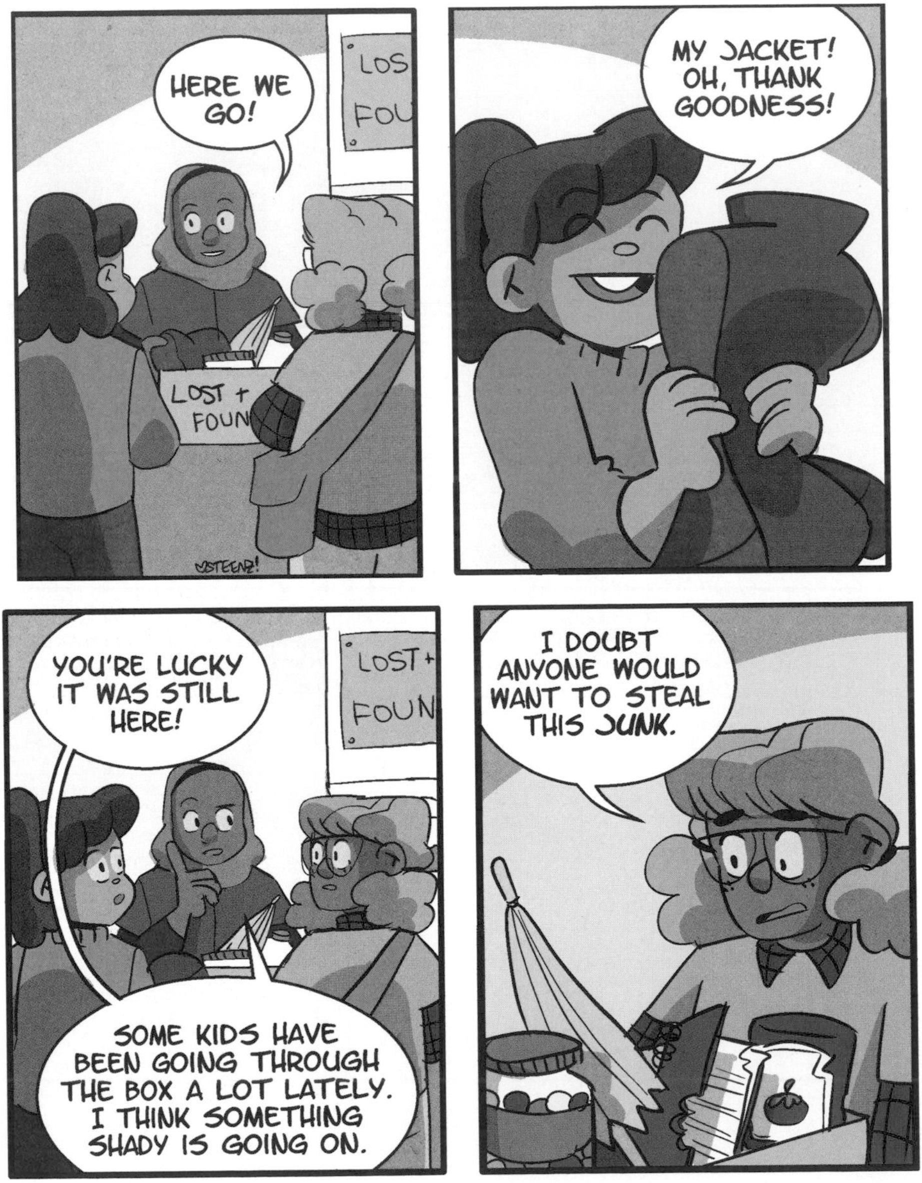
HERE WE GO!
LOS
FOU
LOST + FOUN
©STEENZ!
MY JACKET! OH, THANK GOODNESS!
LOST +
FOUN
YOU'RE LUCKY IT WAS STILL HERE!
SOME KIDS HAVE BEEN GOING THROUGH THE BOX A LOT LATELY. I THINK SOMETHING SHADY IS GOING ON.
I DOUBT ANYONE WOULD WANT TO STEAL THIS JUNK.

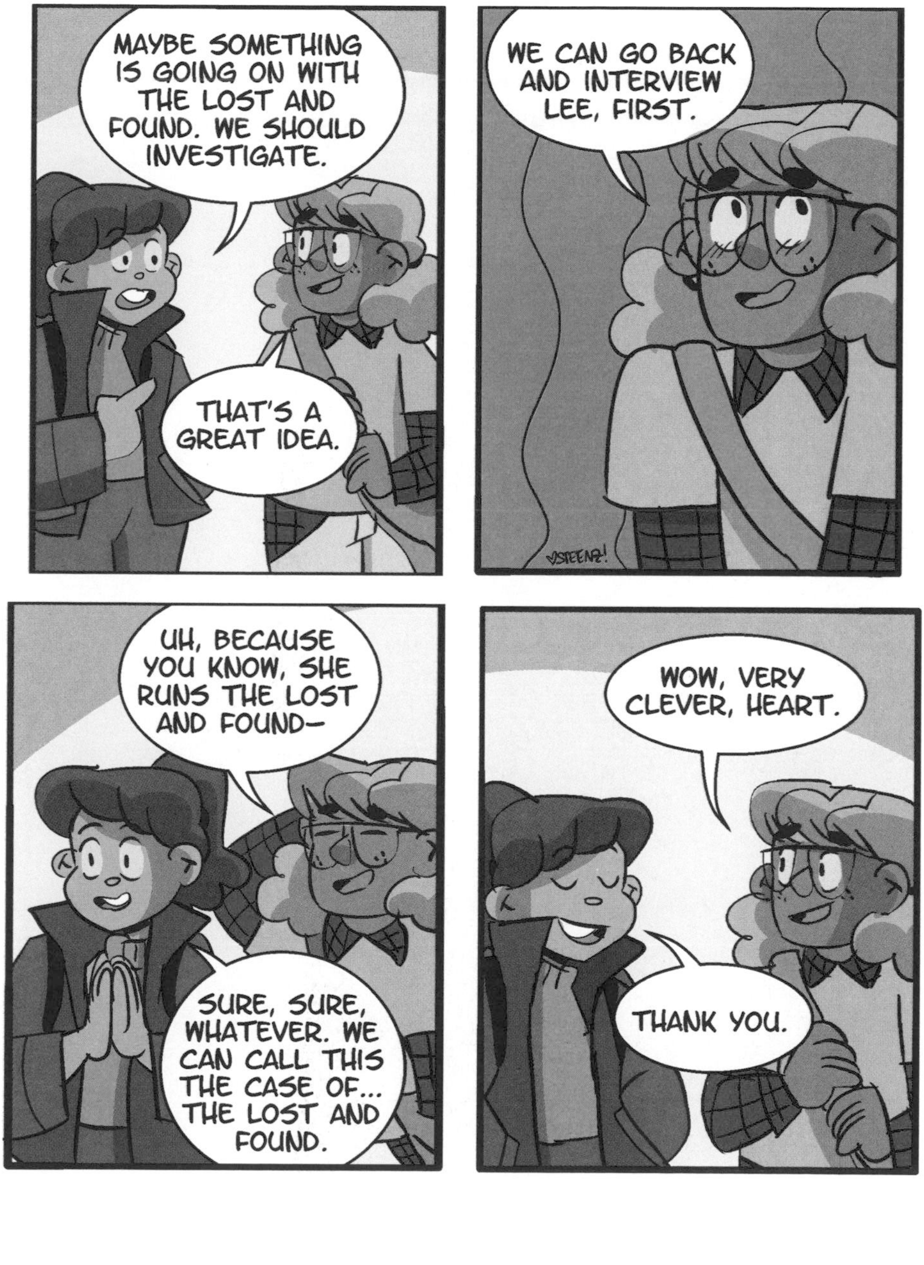
MAYBE SOMETHING IS GOING ON WITH THE LOST AND FOUND. WE SHOULD INVESTIGATE.
THAT'S A GREAT IDEA.
WE CAN GO BACK AND INTERVIEW LEE, FIRST.
♡STEENZ!
UH, BECAUSE YOU KNOW, SHE RUNS THE LOST AND FOUND–
SURE, SURE, WHATEVER. WE CAN CALL THIS THE CASE OF... THE LOST AND FOUND.
WOW, VERY CLEVER, HEART.
THANK YOU.

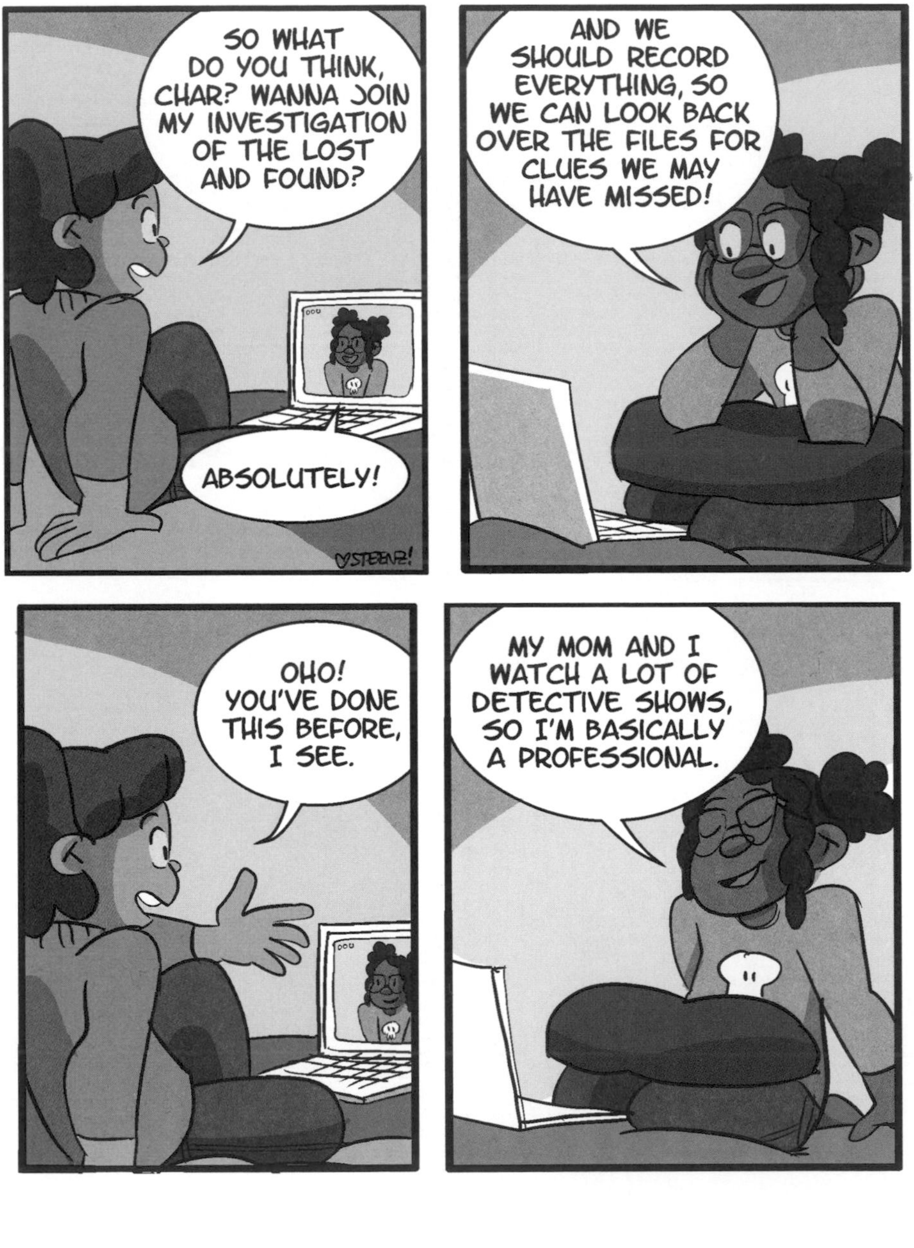
SO WHAT DO YOU THINK, CHAR? WANNA JOIN MY INVESTIGATION OF THE LOST AND FOUND?
ABSOLUTELY!
AND WE SHOULD RECORD EVERYTHING, SO WE CAN LOOK BACK OVER THE FILES FOR CLUES WE MAY HAVE MISSED!
OHO! YOU'VE DONE THIS BEFORE, I SEE.
MY MOM AND I WATCH A LOT OF DETECTIVE SHOWS, SO I'M BASICALLY A PROFESSIONAL.

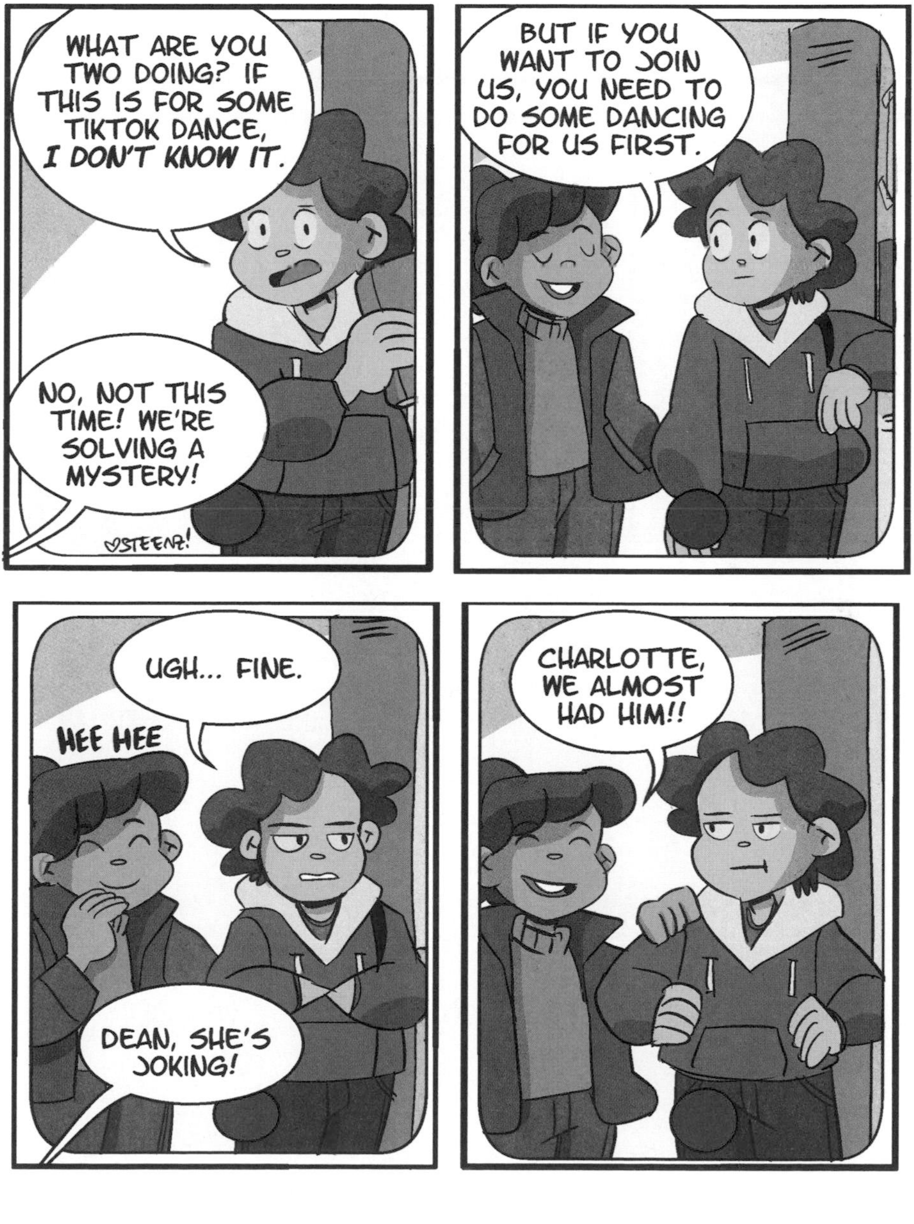
WHAT ARE YOU TWO DOING? IF THIS IS FOR SOME TIKTOK DANCE, *I DON'T KNOW IT.*
NO, NOT THIS TIME! WE'RE SOLVING A MYSTERY!
♡STEENZ!
BUT IF YOU WANT TO JOIN US, YOU NEED TO DO SOME DANCING FOR US FIRST.
HEE HEE
UGH... FINE.
DEAN, SHE'S JOKING!
CHARLOTTE, WE ALMOST HAD HIM!!

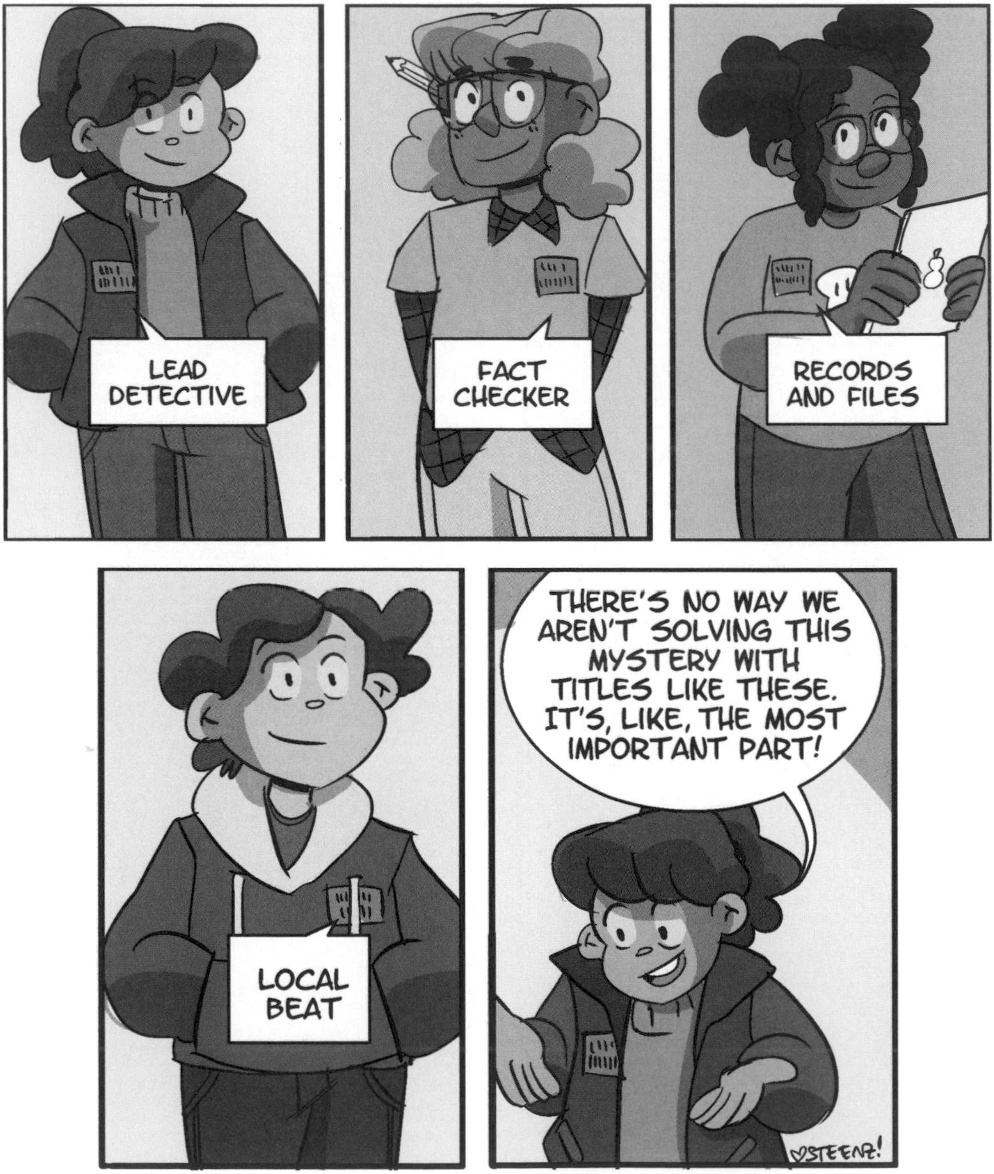
LEAD DETECTIVE
FACT CHECKER
RECORDS AND FILES
LOCAL BEAT
THERE'S NO WAY WE AREN'T SOLVING THIS MYSTERY WITH TITLES LIKE THESE. IT'S, LIKE, THE MOST IMPORTANT PART!
STEENZ!

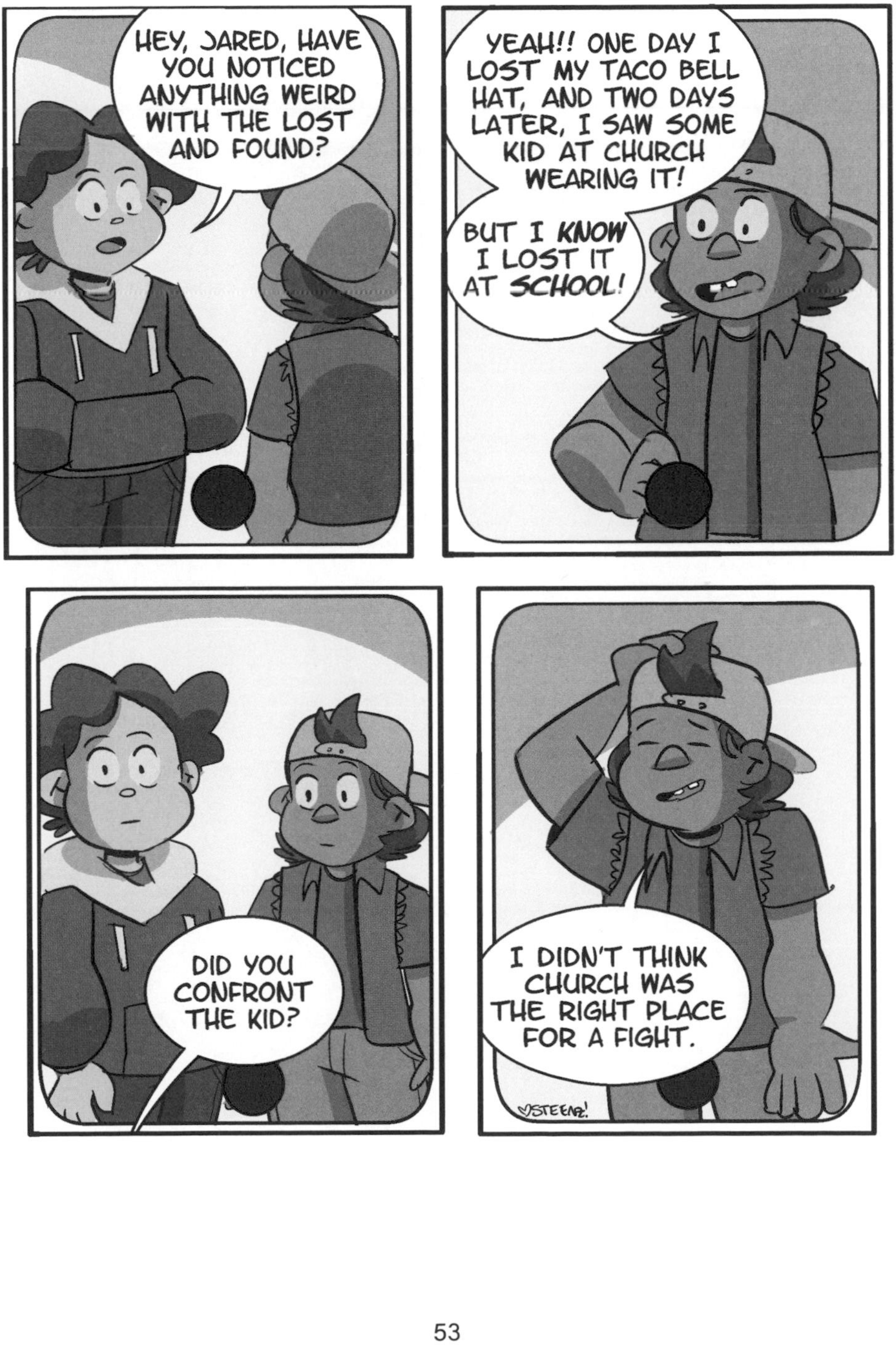
HEY, JARED, HAVE YOU NOTICED ANYTHING WEIRD WITH THE LOST AND FOUND?
YEAH!! ONE DAY I LOST MY TACO BELL HAT, AND TWO DAYS LATER, I SAW SOME KID AT CHURCH WEARING IT!
BUT I *KNOW* I LOST IT AT *SCHOOL*!
DID YOU CONFRONT THE KID?
I DIDN'T THINK CHURCH WAS THE RIGHT PLACE FOR A FIGHT.
♡STEENZ!

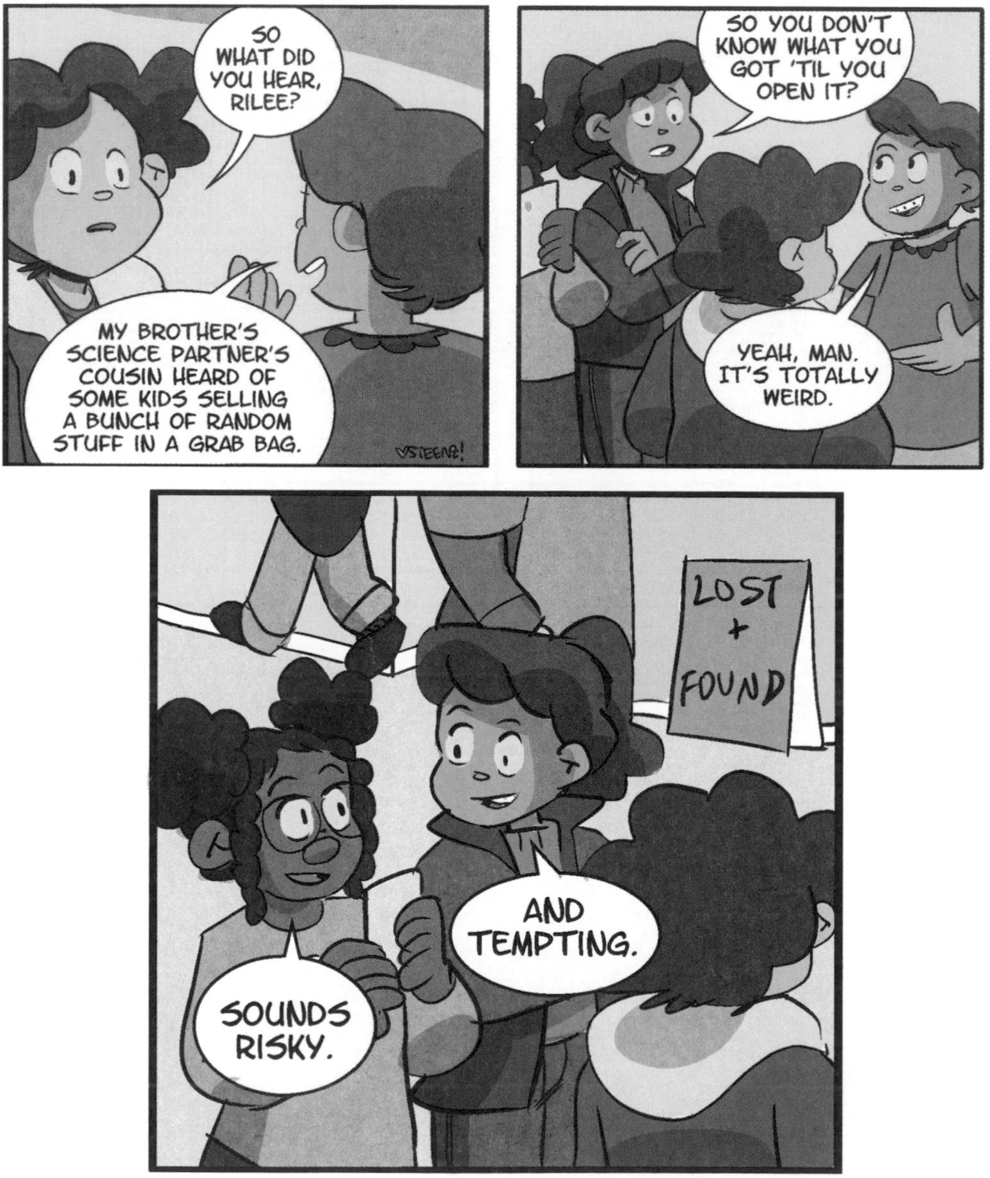
SO WHAT DID YOU HEAR, RILEE?
MY BROTHER'S SCIENCE PARTNER'S COUSIN HEARD OF SOME KIDS SELLING A BUNCH OF RANDOM STUFF IN A GRAB BAG.
SO YOU DON'T KNOW WHAT YOU GOT 'TIL YOU OPEN IT?
YEAH, MAN. IT'S TOTALLY WEIRD.
LOST + FOUND
SOUNDS RISKY.
AND TEMPTING.

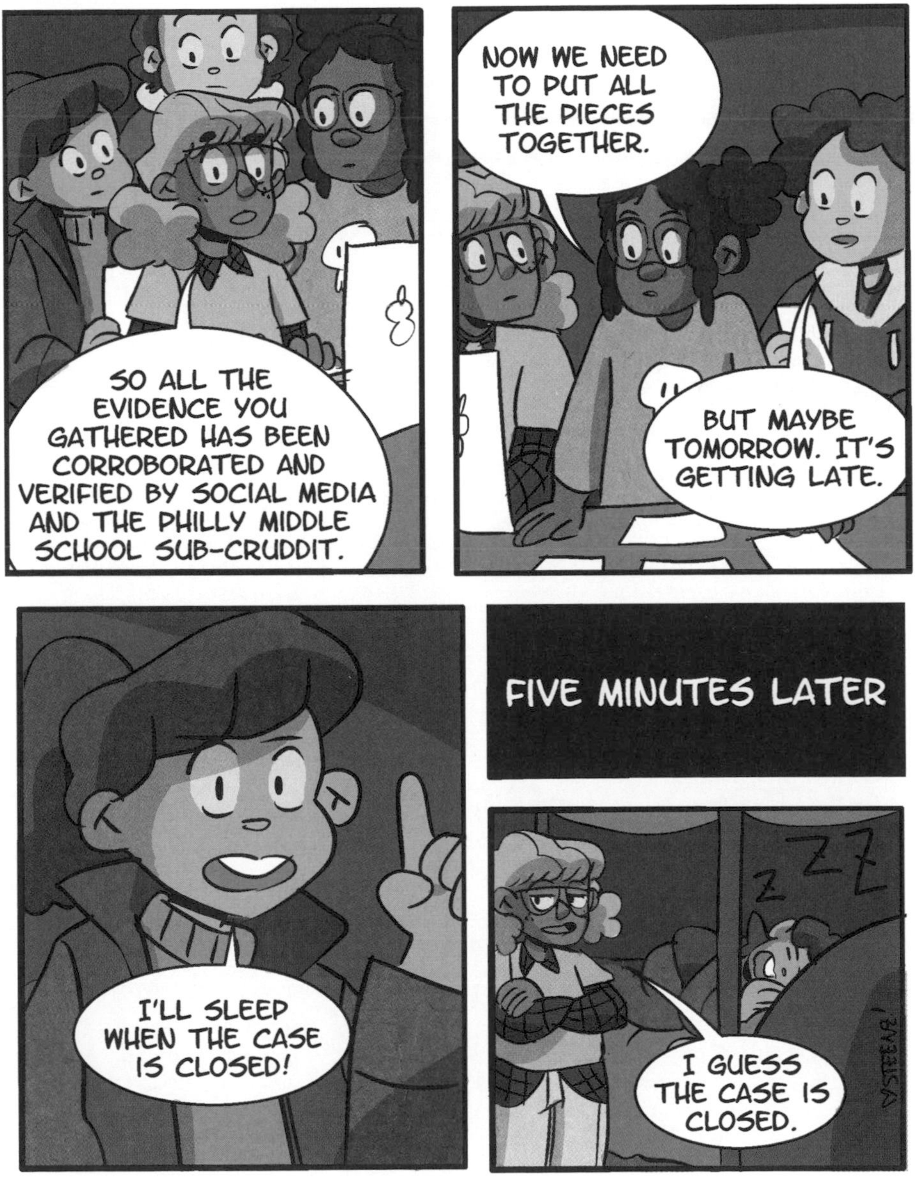
SO ALL THE EVIDENCE YOU GATHERED HAS BEEN CORROBORATED AND VERIFIED BY SOCIAL MEDIA AND THE PHILLY MIDDLE SCHOOL SUB-CRUDDIT.
NOW WE NEED TO PUT ALL THE PIECES TOGETHER.
BUT MAYBE TOMORROW. IT'S GETTING LATE.
I'LL SLEEP WHEN THE CASE IS CLOSED!
FIVE MINUTES LATER
ZZZ
I GUESS THE CASE IS CLOSED.

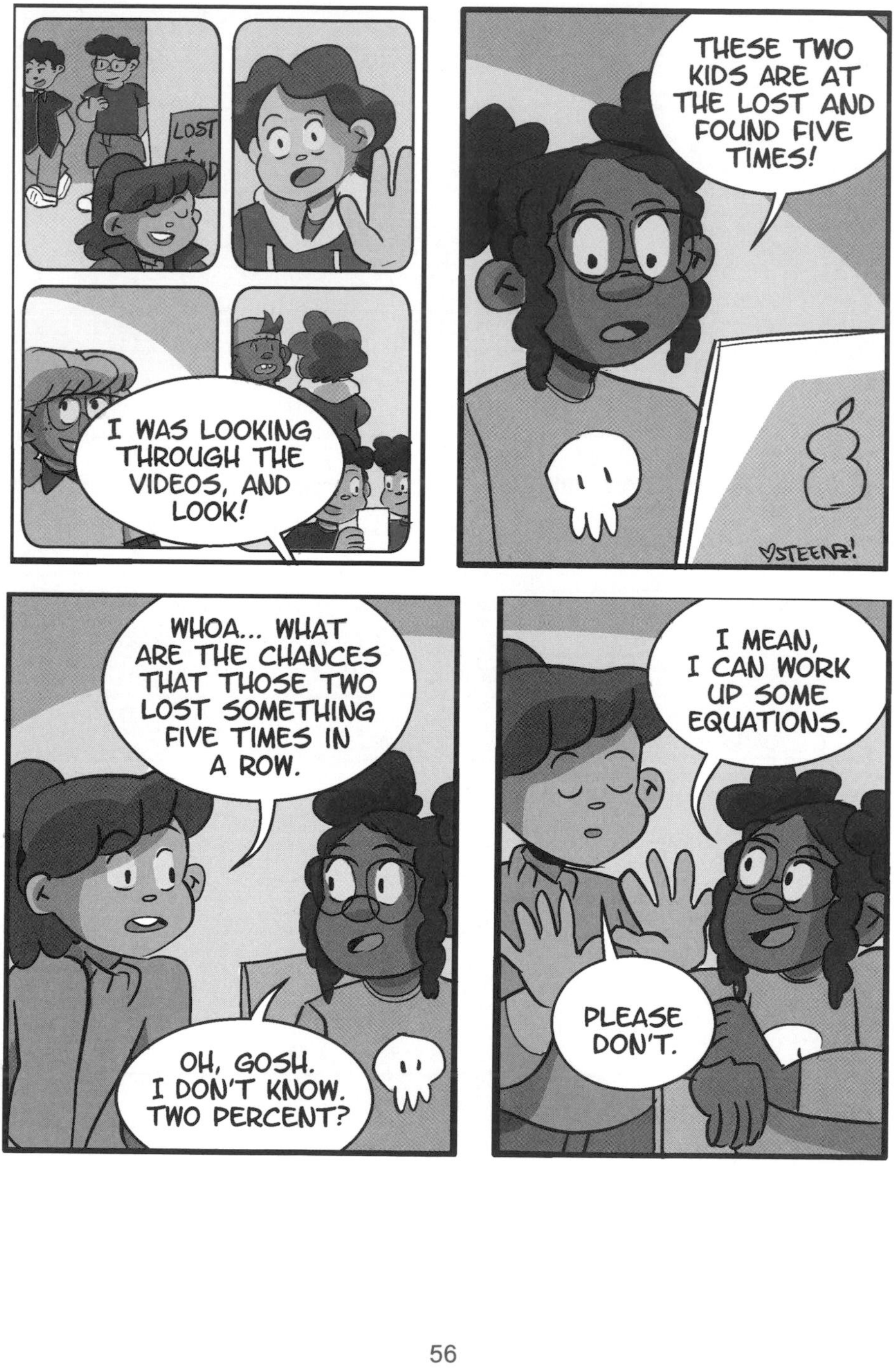
LOST
+
I WAS LOOKING THROUGH THE VIDEOS, AND LOOK!
THESE TWO KIDS ARE AT THE LOST AND FOUND FIVE TIMES!
♥STEENZ!
WHOA... WHAT ARE THE CHANCES THAT THOSE TWO LOST SOMETHING FIVE TIMES IN A ROW.
OH, GOSH. I DON'T KNOW. TWO PERCENT?
I MEAN, I CAN WORK UP SOME EQUATIONS.
PLEASE DON'T.

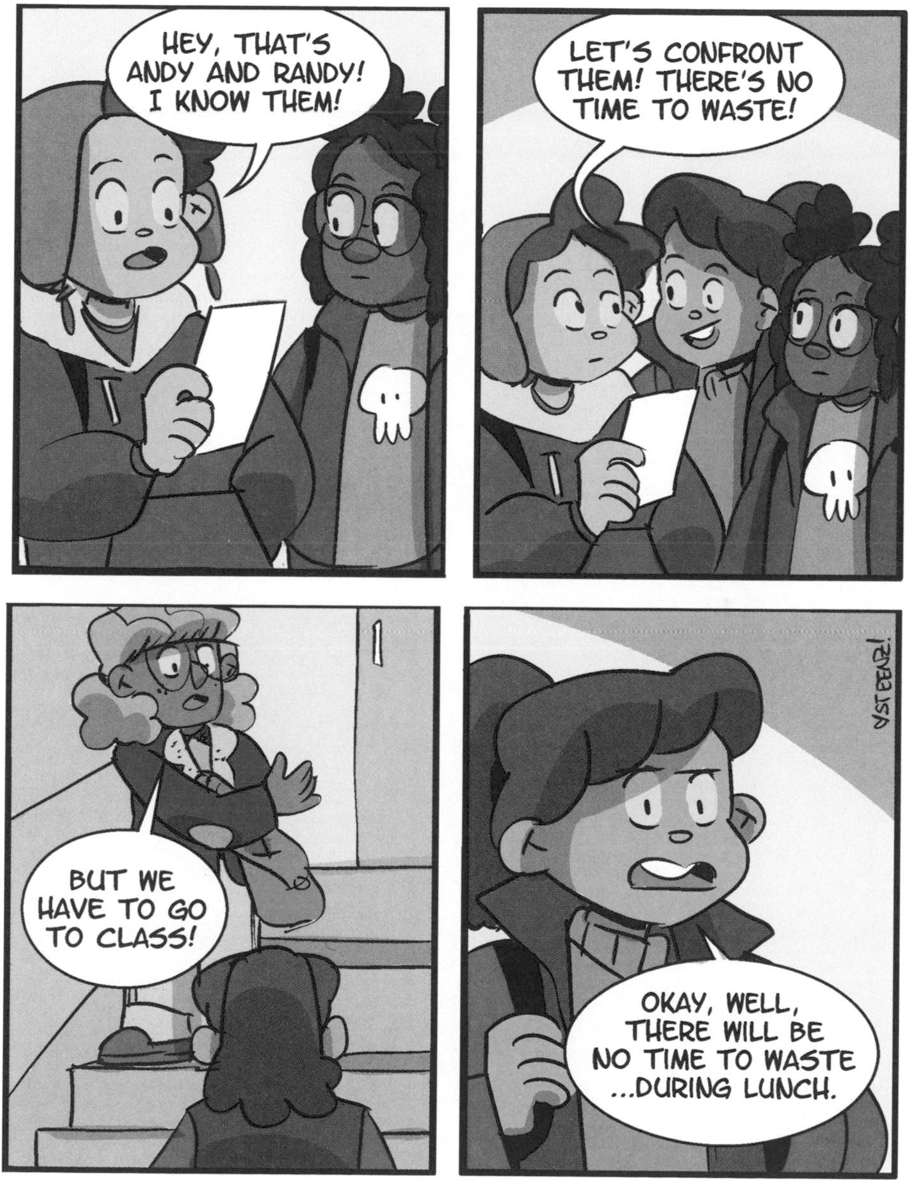
HEY, THAT'S ANDY AND RANDY! I KNOW THEM!
LET'S CONFRONT THEM! THERE'S NO TIME TO WASTE!
BUT WE HAVE TO GO TO CLASS!
OKAY, WELL, THERE WILL BE NO TIME TO WASTE ...DURING LUNCH.

HI AGAIN!
HAHA, S-SAME... WORDS.
ANYWAY.
CAN WE SEE THE LUNCH SCHEDULES FOR ANDY AND RANDY MORRIS?
SORRY, HEART. THAT'S CONFIDENTIAL INFORMATION.
I GOT YOU. I WON'T TELL A SOUL.
STEENZ!

YOU GOTTA HELP US!

ANDY AND RANDY MIGHT BE INVOLVED IN THEFT AND DISTRIBUTION OF STOLEN ITEMS!

I CAN'T.

I CAN'T TELL YOU THAT THEY GO TO LUNCH IN TEN MINUTES.

♡STEEVZ!

GREAT JOB GETTING INFO OUT OF LEE!

ANYTHING FOR THE CASE!

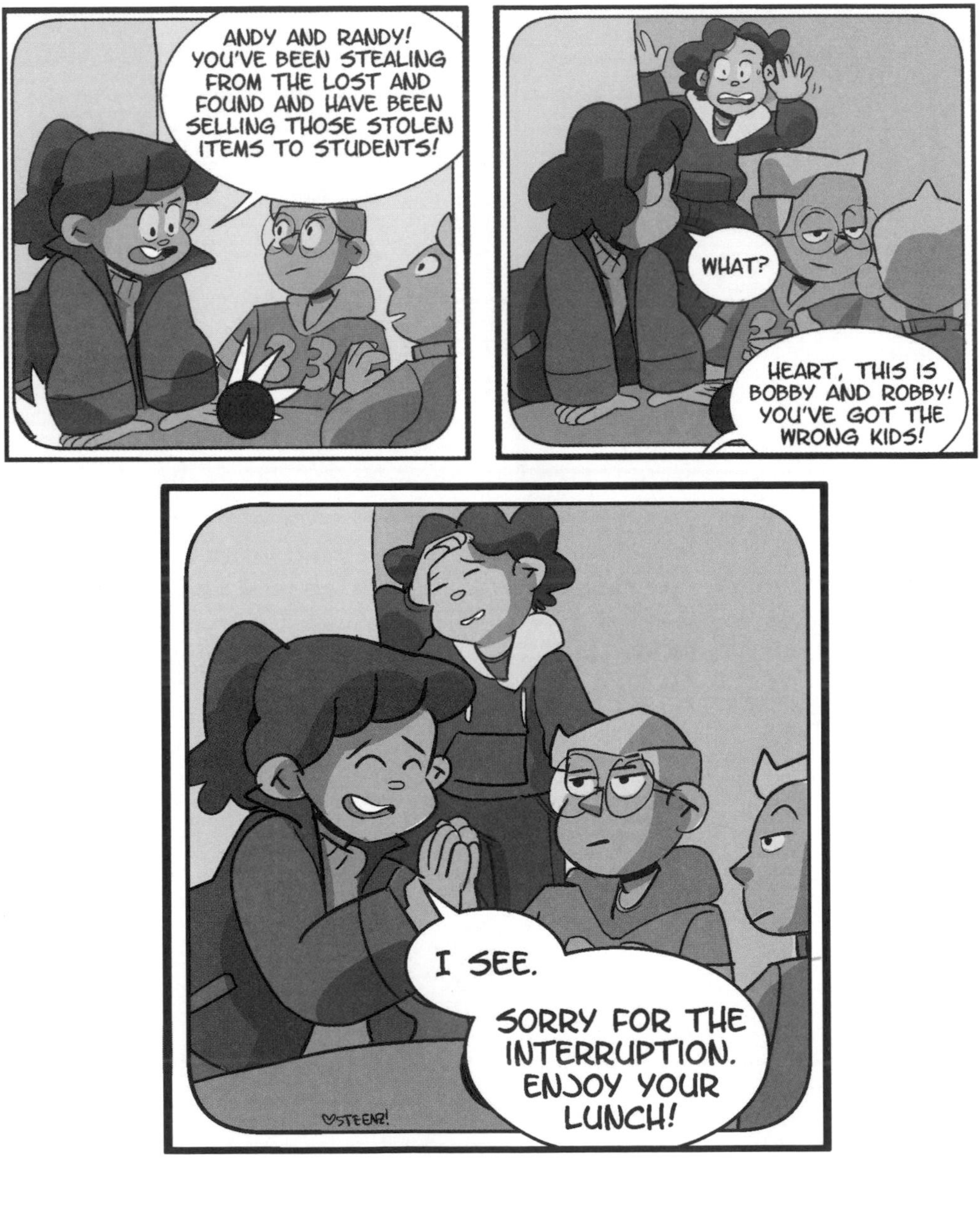
ANDY AND RANDY! YOU'VE BEEN STEALING FROM THE LOST AND FOUND AND HAVE BEEN SELLING THOSE STOLEN ITEMS TO STUDENTS!
WHAT?
HEART, THIS IS BOBBY AND ROBBY! YOU'VE GOT THE WRONG KIDS!
I SEE.
SORRY FOR THE INTERRUPTION. ENJOY YOUR LUNCH!
♡STEENZ!

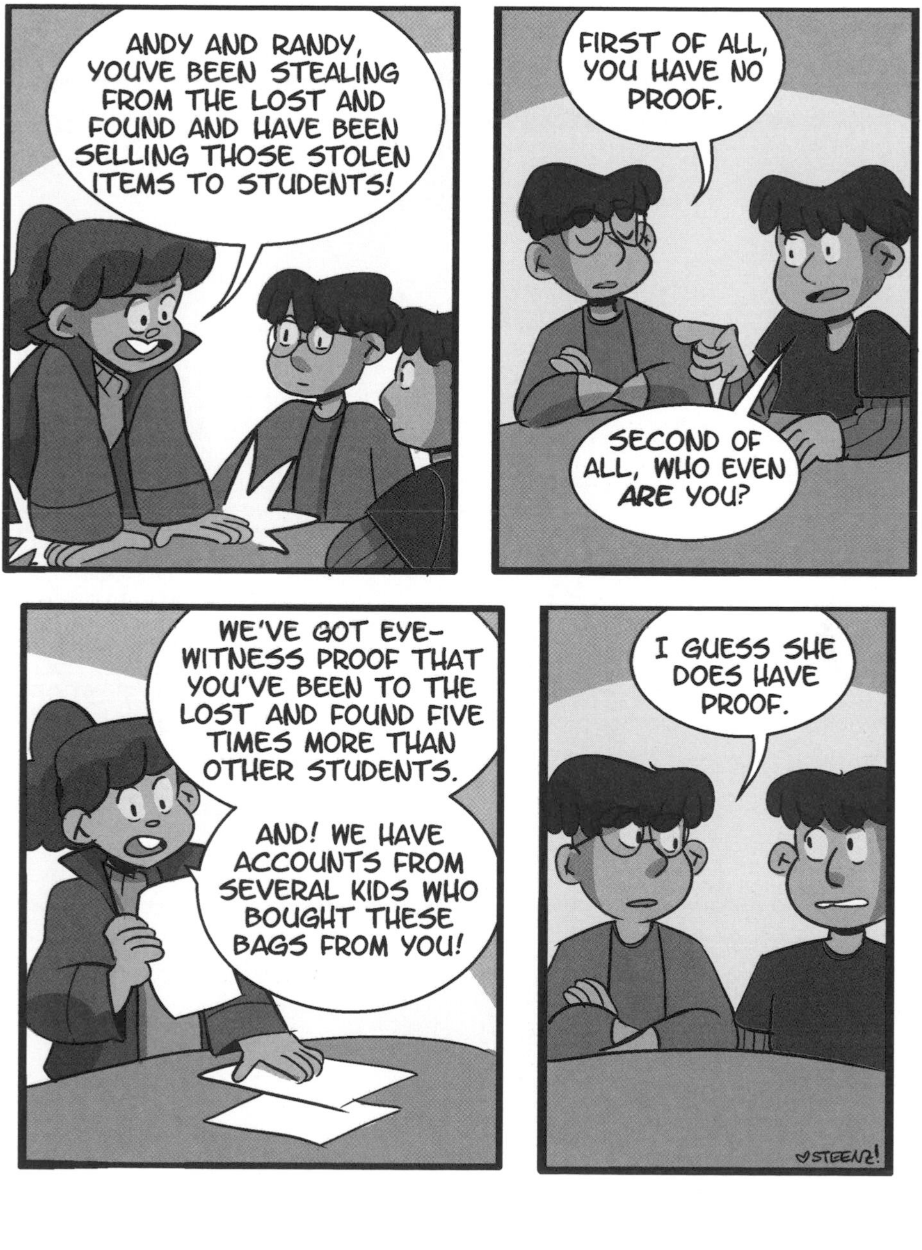
ANDY AND RANDY, YOUVE BEEN STEALING FROM THE LOST AND FOUND AND HAVE BEEN SELLING THOSE STOLEN ITEMS TO STUDENTS!
FIRST OF ALL, YOU HAVE NO PROOF.
SECOND OF ALL, WHO EVEN ARE YOU?
WE'VE GOT EYE-WITNESS PROOF THAT YOU'VE BEEN TO THE LOST AND FOUND FIVE TIMES MORE THAN OTHER STUDENTS.
AND! WE HAVE ACCOUNTS FROM SEVERAL KIDS WHO BOUGHT THESE BAGS FROM YOU!
I GUESS SHE DOES HAVE PROOF.
♡STEENZ!

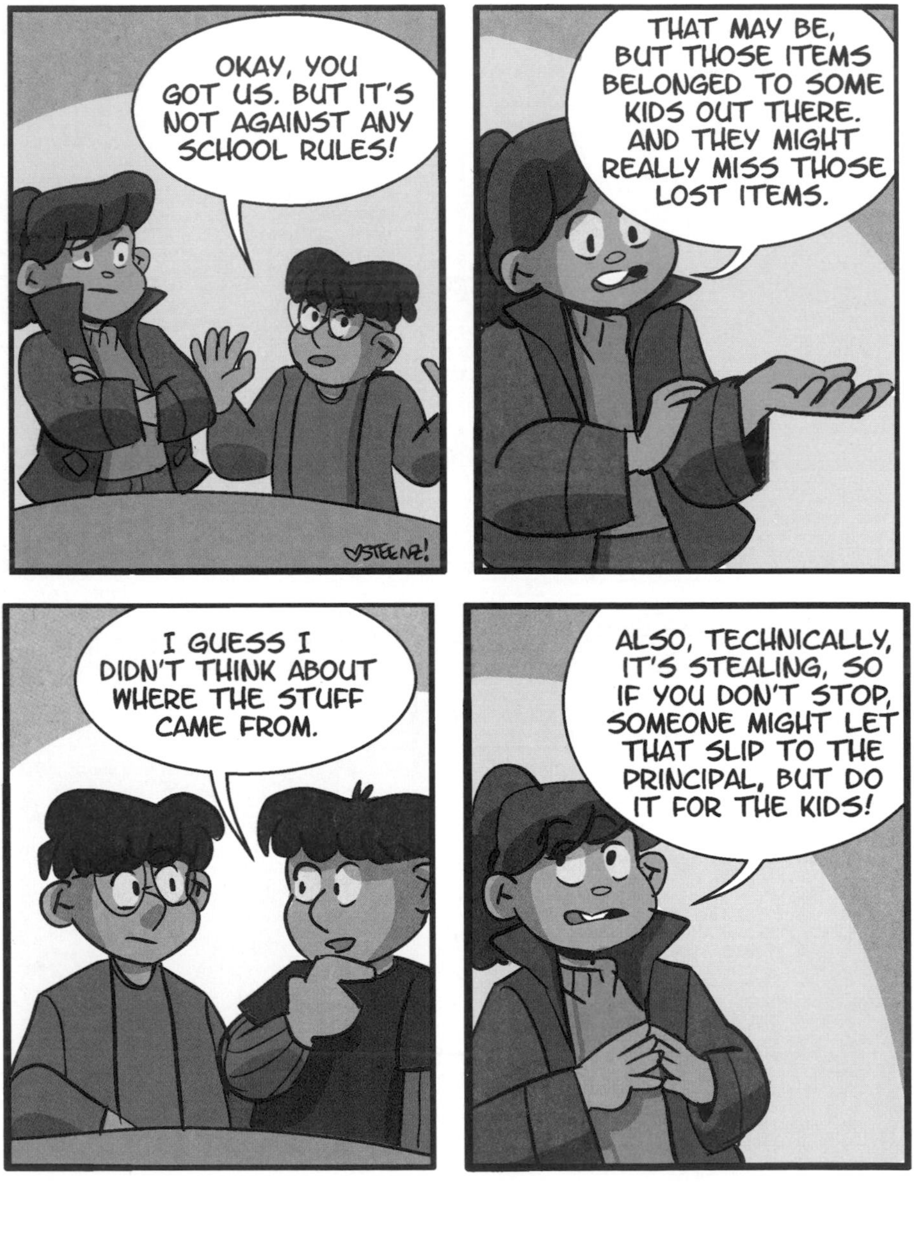
OKAY, YOU GOT US. BUT IT'S NOT AGAINST ANY SCHOOL RULES!
STEENZ!
THAT MAY BE, BUT THOSE ITEMS BELONGED TO SOME KIDS OUT THERE. AND THEY MIGHT REALLY MISS THOSE LOST ITEMS.
I GUESS I DIDN'T THINK ABOUT WHERE THE STUFF CAME FROM.
ALSO, TECHNICALLY, IT'S STEALING, SO IF YOU DON'T STOP, SOMEONE MIGHT LET THAT SLIP TO THE PRINCIPAL, BUT DO IT FOR THE KIDS!

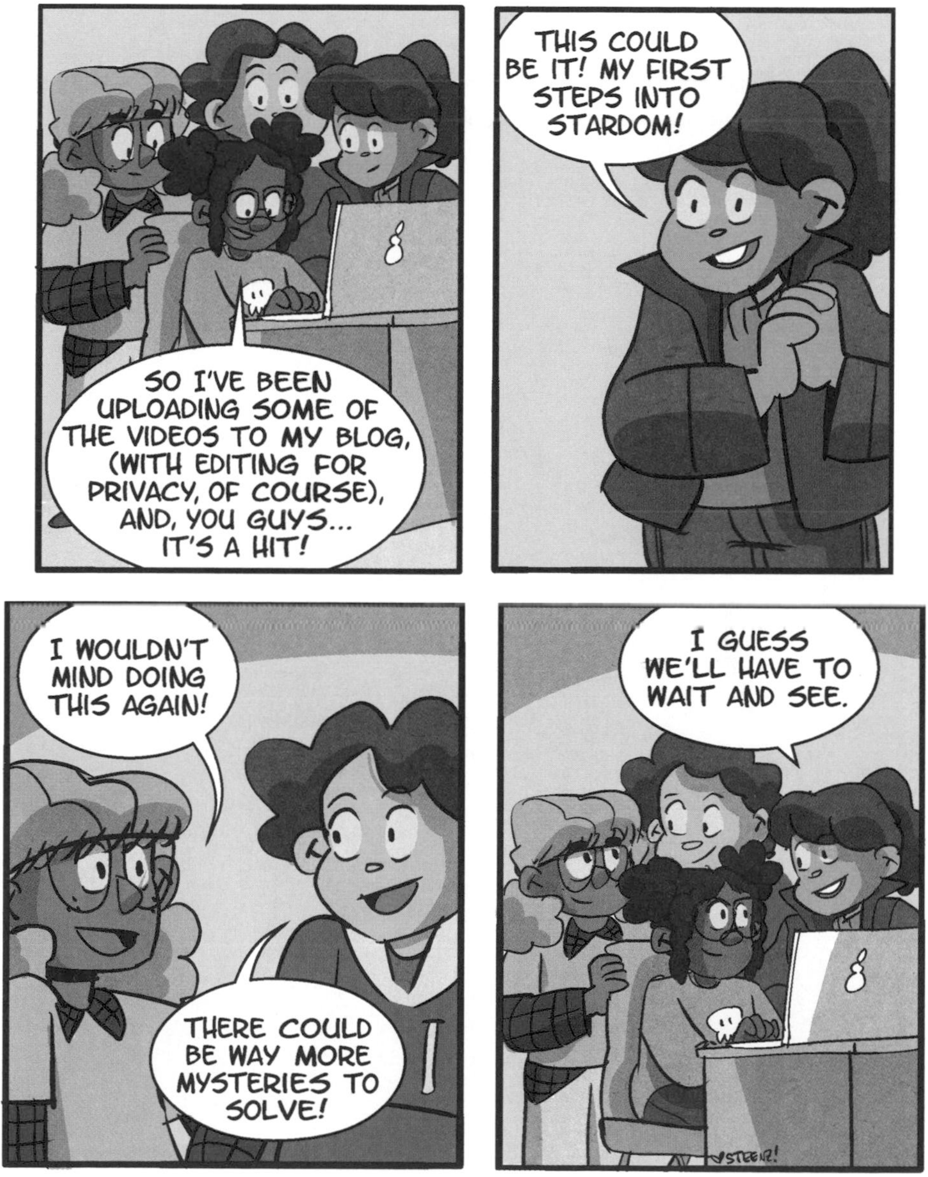
SO I'VE BEEN UPLOADING SOME OF THE VIDEOS TO MY BLOG, (WITH EDITING FOR PRIVACY, OF COURSE), AND, YOU GUYS... IT'S A HIT!
THIS COULD BE IT! MY FIRST STEPS INTO STARDOM!
I WOULDN'T MIND DOING THIS AGAIN!
THERE COULD BE WAY MORE MYSTERIES TO SOLVE!
I GUESS WE'LL HAVE TO WAIT AND SEE.

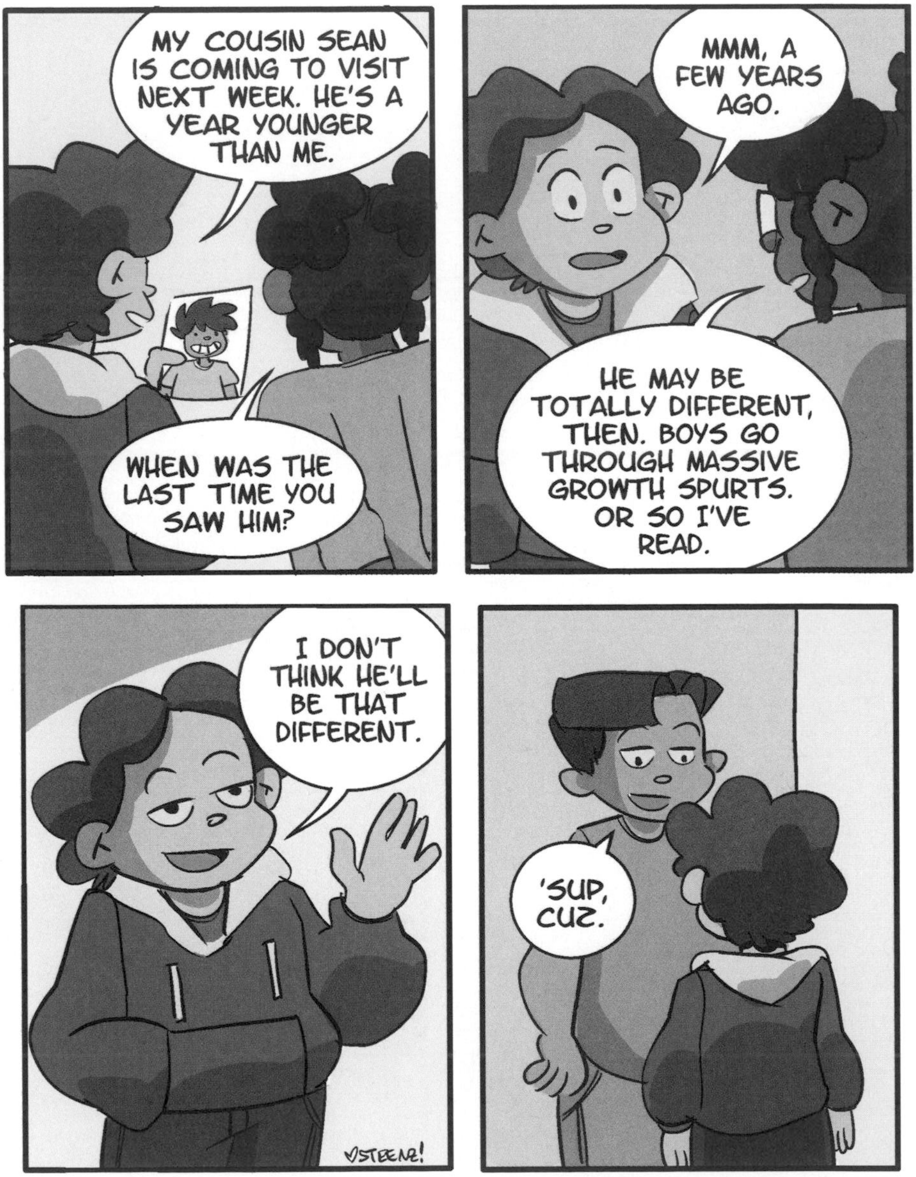
MY COUSIN SEAN IS COMING TO VISIT NEXT WEEK. HE'S A YEAR YOUNGER THAN ME.
WHEN WAS THE LAST TIME YOU SAW HIM?
MMM, A FEW YEARS AGO.
HE MAY BE TOTALLY DIFFERENT, THEN. BOYS GO THROUGH MASSIVE GROWTH SPURTS. OR SO I'VE READ.
I DON'T THINK HE'LL BE THAT DIFFERENT.
♡STEENZ!
'SUP, CUZ.

SEAN, THIS IS HEART!
WHOA! YOU'RE TALL! YOU COULD BE A MODEL!
AND THIS IS KAT!
NICE TO MEET YOU!
AND HERE'S CHARLOTTE!
WHAT VIDEO GAMES DO YOU PLAY?
WHY ARE ALL YOUR FRIENDS *GIRLS*?

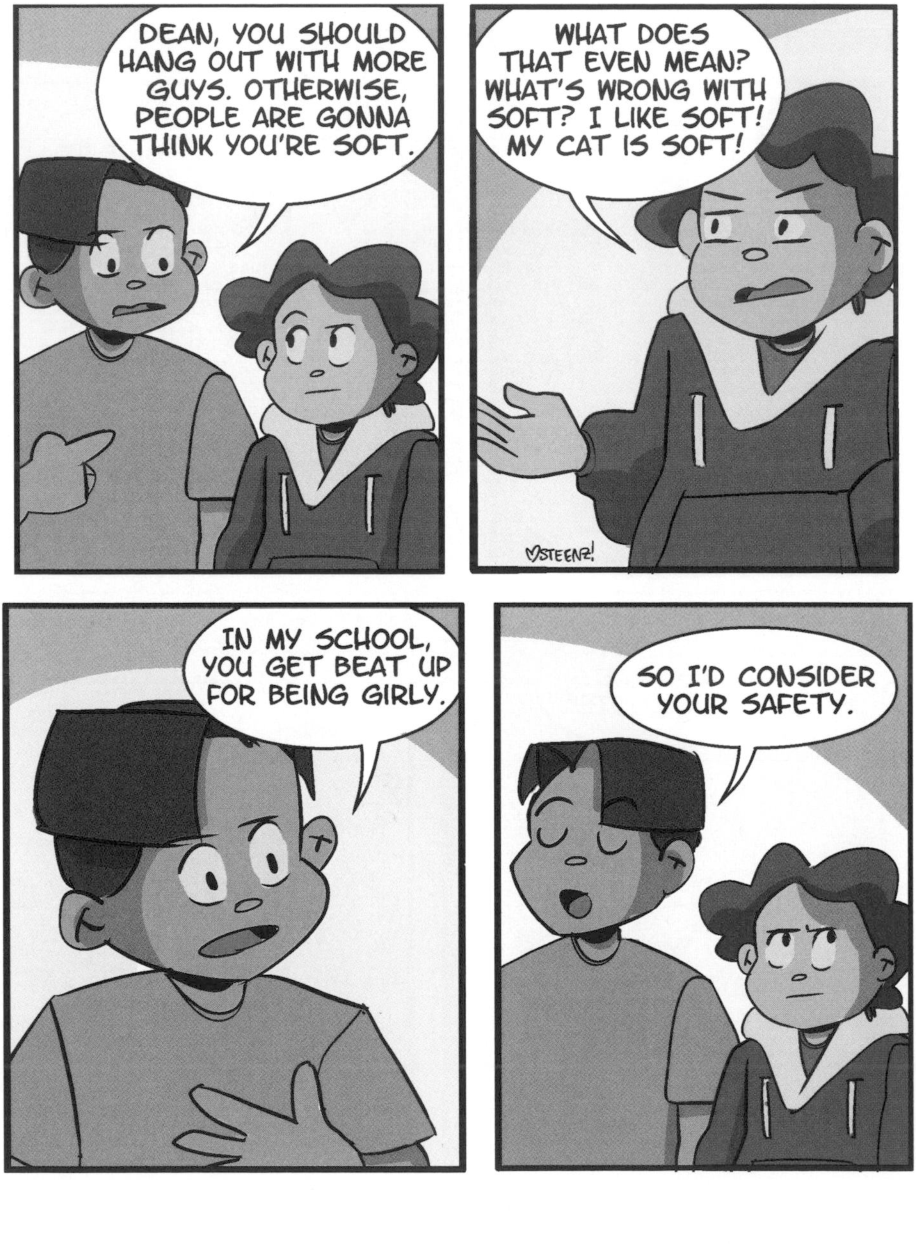
DEAN, YOU SHOULD HANG OUT WITH MORE GUYS. OTHERWISE, PEOPLE ARE GONNA THINK YOU'RE SOFT.
WHAT DOES THAT EVEN MEAN? WHAT'S WRONG WITH SOFT? I LIKE SOFT! MY CAT IS SOFT!
♡STEENZ!
IN MY SCHOOL, YOU GET BEAT UP FOR BEING GIRLY.
SO I'D CONSIDER YOUR SAFETY.

NOT THAT IT *MATTERS*, BUT I DO HAVE FRIENDS WHO ARE GUYS.

HEY, DEAN!

THIS IS CHRIS, BRENT, AND JOHN.

'SUP, DUDE?

HI, I'M BRENT.

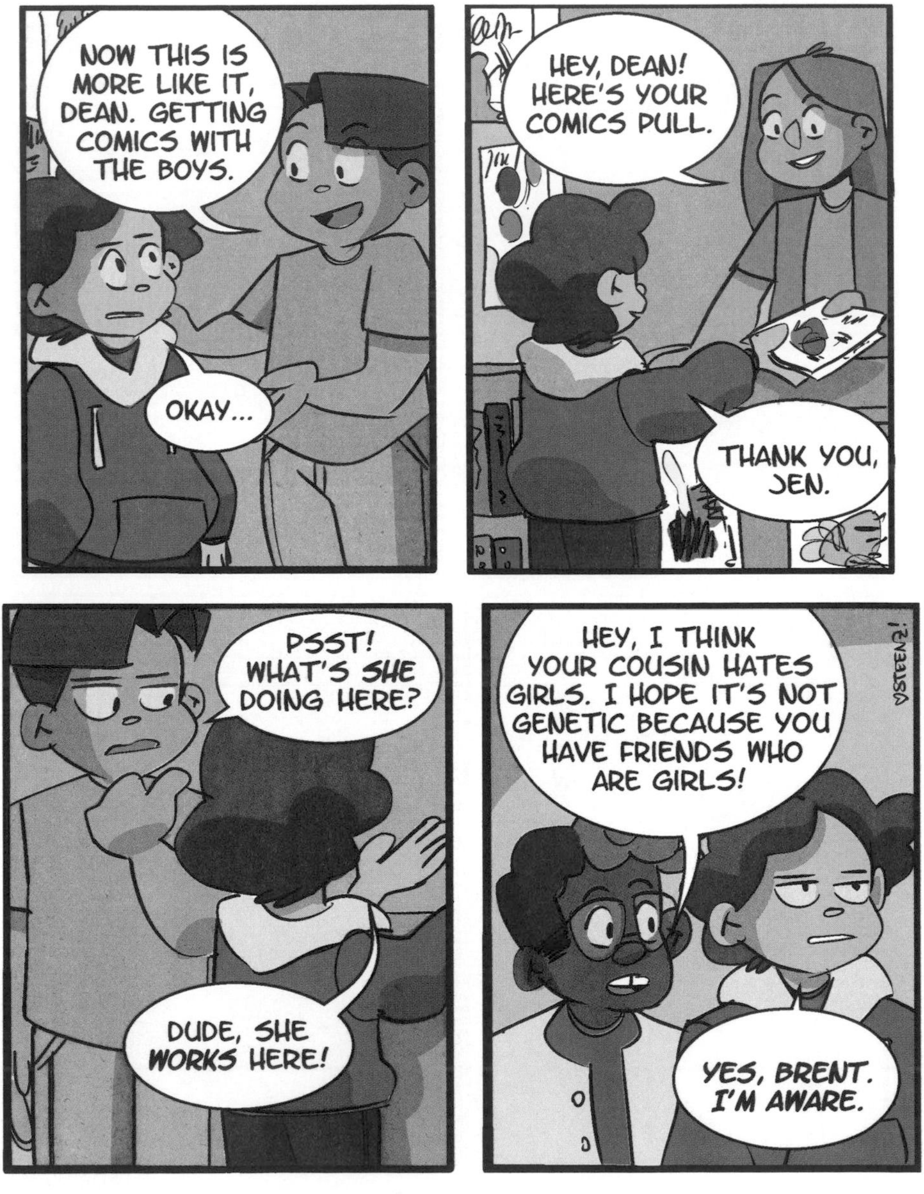
NOW THIS IS MORE LIKE IT, DEAN. GETTING COMICS WITH THE BOYS.
OKAY...
HEY, DEAN! HERE'S YOUR COMICS PULL.
THANK YOU, JEN.
PSST! WHAT'S *SHE* DOING HERE?
DUDE, SHE *WORKS* HERE!
HEY, I THINK YOUR COUSIN HATES GIRLS. I HOPE IT'S NOT GENETIC BECAUSE YOU HAVE FRIENDS WHO ARE GIRLS!
YES, BRENT. I'M AWARE.

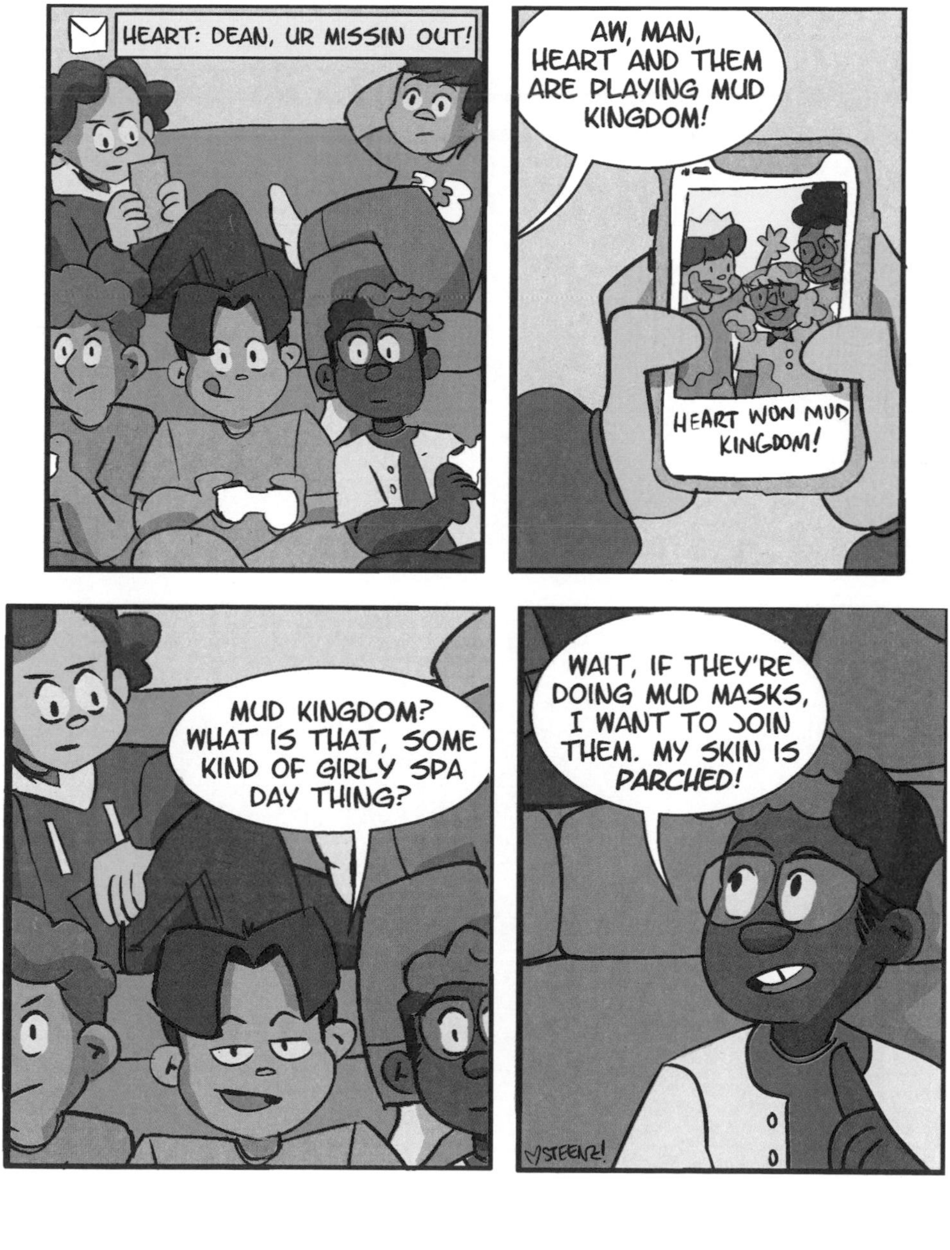
HEART: DEAN, UR MISSIN OUT!
AW, MAN, HEART AND THEM ARE PLAYING MUD KINGDOM!
HEART WON MUD KINGDOM!
MUD KINGDOM? WHAT IS THAT, SOME KIND OF GIRLY SPA DAY THING?
WAIT, IF THEY'RE DOING MUD MASKS, I WANT TO JOIN THEM. MY SKIN IS *PARCHED!*
♡STEENZ!

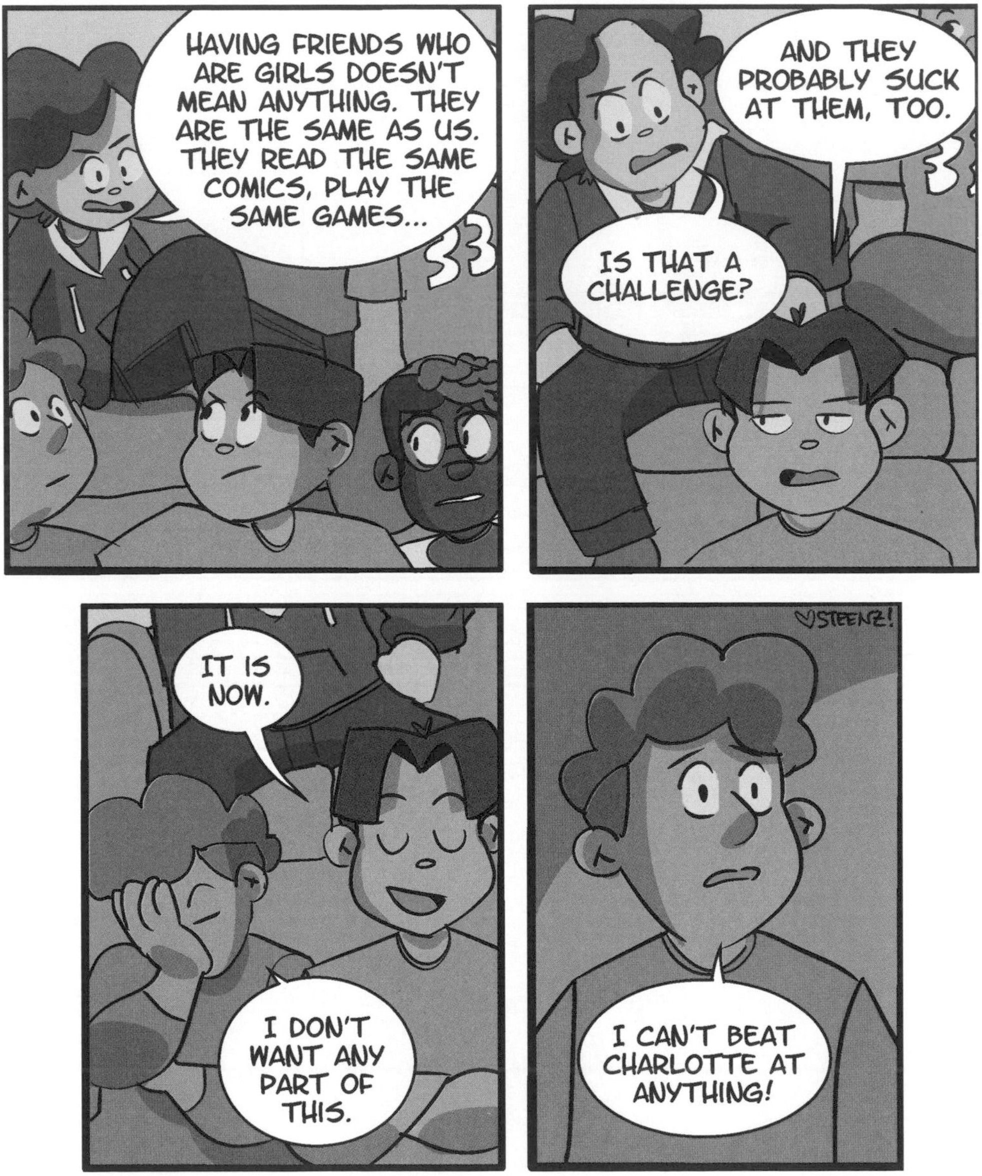
HAVING FRIENDS WHO ARE GIRLS DOESN'T MEAN ANYTHING. THEY ARE THE SAME AS US. THEY READ THE SAME COMICS, PLAY THE SAME GAMES...
AND THEY PROBABLY SUCK AT THEM, TOO.
IS THAT A CHALLENGE?
IT IS NOW.
I DON'T WANT ANY PART OF THIS.
♡STEENZ!
I CAN'T BEAT CHARLOTTE AT ANYTHING!

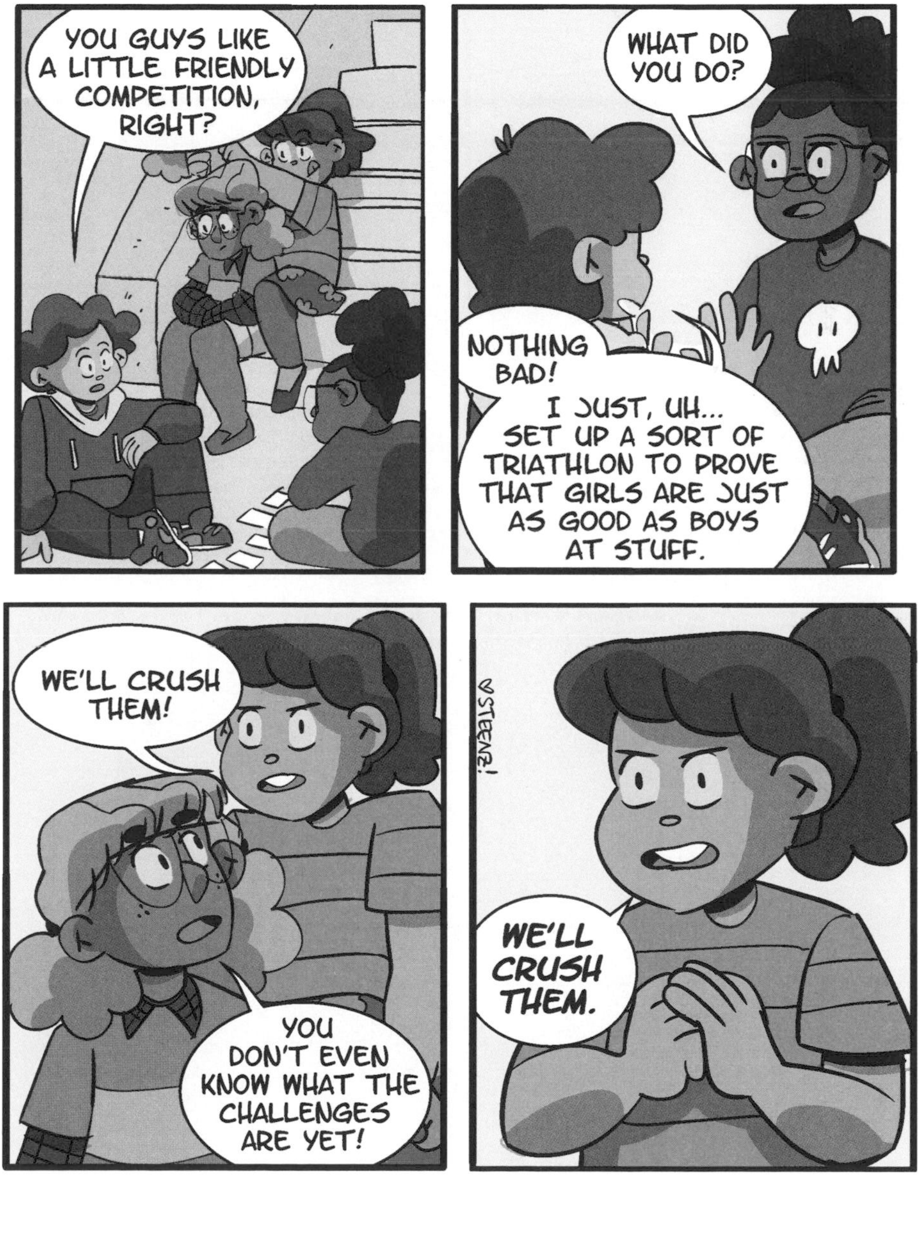
YOU GUYS LIKE A LITTLE FRIENDLY COMPETITION, RIGHT?
WHAT DID YOU DO?
NOTHING BAD!
I JUST, UH... SET UP A SORT OF TRIATHLON TO PROVE THAT GIRLS ARE JUST AS GOOD AS BOYS AT STUFF.
WE'LL CRUSH THEM!
YOU DON'T EVEN KNOW WHAT THE CHALLENGES ARE YET!
@STEENZ!
WE'LL CRUSH THEM.

OKAY!
WE'VE GOT THREE CATEGORIES:
BRAINS, BRAWN, AND DEXTERITY.
IT'S INCREDIBLY DATED TO HAVE A BATTLE OF THE GENDERS, BUT IT'S IN YOUR BEST INTEREST TO GIVE UP NOW.
♡STEENZ!

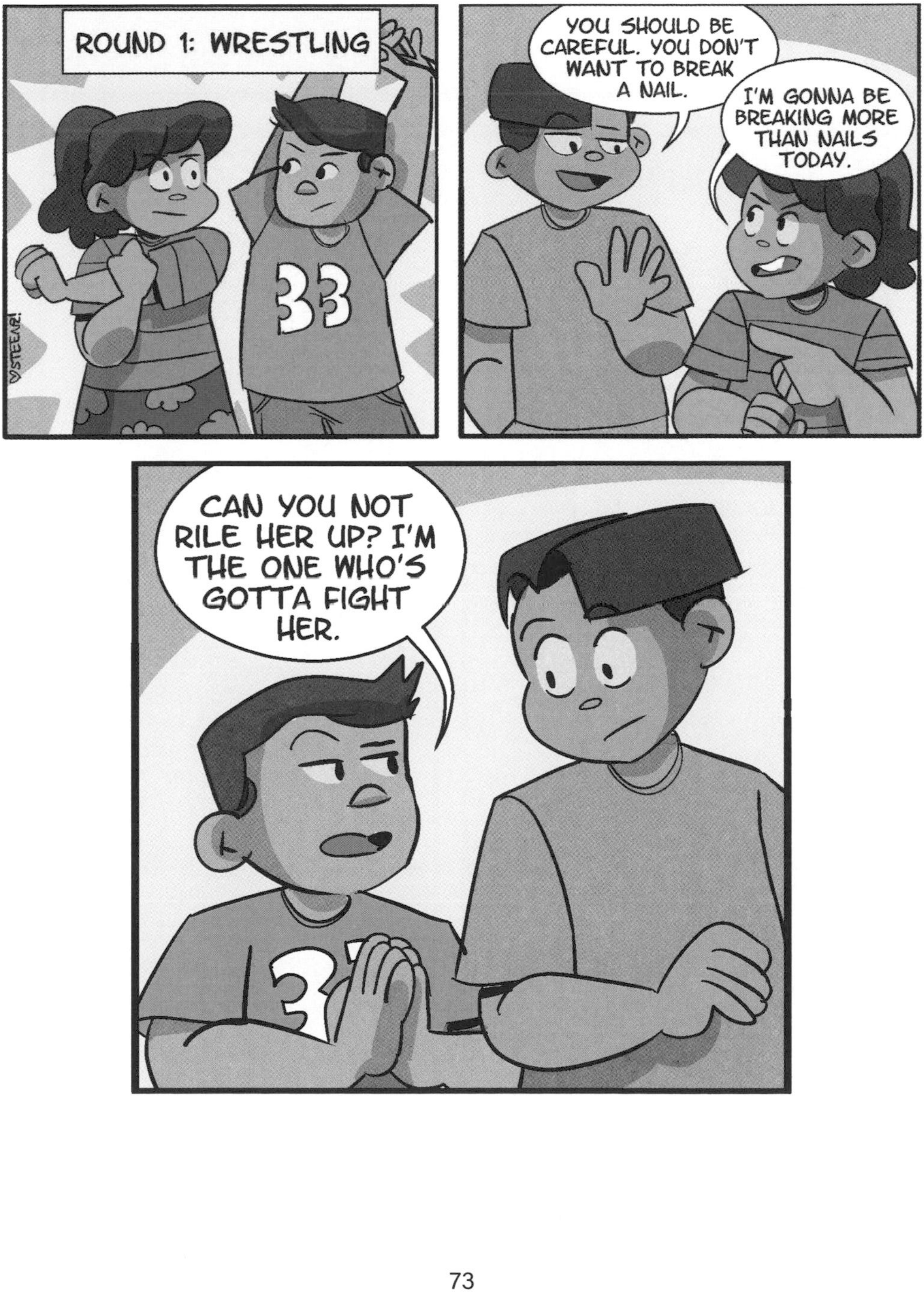
ROUND 1: WRESTLING
YOU SHOULD BE CAREFUL. YOU DON'T WANT TO BREAK A NAIL.
I'M GONNA BE BREAKING MORE THAN NAILS TODAY.
CAN YOU NOT RILE HER UP? I'M THE ONE WHO'S GOTTA FIGHT HER.

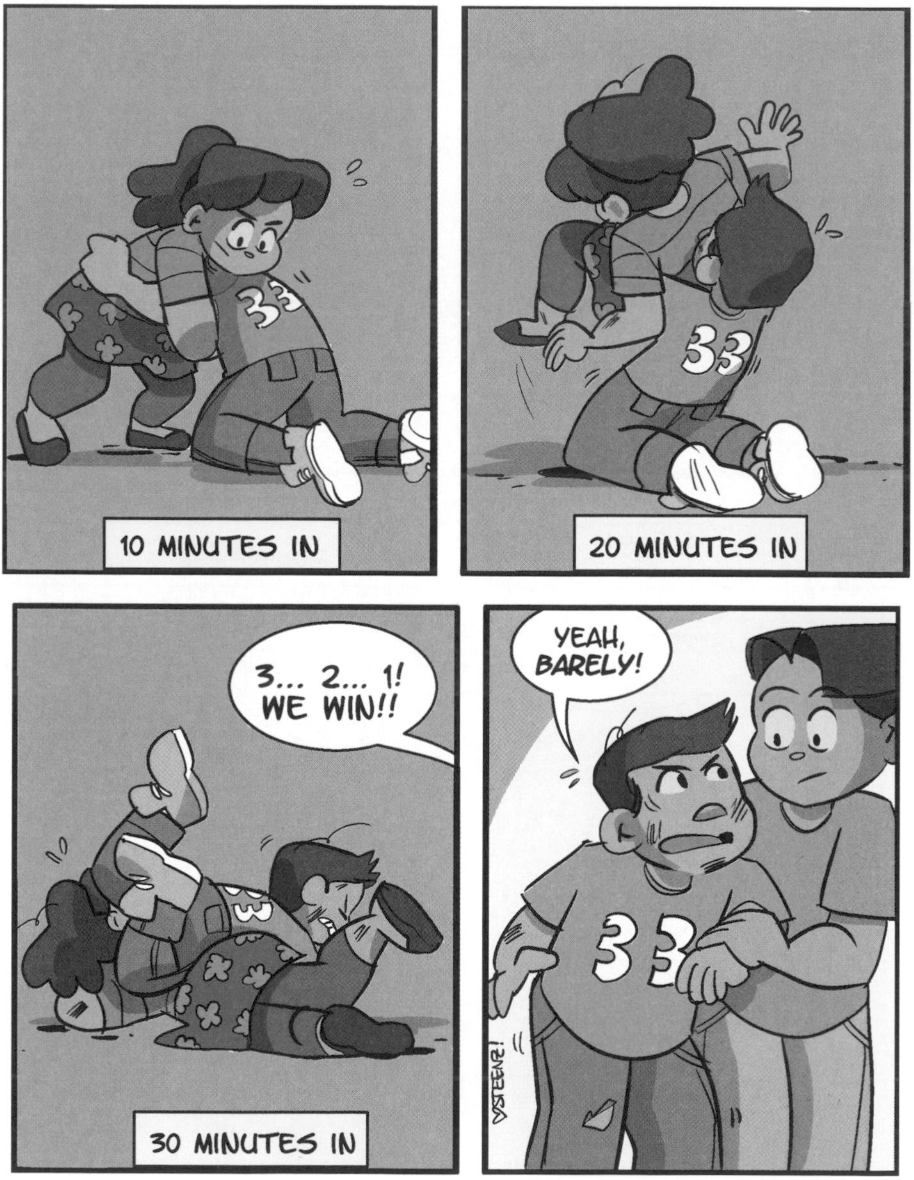
10 MINUTES IN
20 MINUTES IN
3... 2... 1! WE WIN!!
30 MINUTES IN
YEAH, BARELY!

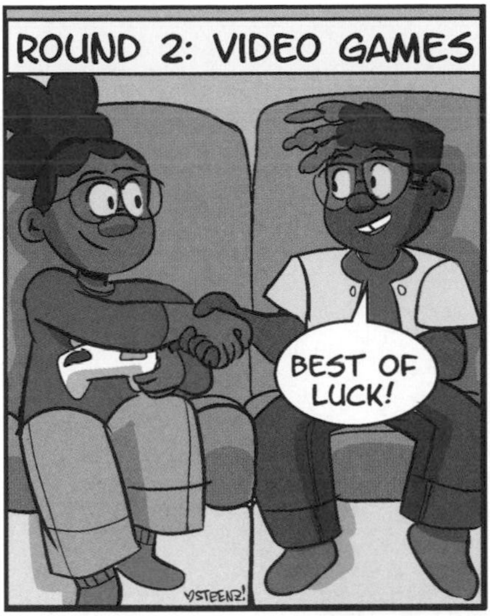
ROUND 2: VIDEO GAMES
BEST OF LUCK!
♡STEENZ!

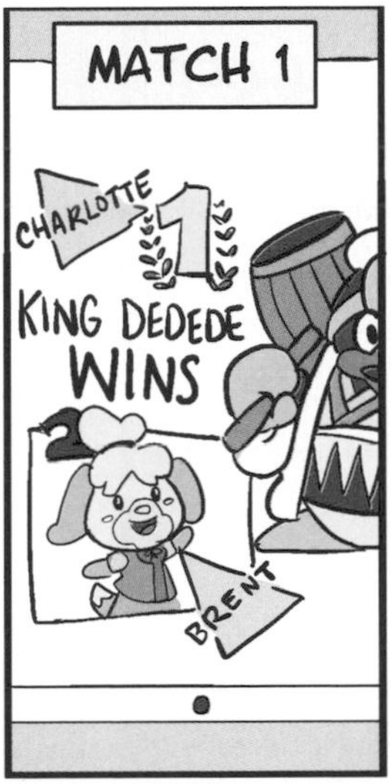
MATCH 1
CHARLOTTE
1
KING DEDEDE WINS
2
BRENT

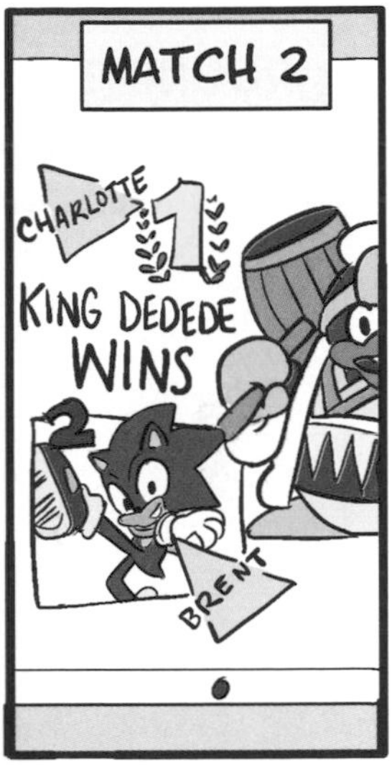
MATCH 2
CHARLOTTE
1
KING DEDEDE WINS
2
BRENT

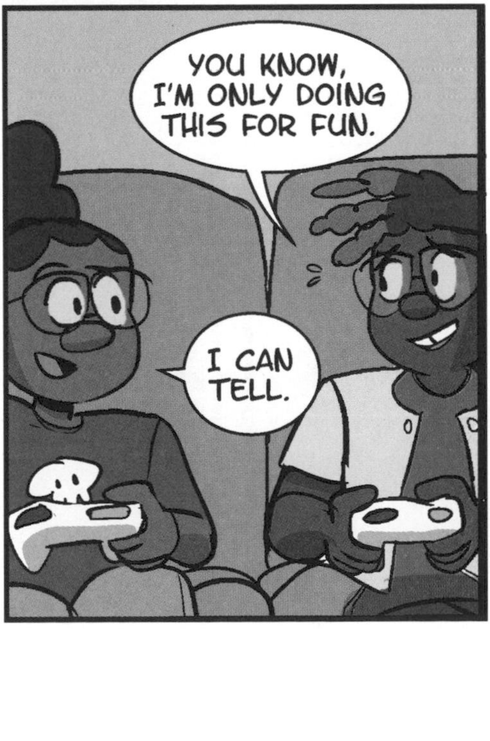
YOU KNOW, I'M ONLY DOING THIS FOR FUN.
I CAN TELL.

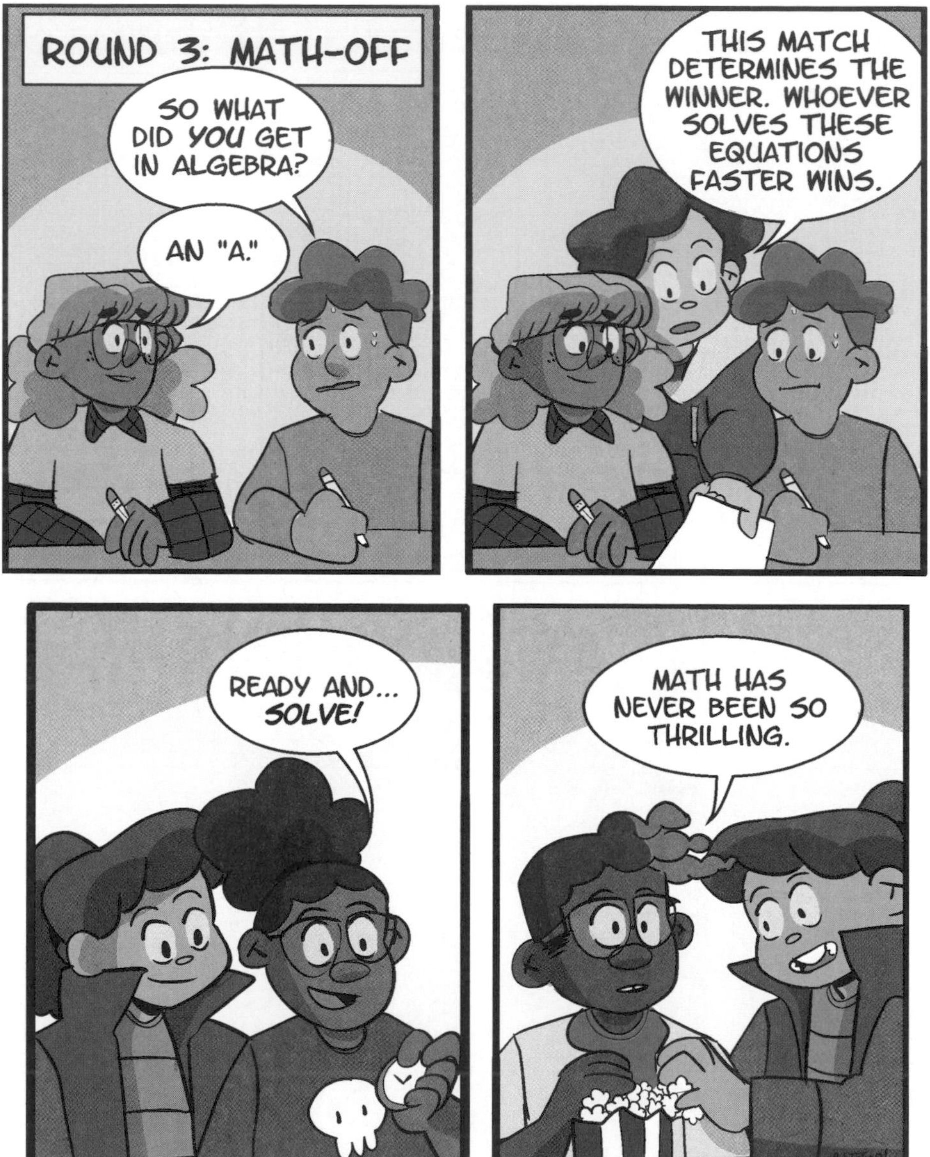
ROUND 3: MATH-OFF
SO WHAT DID YOU GET IN ALGEBRA?
AN "A."
THIS MATCH DETERMINES THE WINNER. WHOEVER SOLVES THESE EQUATIONS FASTER WINS.
READY AND... SOLVE!
MATH HAS NEVER BEEN SO THRILLING.

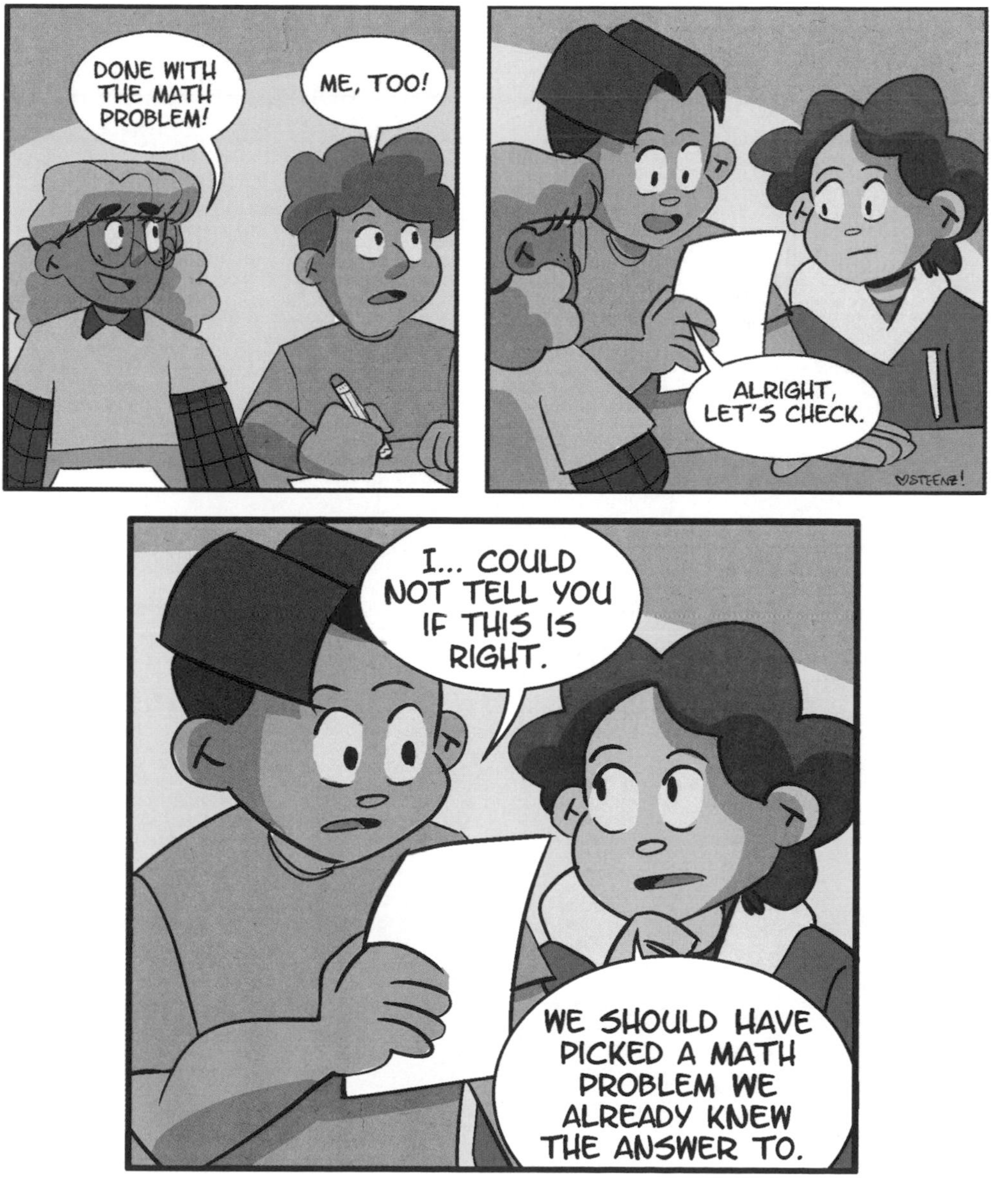
DONE WITH THE MATH PROBLEM!
ME, TOO!
ALRIGHT, LET'S CHECK.
I... COULD NOT TELL YOU IF THIS IS RIGHT.
WE SHOULD HAVE PICKED A MATH PROBLEM WE ALREADY KNEW THE ANSWER TO.

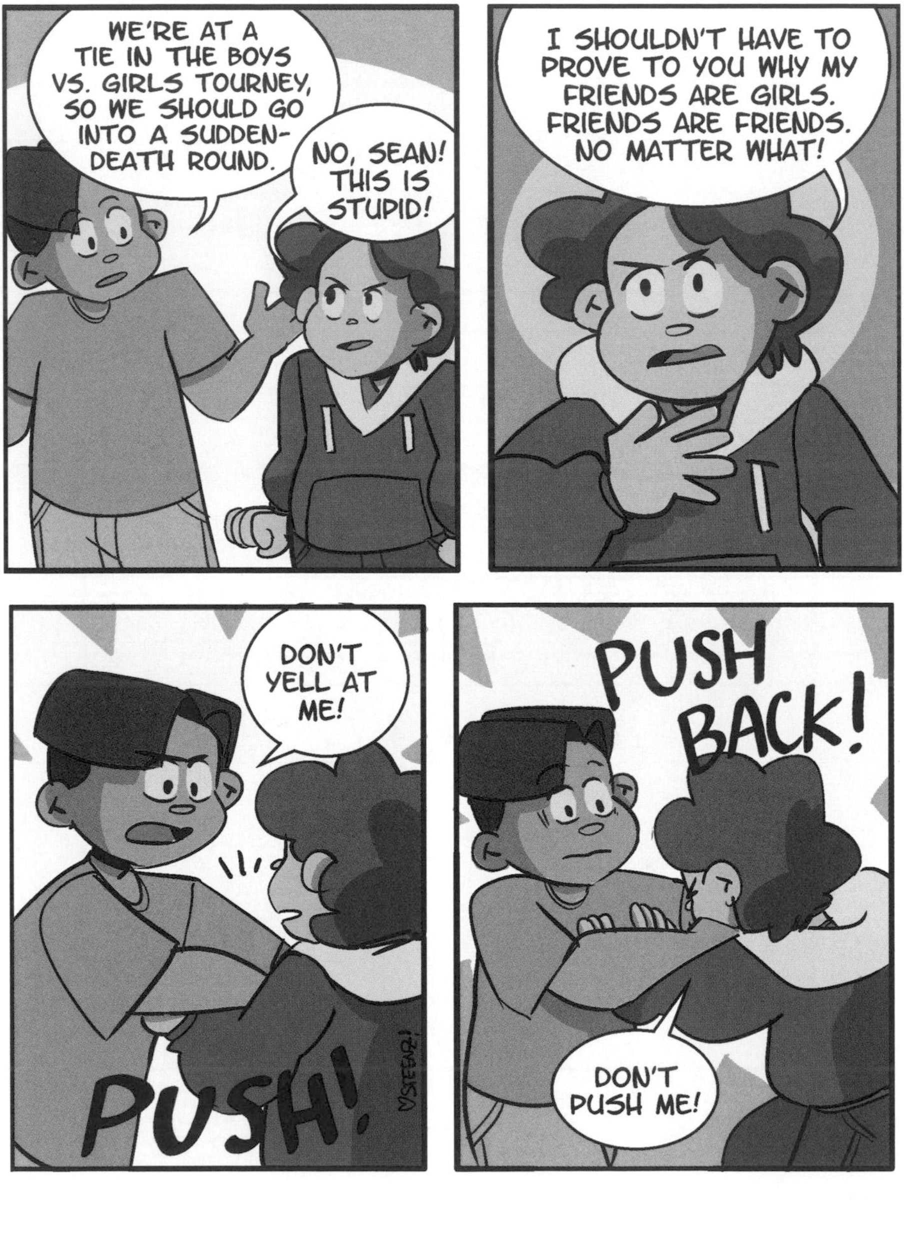
WE'RE AT A TIE IN THE BOYS VS. GIRLS TOURNEY, SO WE SHOULD GO INTO A SUDDEN-DEATH ROUND.
NO, SEAN! THIS IS STUPID!
I SHOULDN'T HAVE TO PROVE TO YOU WHY MY FRIENDS ARE GIRLS. FRIENDS ARE FRIENDS. NO MATTER WHAT!
DON'T YELL AT ME!
PUSH!
PUSH BACK!
DON'T PUSH ME!

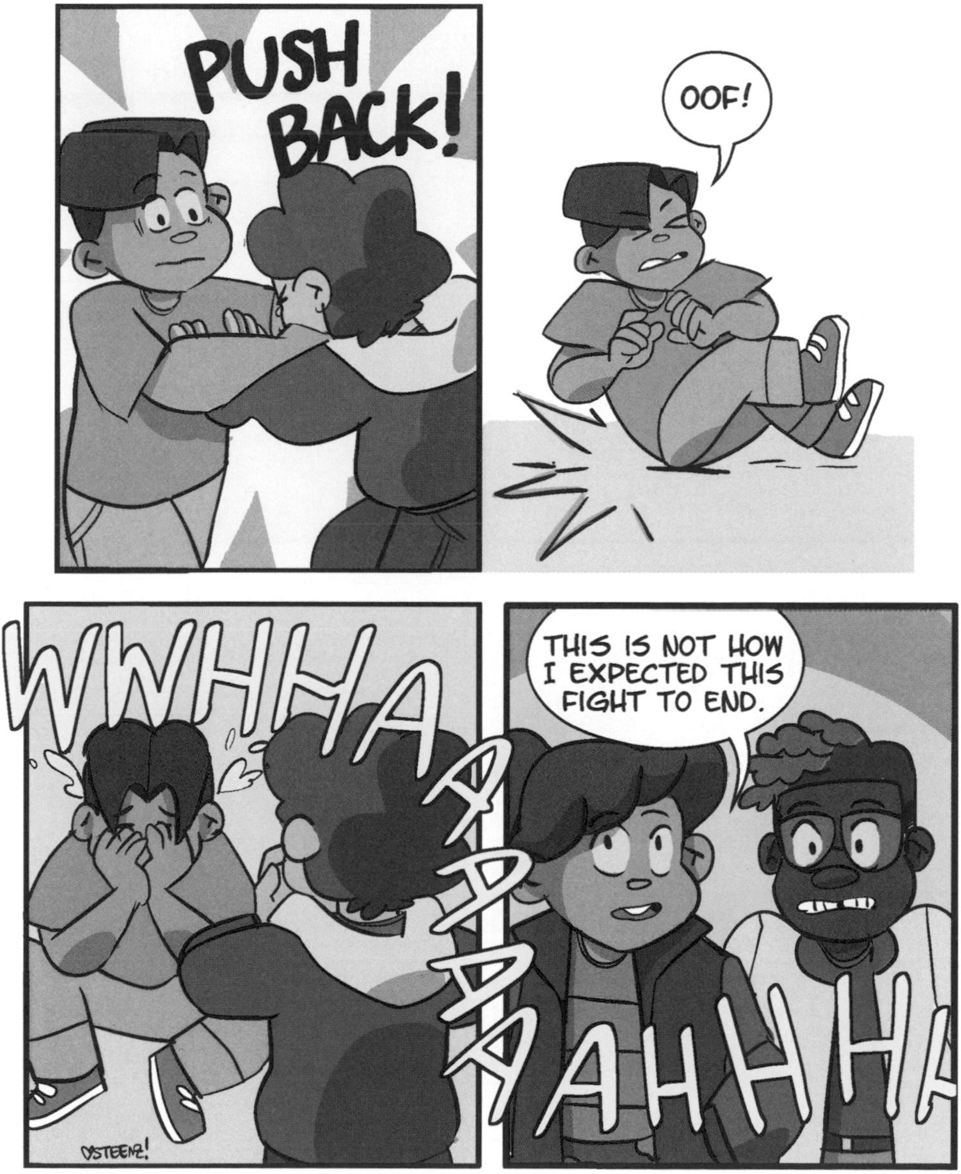
PUSH BACK!
OOF!
WWHHAAAAAAHHHH
THIS IS NOT HOW I EXPECTED THIS FIGHT TO END.
STEENZ!

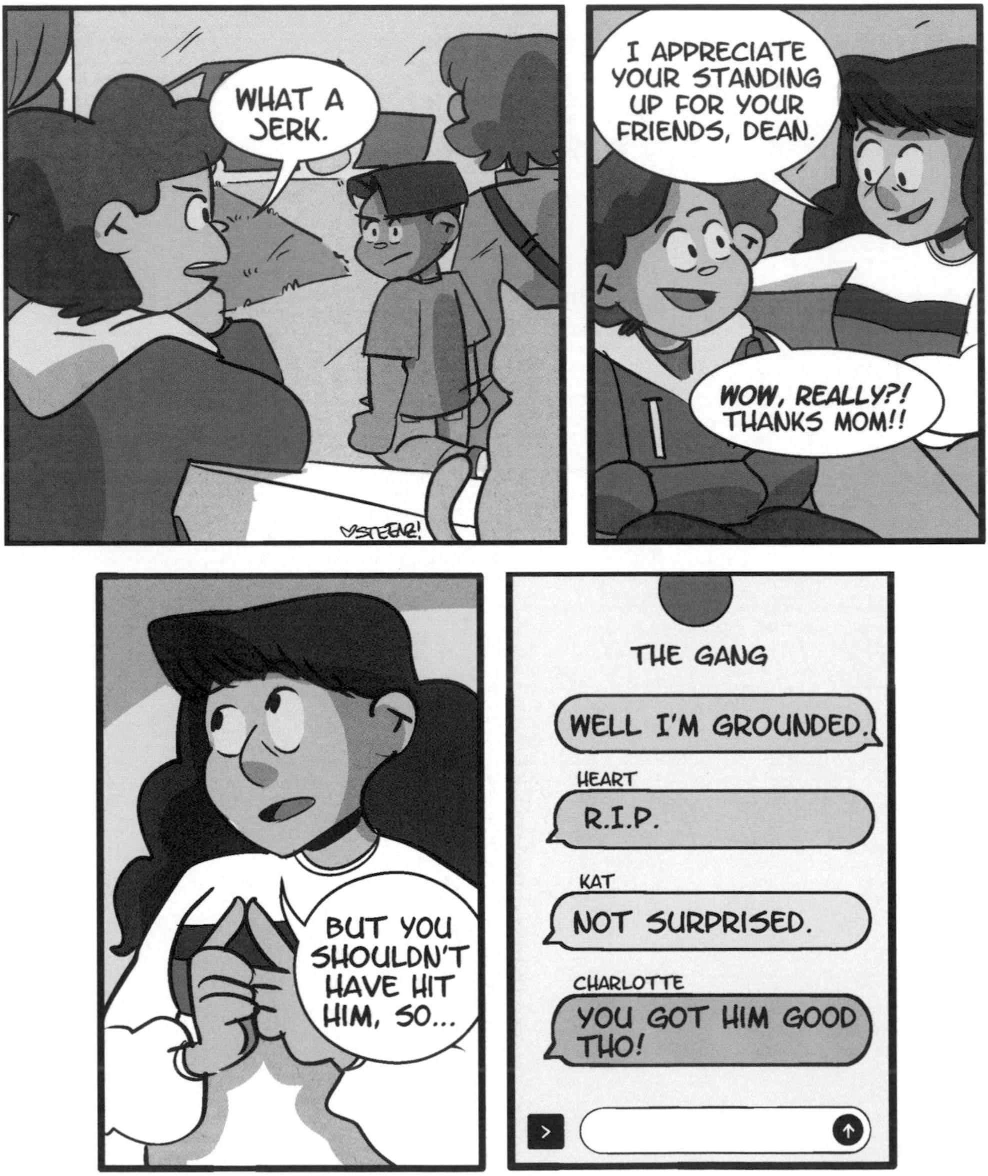
WHAT A JERK.
I APPRECIATE YOUR STANDING UP FOR YOUR FRIENDS, DEAN.
WOW, REALLY?! THANKS MOM!!
BUT YOU SHOULDN'T HAVE HIT HIM, SO...
THE GANG
WELL I'M GROUNDED.
HEART
R.I.P.
KAT
NOT SURPRISED.
CHARLOTTE
YOU GOT HIM GOOD THO!

HEART
OMG, LOOK AT THIS. THIS BABY IS MAKING A PIZZA. A WHOLE PIZZA!!

HEART
OMG, LOOK AT THIS. THIS BABY IS MAKING A PIZZA. A WHOLE PIZZA!!
KAT
THAT'S NOT THE MOST HYGIENIC.

HEART
OMG, LOOK AT THIS. THIS BABY IS MAKING A PIZZA. A WHOLE PIZZA!!
KAT
THAT'S NOT THE MOST HYGIENIC.
HEART
UHHG... THAT'S NOT THE POINT YOU DEBBIE DOWNER.
KAT
A DEBBIE ***WHAT?!***

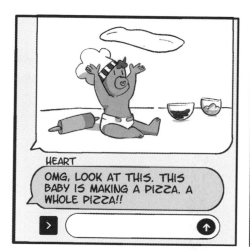

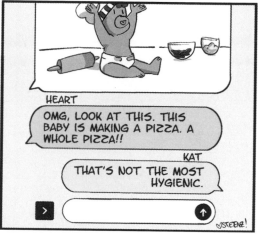

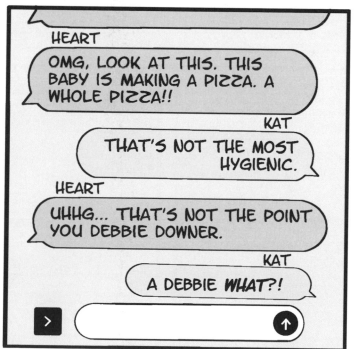

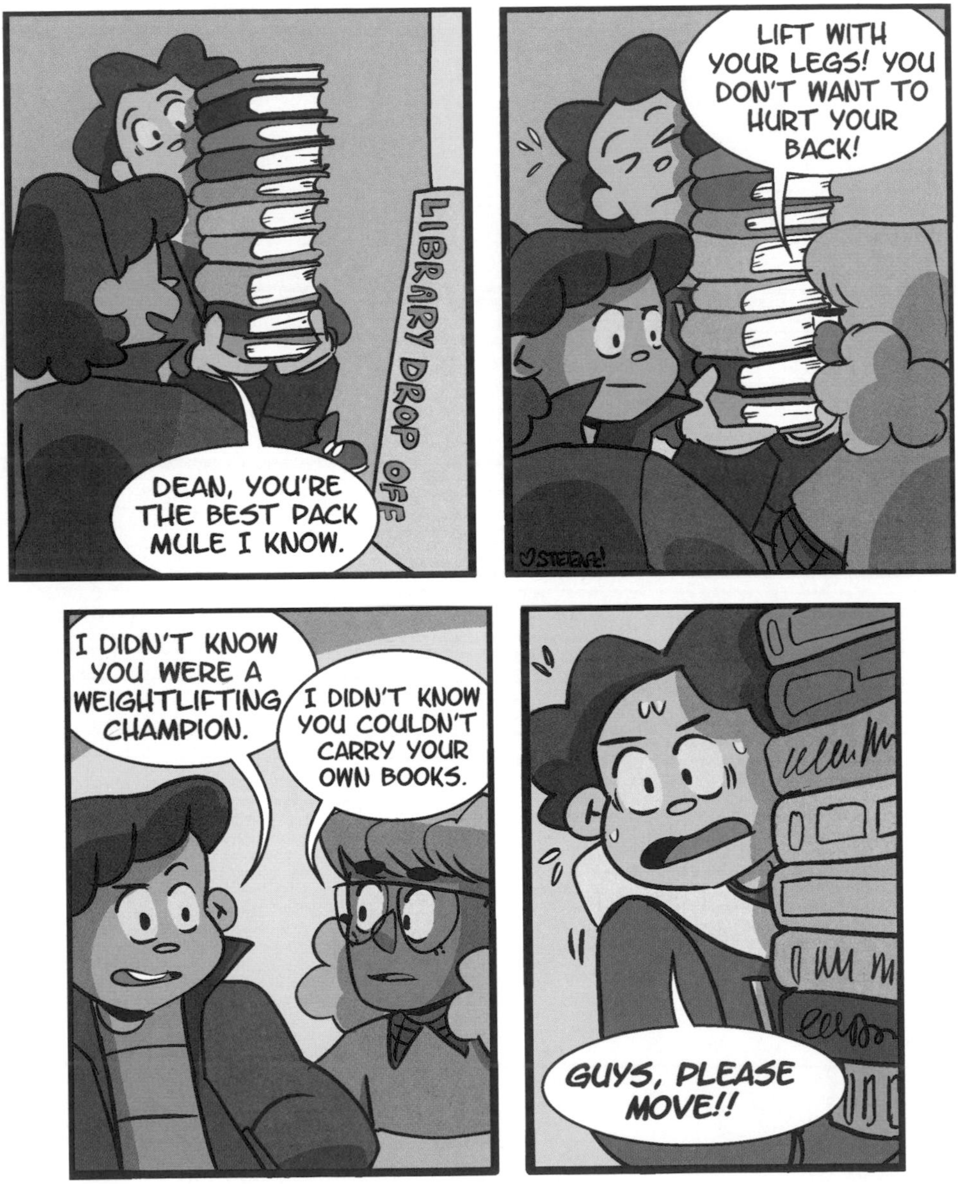
LIBRARY DROP OFF
DEAN, YOU'RE THE BEST PACK MULE I KNOW.
LIFT WITH YOUR LEGS! YOU DON'T WANT TO HURT YOUR BACK!
I DIDN'T KNOW YOU WERE A WEIGHTLIFTING CHAMPION.
I DIDN'T KNOW YOU COULDN'T CARRY YOUR OWN BOOKS.
GUYS, PLEASE MOVE!!

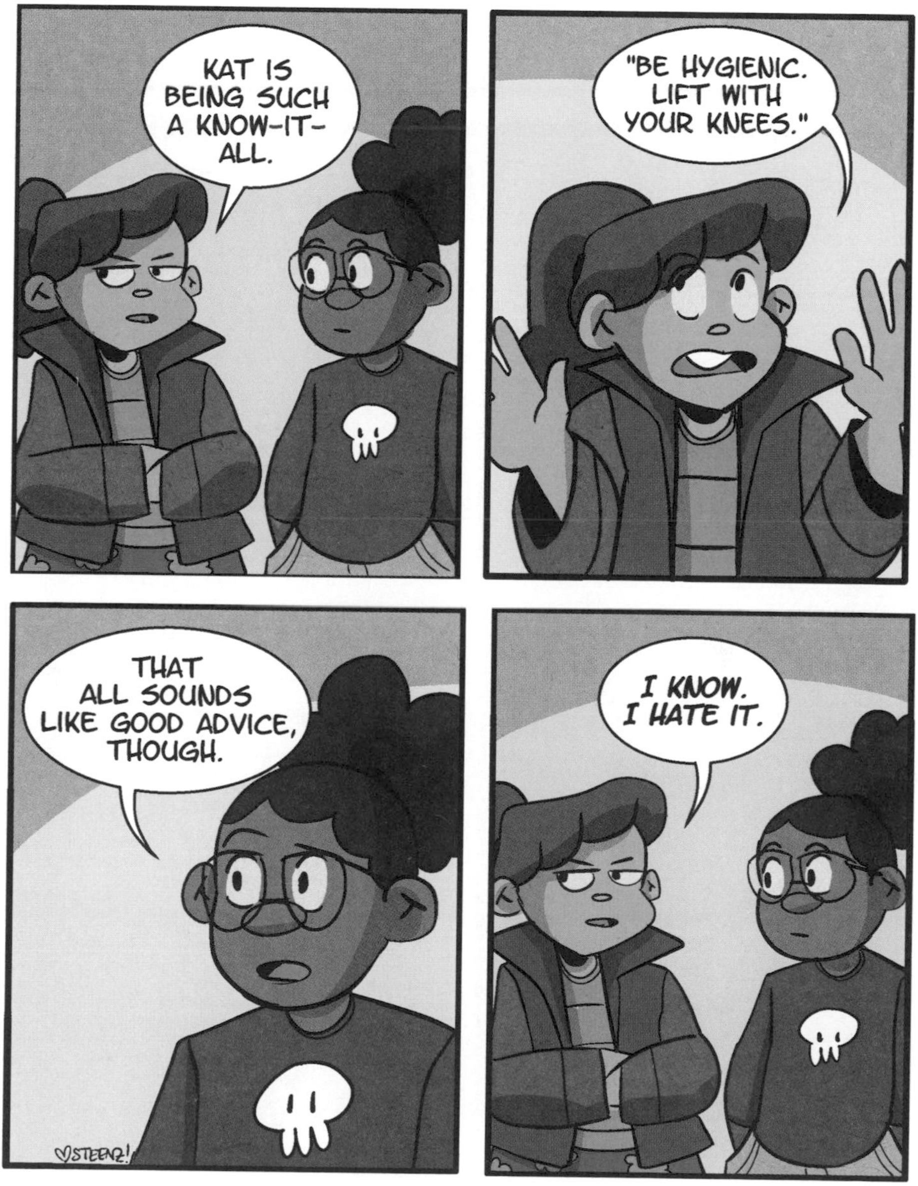
KAT IS BEING SUCH A KNOW-IT-ALL.
"BE HYGIENIC. LIFT WITH YOUR KNEES."
THAT ALL SOUNDS LIKE GOOD ADVICE, THOUGH.
STEENZ!
I KNOW. I HATE IT.

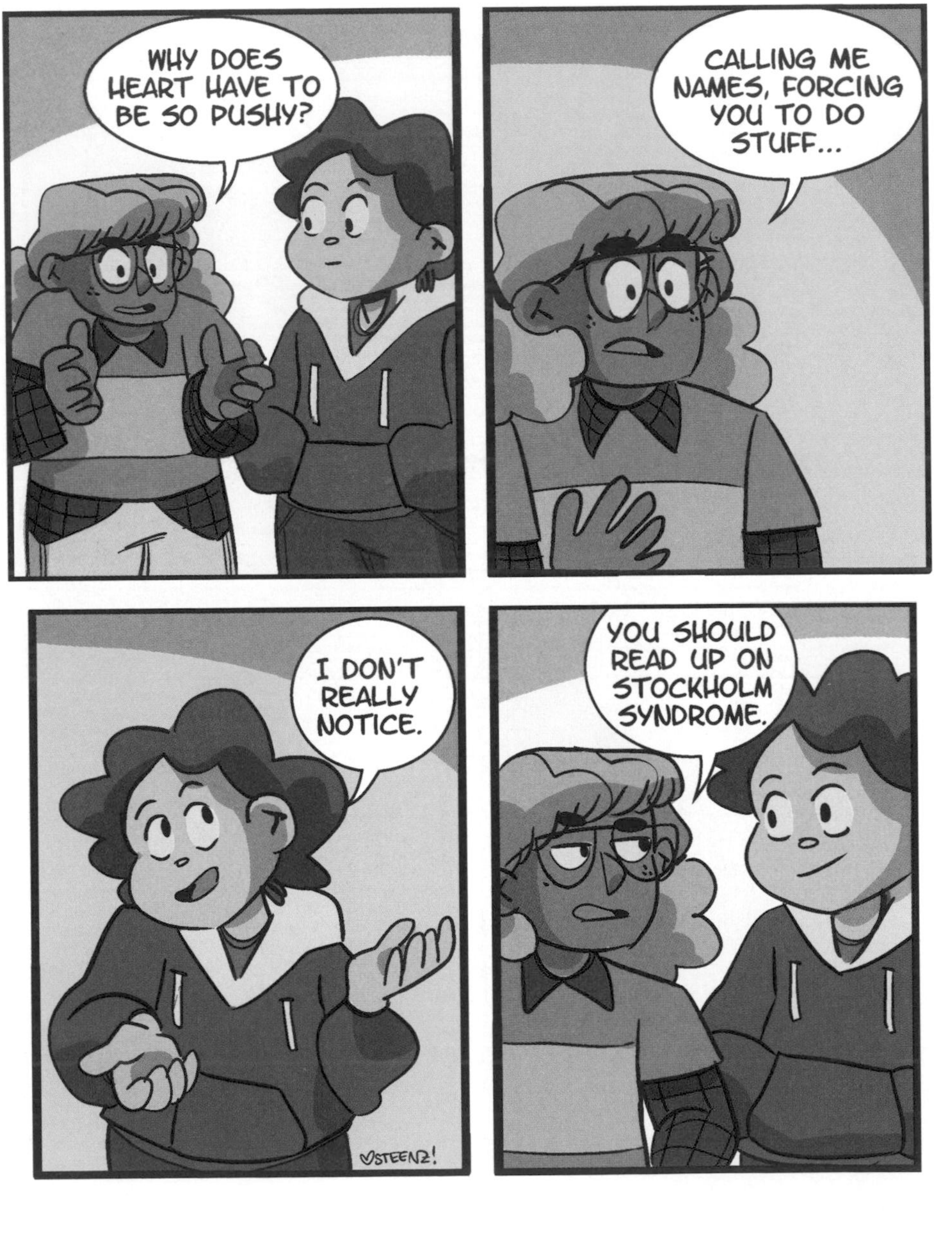
WHY DOES HEART HAVE TO BE SO PUSHY?
CALLING ME NAMES, FORCING YOU TO DO STUFF...
I DON'T REALLY NOTICE.
STEENZ!
YOU SHOULD READ UP ON STOCKHOLM SYNDROME.

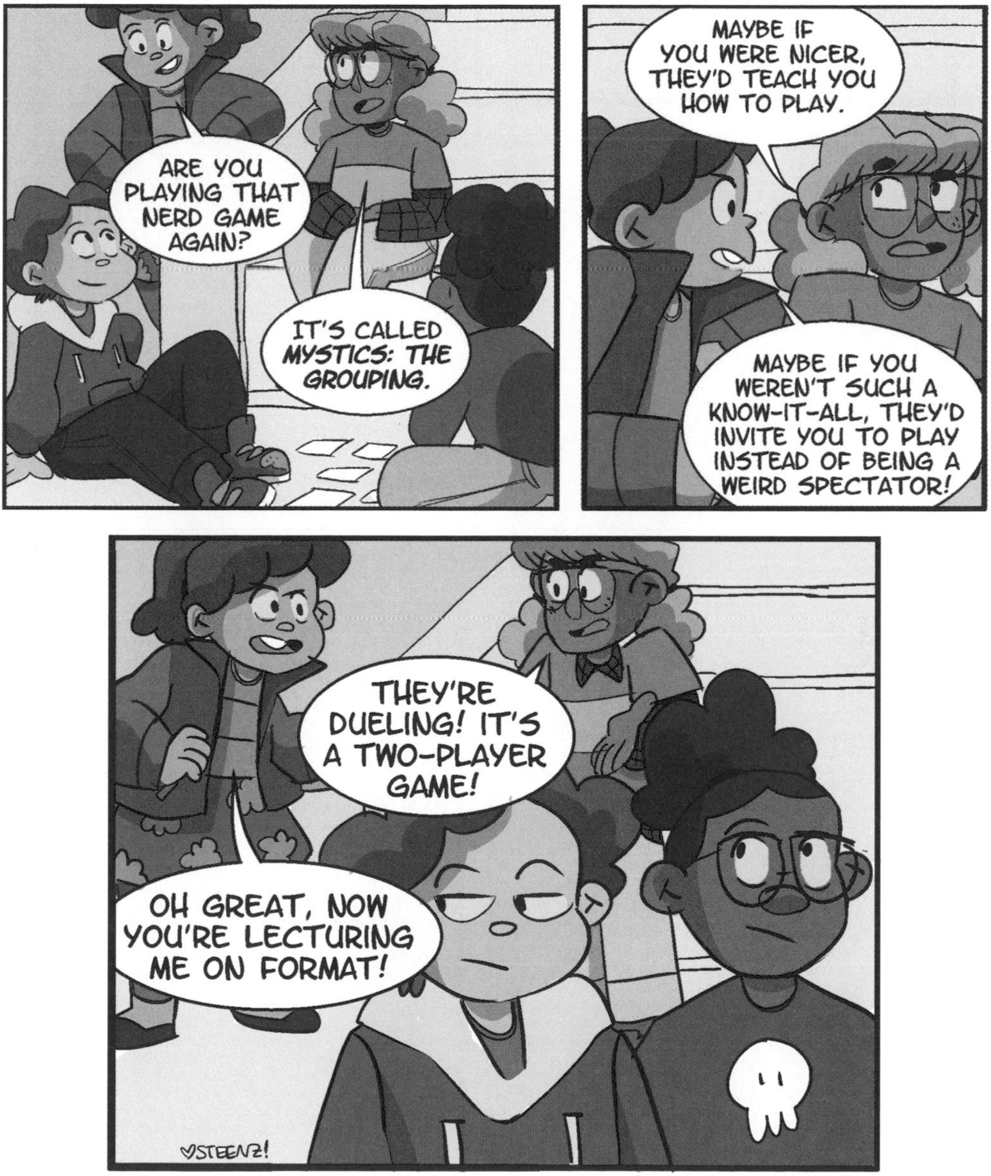
ARE YOU PLAYING THAT NERD GAME AGAIN?
IT'S CALLED *MYSTICS: THE GROUPING.*
MAYBE IF YOU WERE NICER, THEY'D TEACH YOU HOW TO PLAY.
MAYBE IF YOU WEREN'T SUCH A KNOW-IT-ALL, THEY'D INVITE YOU TO PLAY INSTEAD OF BEING A WEIRD SPECTATOR!
THEY'RE DUELING! IT'S A TWO-PLAYER GAME!
OH GREAT, NOW YOU'RE LECTURING ME ON FORMAT!
♡STEENZ!

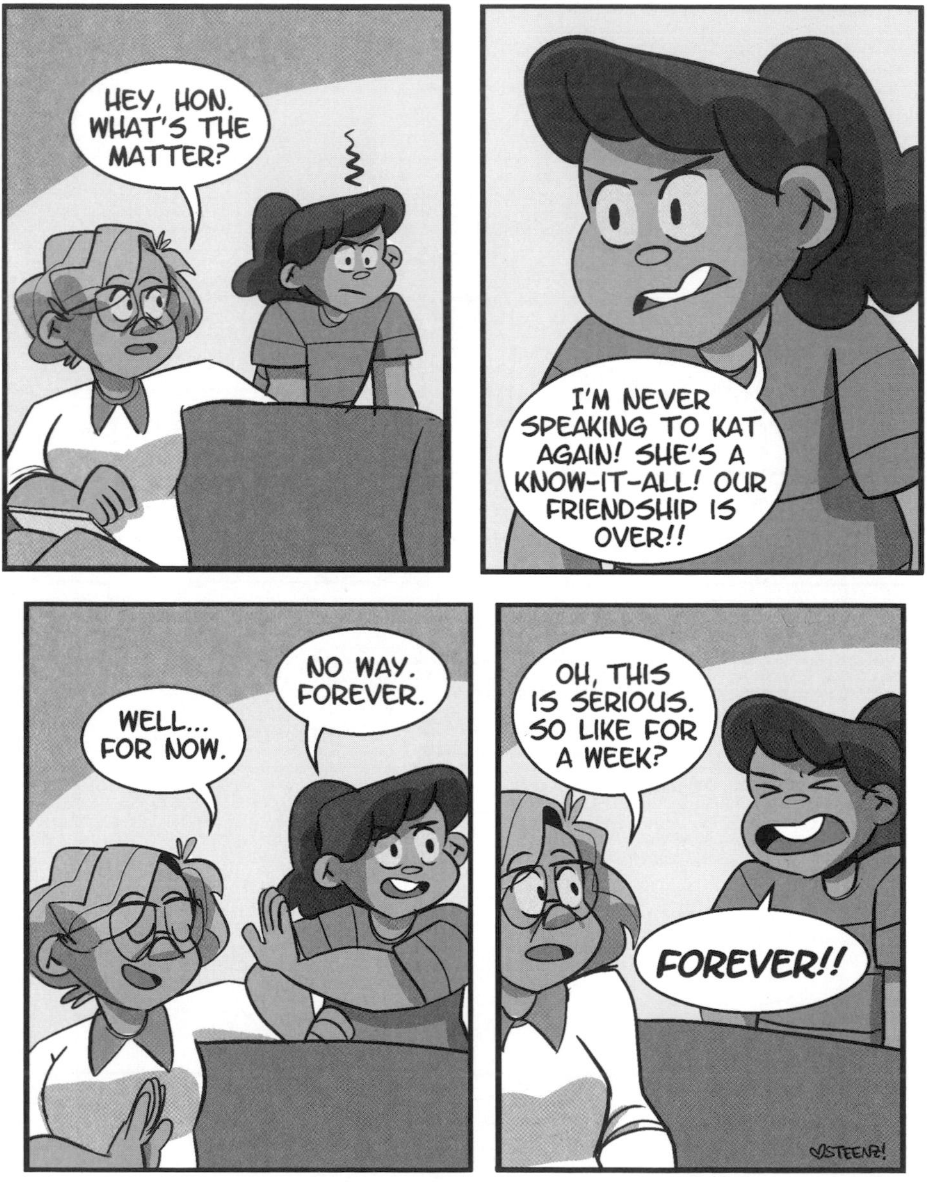
HEY, HON. WHAT'S THE MATTER?
I'M NEVER SPEAKING TO KAT AGAIN! SHE'S A KNOW-IT-ALL! OUR FRIENDSHIP IS OVER!!
WELL... FOR NOW.
NO WAY. FOREVER.
OH, THIS IS SERIOUS. SO LIKE FOR A WEEK?
FOREVER!!
STEENZ!

WHAT'S THE MATTER, KAT?

♥STEENZ!

HEART AND I GOT INTO A FIGHT.

WHOA! DID YOU WIN?

SHARI...

SORRY, SORRY!

BUT YOU DID WIN, RIGHT?

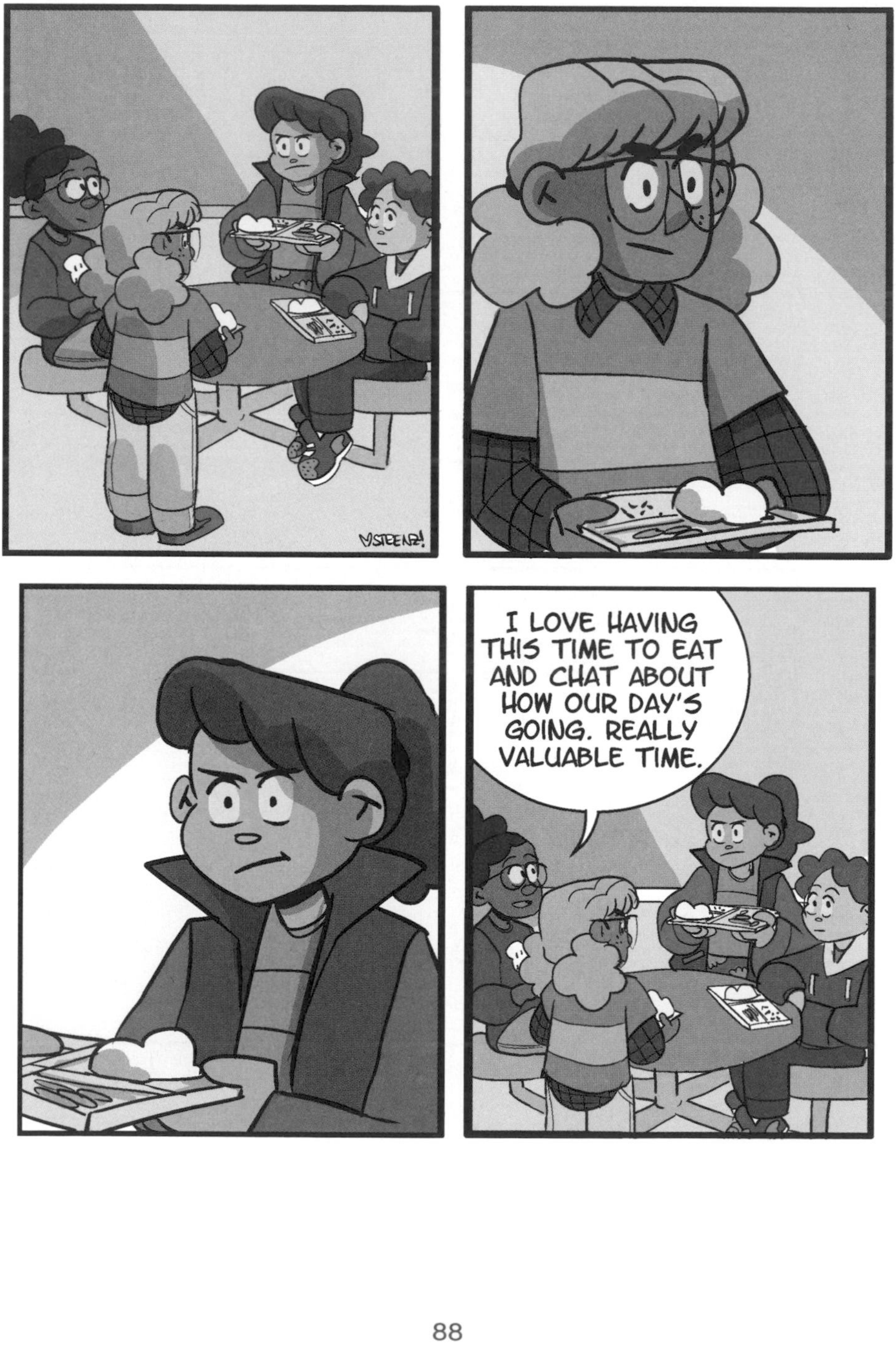
I LOVE HAVING THIS TIME TO EAT AND CHAT ABOUT HOW OUR DAY'S GOING. REALLY VALUABLE TIME.

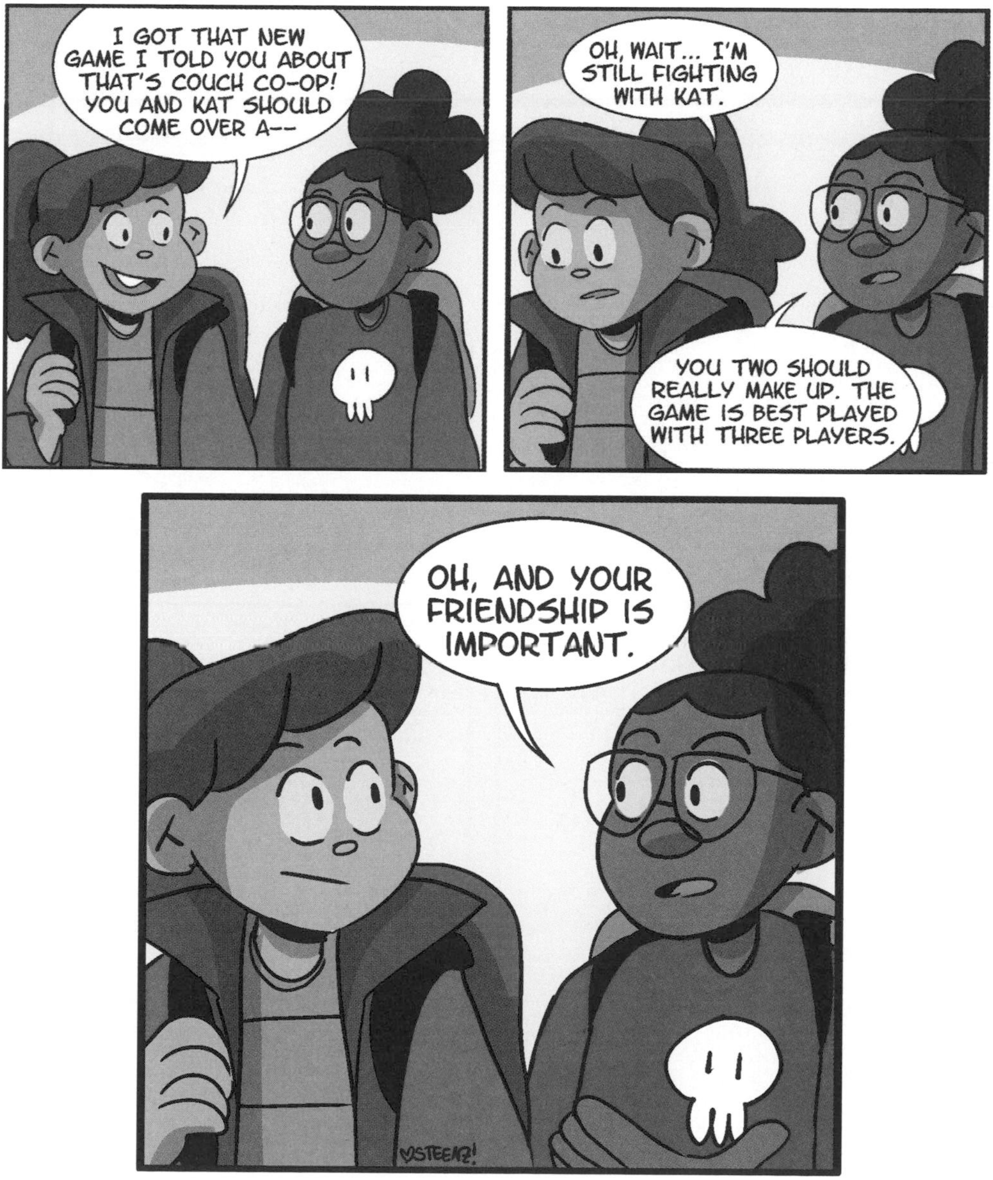
I GOT THAT NEW GAME I TOLD YOU ABOUT THAT'S COUCH CO-OP! YOU AND KAT SHOULD COME OVER A--
OH, WAIT... I'M STILL FIGHTING WITH KAT.
YOU TWO SHOULD REALLY MAKE UP. THE GAME IS BEST PLAYED WITH THREE PLAYERS.
OH, AND YOUR FRIENDSHIP IS IMPORTANT.
STEENZ!

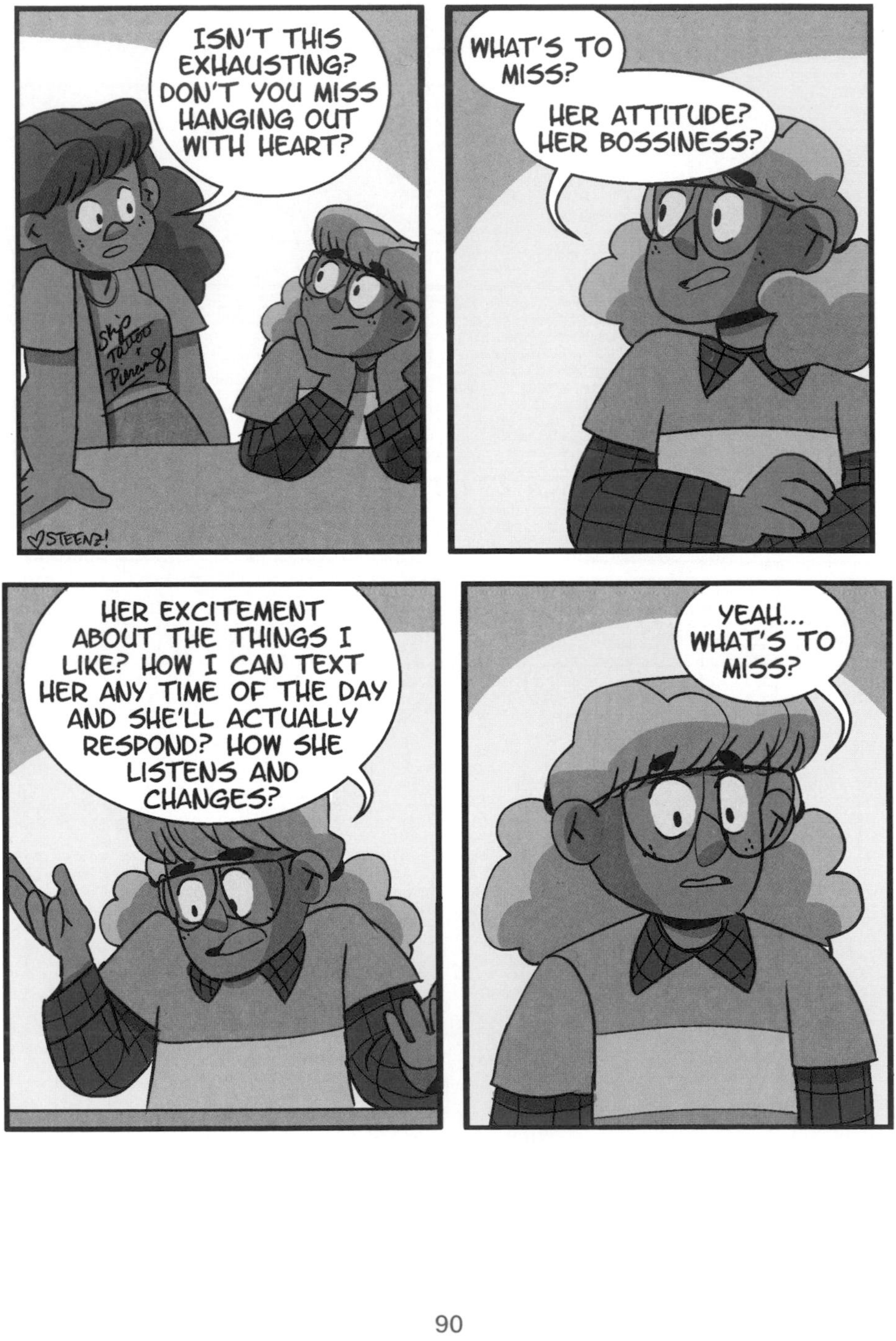
ISN'T THIS EXHAUSTING? DON'T YOU MISS HANGING OUT WITH HEART?
♡STEENZ!
WHAT'S TO MISS?
HER ATTITUDE? HER BOSSINESS?
HER EXCITEMENT ABOUT THE THINGS I LIKE? HOW I CAN TEXT HER ANY TIME OF THE DAY AND SHE'LL ACTUALLY RESPOND? HOW SHE LISTENS AND CHANGES?
YEAH... WHAT'S TO MISS?

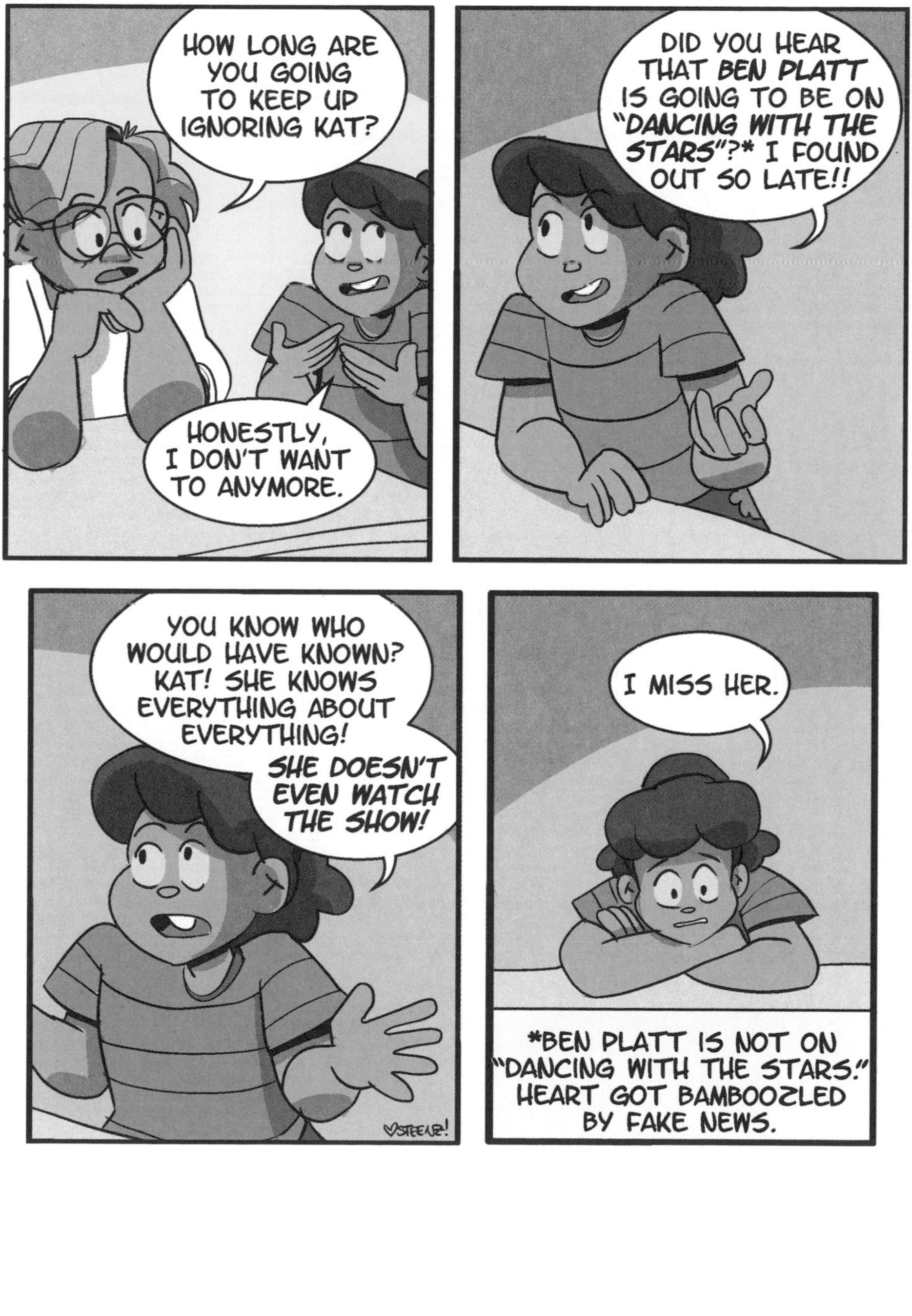
HOW LONG ARE YOU GOING TO KEEP UP IGNORING KAT?
HONESTLY, I DON'T WANT TO ANYMORE.
DID YOU HEAR THAT BEN PLATT IS GOING TO BE ON "DANCING WITH THE STARS"?* I FOUND OUT SO LATE!!
YOU KNOW WHO WOULD HAVE KNOWN? KAT! SHE KNOWS EVERYTHING ABOUT EVERYTHING!
SHE DOESN'T EVEN WATCH THE SHOW!
I MISS HER.
*BEN PLATT IS NOT ON "DANCING WITH THE STARS." HEART GOT BAMBOOZLED BY FAKE NEWS.

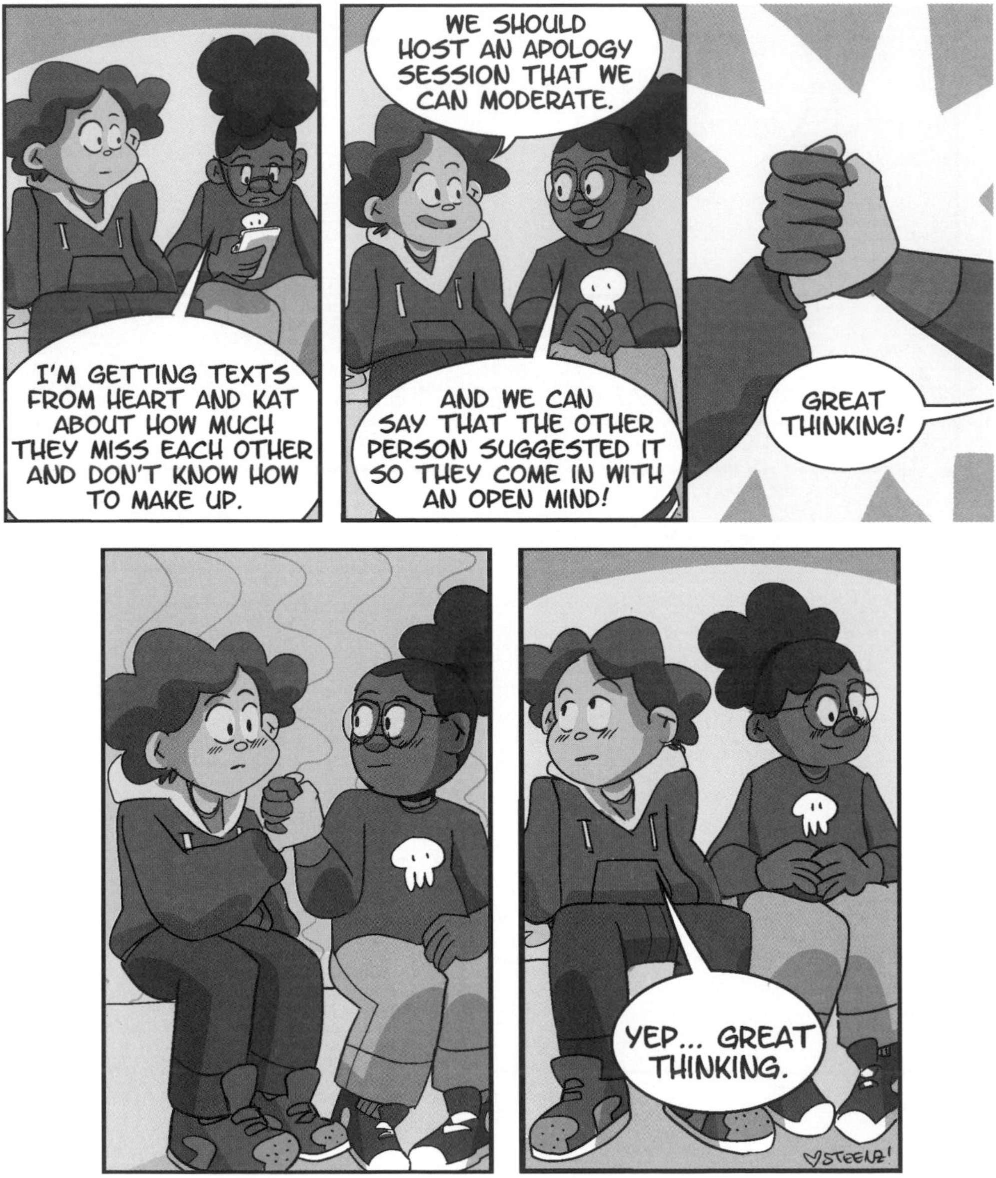
I'M GETTING TEXTS FROM HEART AND KAT ABOUT HOW MUCH THEY MISS EACH OTHER AND DON'T KNOW HOW TO MAKE UP.
WE SHOULD HOST AN APOLOGY SESSION THAT WE CAN MODERATE.
AND WE CAN SAY THAT THE OTHER PERSON SUGGESTED IT SO THEY COME IN WITH AN OPEN MIND!
GREAT THINKING!
YEP... GREAT THINKING.
♡STEENZ!

SO? WHAT DID YOU WANT TO SAY?
WHAT DID YOU WANT TO SAY?
MAYBE YOU SHOULD BOTH SAY IT AT THE SAME TIME.
I'LL COUNT YOU DOWN. 3...2...1!
I THINK YOU BOTH MISSED THE CUE.
♡STEENZ!

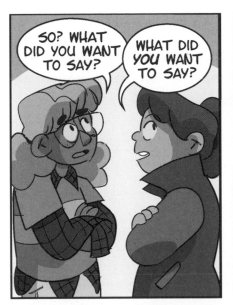

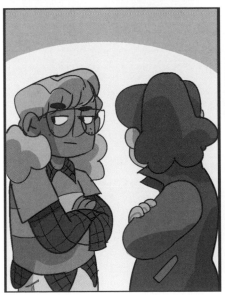

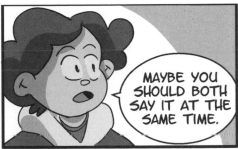

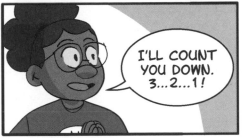

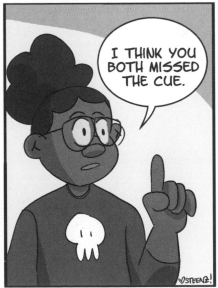

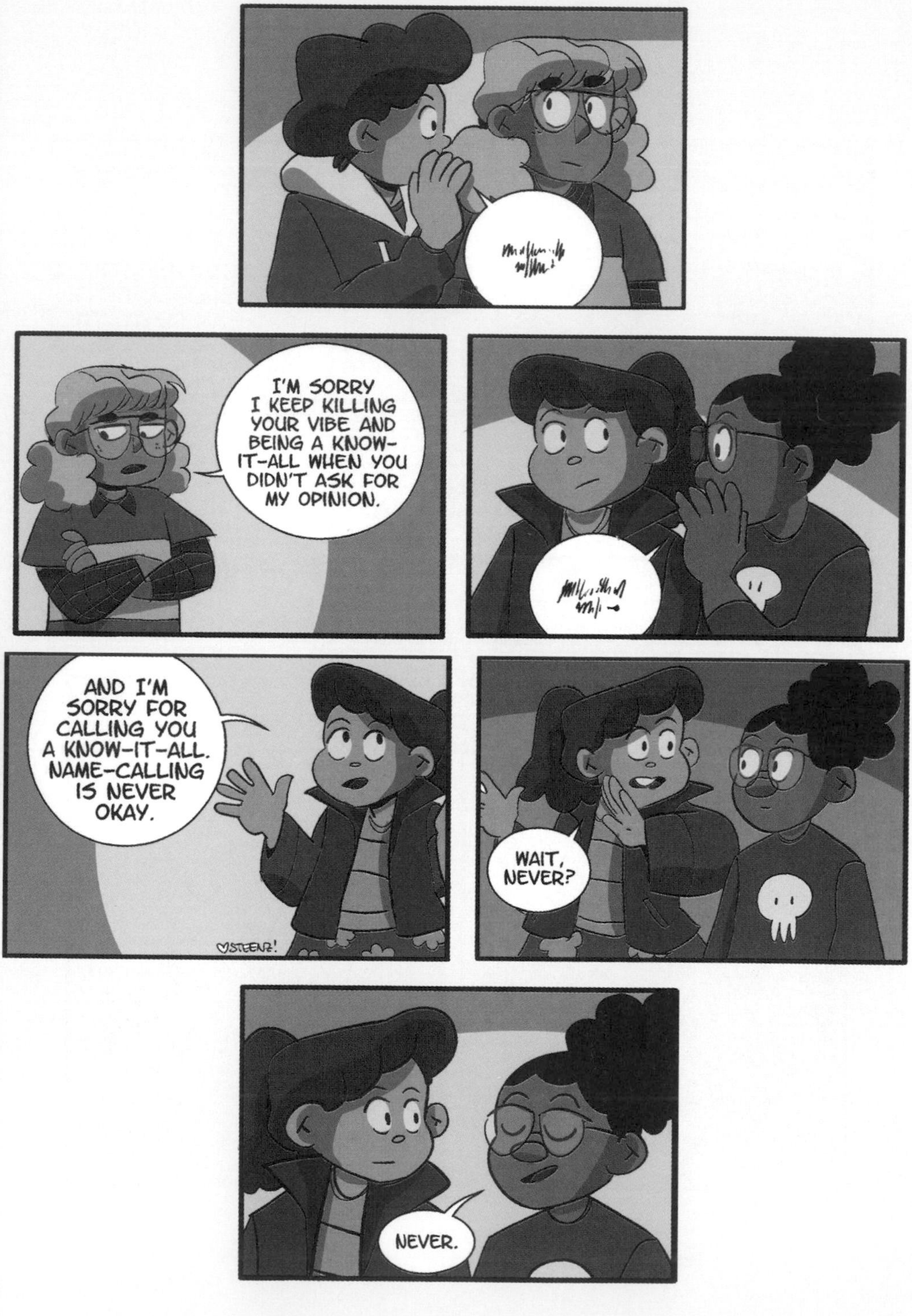
I'M SORRY I KEEP KILLING YOUR VIBE AND BEING A KNOW-IT-ALL WHEN YOU DIDN'T ASK FOR MY OPINION.
AND I'M SORRY FOR CALLING YOU A KNOW-IT-ALL. NAME-CALLING IS NEVER OKAY.
♡STEENZ!
WAIT, NEVER?
NEVER.

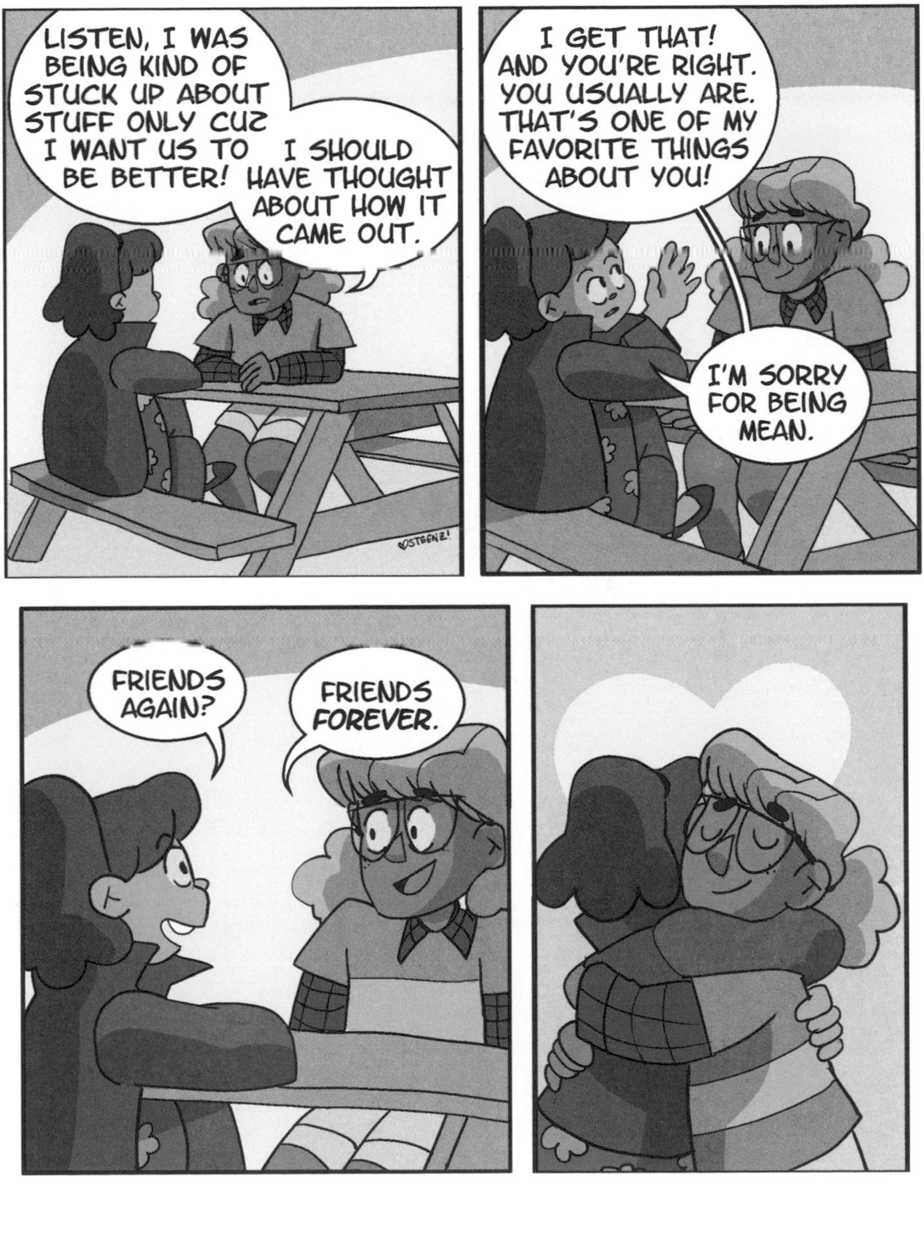
LISTEN, I WAS BEING KIND OF STUCK UP ABOUT STUFF ONLY CUZ I WANT US TO BE BETTER!
I SHOULD HAVE THOUGHT ABOUT HOW IT CAME OUT.
STEENZ!
I GET THAT! AND YOU'RE RIGHT. YOU USUALLY ARE. THAT'S ONE OF MY FAVORITE THINGS ABOUT YOU!
I'M SORRY FOR BEING MEAN.
FRIENDS AGAIN?
FRIENDS FOREVER.

WE'RE SO GOOD AT THIS.

YEAH! WE SHOULD START A COUNSELING BUSINESS.

♡STEENZ!

KNOWING THEM, I'M SURE THEY'LL FIGHT AGAIN. MAYBE THEY'RE OUR EXCLUSIVE CLIENTS.

PROBABLY FOR THE BEST.

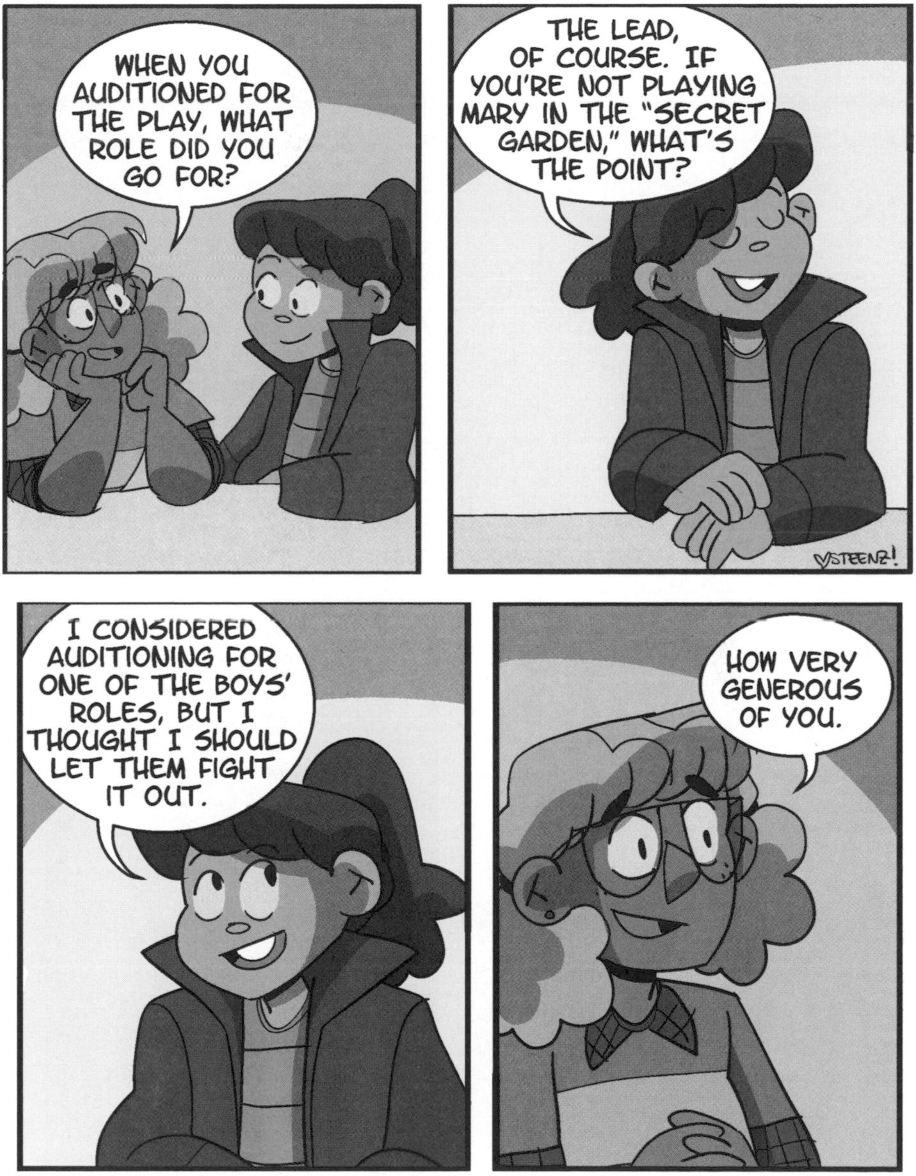
WHEN YOU AUDITIONED FOR THE PLAY, WHAT ROLE DID YOU GO FOR?
THE LEAD, OF COURSE. IF YOU'RE NOT PLAYING MARY IN THE "SECRET GARDEN," WHAT'S THE POINT?
STEENZ!
I CONSIDERED AUDITIONING FOR ONE OF THE BOYS' ROLES, BUT I THOUGHT I SHOULD LET THEM FIGHT IT OUT.
HOW VERY GENEROUS OF YOU.

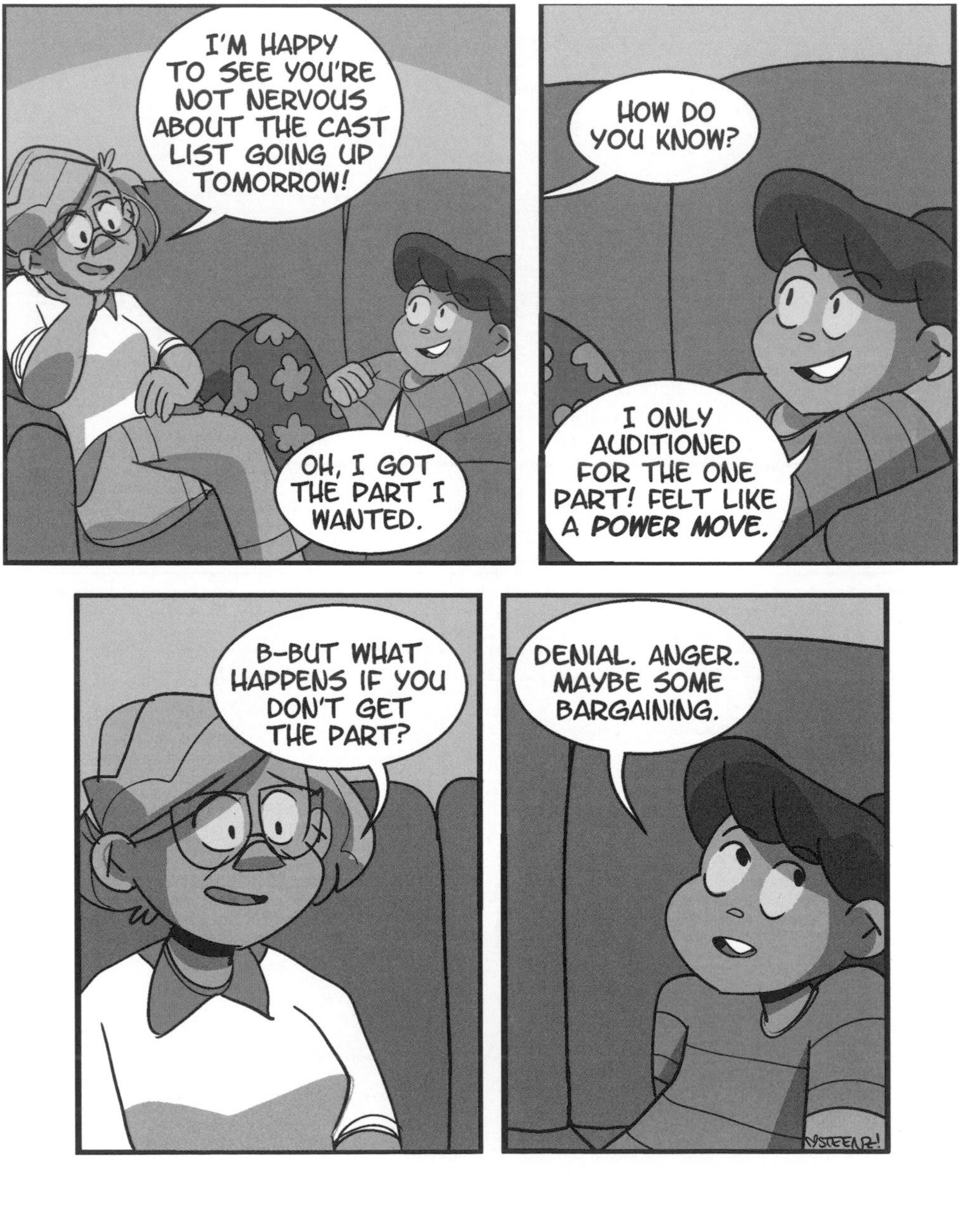
I'M HAPPY TO SEE YOU'RE NOT NERVOUS ABOUT THE CAST LIST GOING UP TOMORROW!
OH, I GOT THE PART I WANTED.
HOW DO YOU KNOW?
I ONLY AUDITIONED FOR THE ONE PART! FELT LIKE A **POWER MOVE.**
B-BUT WHAT HAPPENS IF YOU DON'T GET THE PART?
DENIAL. ANGER. MAYBE SOME BARGAINING.

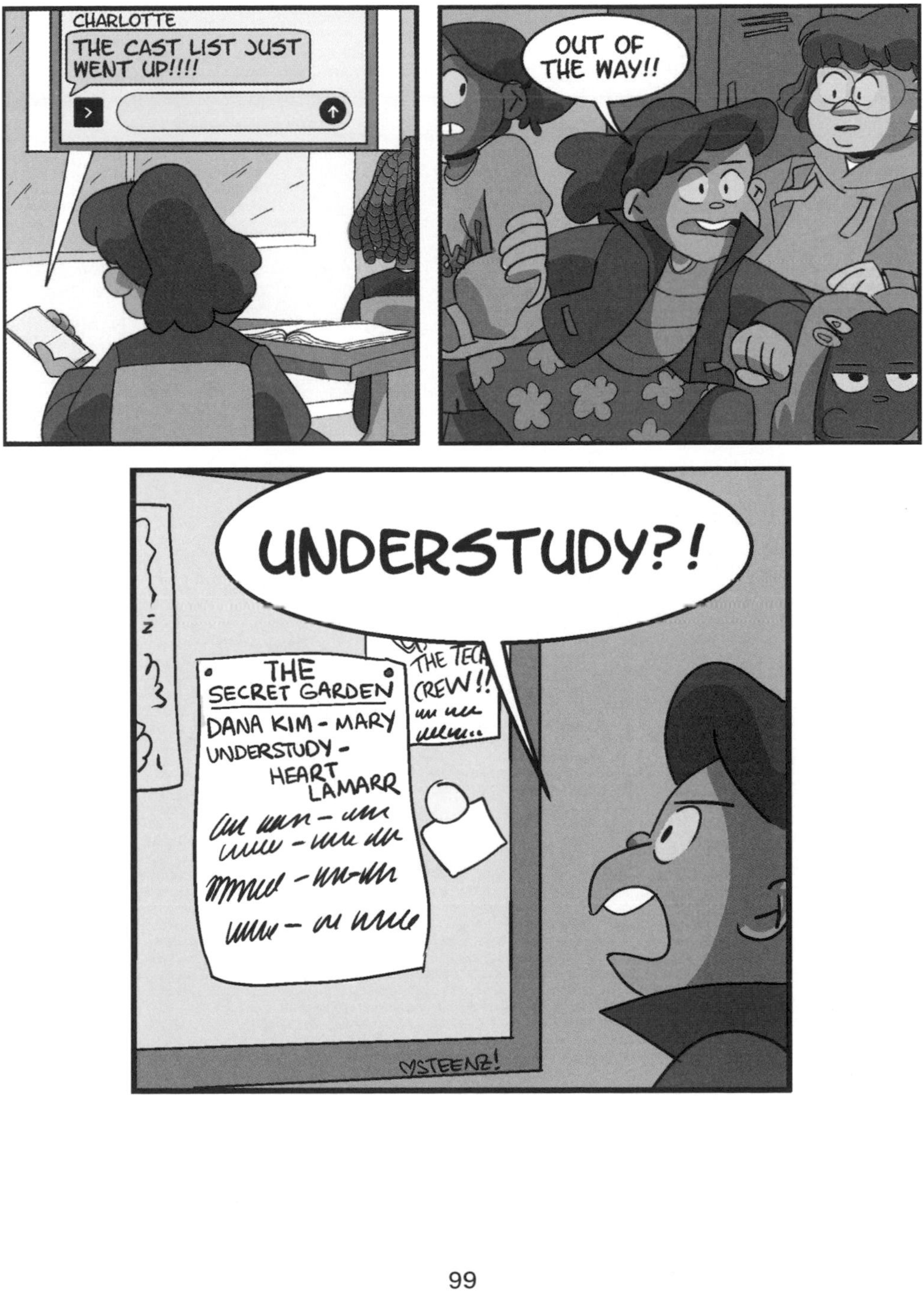
CHARLOTTE
THE CAST LIST JUST WENT UP!!!!
OUT OF THE WAY!!
UNDERSTUDY?!
THE SECRET GARDEN
DANA KIM - MARY
UNDERSTUDY - HEART LAMARR
CREW!!
STEENZ!

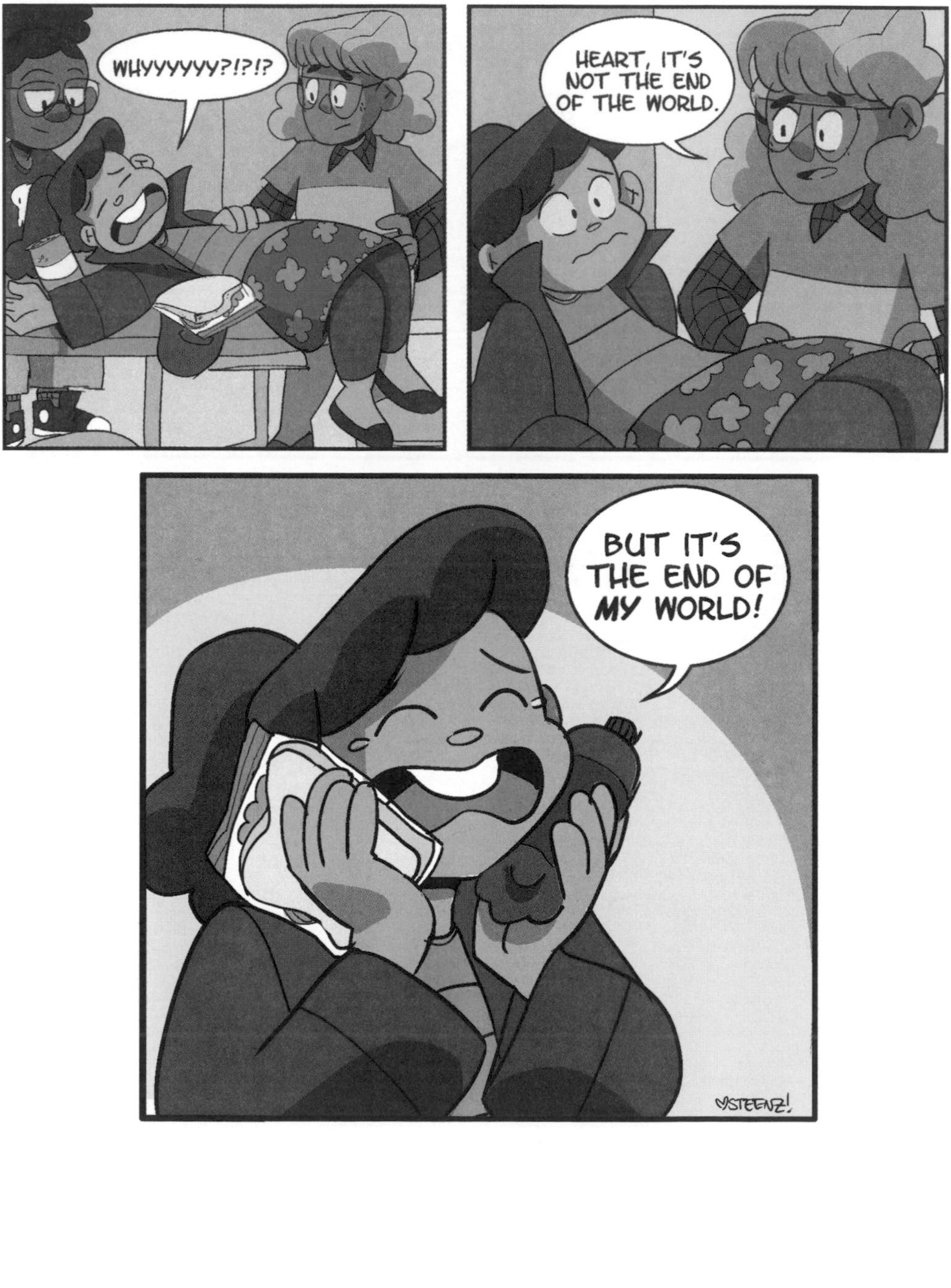
WHYYYYYY?!?!?
HEART, IT'S NOT THE END OF THE WORLD.
BUT IT'S THE END OF MY WORLD!
STEENZ!

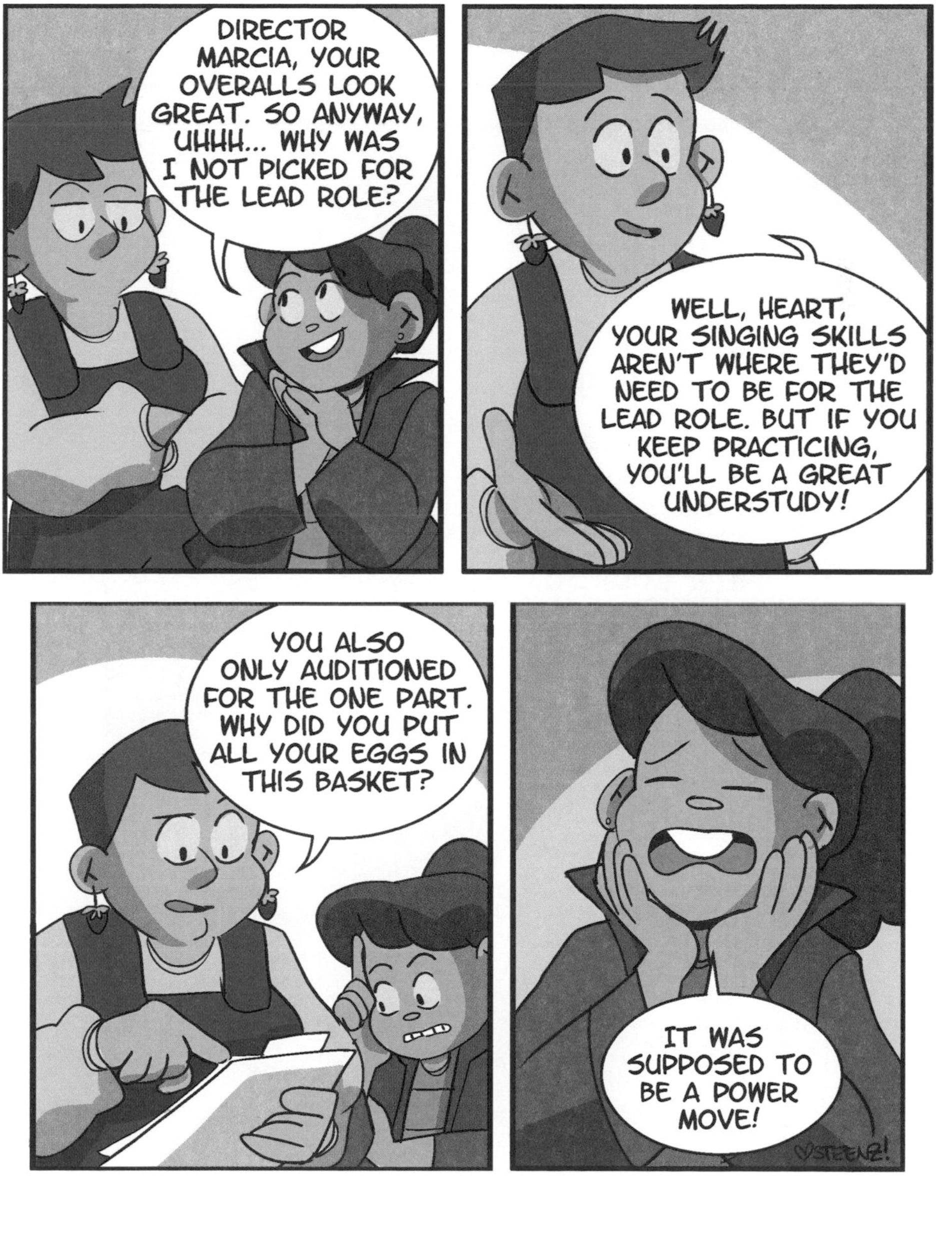
DIRECTOR MARCIA, YOUR OVERALLS LOOK GREAT. SO ANYWAY, UHHH... WHY WAS I NOT PICKED FOR THE LEAD ROLE?
WELL, HEART, YOUR SINGING SKILLS AREN'T WHERE THEY'D NEED TO BE FOR THE LEAD ROLE. BUT IF YOU KEEP PRACTICING, YOU'LL BE A GREAT UNDERSTUDY!
YOU ALSO ONLY AUDITIONED FOR THE ONE PART. WHY DID YOU PUT ALL YOUR EGGS IN THIS BASKET?
IT WAS SUPPOSED TO BE A POWER MOVE!
STEENZ!

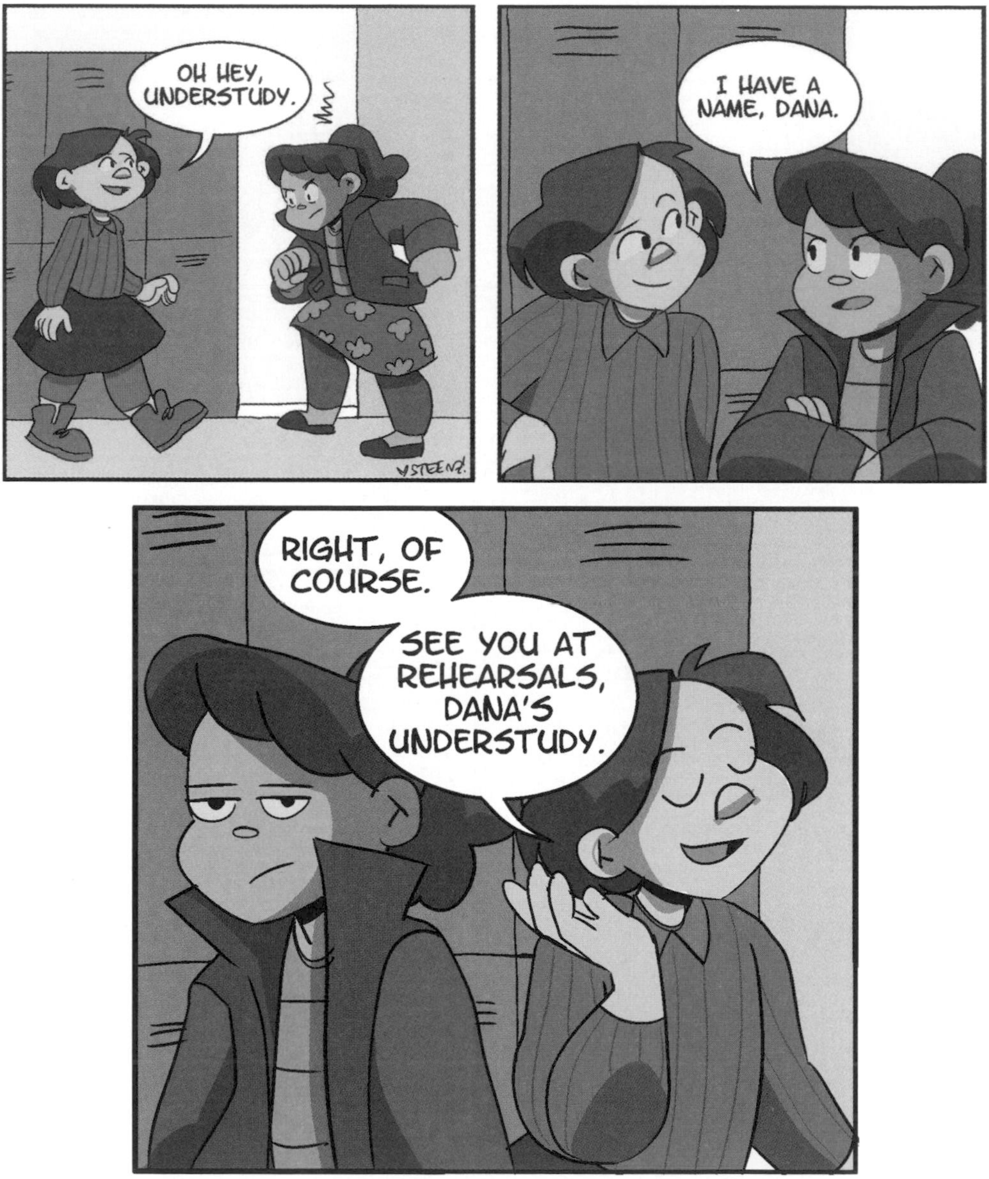
OH HEY, UNDERSTUDY.
STEENZ.
I HAVE A NAME, DANA.
RIGHT, OF COURSE.
SEE YOU AT REHEARSALS, DANA'S UNDERSTUDY.

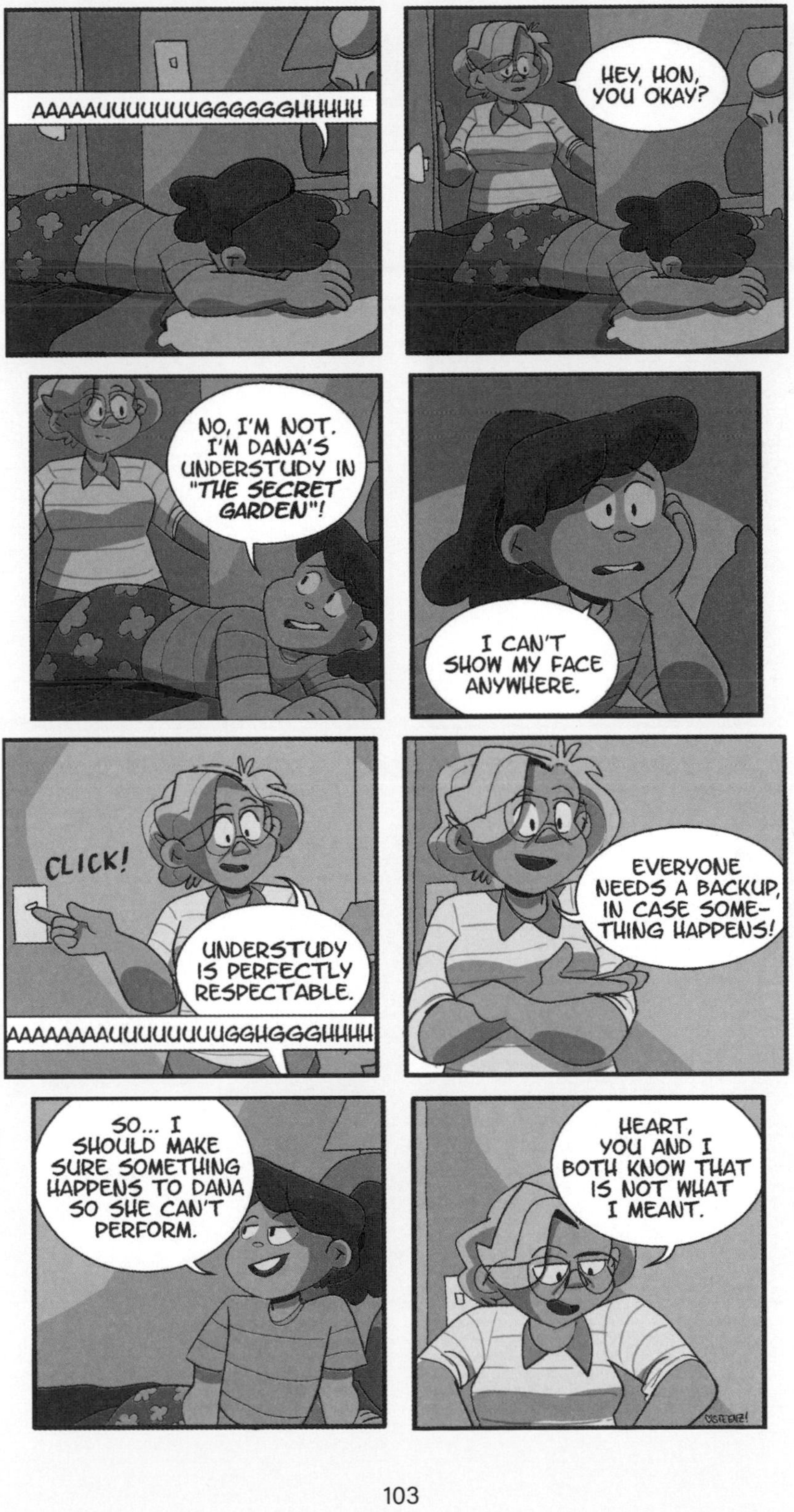
AAAAAUUUUUUUGGGGGGHHHHHH
HEY, HON, YOU OKAY?
NO, I'M NOT. I'M DANA'S UNDERSTUDY IN "THE SECRET GARDEN"!
I CAN'T SHOW MY FACE ANYWHERE.
CLICK!
UNDERSTUDY IS PERFECTLY RESPECTABLE.
AAAAAAAAUUUUUUUUGGHGGGHHHH
EVERYONE NEEDS A BACKUP, IN CASE SOMETHING HAPPENS!
SO... I SHOULD MAKE SURE SOMETHING HAPPENS TO DANA SO SHE CAN'T PERFORM.
HEART, YOU AND I BOTH KNOW THAT IS NOT WHAT I MEANT.

IN THE ACTING PROFESSION, YOU HAVE TO BE A TRIPLE THREAT TO BE COMPETITIVE.

AND SOME PEOPLE JUST DON'T MAKE THE CUT.

♥STEENZ!

I'LL SHOW HER "MAKING THE CUT"...

SNIP! SNIP!

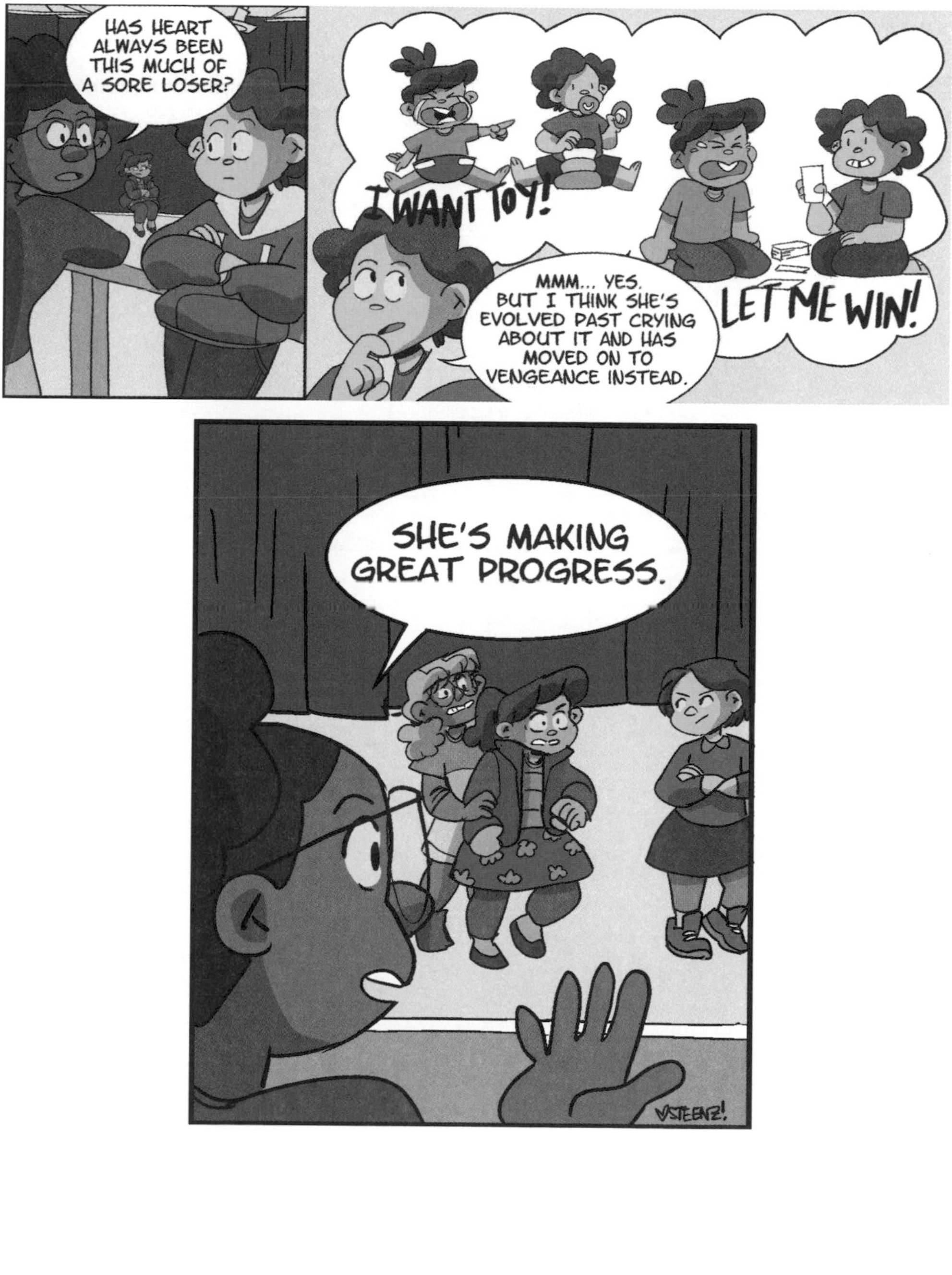
HAS HEART ALWAYS BEEN THIS MUCH OF A SORE LOSER?
I WANT TOY!
MMM... YES. BUT I THINK SHE'S EVOLVED PAST CRYING ABOUT IT AND HAS MOVED ON TO VENGEANCE INSTEAD.
LET ME WIN!
SHE'S MAKING GREAT PROGRESS.
STEENZ!

ALRIGHT, I'LL SABOTAGE THE PLAY SO THAT DANA CAN'T GET HER TIME IN THE SPOTLIGHT!

PLEASE DON'T. WE'VE BEEN WORKING SO HARD ON THE SET THIS YEAR!

HEART, YOU HAVE GOT TO BE LESS VINDICTIVE.

THIS ISN'T EVEN REVENGE! IT'S JUSTICE!

6TH GRADE DRAMA IS AS GOOD AS, IF NOT BETTER THAN, HIGH SCHOOL DRAMA.

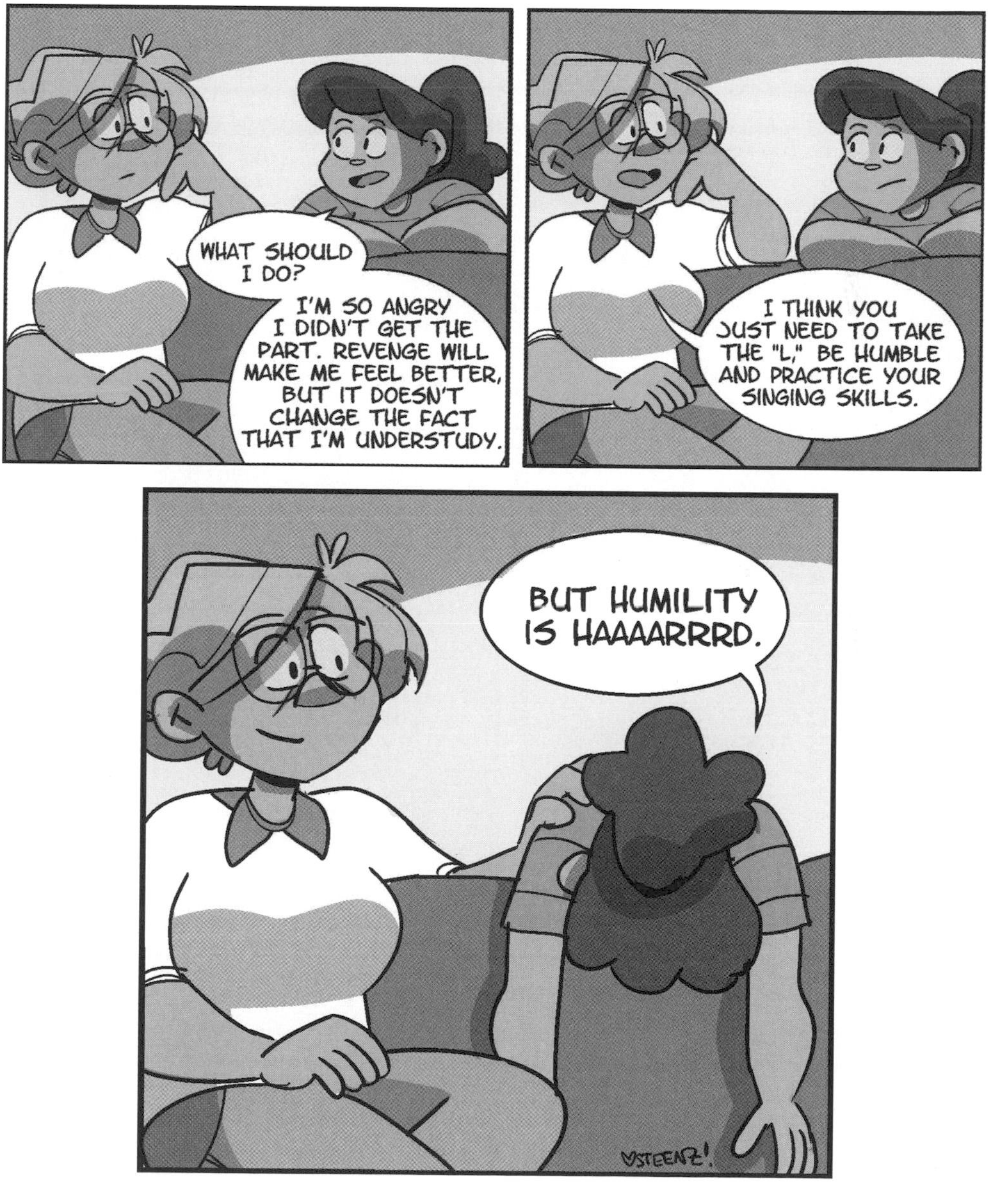
WHAT SHOULD I DO?
I'M SO ANGRY I DIDN'T GET THE PART. REVENGE WILL MAKE ME FEEL BETTER, BUT IT DOESN'T CHANGE THE FACT THAT I'M UNDERSTUDY.
I THINK YOU JUST NEED TO TAKE THE "L," BE HUMBLE AND PRACTICE YOUR SINGING SKILLS.
BUT HUMILITY IS HAAAARRRD.
♡STEENZ!

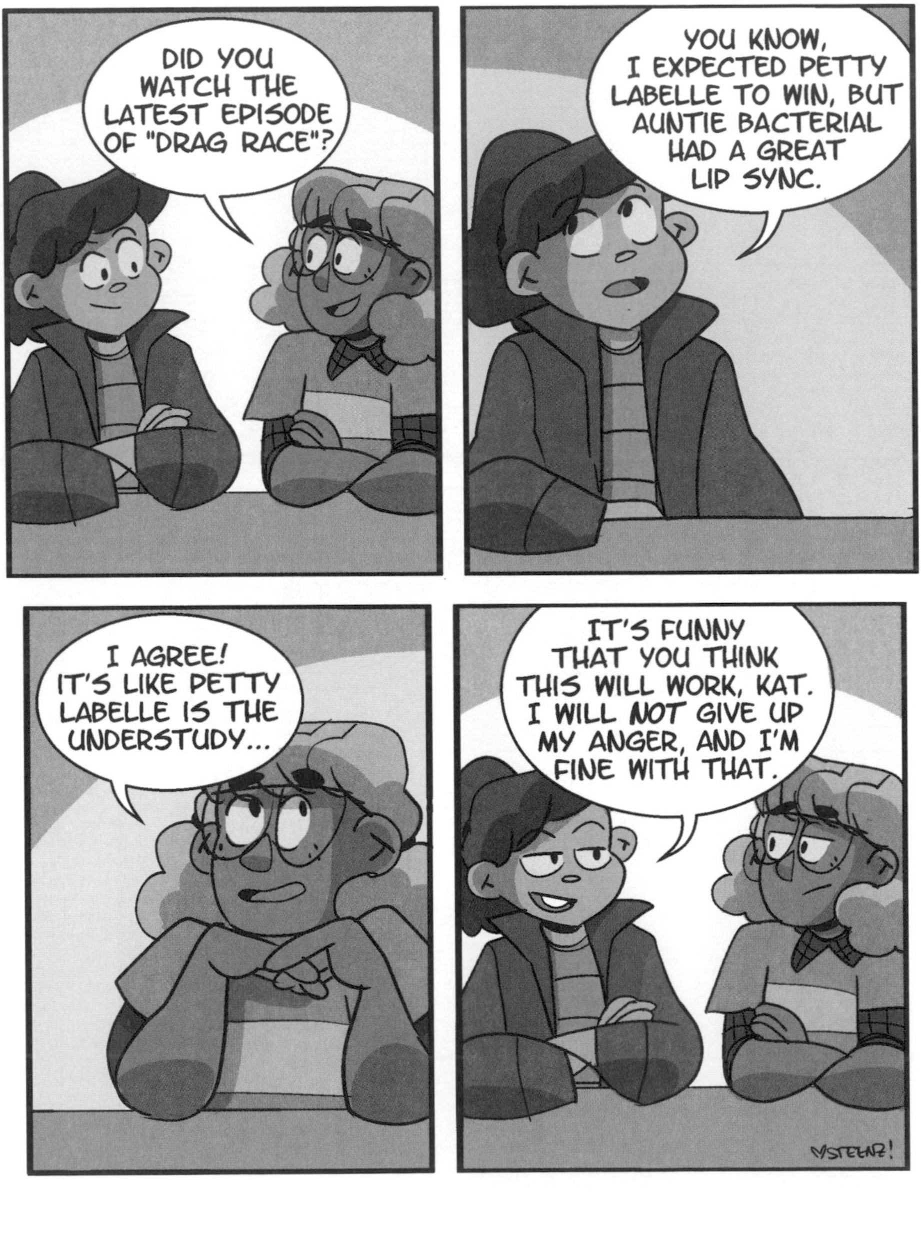
DID YOU WATCH THE LATEST EPISODE OF "DRAG RACE"?
YOU KNOW, I EXPECTED PETTY LABELLE TO WIN, BUT AUNTIE BACTERIAL HAD A GREAT LIP SYNC.
I AGREE! IT'S LIKE PETTY LABELLE IS THE UNDERSTUDY...
IT'S FUNNY THAT YOU THINK THIS WILL WORK, KAT. I WILL NOT GIVE UP MY ANGER, AND I'M FINE WITH THAT.
♡STEENZ!

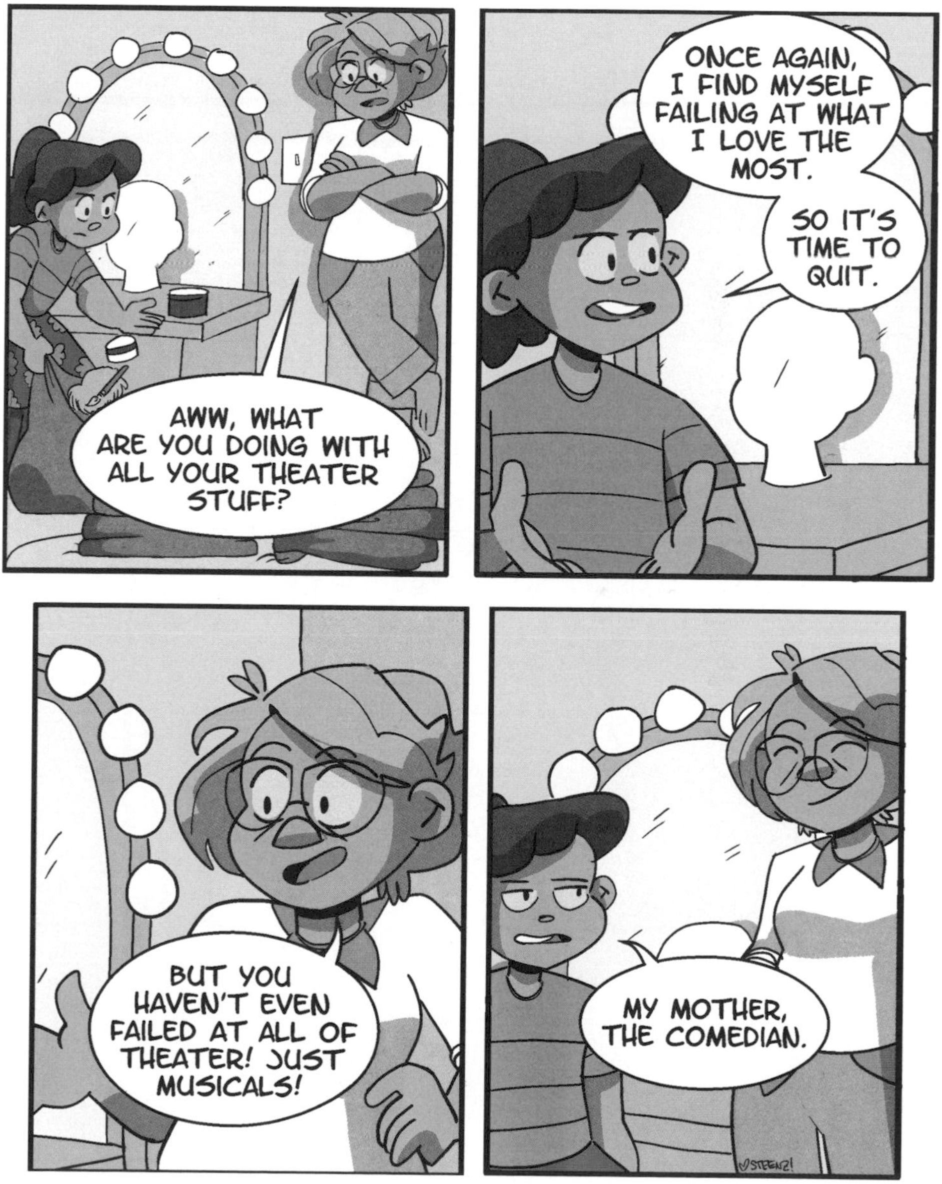
AWW, WHAT ARE YOU DOING WITH ALL YOUR THEATER STUFF?
ONCE AGAIN, I FIND MYSELF FAILING AT WHAT I LOVE THE MOST.
SO IT'S TIME TO QUIT.
BUT YOU HAVEN'T EVEN FAILED AT ALL OF THEATER! JUST MUSICALS!
MY MOTHER, THE COMEDIAN.
STEENZ!

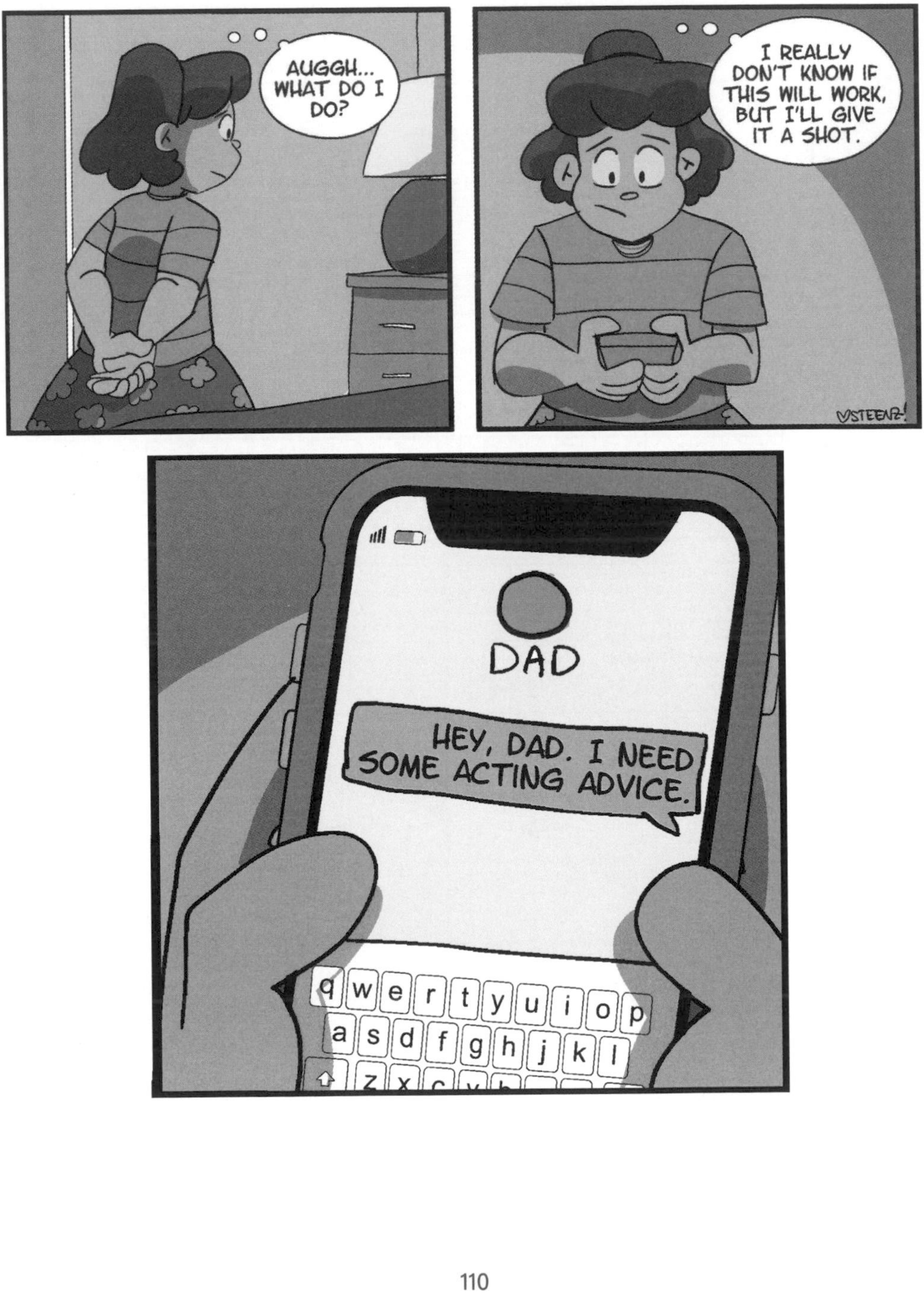
AUGGH... WHAT DO I DO?
I REALLY DON'T KNOW IF THIS WILL WORK, BUT I'LL GIVE IT A SHOT.
DAD
HEY, DAD. I NEED SOME ACTING ADVICE.

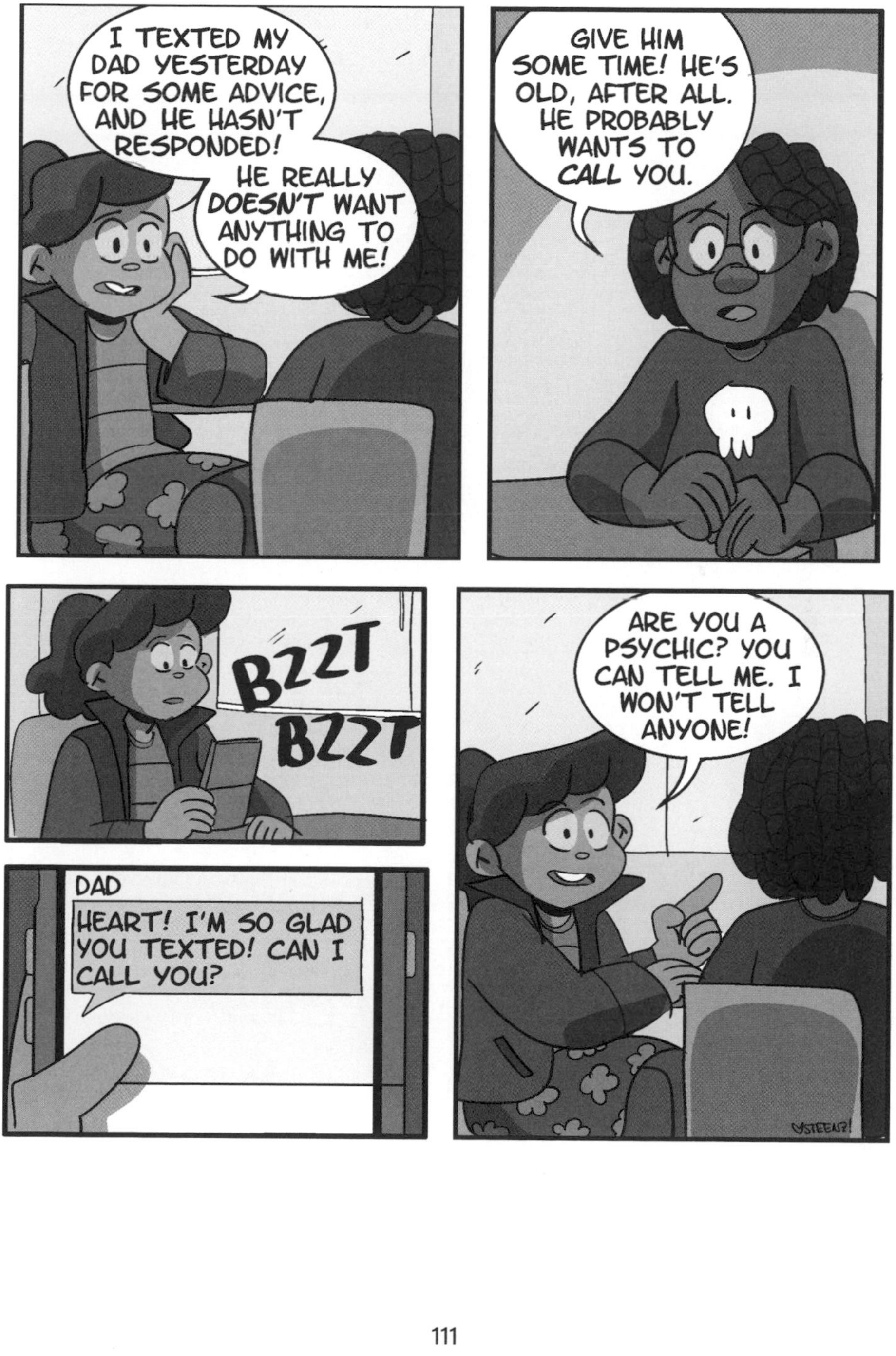
I TEXTED MY DAD YESTERDAY FOR SOME ADVICE, AND HE HASN'T RESPONDED!
HE REALLY DOESN'T WANT ANYTHING TO DO WITH ME!
GIVE HIM SOME TIME! HE'S OLD, AFTER ALL. HE PROBABLY WANTS TO CALL YOU.
BZZT
BZZT
DAD
HEART! I'M SO GLAD YOU TEXTED! CAN I CALL YOU?
ARE YOU A PSYCHIC? YOU CAN TELL ME. I WON'T TELL ANYONE!

I'M HOME!

HEY, HEART! WANNA WATCH A MOVIE AFTER HOMEWORK?

CAN'T! I'VE GOT A CALL!

♥STEENZ!

WELL, PENCIL ME IN WHEN YOUR SCHEDULE IS A LITTLE LESS FULL.

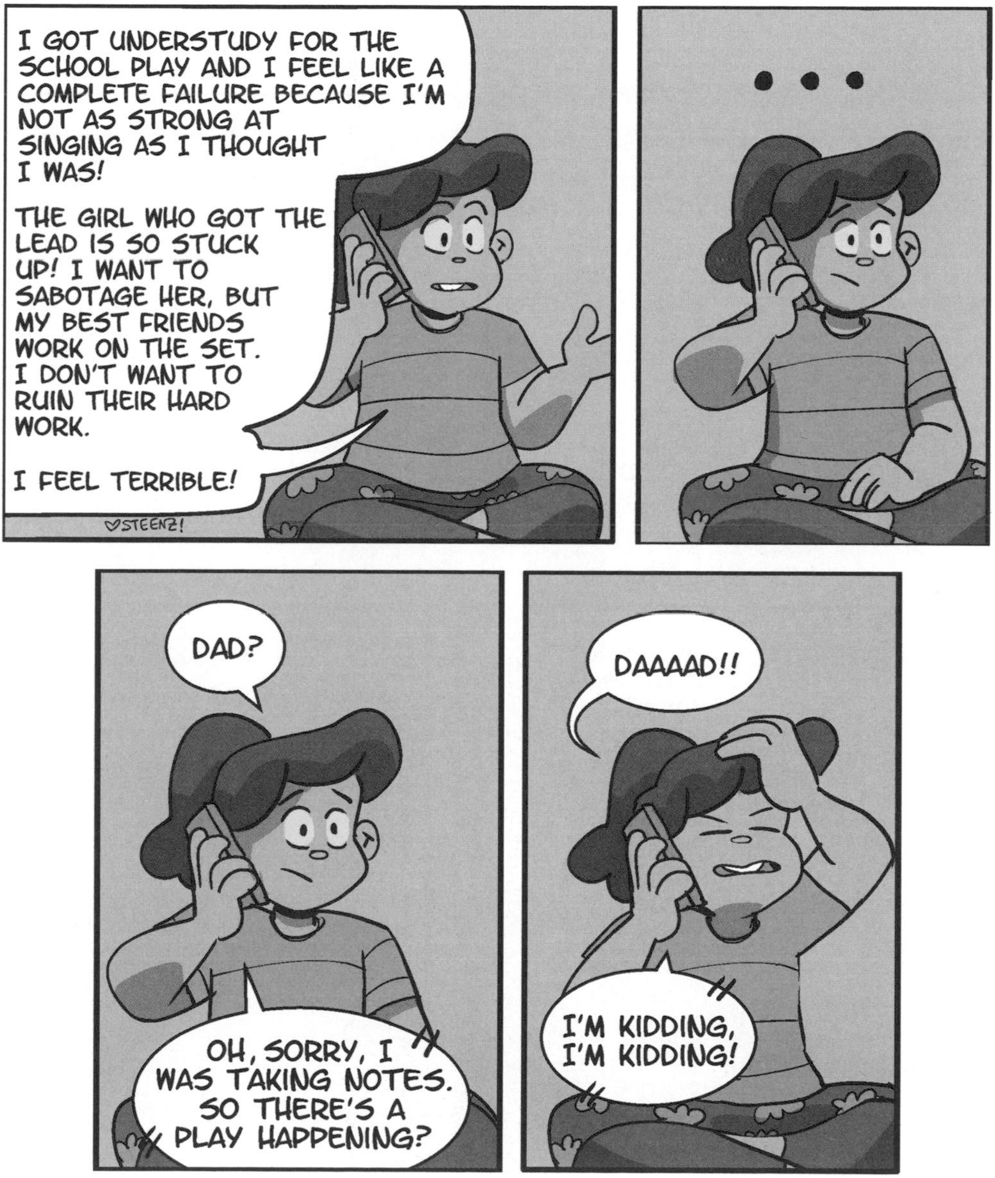
I GOT UNDERSTUDY FOR THE SCHOOL PLAY AND I FEEL LIKE A COMPLETE FAILURE BECAUSE I'M NOT AS STRONG AT SINGING AS I THOUGHT I WAS!
THE GIRL WHO GOT THE LEAD IS SO STUCK UP! I WANT TO SABOTAGE HER, BUT MY BEST FRIENDS WORK ON THE SET. I DON'T WANT TO RUIN THEIR HARD WORK.
I FEEL TERRIBLE!
♡STEENZ!
• • •
DAD?
OH, SORRY, I WAS TAKING NOTES. SO THERE'S A PLAY HAPPENING?
DAAAAD!!
I'M KIDDING, I'M KIDDING!

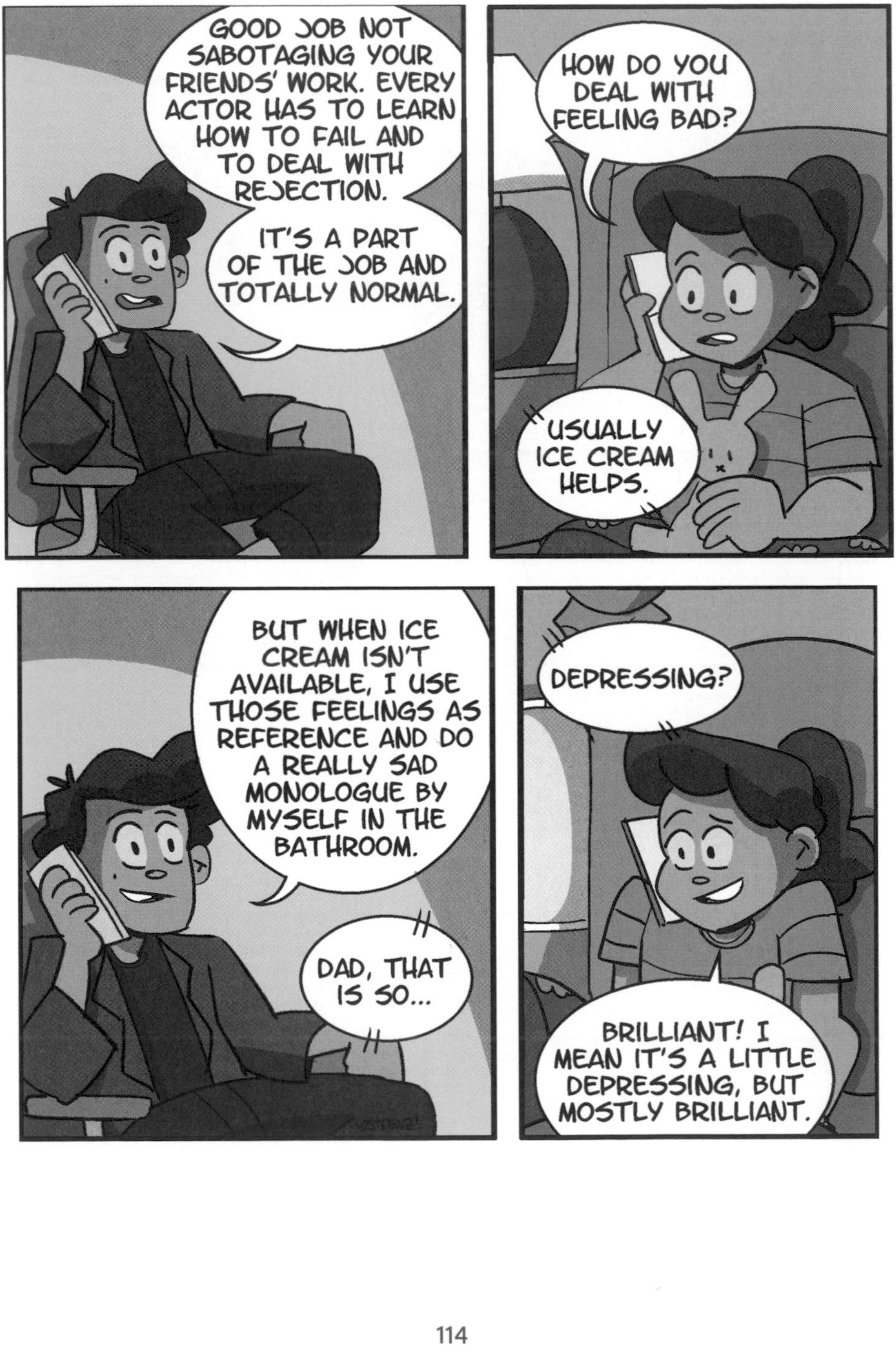
GOOD JOB NOT SABOTAGING YOUR FRIENDS' WORK. EVERY ACTOR HAS TO LEARN HOW TO FAIL AND TO DEAL WITH REJECTION.
IT'S A PART OF THE JOB AND TOTALLY NORMAL.
HOW DO YOU DEAL WITH FEELING BAD?
USUALLY ICE CREAM HELPS.
BUT WHEN ICE CREAM ISN'T AVAILABLE, I USE THOSE FEELINGS AS REFERENCE AND DO A REALLY SAD MONOLOGUE BY MYSELF IN THE BATHROOM.
DAD, THAT IS SO...
DEPRESSING?
BRILLIANT! I MEAN IT'S A LITTLE DEPRESSING, BUT MOSTLY BRILLIANT.

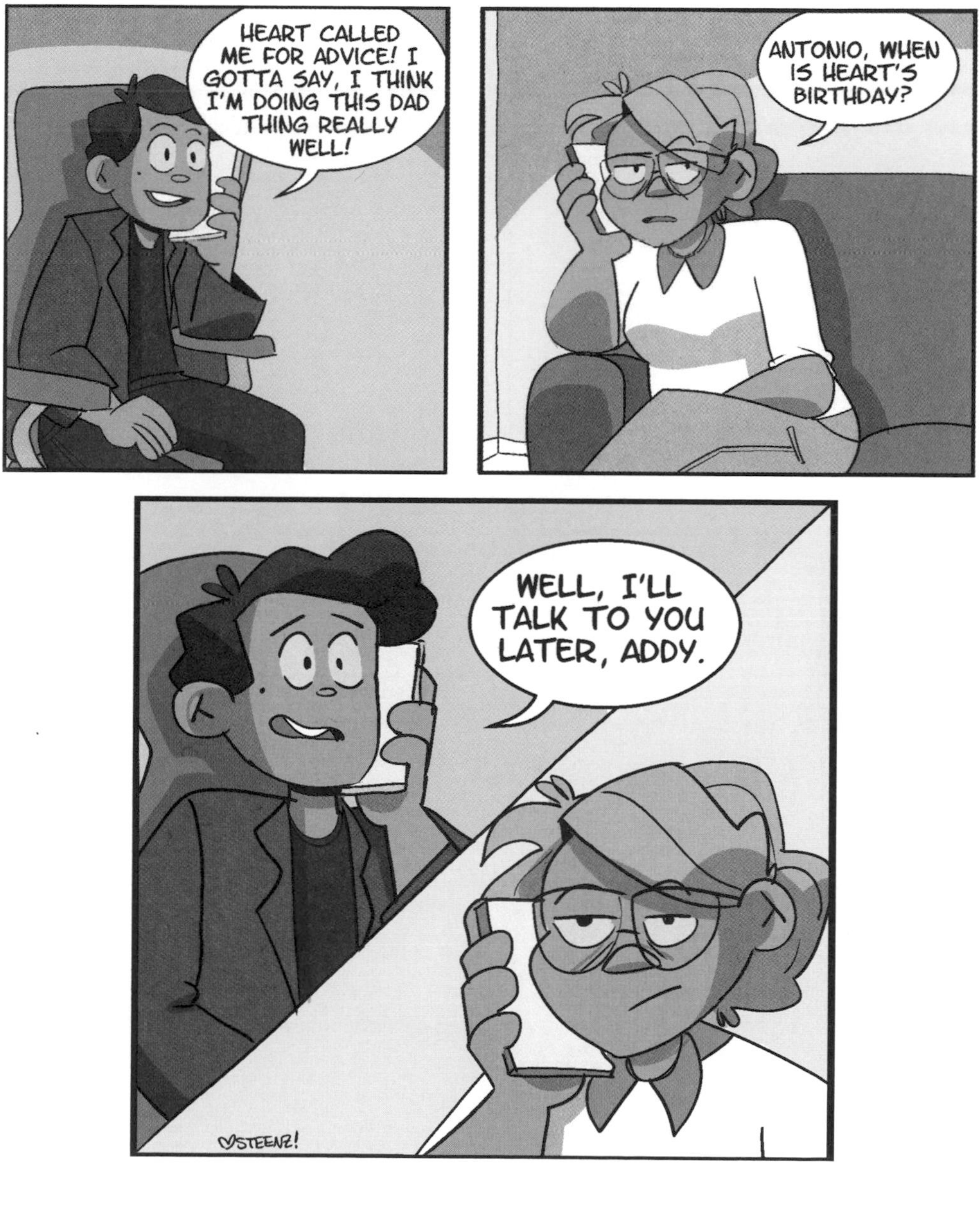
HEART CALLED ME FOR ADVICE! I GOTTA SAY, I THINK I'M DOING THIS DAD THING REALLY WELL!
ANTONIO, WHEN IS HEART'S BIRTHDAY?
WELL, I'LL TALK TO YOU LATER, ADDY.
STEENZ!

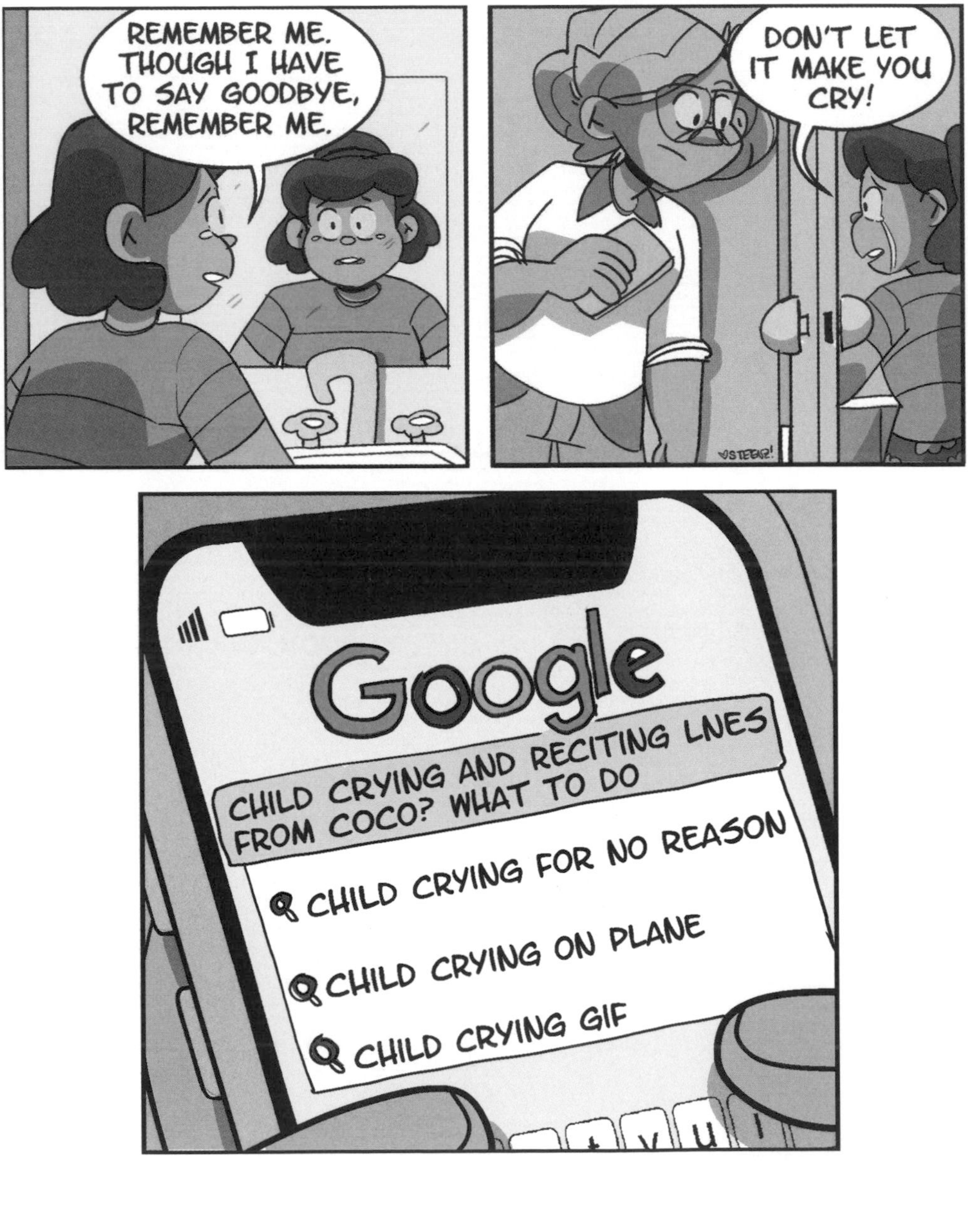
REMEMBER ME. THOUGH I HAVE TO SAY GOODBYE, REMEMBER ME.
DON'T LET IT MAKE YOU CRY!
Google
CHILD CRYING AND RECITING LNES FROM COCO? WHAT TO DO
CHILD CRYING FOR NO REASON
CHILD CRYING ON PLANE
CHILD CRYING GIF

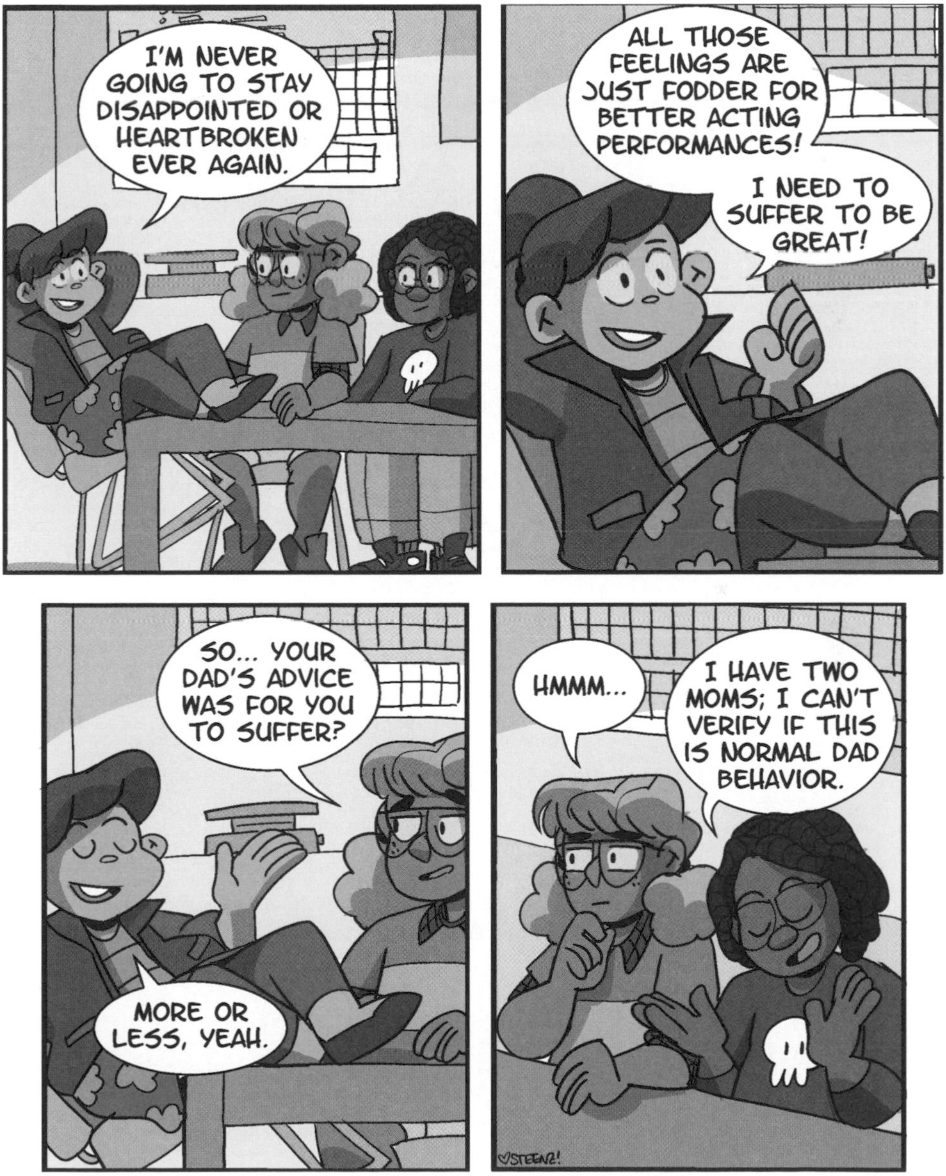
I'M NEVER GOING TO STAY DISAPPOINTED OR HEARTBROKEN EVER AGAIN.
ALL THOSE FEELINGS ARE JUST FODDER FOR BETTER ACTING PERFORMANCES!
I NEED TO SUFFER TO BE GREAT!
SO... YOUR DAD'S ADVICE WAS FOR YOU TO SUFFER?
MORE OR LESS, YEAH.
HMMM...
I HAVE TWO MOMS; I CAN'T VERIFY IF THIS IS NORMAL DAD BEHAVIOR.
♡STEENZ!

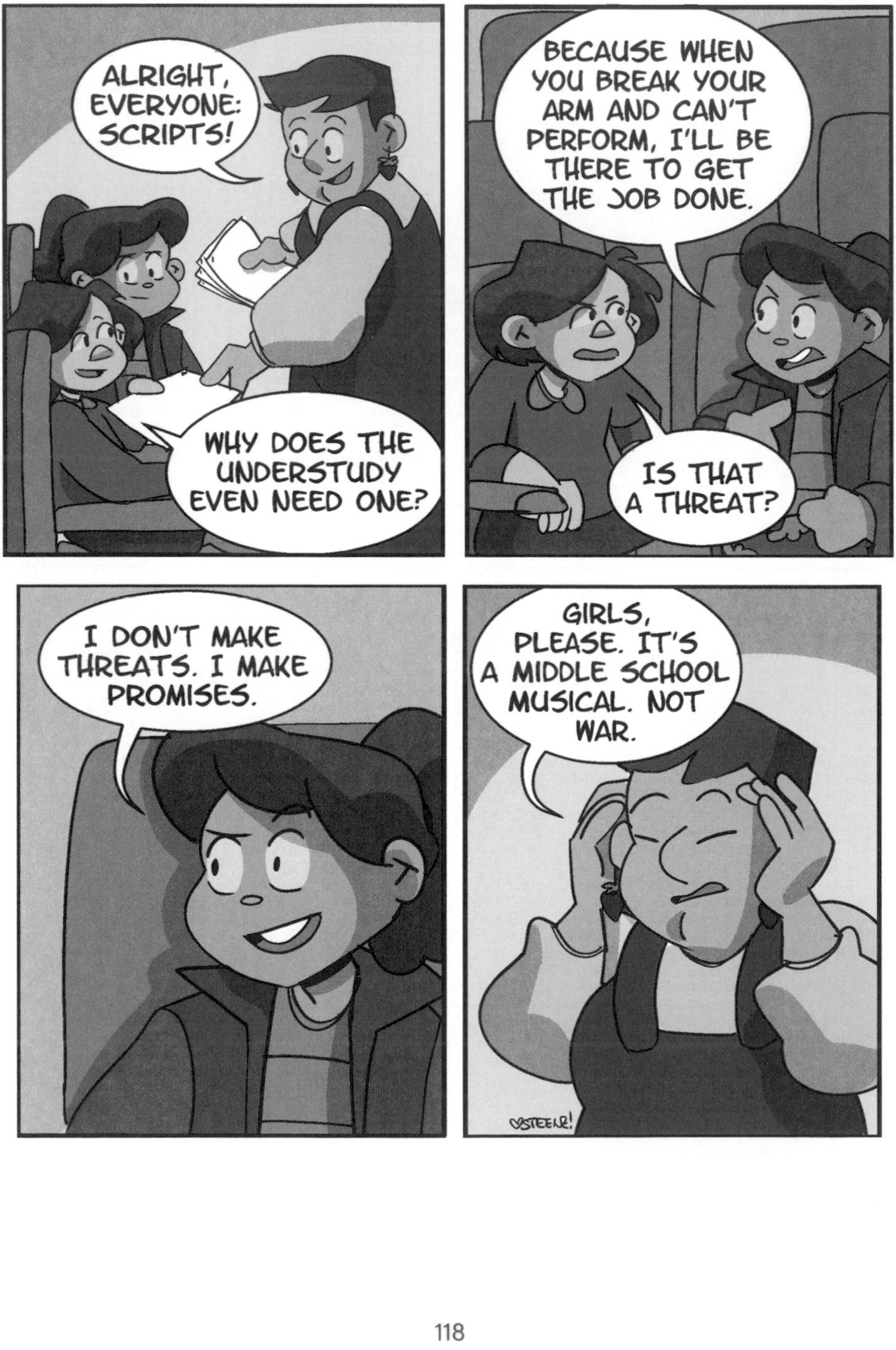
ALRIGHT, EVERYONE: SCRIPTS!
WHY DOES THE UNDERSTUDY EVEN NEED ONE?
BECAUSE WHEN YOU BREAK YOUR ARM AND CAN'T PERFORM, I'LL BE THERE TO GET THE JOB DONE.
IS THAT A THREAT?
I DON'T MAKE THREATS. I MAKE PROMISES.
GIRLS, PLEASE. IT'S A MIDDLE SCHOOL MUSICAL. NOT WAR.
♡STEENZ!

DOES ANYONE WANNA COME OVER AFTER SCHOOL?
I HAVE REHEARSAL.
SORRY. GOT A MYSTICS: THE GROUPING TOURNEY.
YOU CAN STAY LATE WITH ME AND MEET THE THEATER TECHIES!
HMM... HANGING OUT AT SCHOOL *AFTER* SCHOOL...

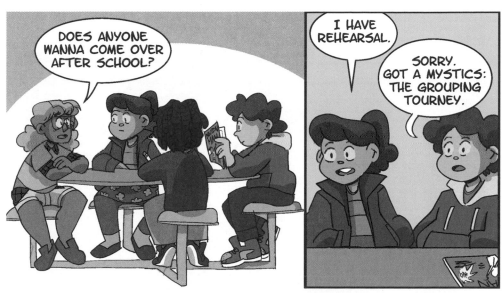

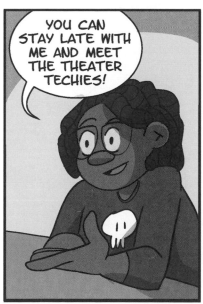

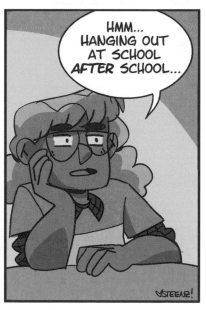

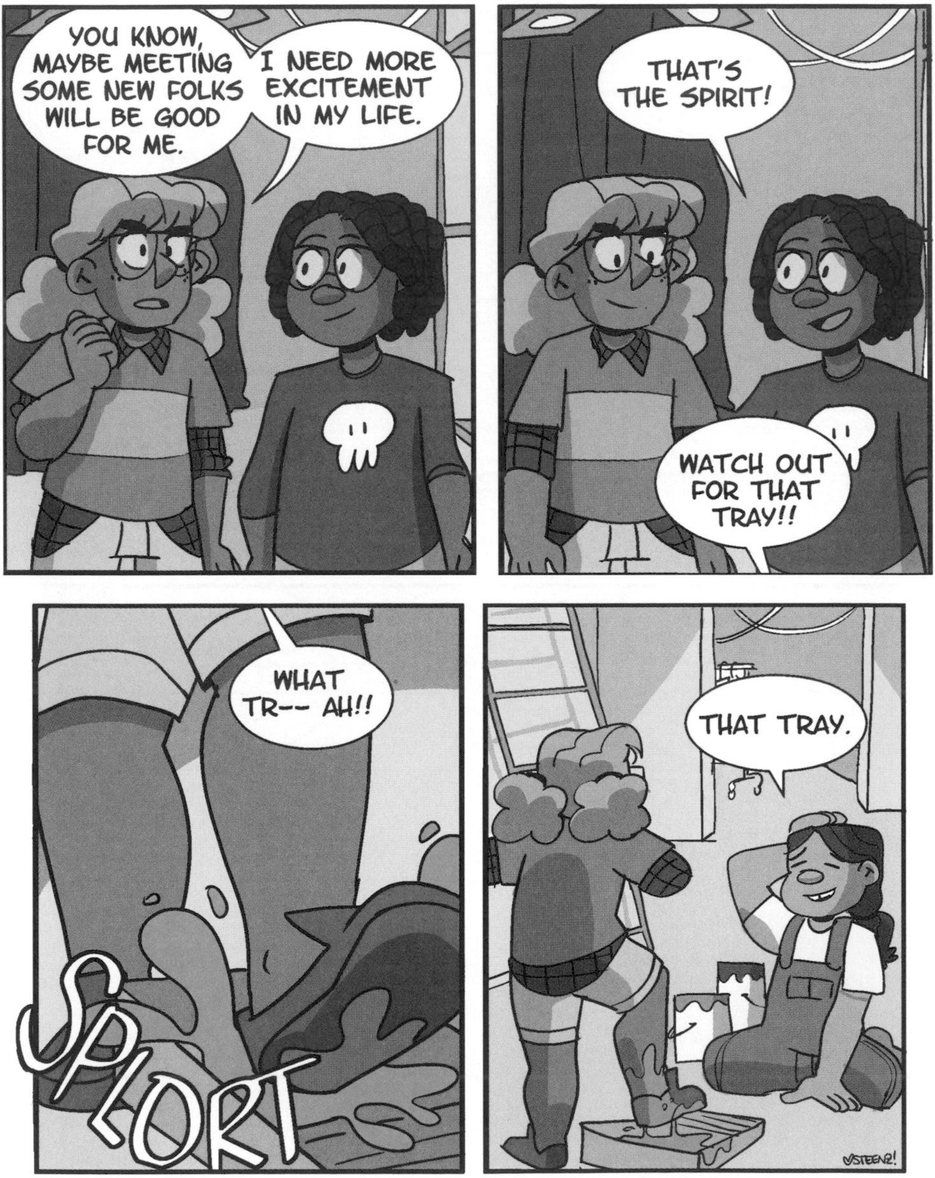
YOU KNOW, MAYBE MEETING SOME NEW FOLKS WILL BE GOOD FOR ME.
I NEED MORE EXCITEMENT IN MY LIFE.
THAT'S THE SPIRIT!
WATCH OUT FOR THAT TRAY!!
WHAT TR-- AH!!
SPLORT
THAT TRAY.
©STEENZ!

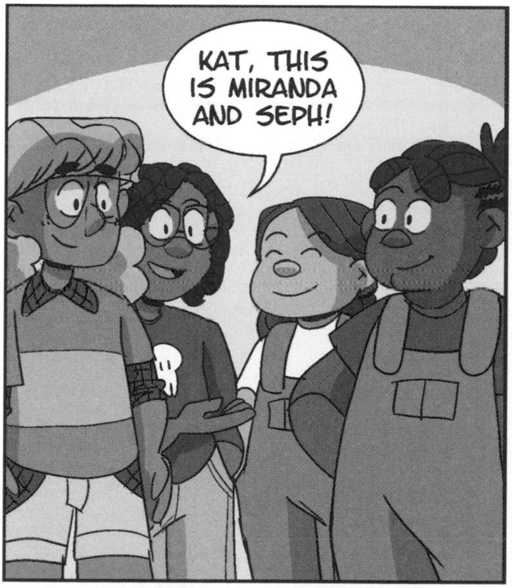
KAT, THIS IS MIRANDA AND SEPH!

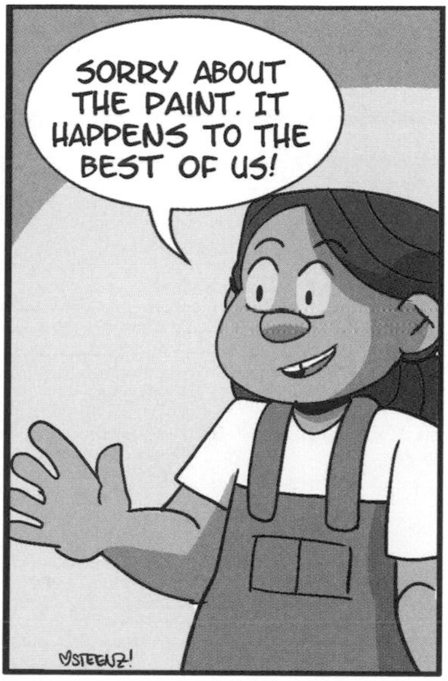
SORRY ABOUT THE PAINT. IT HAPPENS TO THE BEST OF US!
♡STEENZ!

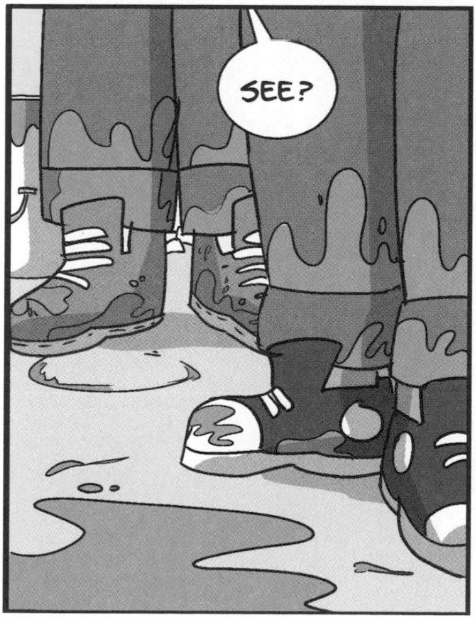
SEE?

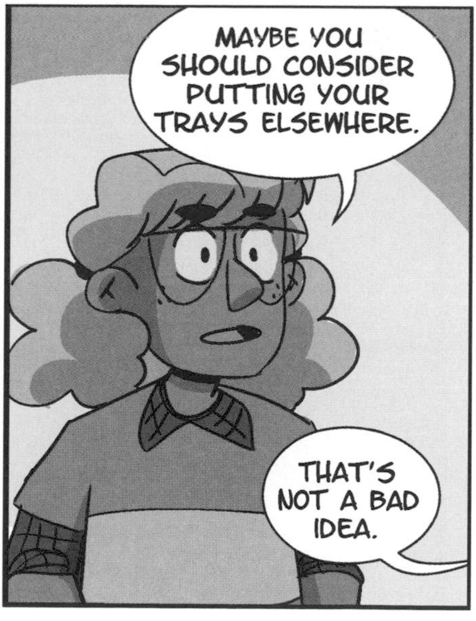
MAYBE YOU SHOULD CONSIDER PUTTING YOUR TRAYS ELSEWHERE.
THAT'S NOT A BAD IDEA.

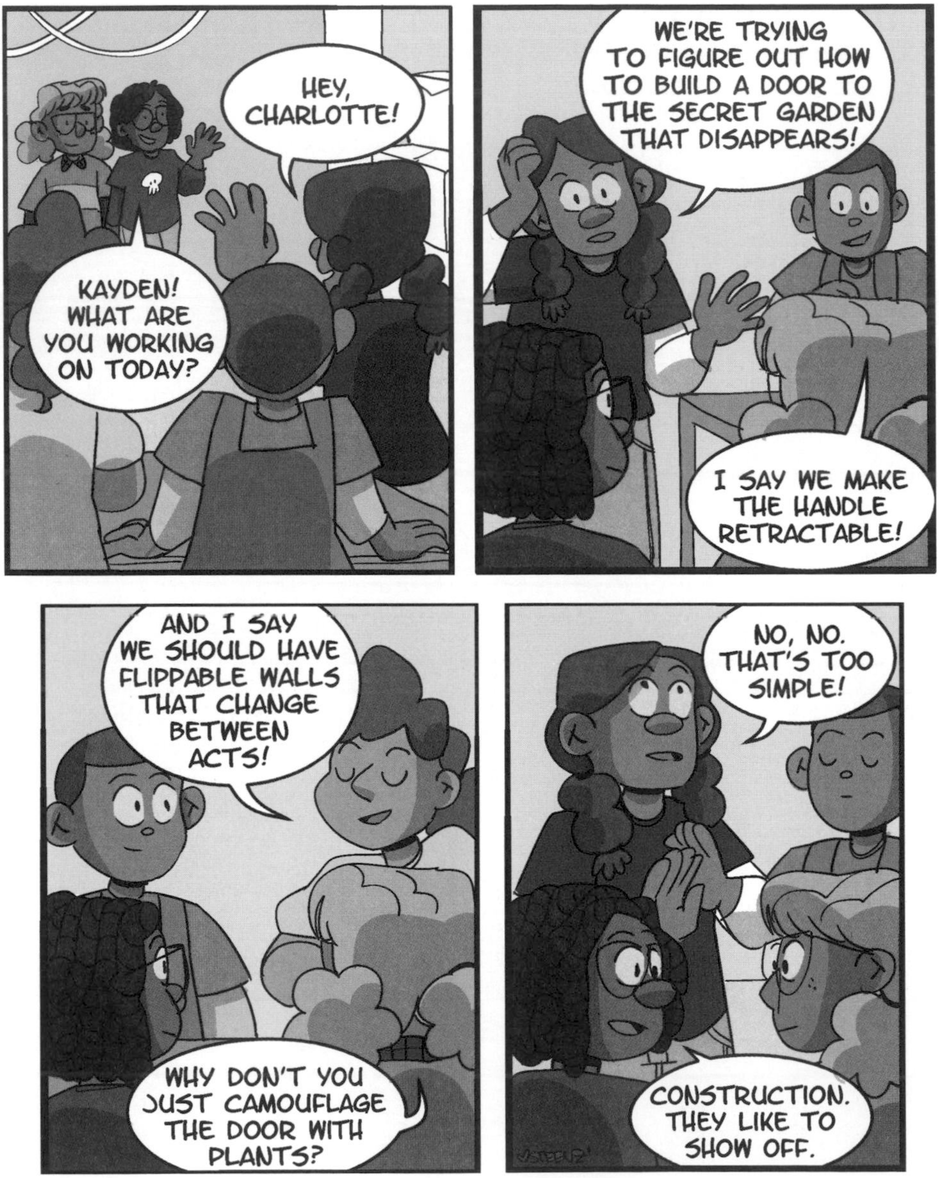
HEY, CHARLOTTE!
KAYDEN! WHAT ARE YOU WORKING ON TODAY?
WE'RE TRYING TO FIGURE OUT HOW TO BUILD A DOOR TO THE SECRET GARDEN THAT DISAPPEARS!
I SAY WE MAKE THE HANDLE RETRACTABLE!
AND I SAY WE SHOULD HAVE FLIPPABLE WALLS THAT CHANGE BETWEEN ACTS!
WHY DON'T YOU JUST CAMOUFLAGE THE DOOR WITH PLANTS?
NO, NO. THAT'S TOO SIMPLE!
CONSTRUCTION. THEY LIKE TO SHOW OFF.

THIS IS WHERE THE LIGHTING TEAM AND I WORK!

EVERY COMBINATION OF BUTTONS AND SWITCHES DOES SOMETHING DIFFERENT. AND I CAN GET REALLY CREATIVE WITH EACH SCENE!

IT'S COOL TO SEE FOLKS PASSIONATE ABOUT LIGHT.

LIGHT IS EVERYTHING! IT SETS THE MOOD, IT WARMS YOU, AND IT SIGNALS WHAT'S TO COME!

WHAT'S NOT TO LOVE?

OH, HEY, CHARLOTTE! WHO'S YOUR FRIEND?

HI, OLIVE! THIS IS KAT!

HEY, IT'S YOU AGAIN!

H-HAHA. ME...

CHARLOTTE CONVINCED ME THAT COSTUME DESIGN WAS MORE FUN THAN WATCHING THE LOST AND FOUND. SHE WAS RIGHT!

WOW, WHAT A COINCIDENCE. I'M SIGNING UP TODAY!

SINCE WHEN?

SINCE NOW.

DID YOU REALLY WANT TO JOIN COSTUMING?
I HAVE NO IDEA WHY I SAID THAT TO HER...
OHOHOHHOHOOHO I THINK I KNOW!
I'M NUDGING YOU BECAUSE YOU THINK LEE IS CUTE. A BIT OF FUN AT YOUR EXPENSE.
CHARLOTTE, I GOT IT.

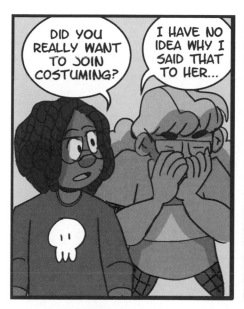

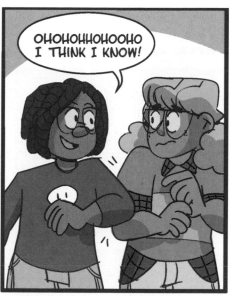

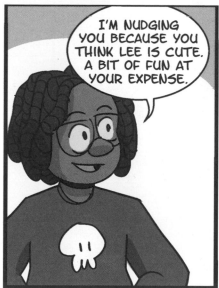

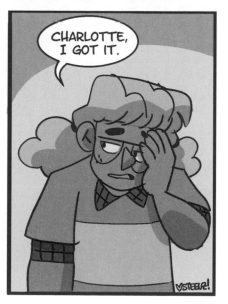

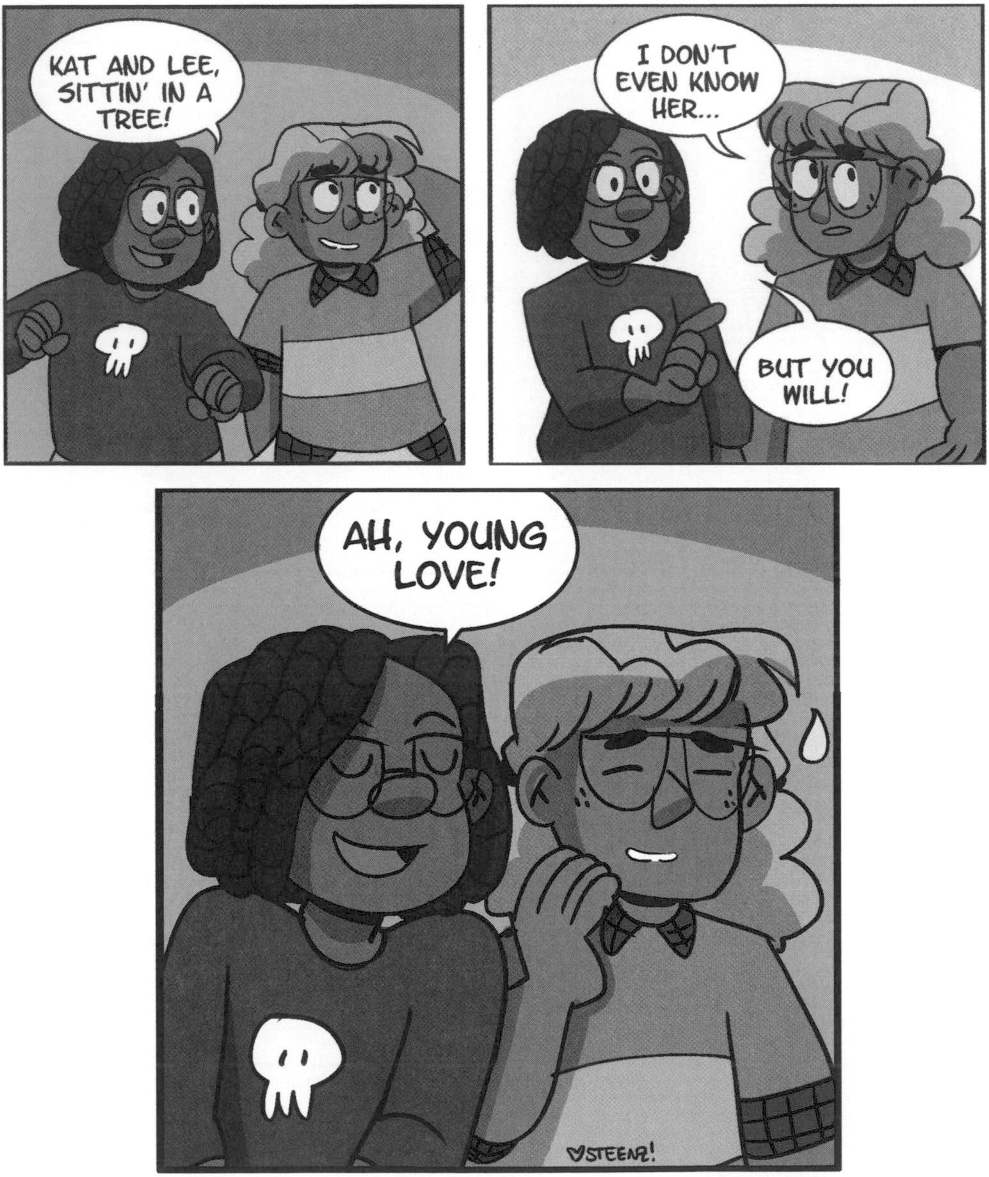
KAT AND LEE, SITTIN' IN A TREE!
I DON'T EVEN KNOW HER...
BUT YOU WILL!
AH, YOUNG LOVE!
STEENZ!

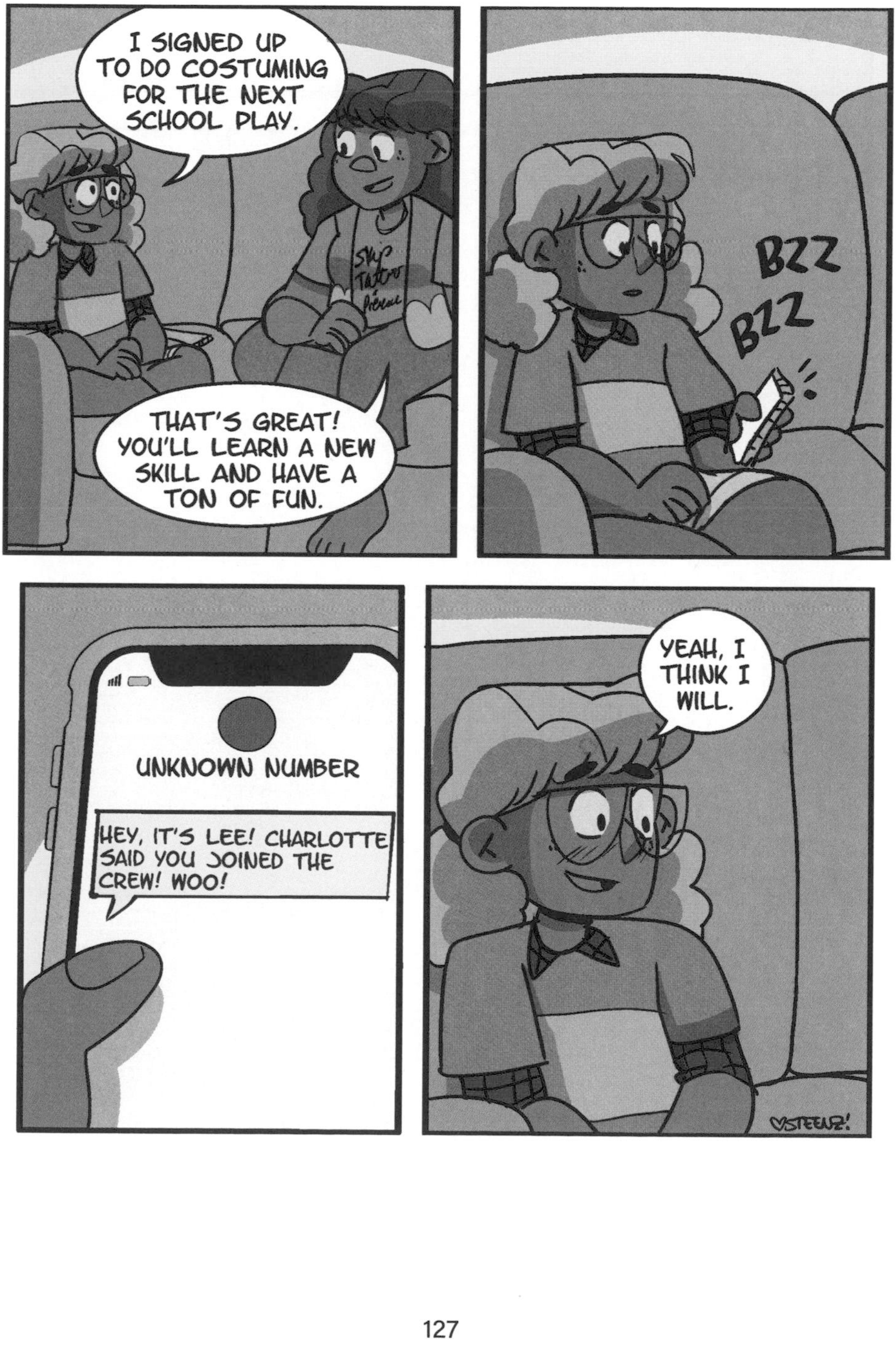
I SIGNED UP TO DO COSTUMING FOR THE NEXT SCHOOL PLAY.
THAT'S GREAT! YOU'LL LEARN A NEW SKILL AND HAVE A TON OF FUN.
BZZ
BZZ
UNKNOWN NUMBER
HEY, IT'S LEE! CHARLOTTE SAID YOU JOINED THE CREW! WOO!
YEAH, I THINK I WILL.
♡STEENZ!

I'M BORED.
I'M BORED.
CHIPPY
I'M BORED.
SO YOU'VE SAID.
STEENZ!

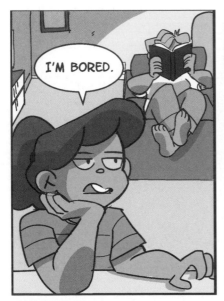

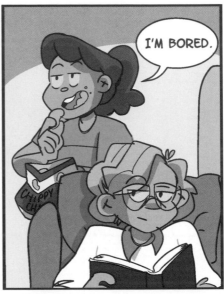

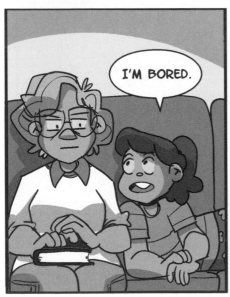

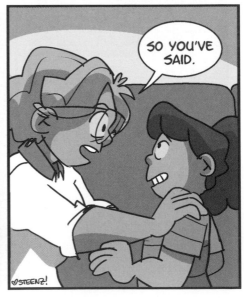

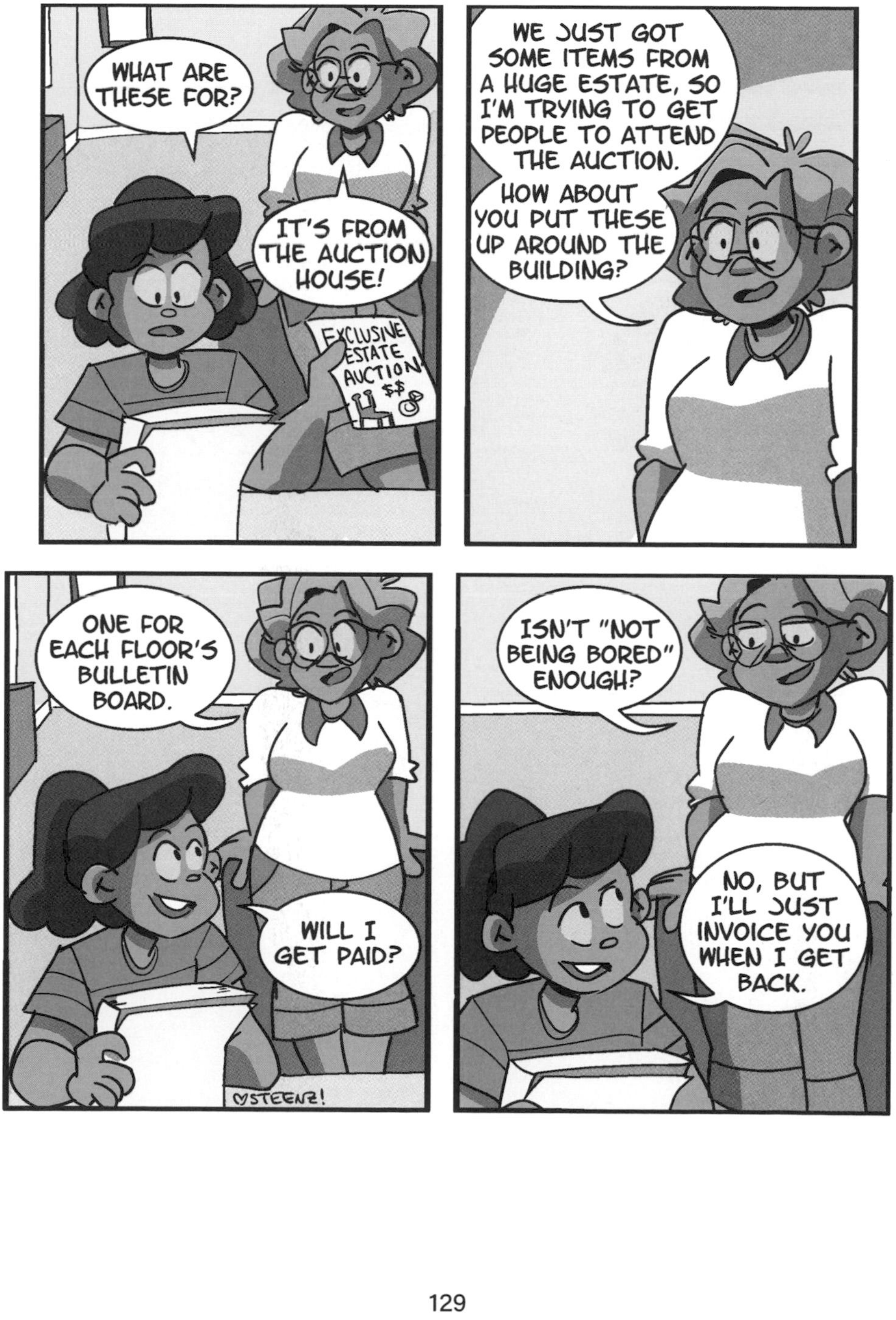
WHAT ARE THESE FOR?
IT'S FROM THE AUCTION HOUSE!
EXCLUSIVE ESTATE AUCTION $$
WE JUST GOT SOME ITEMS FROM A HUGE ESTATE, SO I'M TRYING TO GET PEOPLE TO ATTEND THE AUCTION.
HOW ABOUT YOU PUT THESE UP AROUND THE BUILDING?
ONE FOR EACH FLOOR'S BULLETIN BOARD.
WILL I GET PAID?
STEENZ!
ISN'T "NOT BEING BORED" ENOUGH?
NO, BUT I'LL JUST INVOICE YOU WHEN I GET BACK.

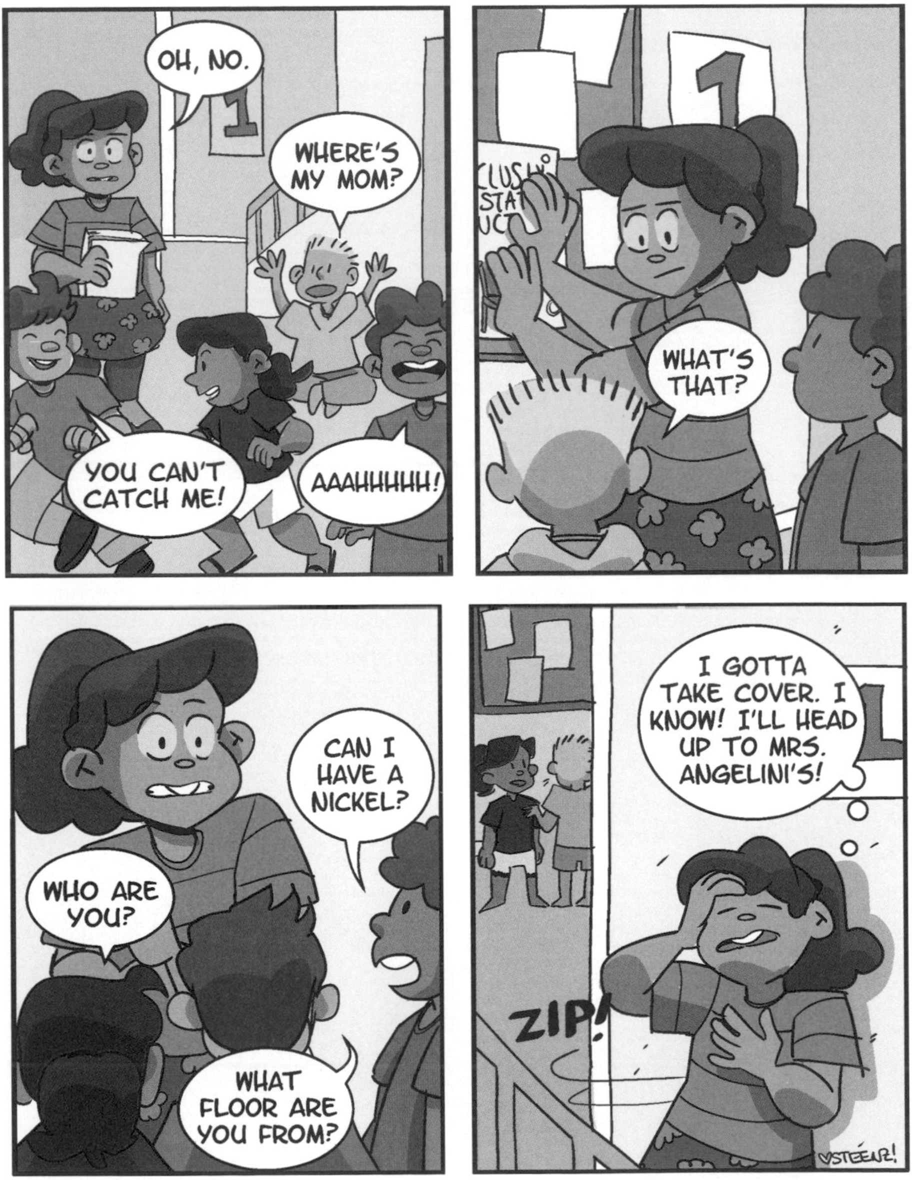
OH, NO.
WHERE'S MY MOM?
YOU CAN'T CATCH ME!
AAAHHHHH!
WHAT'S THAT?
CAN I HAVE A NICKEL?
WHO ARE YOU?
WHAT FLOOR ARE YOU FROM?
I GOTTA TAKE COVER. I KNOW! I'LL HEAD UP TO MRS. ANGELINI'S!
ZIP!

HI, MRS. ANGELINI!
HEART! COME IN! I CAN TELL YOU MORE STORIES ABOUT THE OLD COUNTRY, LIKE WHEN YOU WERE LITTLE!
JUST FOR A FEW MINUTES. I'M HELPING MY MOM PUT UP FLYERS!
THAT'S SO THOUGHTFUL! YOU'RE GROWING UP SO FAST.
IT REMINDS ME OF WHEN I WAS YOUR AGE IN THE OLD COUNTRY.
30 MINUTES LATER
AND YOU WOULDN'T BELIEVE HOW MANY FLYERS FLEW ACROSS THE SKY! BLAH BLAH BLAH? BLAH, BLAH BLAH!
ZZZ

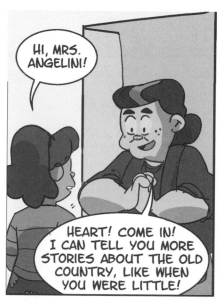

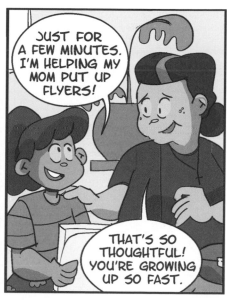

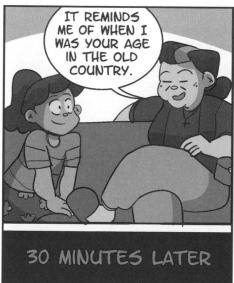

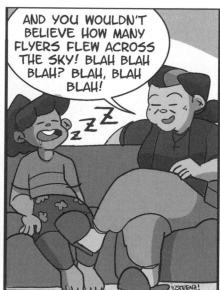

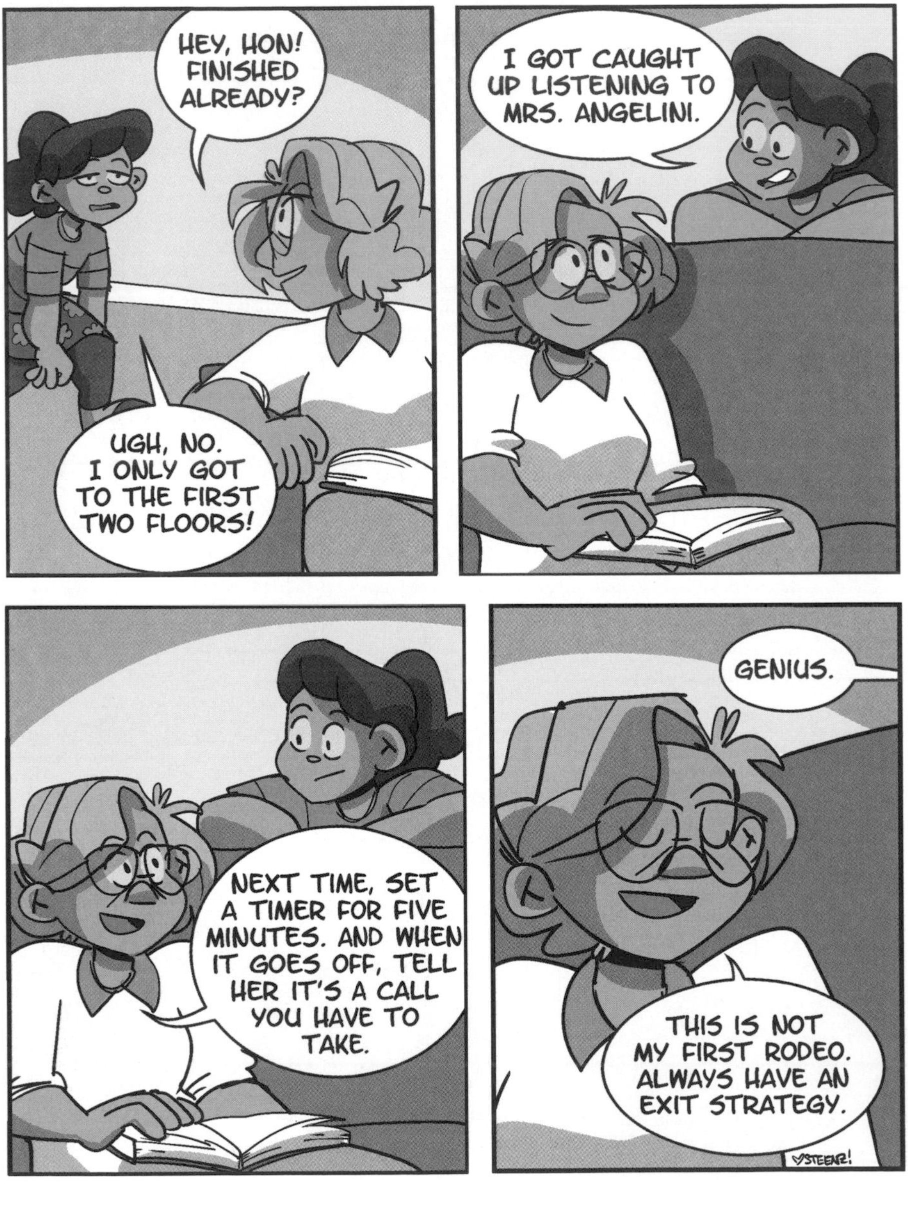
HEY, HON! FINISHED ALREADY?
UGH, NO. I ONLY GOT TO THE FIRST TWO FLOORS!
I GOT CAUGHT UP LISTENING TO MRS. ANGELINI.
NEXT TIME, SET A TIMER FOR FIVE MINUTES. AND WHEN IT GOES OFF, TELL HER IT'S A CALL YOU HAVE TO TAKE.
GENIUS.
THIS IS NOT MY FIRST RODEO. ALWAYS HAVE AN EXIT STRATEGY.
♡STEENZ!

ALRIGHT. FOUR FLOORS DOWN, TWO MORE TO GO.
FWOOM
ACK! THE LIGHTS! THE HAIRS ARE STANDING ON THE BACK OF MY NECK!
IS... IS THERE SOMEONE BEHIND ME???
HELLO? IS ANYONE THERE?
FOURTH FLOOR'S HAUNTED! NOTED!!

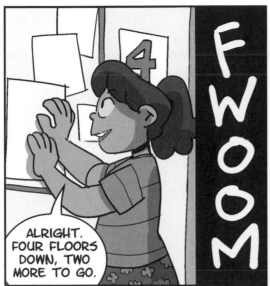

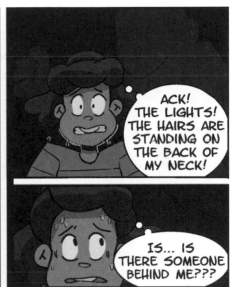

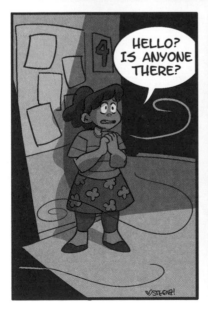

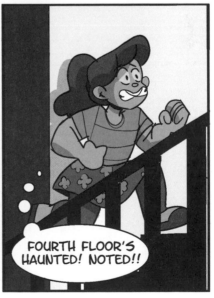

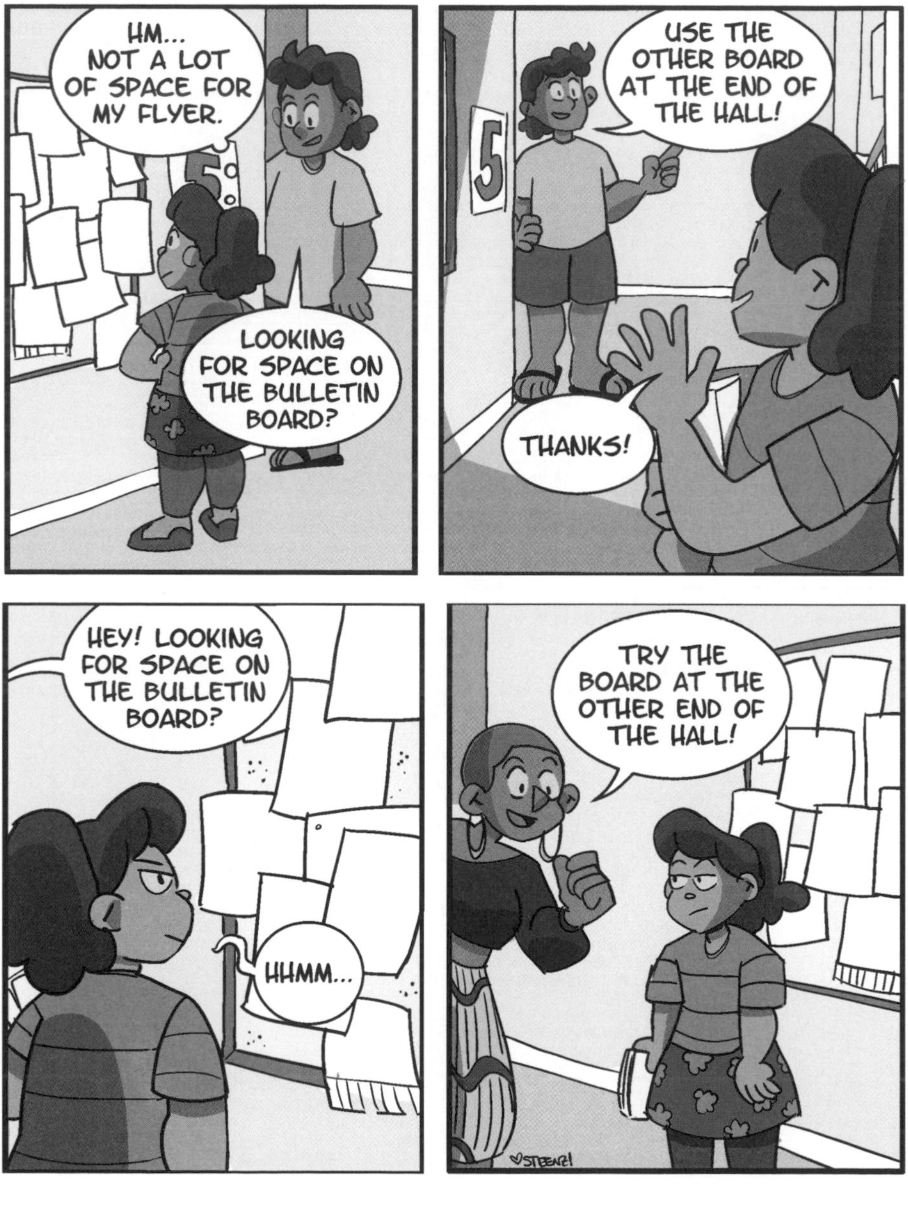
HM...
NOT A LOT OF SPACE FOR MY FLYER.
LOOKING FOR SPACE ON THE BULLETIN BOARD?
USE THE OTHER BOARD AT THE END OF THE HALL!
THANKS!
HEY! LOOKING FOR SPACE ON THE BULLETIN BOARD?
HHMM...
TRY THE BOARD AT THE OTHER END OF THE HALL!
♡STEENZ!

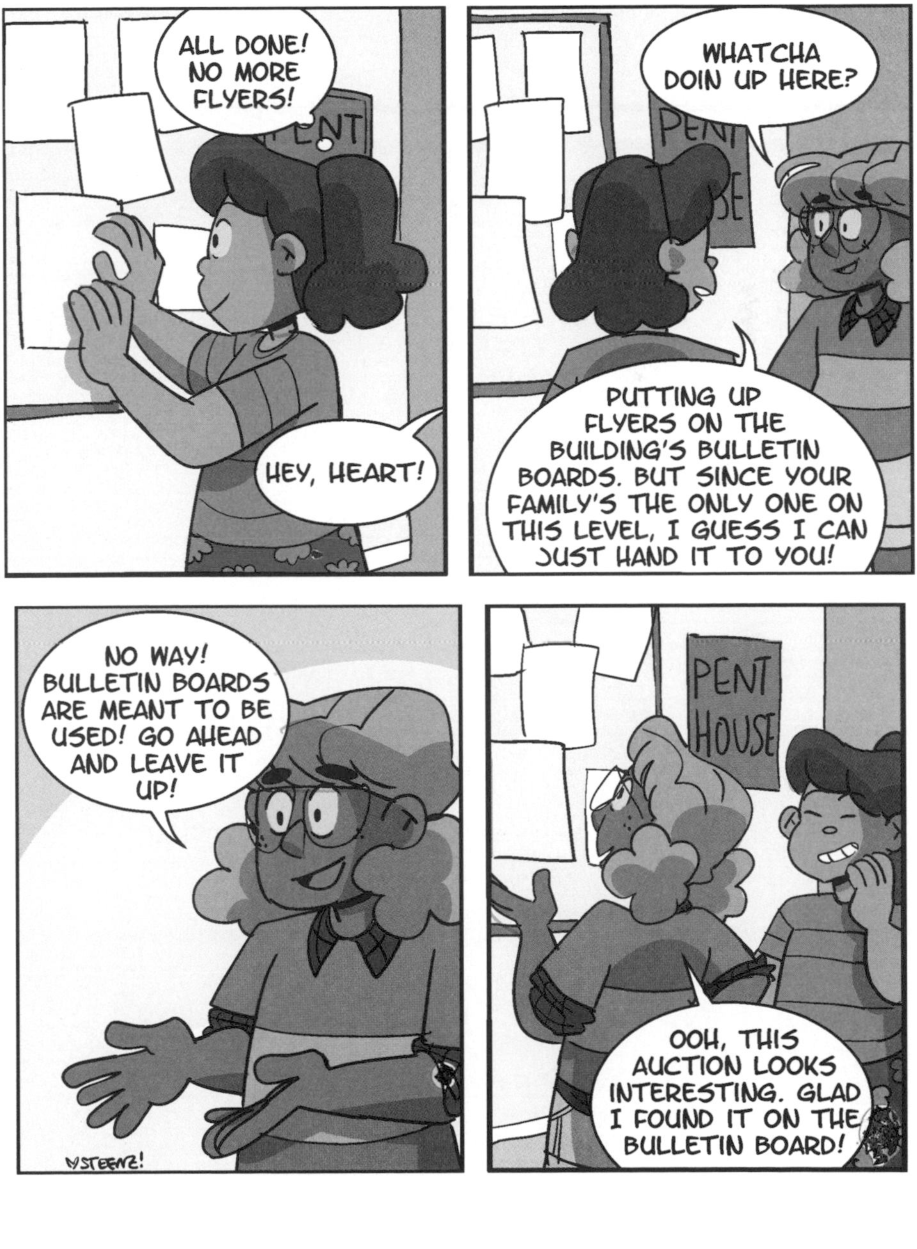
ALL DONE! NO MORE FLYERS!
PENT
HEY, HEART!
WHATCHA DOIN UP HERE?
PUTTING UP FLYERS ON THE BUILDING'S BULLETIN BOARDS. BUT SINCE YOUR FAMILY'S THE ONLY ONE ON THIS LEVEL, I GUESS I CAN JUST HAND IT TO YOU!
NO WAY! BULLETIN BOARDS ARE MEANT TO BE USED! GO AHEAD AND LEAVE IT UP!
♡STEENZ!
PENT HOUSE
OOH, THIS AUCTION LOOKS INTERESTING. GLAD I FOUND IT ON THE BULLETIN BOARD!

ARE YOU... SCRATCHING YOUR ARM-PITS?
UH, WELL...
NO, IT'S OKAY! MINE ITCH TOO!
STEENZ!
NO WAY! MINE TOO!
ARE WE ALL GROWING HAIR UNDER OUR ARMS?
YES!
WE'RE NOT WEIRD!

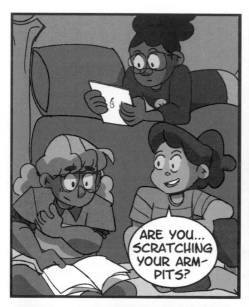

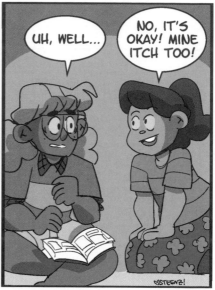

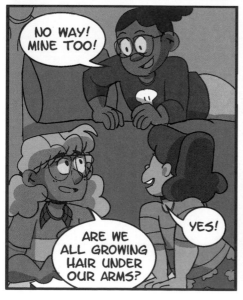

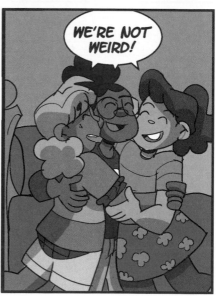

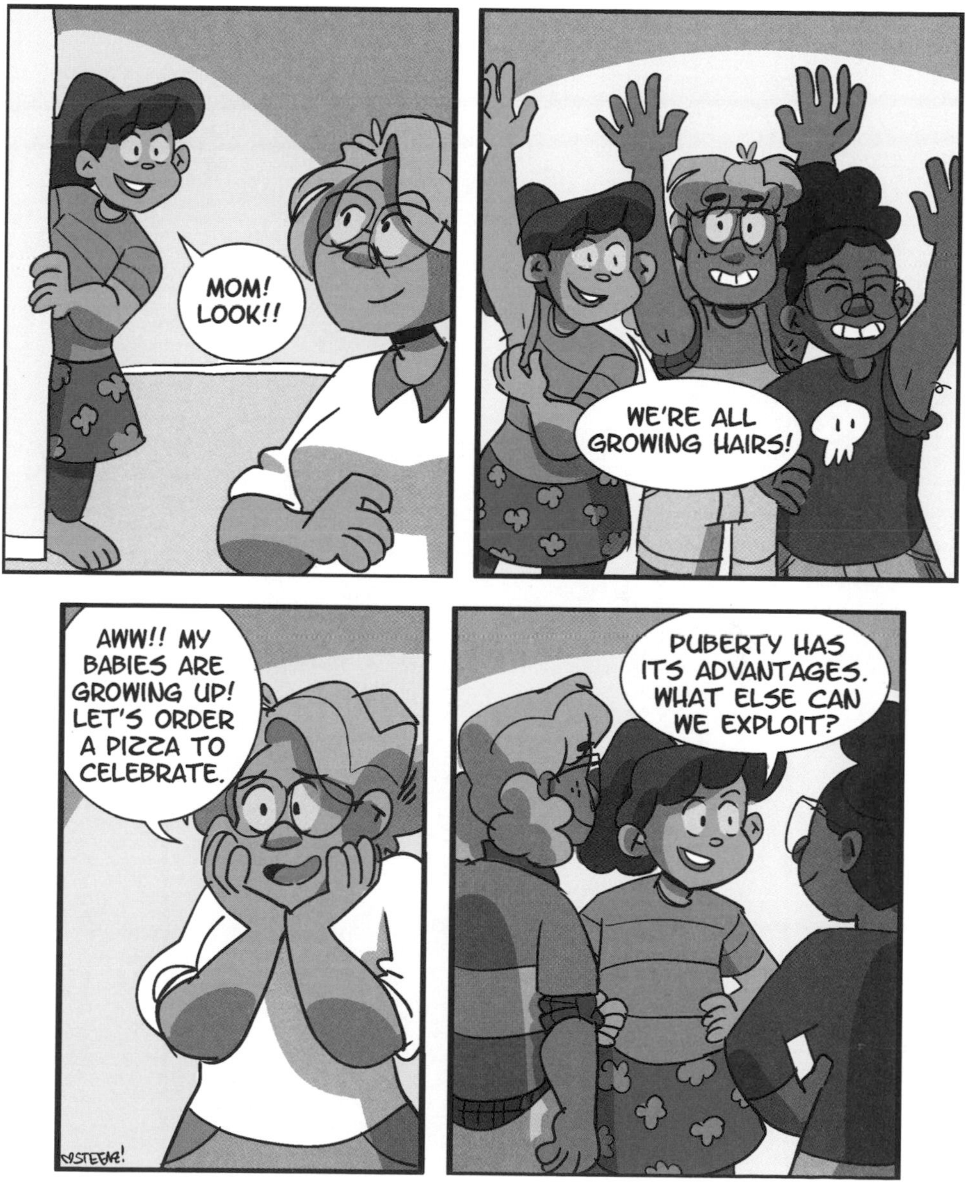
MOM! LOOK!!
WE'RE ALL GROWING HAIRS!
AWW!! MY BABIES ARE GROWING UP! LET'S ORDER A PIZZA TO CELEBRATE.
PUBERTY HAS ITS ADVANTAGES. WHAT ELSE CAN WE EXPLOIT?

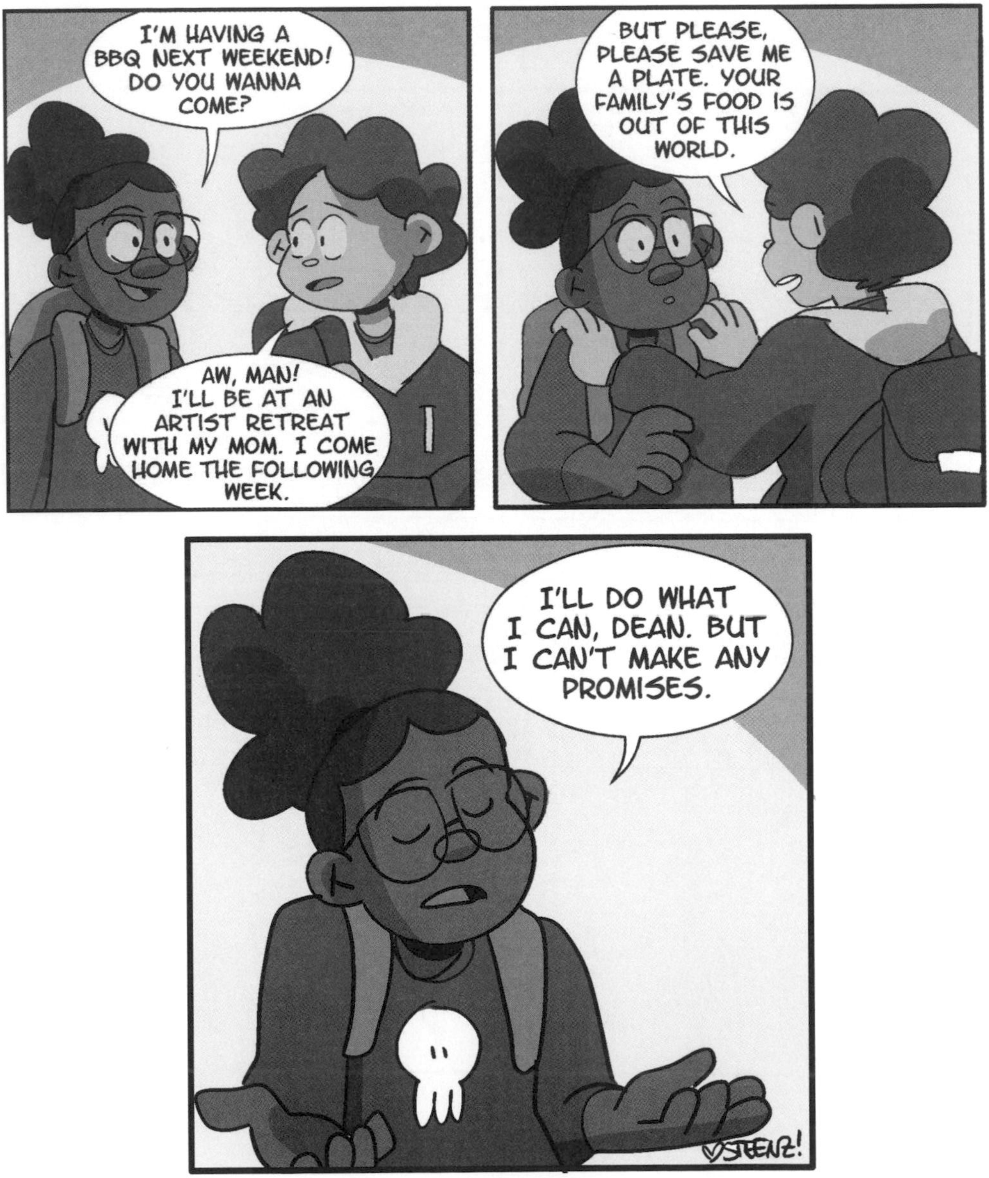
I'M HAVING A BBQ NEXT WEEKEND! DO YOU WANNA COME?
AW, MAN! I'LL BE AT AN ARTIST RETREAT WITH MY MOM. I COME HOME THE FOLLOWING WEEK.
BUT PLEASE, PLEASE SAVE ME A PLATE. YOUR FAMILY'S FOOD IS OUT OF THIS WORLD.
I'LL DO WHAT I CAN, DEAN. BUT I CAN'T MAKE ANY PROMISES.
STEENZ!

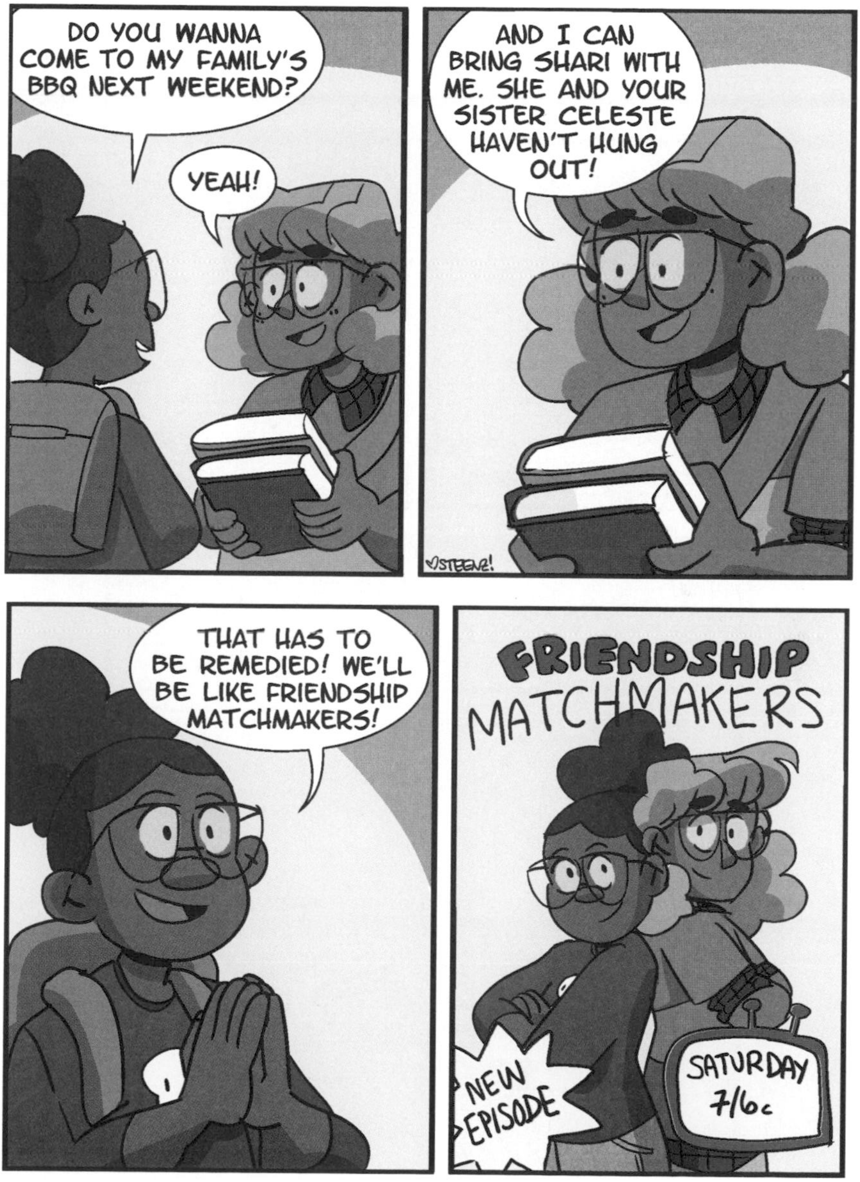
DO YOU WANNA COME TO MY FAMILY'S BBQ NEXT WEEKEND?
YEAH!
AND I CAN BRING SHARI WITH ME. SHE AND YOUR SISTER CELESTE HAVEN'T HUNG OUT!
♡STEENZ!
THAT HAS TO BE REMEDIED! WE'LL BE LIKE FRIENDSHIP MATCHMAKERS!
FRIENDSHIP MATCHMAKERS
NEW EPISODE
SATURDAY 7/6c

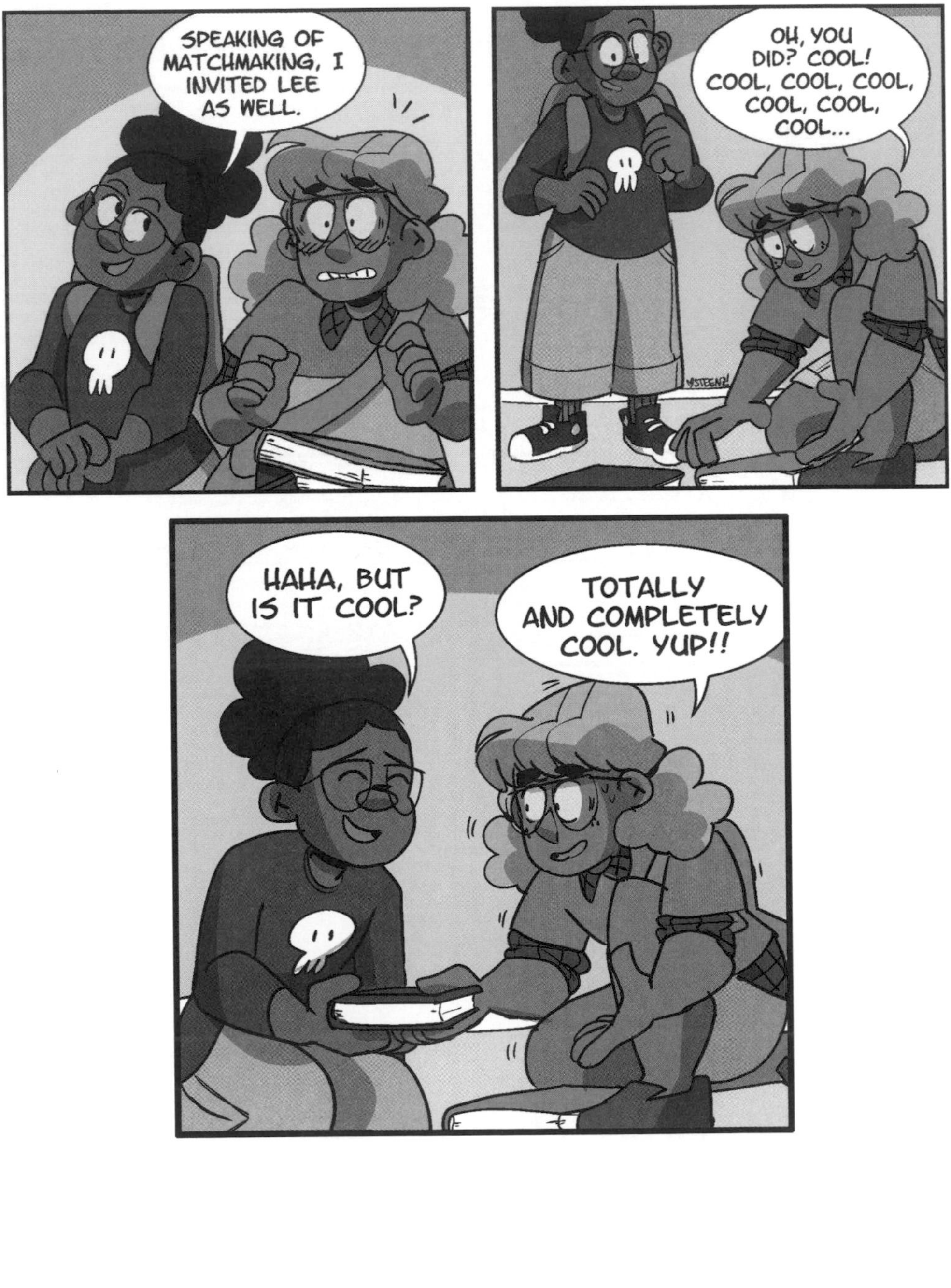
SPEAKING OF MATCHMAKING, I INVITED LEE AS WELL.
OH, YOU DID? COOL! COOL, COOL, COOL, COOL, COOL, COOL...
HAHA, BUT IS IT COOL?
TOTALLY AND COMPLETELY COOL. YUP!!

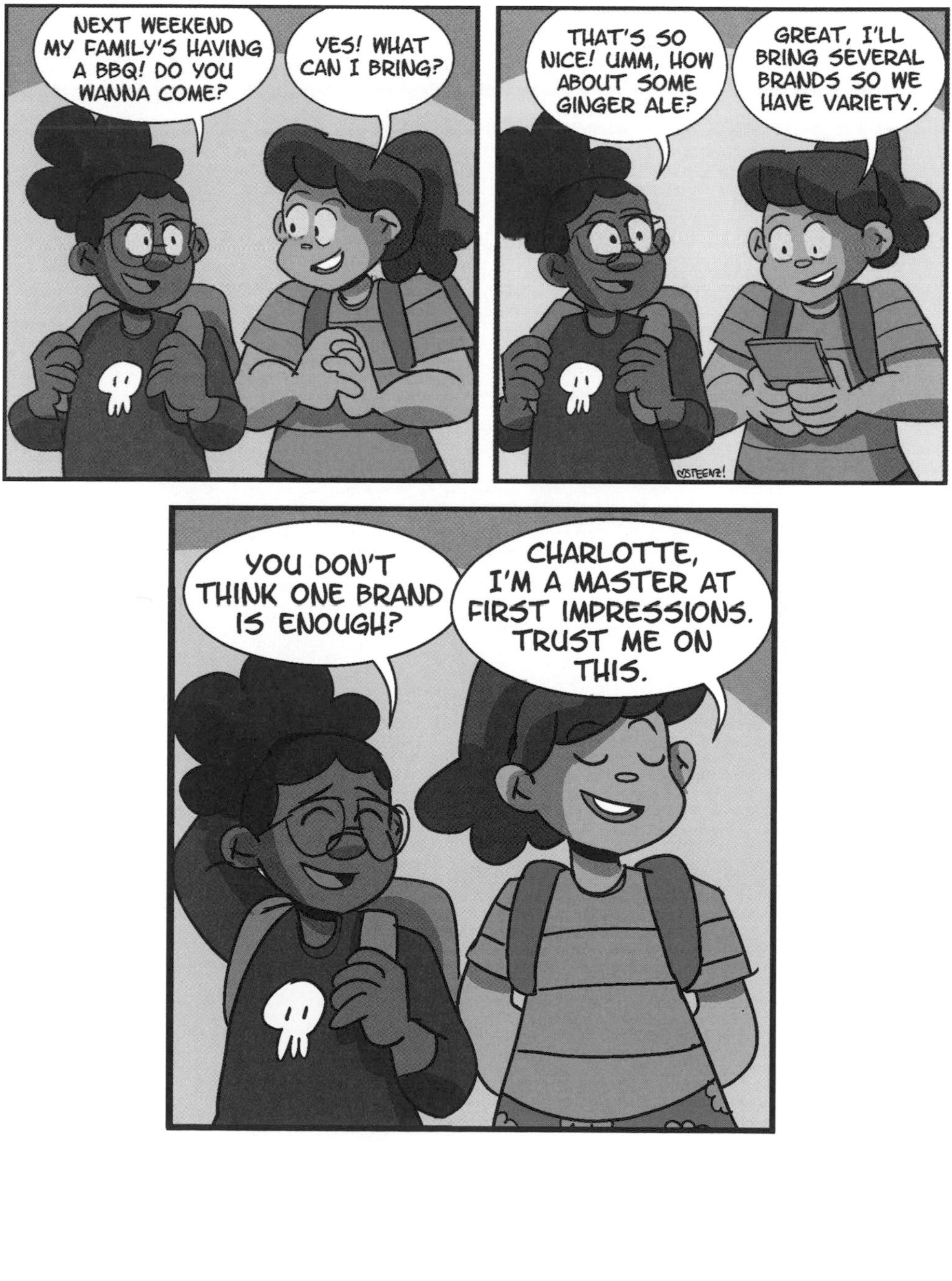
NEXT WEEKEND MY FAMILY'S HAVING A BBQ! DO YOU WANNA COME?
YES! WHAT CAN I BRING?
THAT'S SO NICE! UMM, HOW ABOUT SOME GINGER ALE?
GREAT, I'LL BRING SEVERAL BRANDS SO WE HAVE VARIETY.
YOU DON'T THINK ONE BRAND IS ENOUGH?
CHARLOTTE, I'M A MASTER AT FIRST IMPRESSIONS. TRUST ME ON THIS.

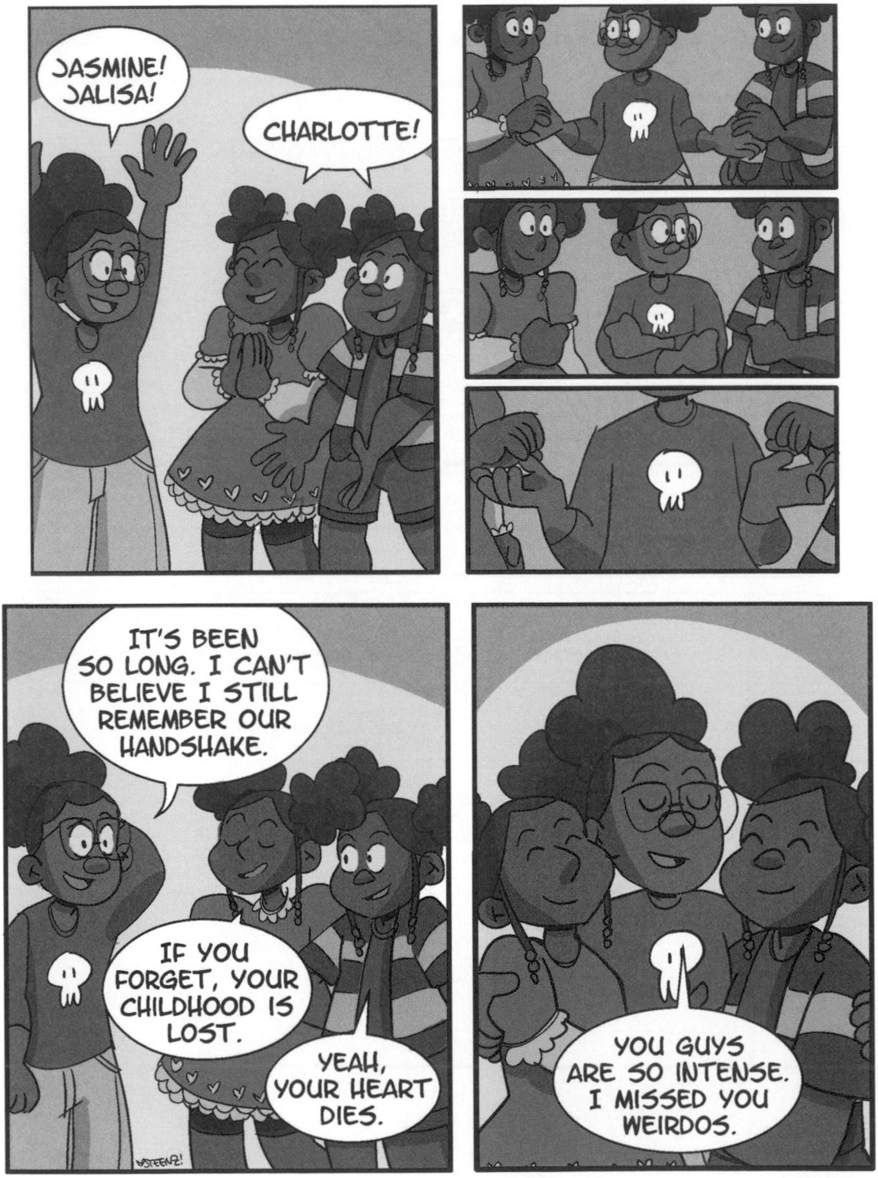
JASMINE! JALISA!
CHARLOTTE!
IT'S BEEN SO LONG. I CAN'T BELIEVE I STILL REMEMBER OUR HANDSHAKE.
IF YOU FORGET, YOUR CHILDHOOD IS LOST.
YEAH, YOUR HEART DIES.
©STEENZ!
YOU GUYS ARE SO INTENSE. I MISSED YOU WEIRDOS.

HEY, CHARLOTTE!
AUNTIE!!
YOU'RE GETTING SO TALL! YOU GON' BE TALLER THAN ME SOON!
AUNTIE! I ONLY GREW AN INCH!
WHEN YOU GET TO MY AGE, YOU START LOSING INCHES.
SO LET'S AGREE TO MEET EACH OTHER IN THE MIDDLE.

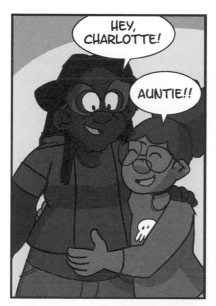

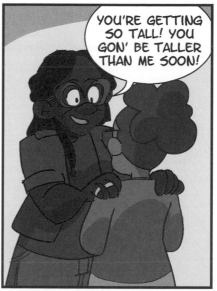

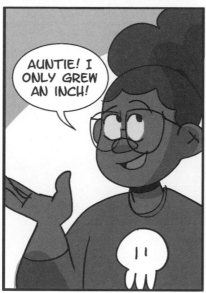

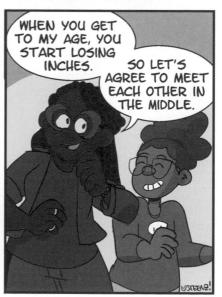

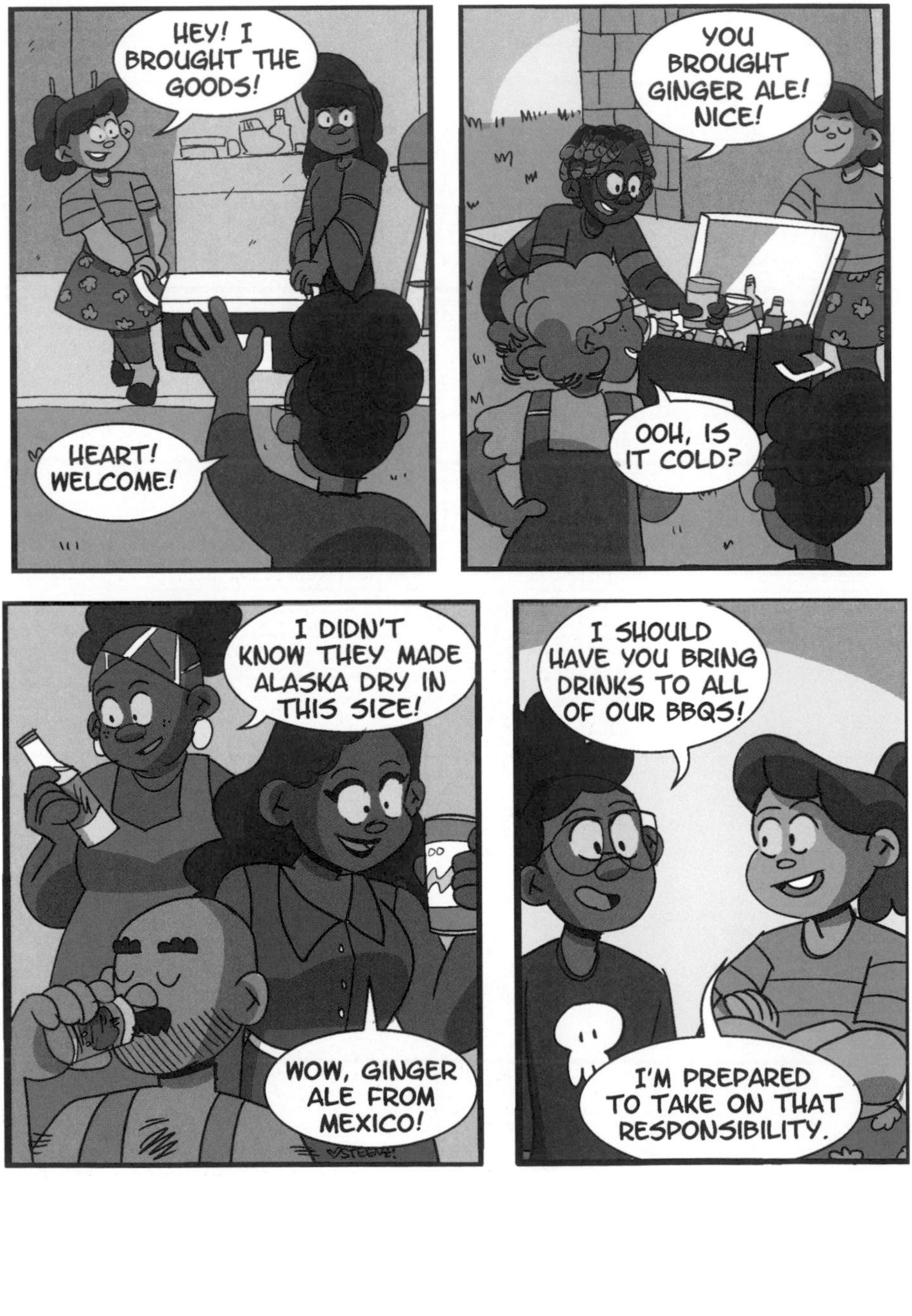
HEY! I BROUGHT THE GOODS!
HEART! WELCOME!
YOU BROUGHT GINGER ALE! NICE!
OOH, IS IT COLD?
I DIDN'T KNOW THEY MADE ALASKA DRY IN THIS SIZE!
WOW, GINGER ALE FROM MEXICO!
I SHOULD HAVE YOU BRING DRINKS TO ALL OF OUR BBQS!
I'M PREPARED TO TAKE ON THAT RESPONSIBILITY.

YOU'RE CHARLOTTE'S SISTER, RIGHT? YOUR WHOLE VIBE IS EXCELLENT!
ME? LOOK AT YOU! GIVING ME CAREFREE BLACK GIRL ENERGY. WHY HAVEN'T WE HUNG OUT YET?
LET'S REMEDY THAT. SELFIE TIME!
ANOTHER FRIENDSHIP FOUND. WE'RE PROS AT THIS.
♡STEENZ!
FRIENDSHIP
MATCHMAKERS
NEW EPISODE
SATURDAY 7/6c

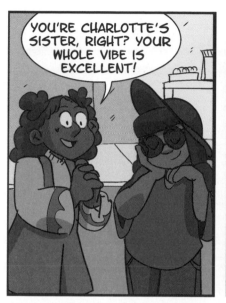

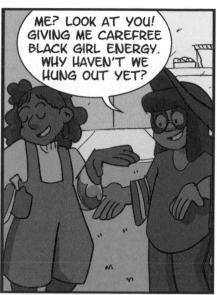

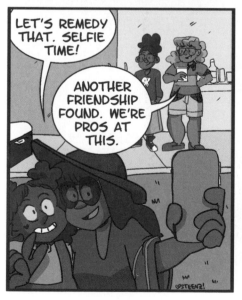

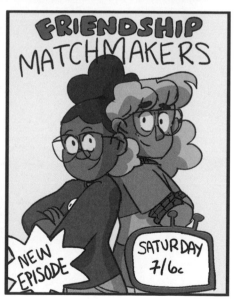

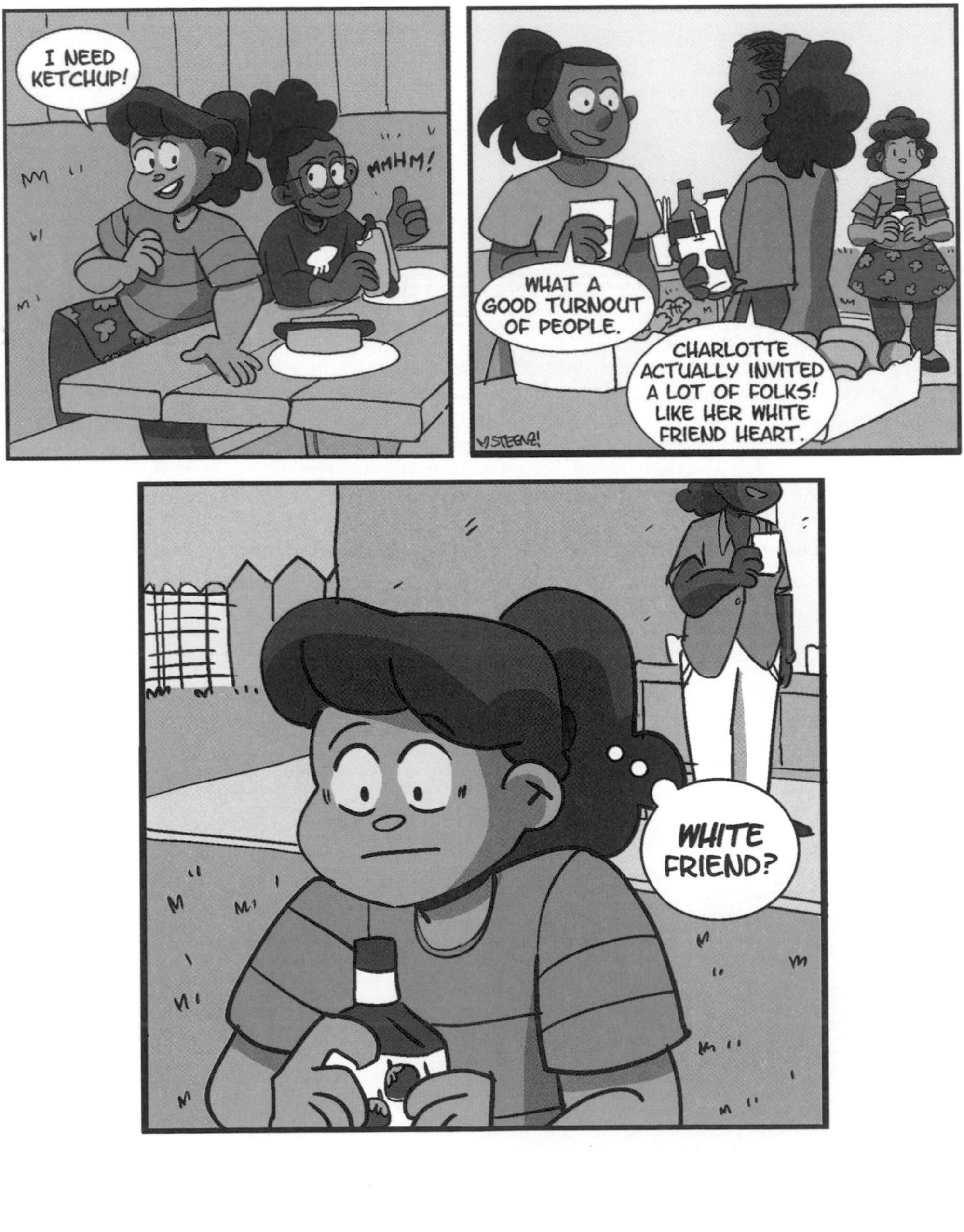
I NEED KETCHUP!
MMHM!
WHAT A GOOD TURNOUT OF PEOPLE.
CHARLOTTE ACTUALLY INVITED A LOT OF FOLKS! LIKE HER WHITE FRIEND HEART.
WHITE FRIEND?

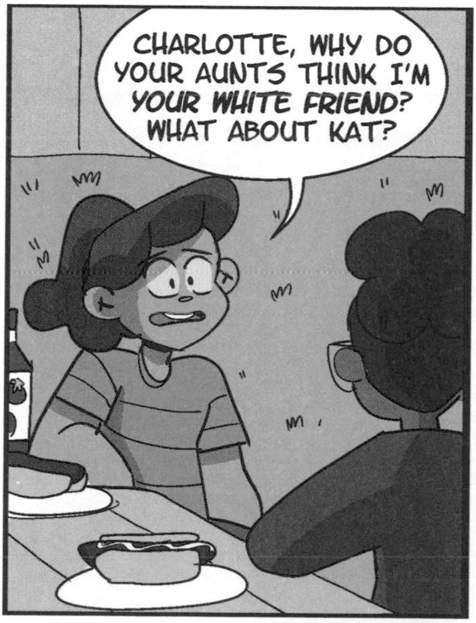
CHARLOTTE, WHY DO YOUR AUNTS THINK I'M *YOUR WHITE FRIEND*? WHAT ABOUT KAT?
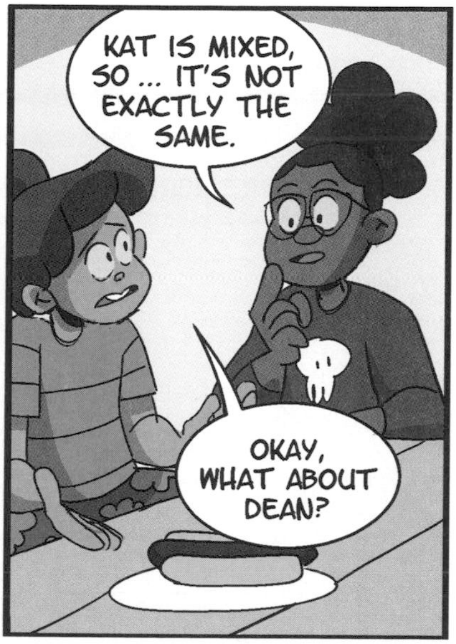
KAT IS MIXED, SO ... IT'S NOT EXACTLY THE SAME.
OKAY, WHAT ABOUT DEAN?
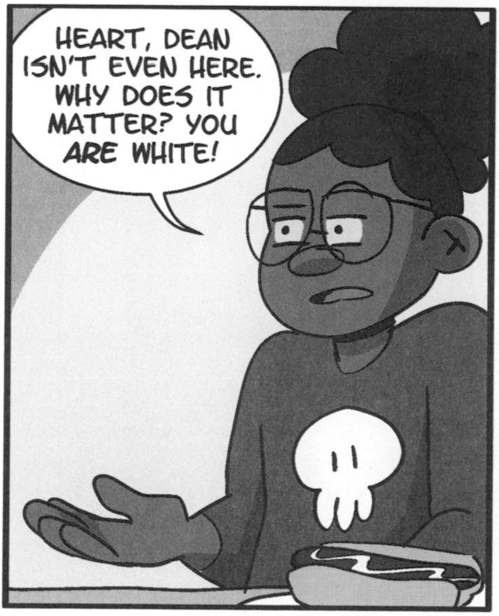
HEART, DEAN ISN'T EVEN HERE. WHY DOES IT MATTER? YOU *ARE* WHITE!
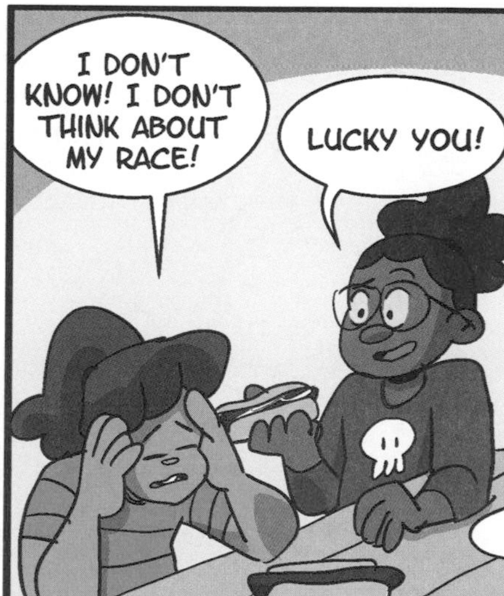
I DON'T KNOW! I DON'T THINK ABOUT MY RACE!
LUCKY YOU!
STEENZ!

HEART, I THINK YOU'RE JUST EMBARRASSED. BUT YOU'RE STILL ONE OF MY BEST FRIENDS. THAT'S WHY YOU'RE HERE!
YOU'RE RIGHT. I DIDN'T MEAN TO BE WEIRD ABOUT IT.
I LIKE WEIRD!
YOU KNOW WHAT? THIS IS AN OPPORTUNITY FOR ME TO BE YOUR COOLEST WHITE FRIEND!
♡STEENZ!
GO FOR THE GOLD!

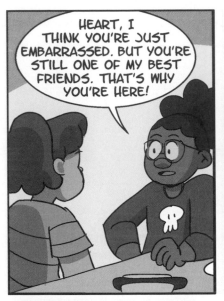

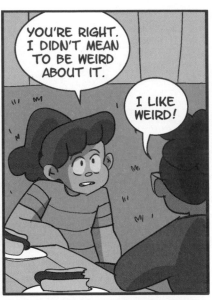

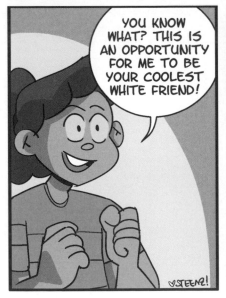

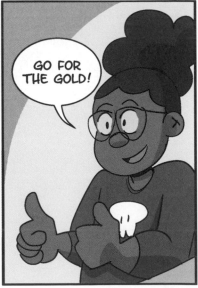

UM ... ARE ANY OF THOSE BURGERS VEGETARIAN?
NO, THEY AREN'T.
OH.
BUT ALL OF THOSE ARE!
WOW! THANKS!
WE WEREN'T GONNA FORGET YA!

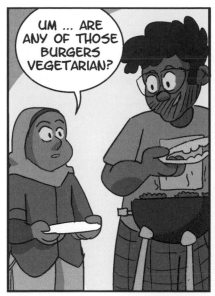

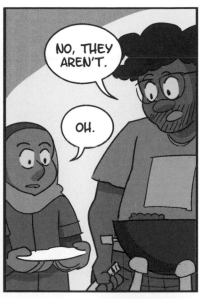

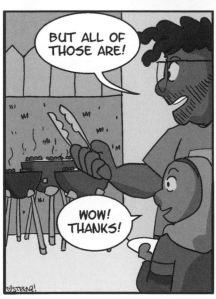

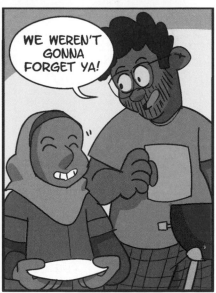

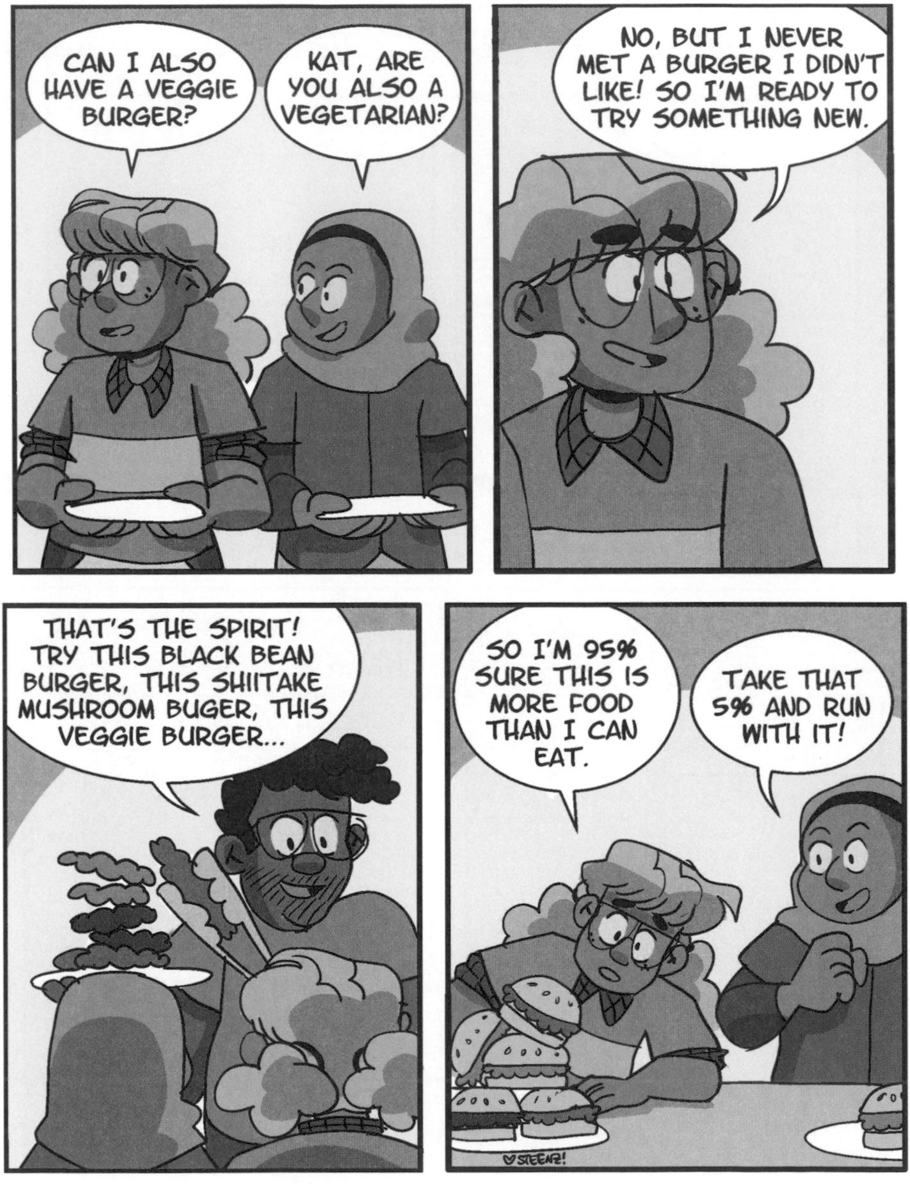
CAN I ALSO HAVE A VEGGIE BURGER?
KAT, ARE YOU ALSO A VEGETARIAN?
NO, BUT I NEVER MET A BURGER I DIDN'T LIKE! SO I'M READY TO TRY SOMETHING NEW.
THAT'S THE SPIRIT! TRY THIS BLACK BEAN BURGER, THIS SHIITAKE MUSHROOM BUGER, THIS VEGGIE BURGER...
SO I'M 95% SURE THIS IS MORE FOOD THAN I CAN EAT.
TAKE THAT 5% AND RUN WITH IT!
♡STEENZ!

I'M SO FULL.
SO MANY DELICIOUS FOODS.
I DON'T EVEN REMEMBER WHAT IT WAS LIKE TO BE HUNGRY.
THAT'S HOW YOU KNOW YOU HAD A GOOD MEAL!

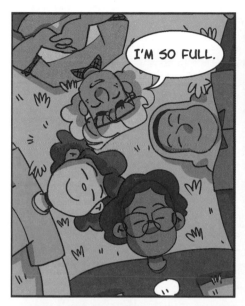

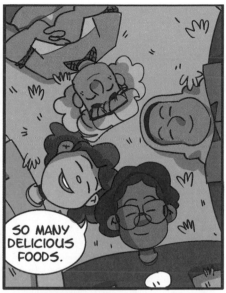

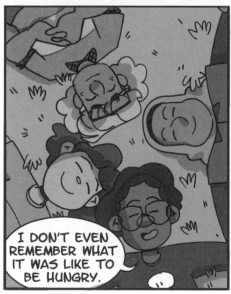

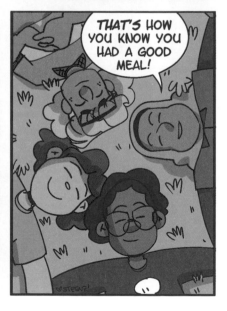

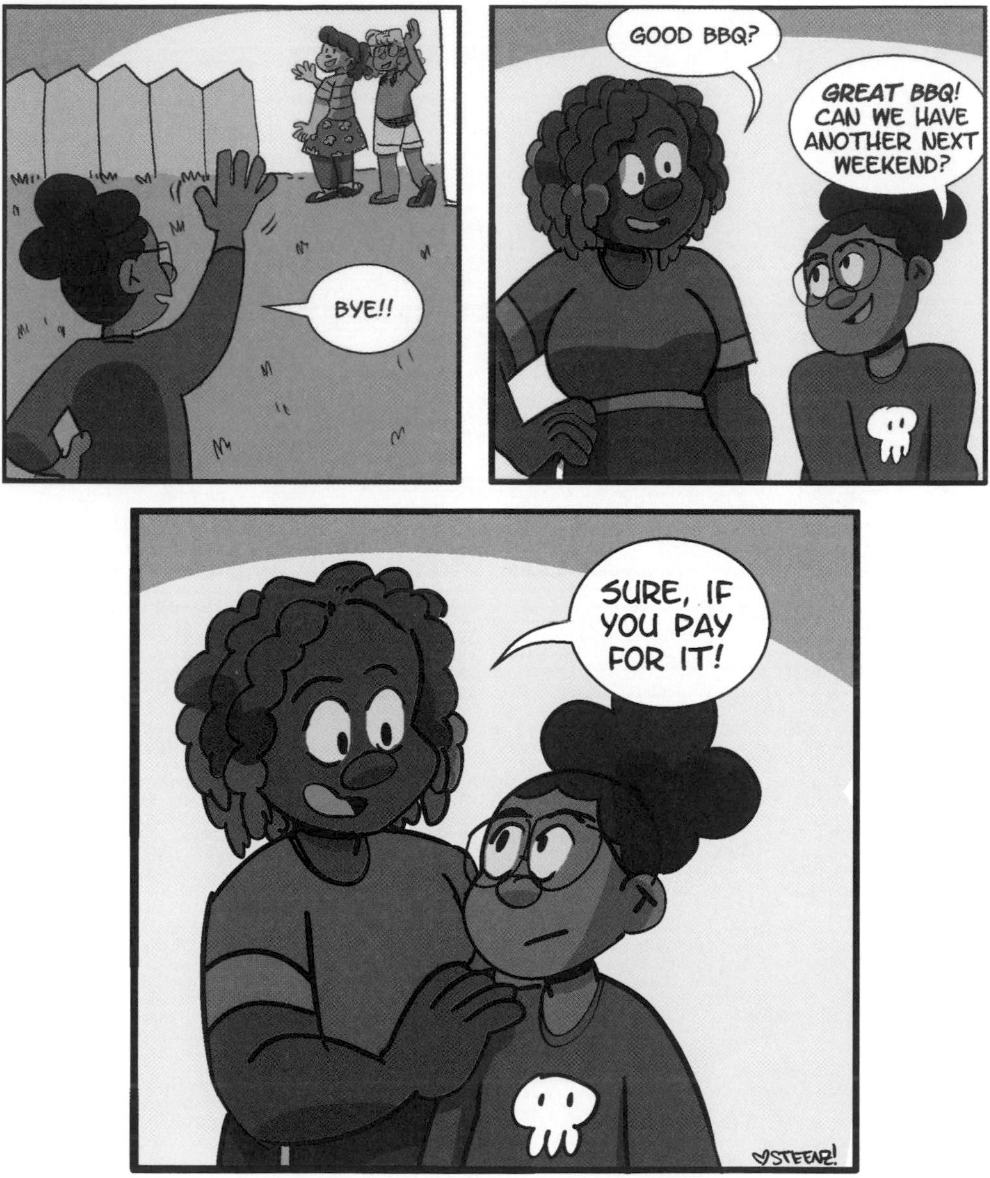
BYE!!
GOOD BBQ?
GREAT BBQ! CAN WE HAVE ANOTHER NEXT WEEKEND?
SURE, IF YOU PAY FOR IT!
♡STEENZ!

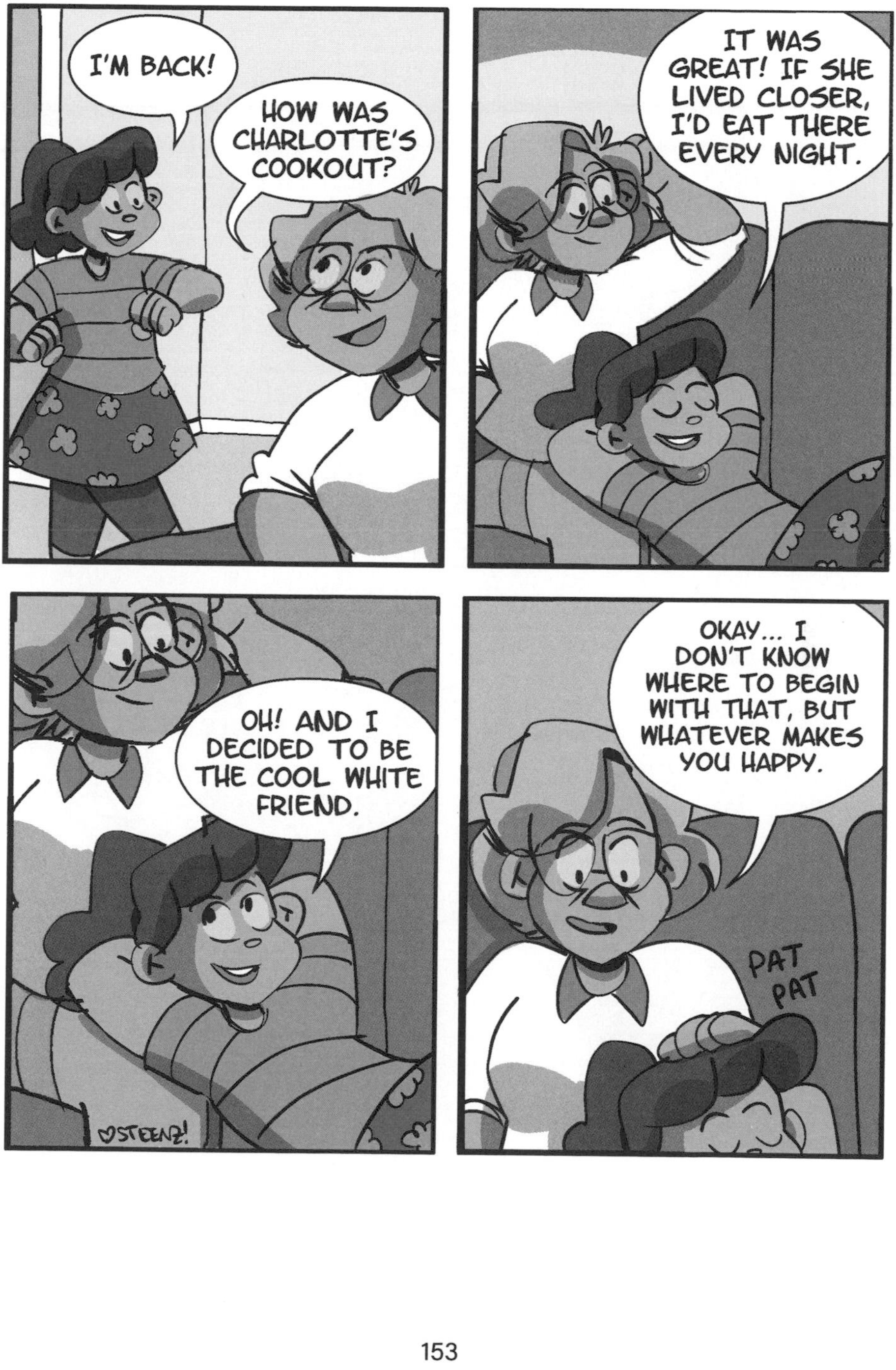
I'M BACK!
HOW WAS CHARLOTTE'S COOKOUT?
IT WAS GREAT! IF SHE LIVED CLOSER, I'D EAT THERE EVERY NIGHT.
OH! AND I DECIDED TO BE THE COOL WHITE FRIEND.
♡STEENZ!
OKAY... I DON'T KNOW WHERE TO BEGIN WITH THAT, BUT WHATEVER MAKES YOU HAPPY.
PAT PAT

BROWNIES! SO, UH... WHEN ARE THESE FREE TO THE PUBLIC?
NOT TILL AFTER DINNER.
YOU PUT THESE IN FRONT OF US, AND WE CAN'T HAVE ANY FOR HOURS?
IT'S A LESSON IN RESTRAINT!
♡STEENZ!
IT'S THE WEEKEND. I'M NOT ALLOWED TO LEARN WHEN I'M NOT IN SCHOOL.

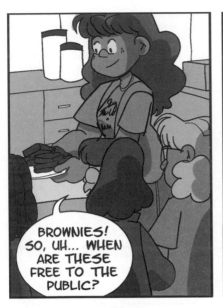

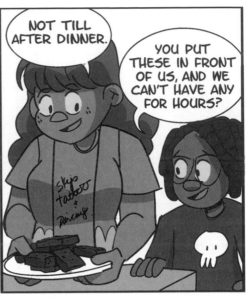

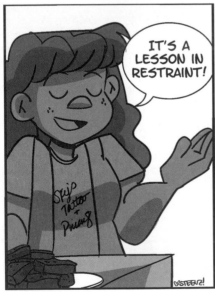

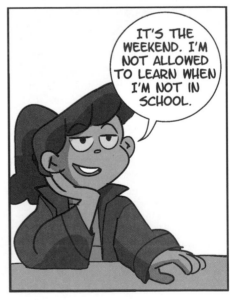

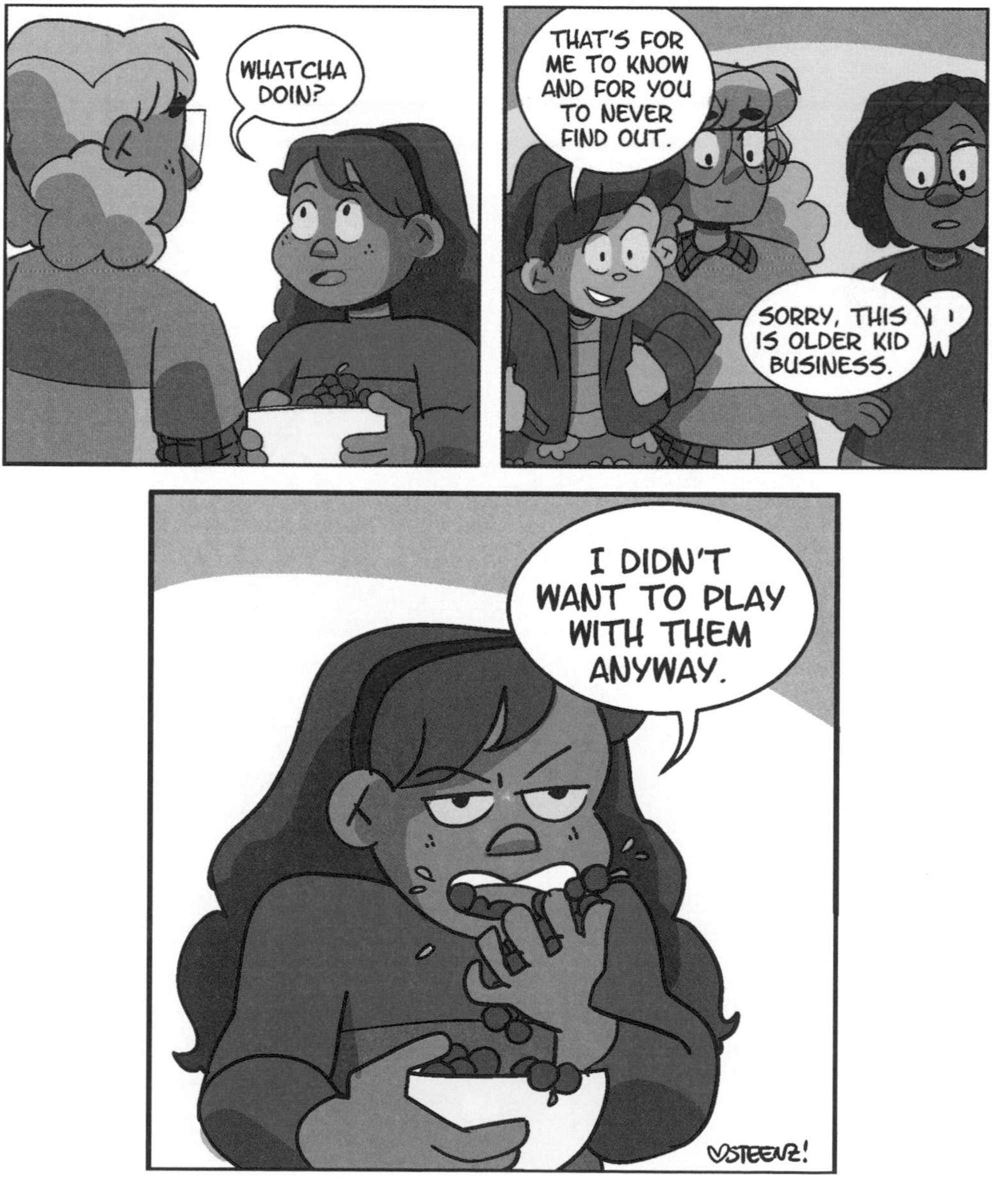
WHATCHA DOIN?
THAT'S FOR ME TO KNOW AND FOR YOU TO NEVER FIND OUT.
SORRY, THIS IS OLDER KID BUSINESS.
I DIDN'T WANT TO PLAY WITH THEM ANYWAY.
♡STEENZ!

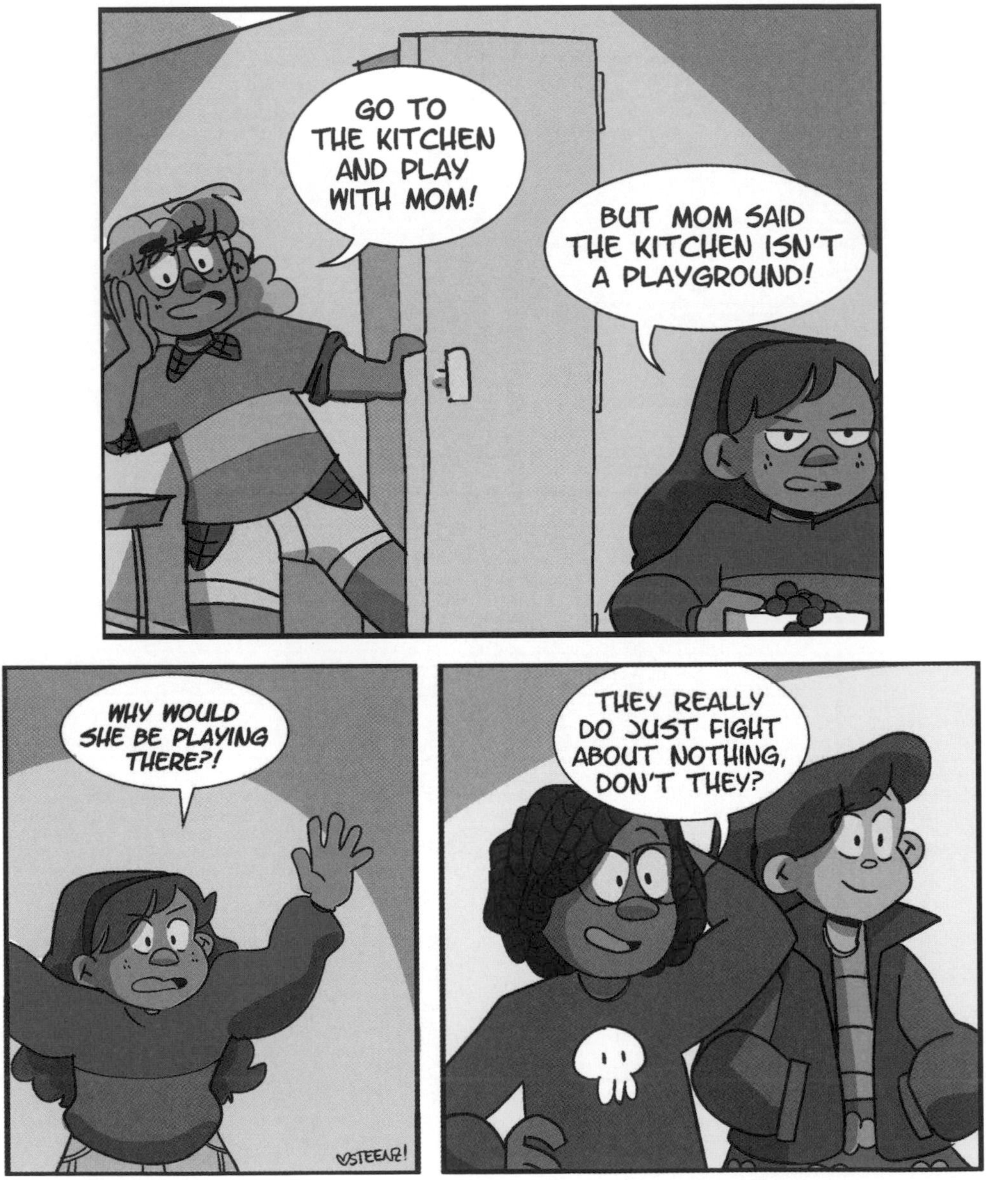
GO TO THE KITCHEN AND PLAY WITH MOM!
BUT MOM SAID THE KITCHEN ISN'T A PLAYGROUND!
WHY WOULD SHE BE PLAYING THERE?!
♡STEENZ!
THEY REALLY DO JUST FIGHT ABOUT NOTHING, DON'T THEY?

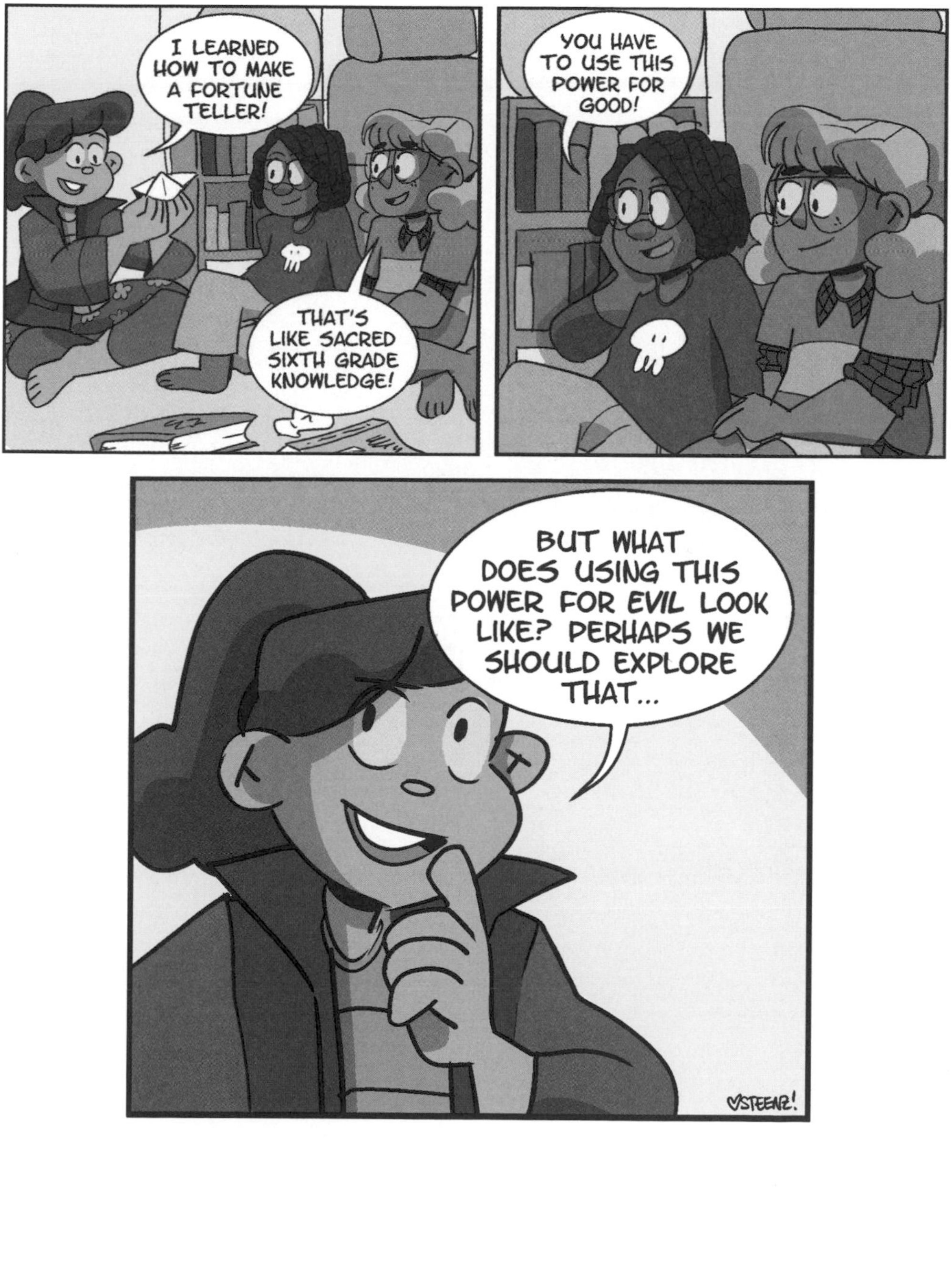
I LEARNED HOW TO MAKE A FORTUNE TELLER!
THAT'S LIKE SACRED SIXTH GRADE KNOWLEDGE!
YOU HAVE TO USE THIS POWER FOR GOOD!
BUT WHAT DOES USING THIS POWER FOR *EVIL* LOOK LIKE? PERHAPS WE SHOULD EXPLORE THAT...
♡STEENZ!

RED

FOUR

EIGHT

CHARLOTTE, YOU WILL FIND TRUE LOVE THIS YEAR!

WE'LL SEE! MY SCHEDULE IS PRETTY PACKED.

SHOULD WE SEE IF DEAN'S SCHEDULE IS FREE?

HA HA HA HA

GIVE ME THAT!!

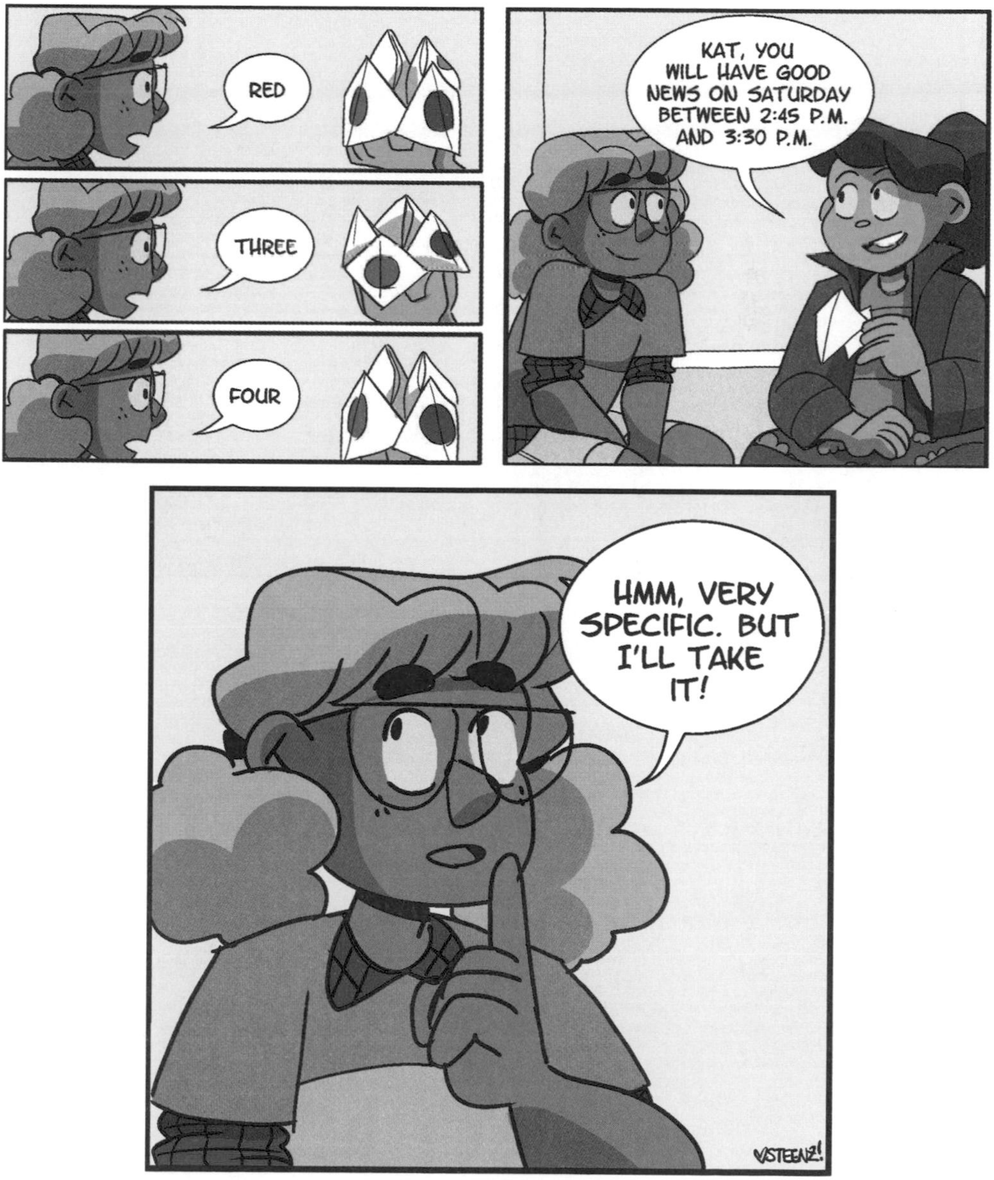
RED
THREE
FOUR
KAT, YOU WILL HAVE GOOD NEWS ON SATURDAY BETWEEN 2:45 P.M. AND 3:30 P.M.
HMM, VERY SPECIFIC. BUT I'LL TAKE IT!

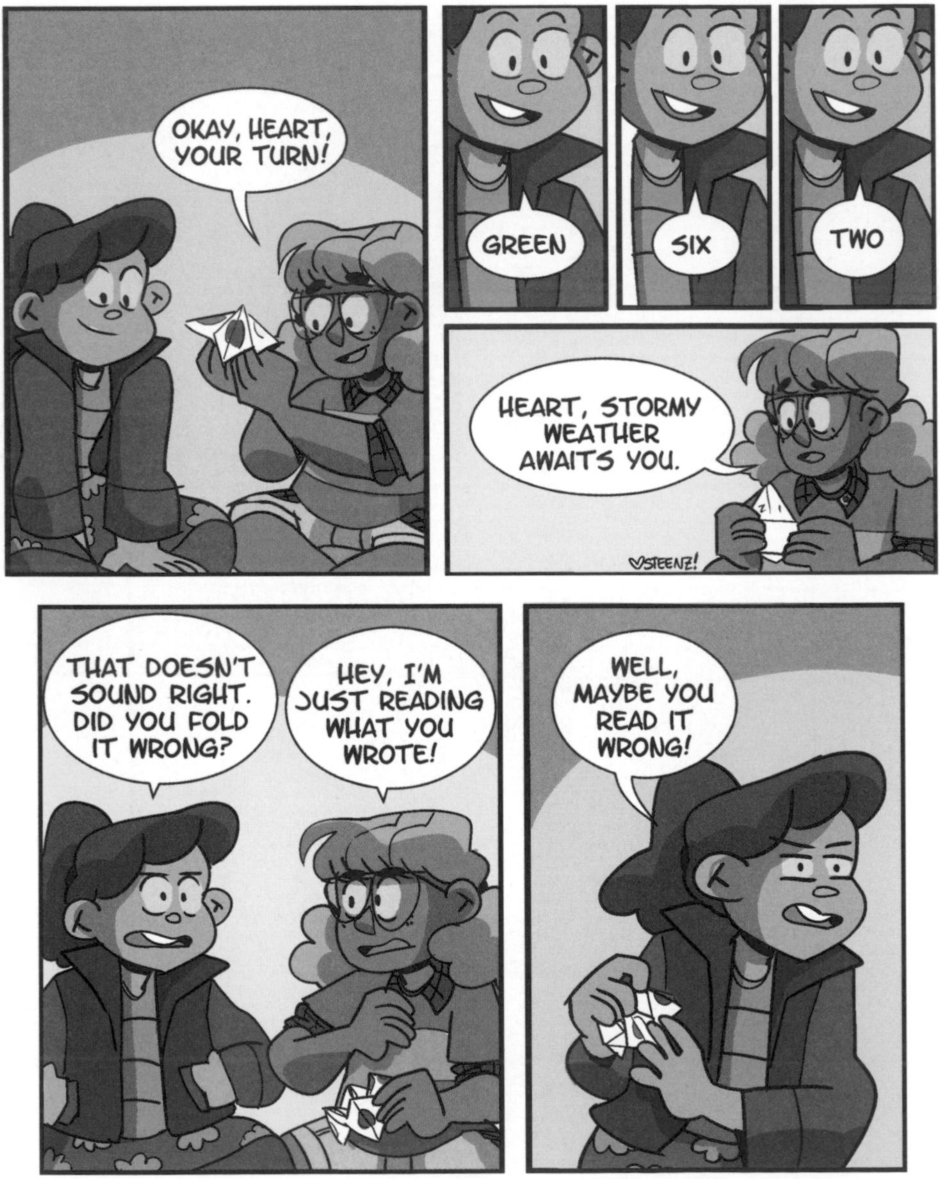
OKAY, HEART, YOUR TURN!
GREEN
SIX
TWO
HEART, STORMY WEATHER AWAITS YOU.
STEENZ!
THAT DOESN'T SOUND RIGHT. DID YOU FOLD IT WRONG?
HEY, I'M JUST READING WHAT YOU WROTE!
WELL, MAYBE YOU READ IT WRONG!

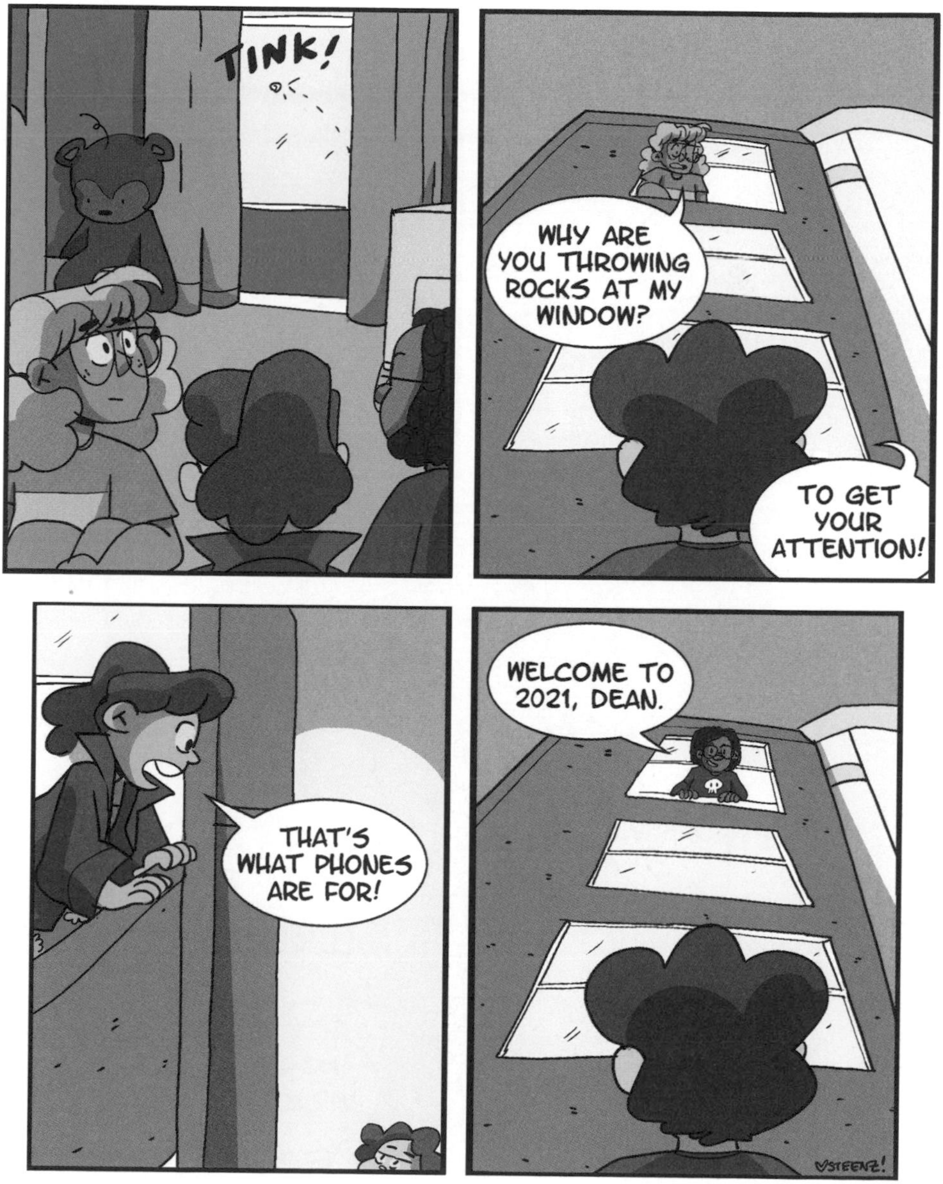
TINK!
WHY ARE YOU THROWING ROCKS AT MY WINDOW?
TO GET YOUR ATTENTION!
THAT'S WHAT PHONES ARE FOR!
WELCOME TO 2021, DEAN.
♡STEENZ!

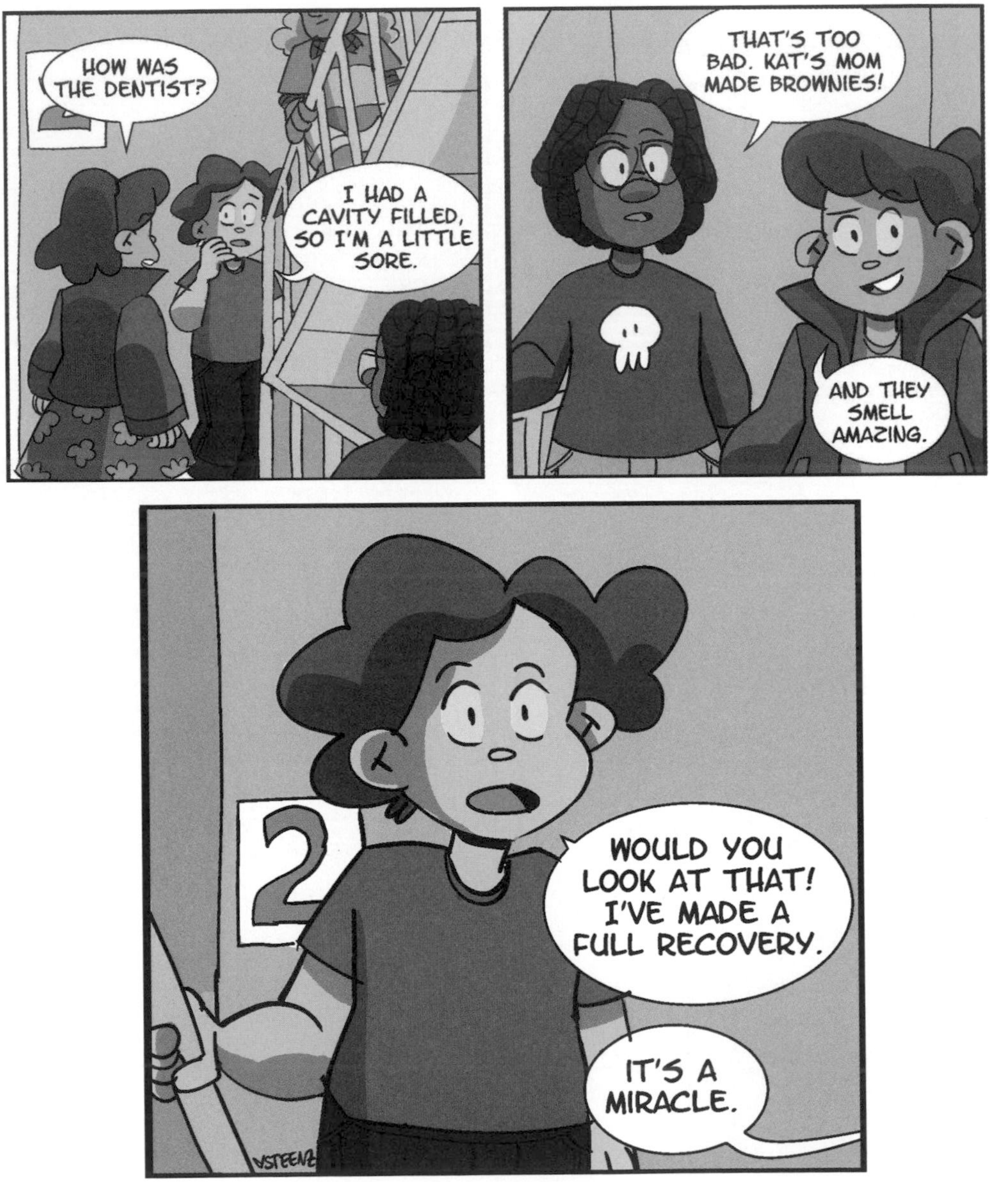
HOW WAS THE DENTIST?
I HAD A CAVITY FILLED, SO I'M A LITTLE SORE.
THAT'S TOO BAD. KAT'S MOM MADE BROWNIES!
AND THEY SMELL AMAZING.
WOULD YOU LOOK AT THAT! I'VE MADE A FULL RECOVERY.
IT'S A MIRACLE.
VSTEENZ

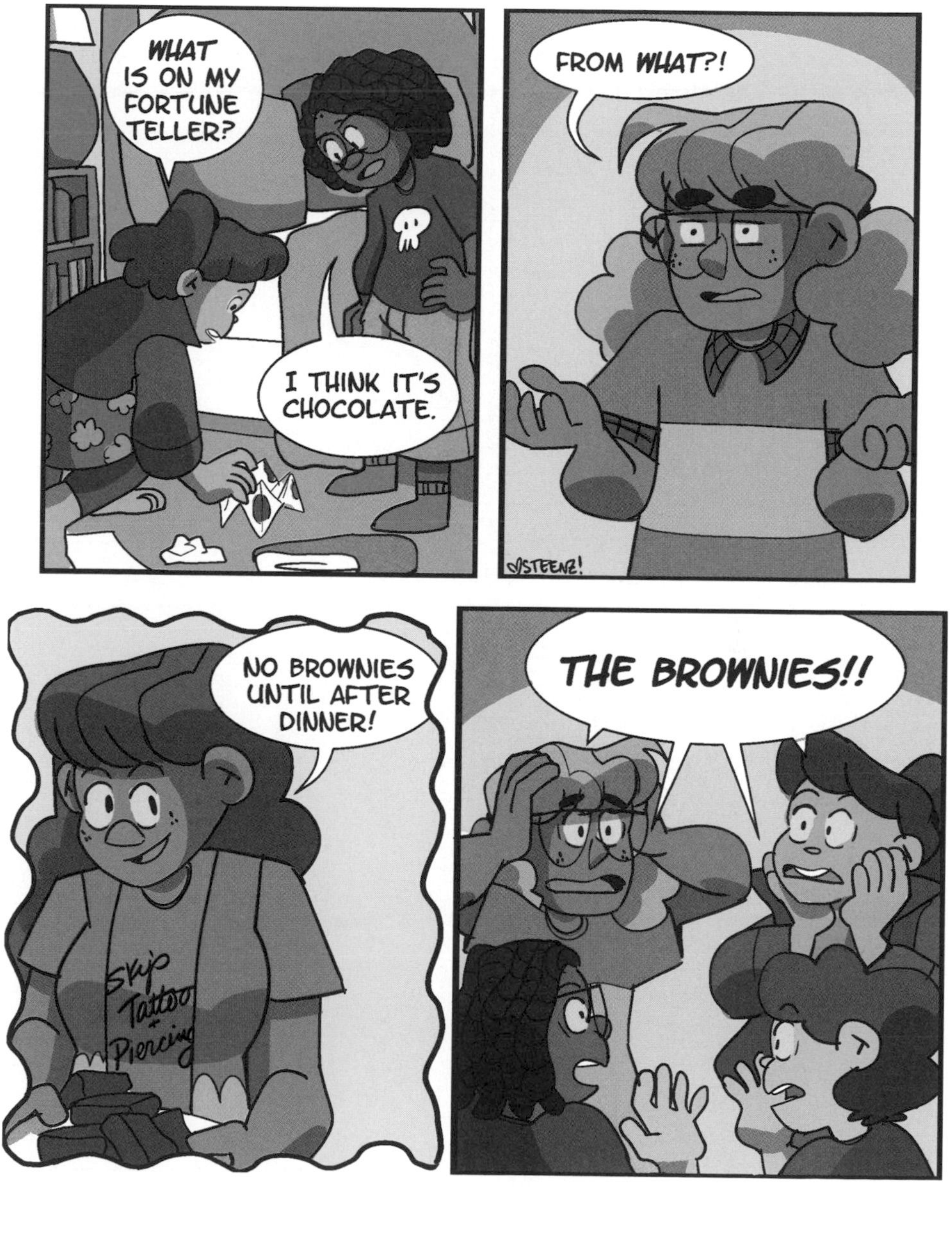
WHAT IS ON MY FORTUNE TELLER?
I THINK IT'S CHOCOLATE.
FROM WHAT?!
STEENZ!
NO BROWNIES UNTIL AFTER DINNER!
Skip's Tattoo + Piercing
THE BROWNIES!!

ALYSSA!

MOM SAID NO BROWNIES TILL AFTER DINNER!

I DIDN'T KNOW! I MEAN, I DIDN'T EAT IT! YOU HAVE NO PROOF!

I THINK THE CHOCOLATE ALL OVER YOUR FACE IS PRETTY GOOD PROOF.

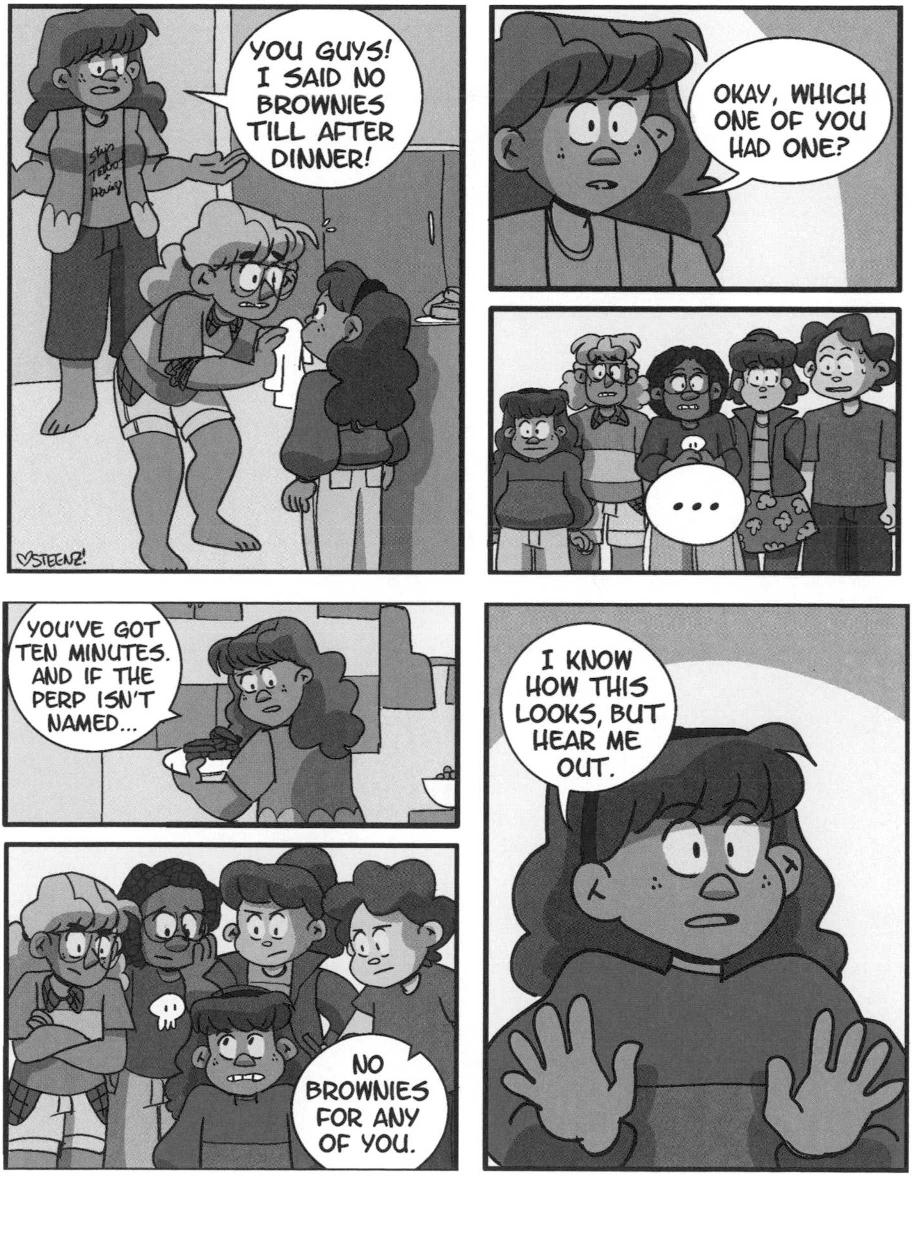
YOU GUYS! I SAID NO BROWNIES TILL AFTER DINNER!
♡STEENZ!
OKAY, WHICH ONE OF YOU HAD ONE?
...
YOU'VE GOT TEN MINUTES. AND IF THE PERP ISN'T NAMED...
NO BROWNIES FOR ANY OF YOU.
I KNOW HOW THIS LOOKS, BUT HEAR ME OUT.

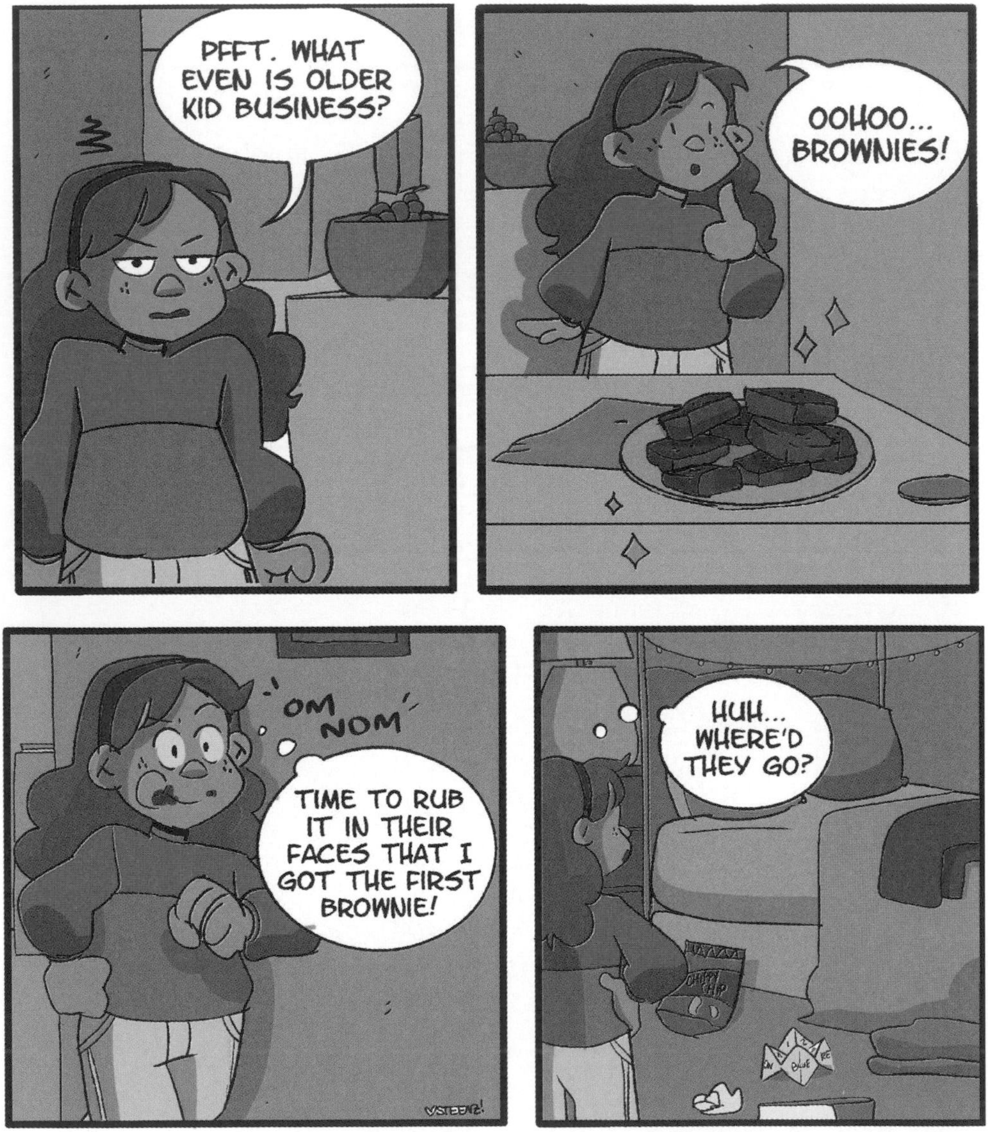
PFFT. WHAT EVEN IS OLDER KID BUSINESS?
OOHOO... BROWNIES!
OM NOM
TIME TO RUB IT IN THEIR FACES THAT I GOT THE FIRST BROWNIE!
HUH... WHERE'D THEY GO?

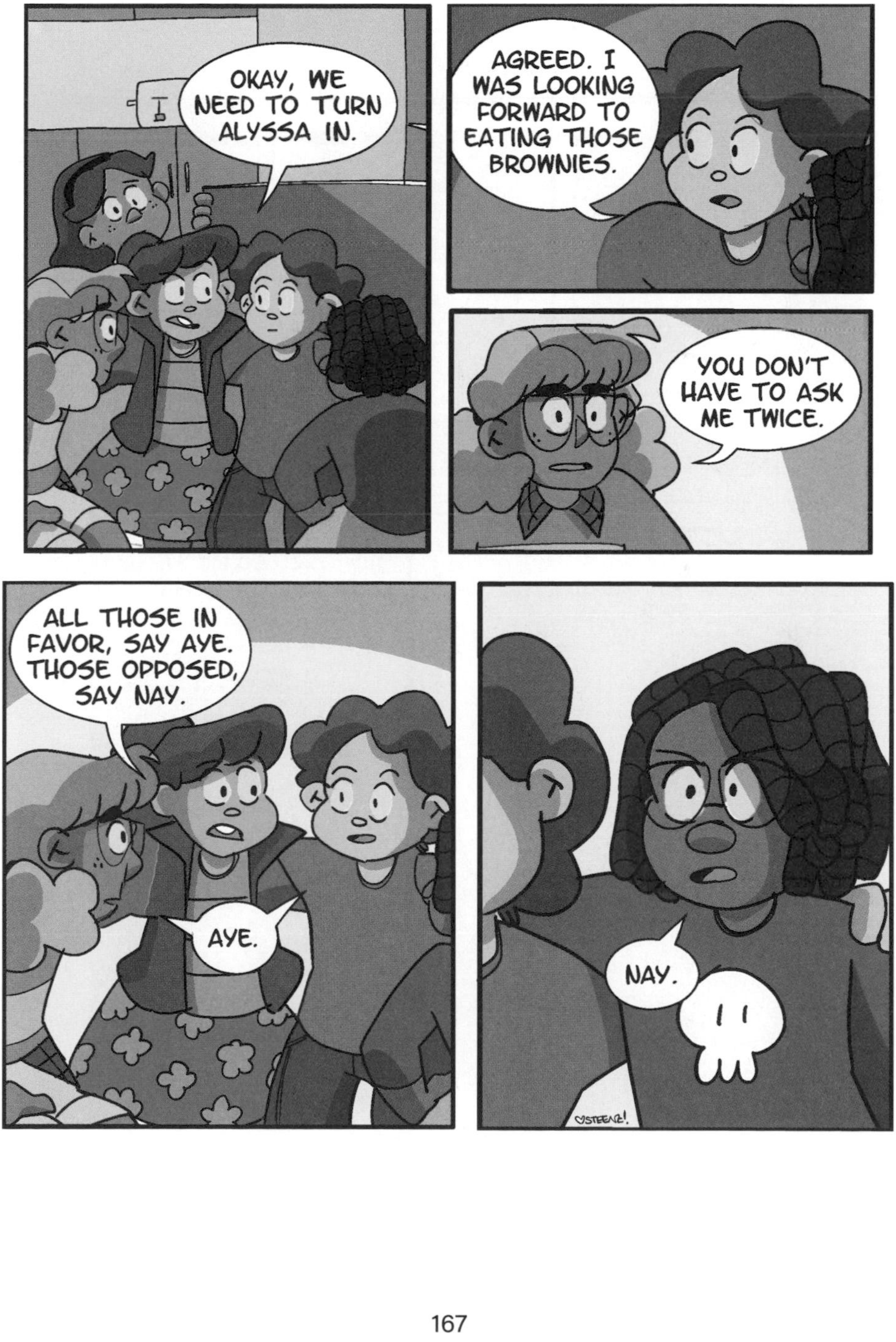
OKAY, WE NEED TO TURN ALYSSA IN.
AGREED. I WAS LOOKING FORWARD TO EATING THOSE BROWNIES.
YOU DON'T HAVE TO ASK ME TWICE.
ALL THOSE IN FAVOR, SAY AYE. THOSE OPPOSED, SAY NAY.
AYE.
NAY.
♡STEENZ!

WHY DON'T YOU THINK WE SHOULD TURN ALYSSA IN?
AND WE ONLY HAVE EIGHT MINUTES TO GET ON THE SAME PAGE.
ALYSSA DIDN'T KNOW THAT SHE WASN'T ALLOWED TO EAT THE BROWNIE!
BUT I DON'T WANT TO GET PUNISHED BECAUSE OF SOMEONE ELSE.
LITTLE SISTERS ARE MENACES! I HAVE NO SYMPATHY FOR HER.
HEY! I'M A LITTLE SISTER! WE'RE ONLY MENACES *SOME* OF THE TIME!

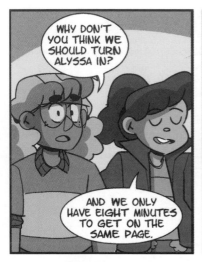

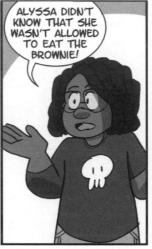

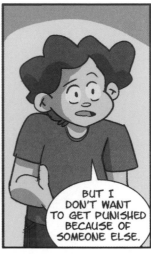

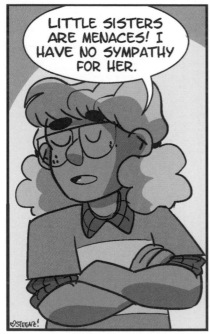

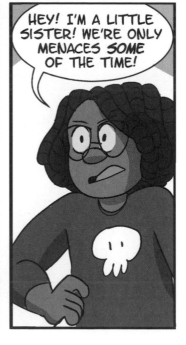

AS AN ONLY CHILD, I DON'T UNDERSTAND THE INNER WORKINGS OF SIBLING RIVALRY...

BUT I'VE STOLEN A BROWNIE OR TWO IN MY TIME. AND IN THIS CASE, ALYSSA DIDN'T EVEN KNOW SHE WAS STEALING.

OKAY, THAT'S TWO AGAINST TWO NOW!

DEAN, DON'T BE SWAYED BY HER DOE EYES!

I'VE BEEN SWAYED. WE CAN'T TURN HER IN.

COME ON! WE'RE GOING TO GIVE UP BROWNIES CUZ ALYSSA MADE A MISTAKE?
THERE! YOU SAID IT. SHE MADE A MISTAKE. WE CAN'T PUNISH HER FOR THAT!
SIGH.
YOU'RE RIGHT. THAT WOULDN'T BE FAIR.
I LET CHOCOLATE CLOUD MY THOUGHTS.
WHAT SHOULD WE DO?
I KNOW EXACTLY WHAT TO DO.

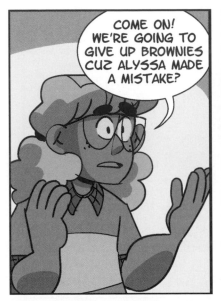

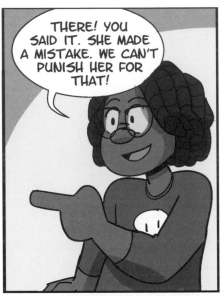

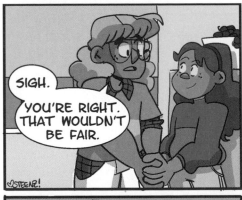

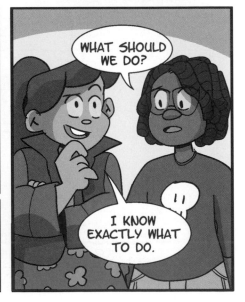

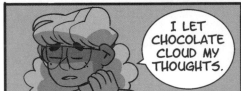

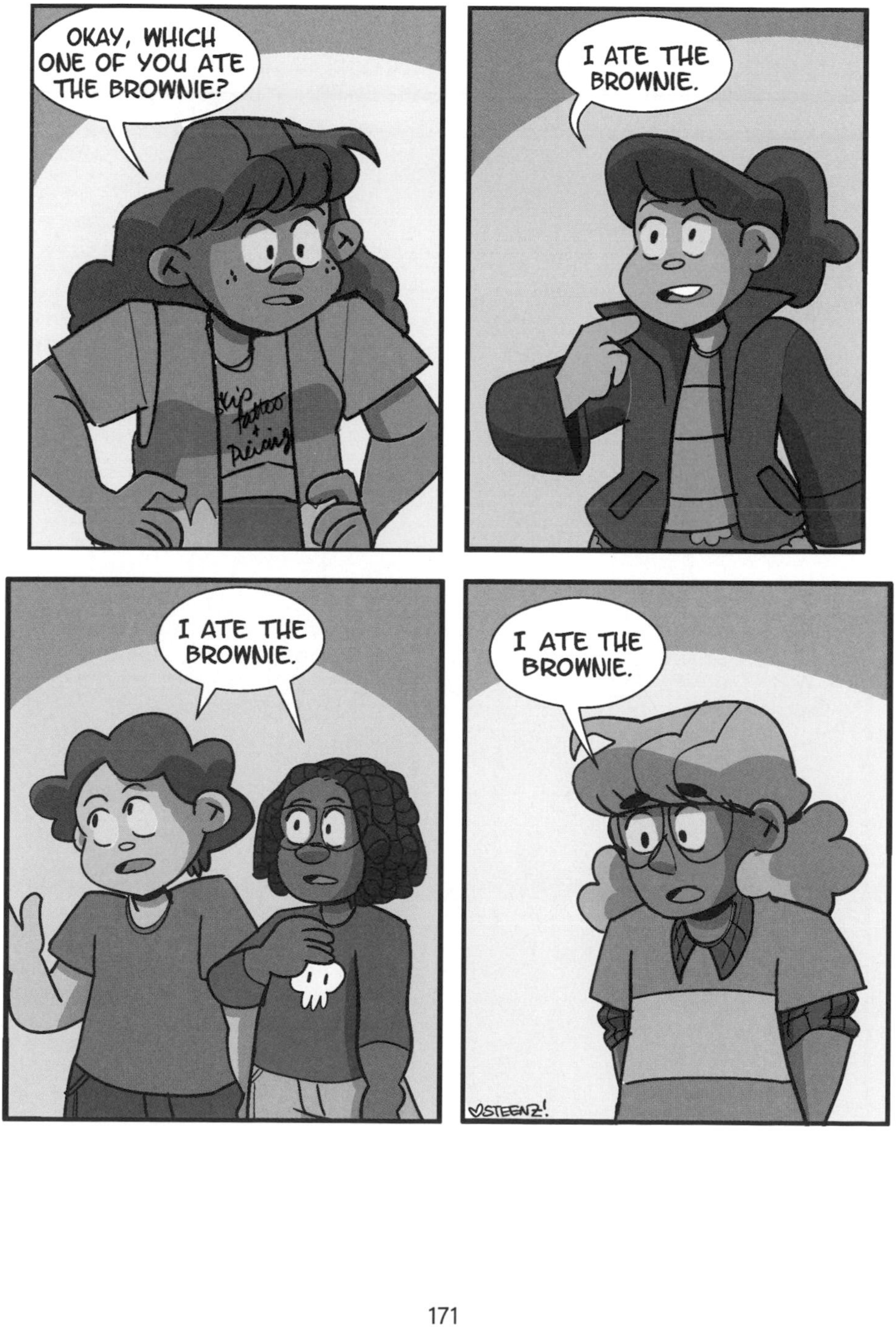
OKAY, WHICH ONE OF YOU ATE THE BROWNIE?
I ATE THE BROWNIE.
I ATE THE BROWNIE.
I ATE THE BROWNIE.
STEENZ!

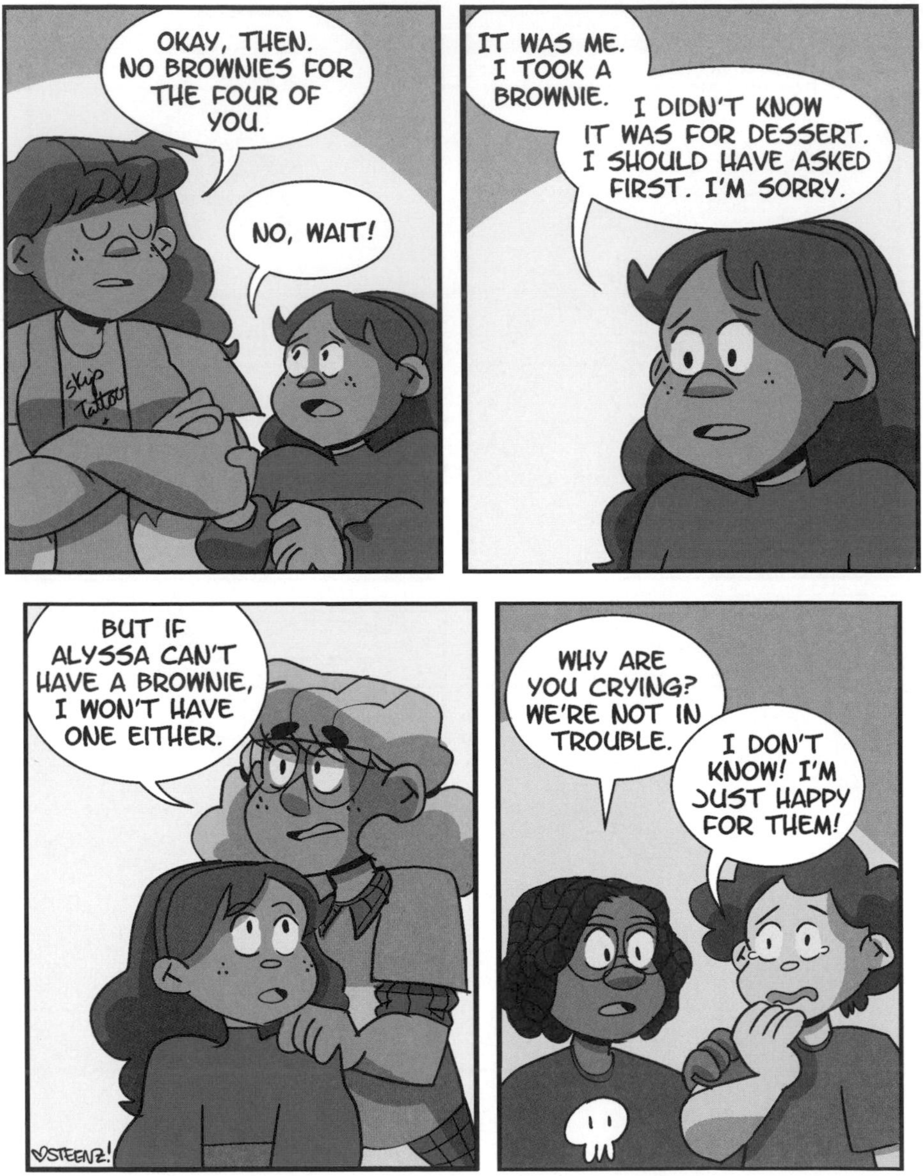
OKAY, THEN. NO BROWNIES FOR THE FOUR OF YOU.
NO, WAIT!
IT WAS ME. I TOOK A BROWNIE.
I DIDN'T KNOW IT WAS FOR DESSERT. I SHOULD HAVE ASKED FIRST. I'M SORRY.
BUT IF ALYSSA CAN'T HAVE A BROWNIE, I WON'T HAVE ONE EITHER.
STEENZ!
WHY ARE YOU CRYING? WE'RE NOT IN TROUBLE.
I DON'T KNOW! I'M JUST HAPPY FOR THEM!

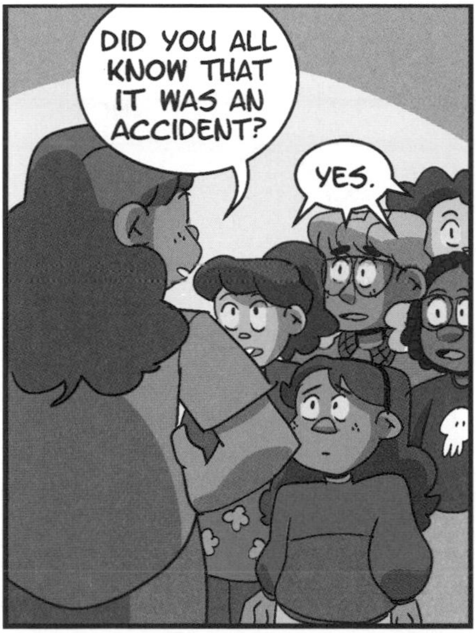
DID YOU ALL KNOW THAT IT WAS AN ACCIDENT?
YES.

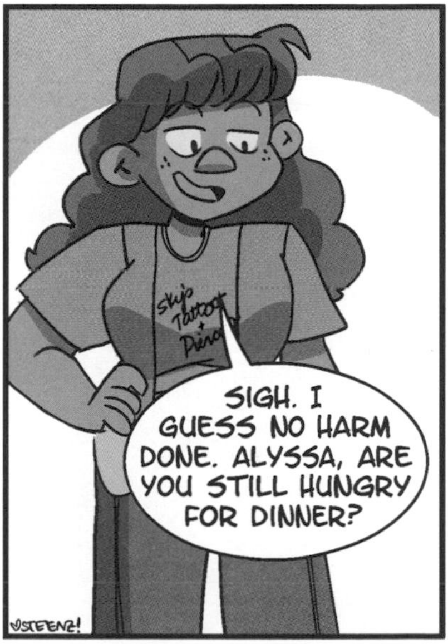
SIGH. I GUESS NO HARM DONE. ALYSSA, ARE YOU STILL HUNGRY FOR DINNER?
STEENZ!

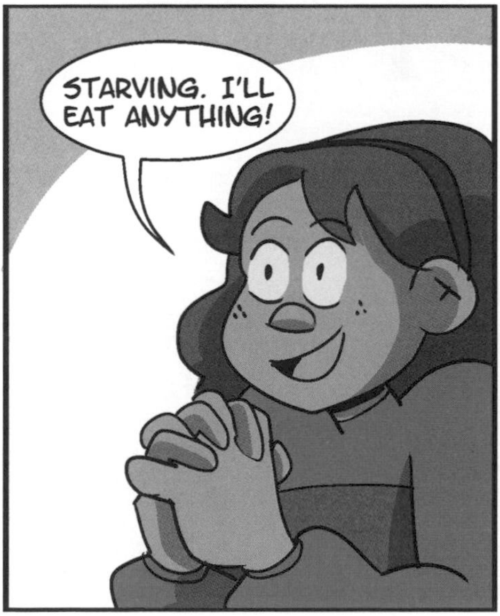
STARVING. I'LL EAT ANYTHING!

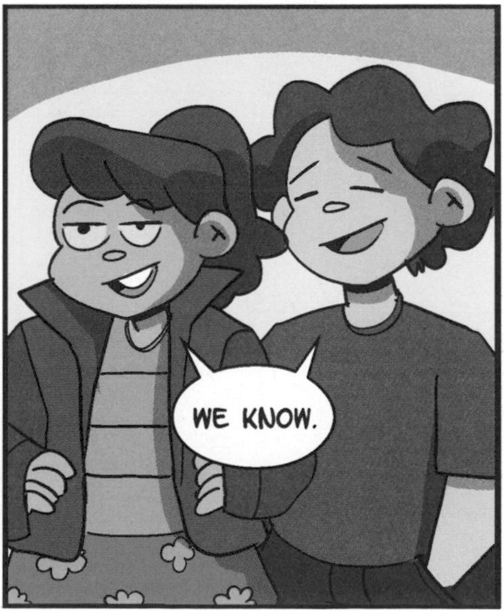
WE KNOW.

ALRIGHT, EVERYONE, GO WASH YOUR HANDS FOR DINNERTIME. AND AFTER...
WE'LL ALL HAVE BROWNIES.
YES!
THANKS FOR HAVING MY BACK.
ANYTIME.

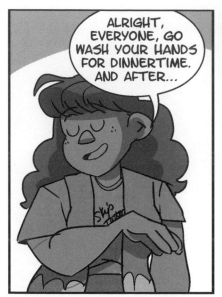

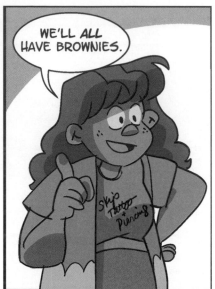

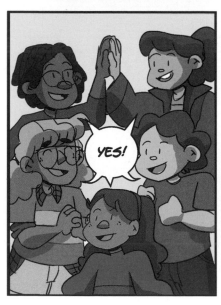

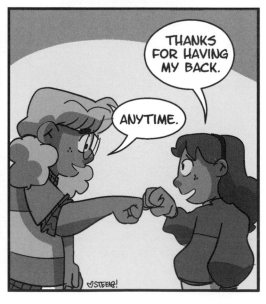

Andrews McMeel Publishing
a division of Andrews McMeel Universal
1130 Walnut Street, Kansas City, Missouri 64106

www.andrewsmcmeel.com

23 24 25 26 27 SDB 10 9 8 7 6 5 4 3 2 1

ISBN: 978-1-5248-7930-3

Library of Congress Control Number: 2021946301

Made by:
RR Donnelley (Guangdong) Printing Solutions Company Ltd
Address and location of manufacturer:
No. 2, Minzhu Road, Daning, Humen Town,
Dongguan City, Guangdong Province, China 523930
1st Printing—11/21/22

ATTENTION: SCHOOLS AND BUSINESSES
Andrews McMeel books are available at quantity discounts with bulk purchase for educational, business, or sales promotional use. For information, please e-mail the Andrews McMeel Publishing Special Sales Department: sales@amuniversal.com.

Look for these books!

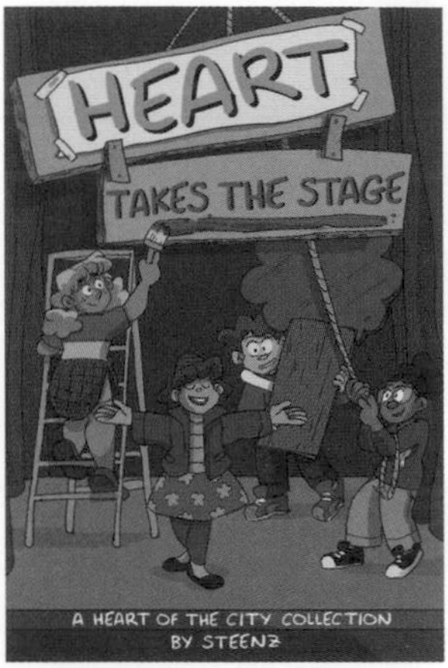
HEART
TAKES THE STAGE
A HEART OF THE CITY COLLECTION
BY STEENZ

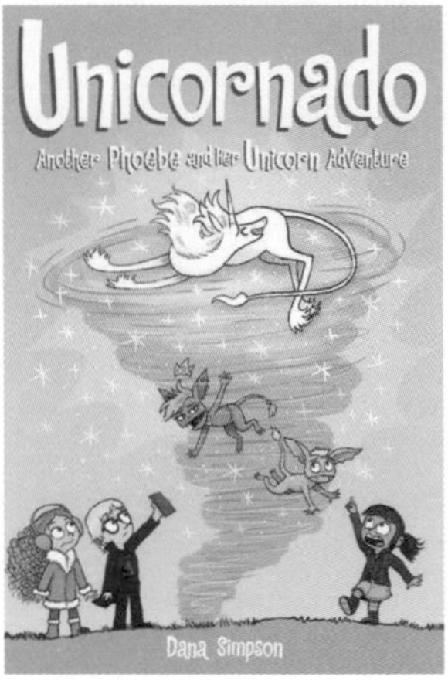
Unicornado
Another Phoebe and her Unicorn Adventure
Dana Simpson

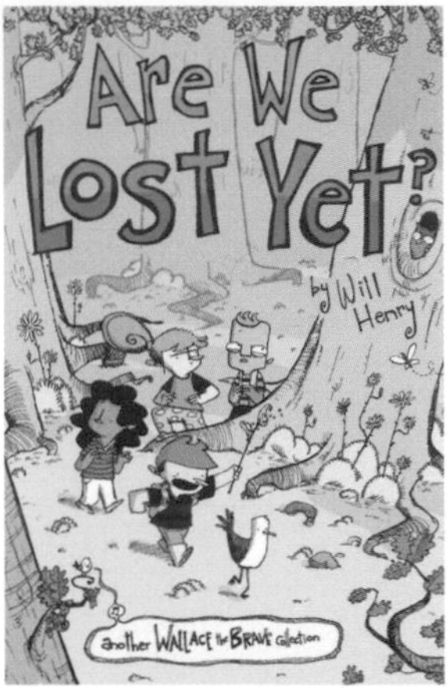
Are We Lost Yet?
by Will Henry
another WALLACE the BRAVE collection

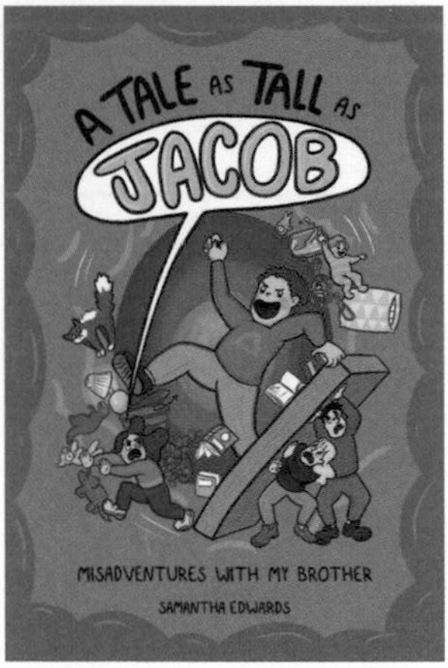
A TALE AS TALL AS JACOB
MISADVENTURES WITH MY BROTHER
SAMANTHA EDWARDS

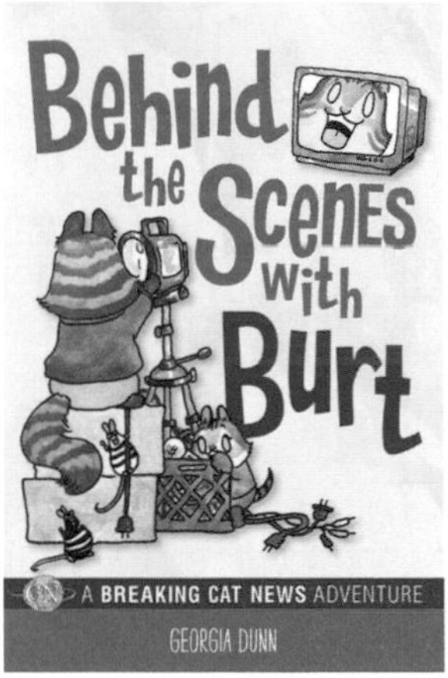
Behind the Scenes with Burt
A BREAKING CAT NEWS ADVENTURE
GEORGIA DUNN

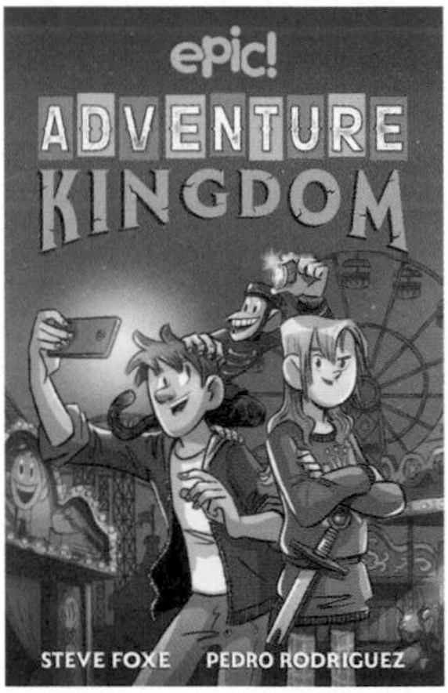
epic!
ADVENTURE KINGDOM
STEVE FOXE
PEDRO RODRIGUEZ

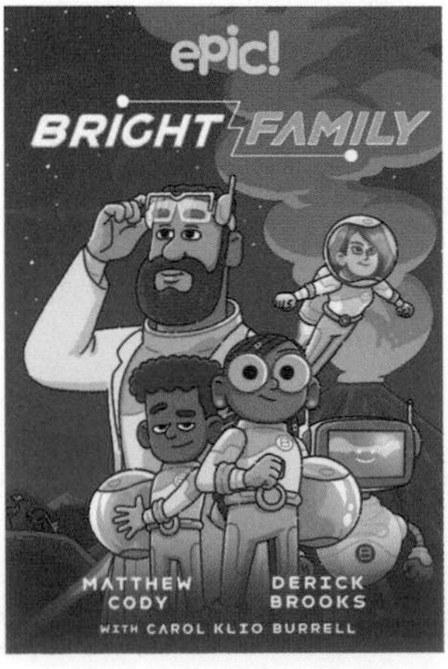
epic!
BRIGHT FAMILY
MATTHEW CODY
DERICK BROOKS
WITH CAROL KLIO BURRELL

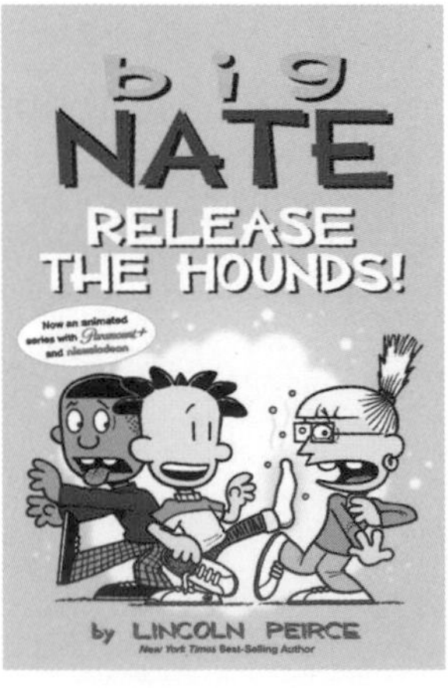
big NATE
RELEASE THE HOUNDS!
by LINCOLN PEIRCE
New York Times Best-Selling Author

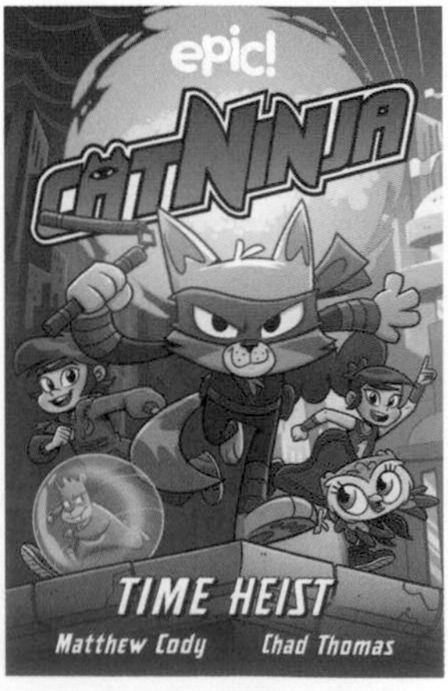
epic!
CATNINJA
TIME HEIST
Matthew Cody
Chad Thomas